Books by Jack Valenti

Nonfiction

THE BITTER TASTE OF GLORY

A VERY HUMAN PRESIDENT

SPEAK UP WITH CONFIDENCE

Fiction

PROTECT AND DEFEND

JACK VALENTI

and Defend

DOUBLEDAY
New York   London   Toronto   Sydney   Auckland

PUBLISHED BY DOUBLEDAY
a division of Bantam Doubleday Dell Publishing Group, Inc.
666 Fifth Avenue, New York, New York 10103

DOUBLEDAY and the portrayal of an anchor
with a dolphin are trademarks of Doubleday,
a division of Bantam Doubleday Dell Publishing Group, Inc.

Library of Congress Cataloging-in-Publication Data

Valenti, Jack.
Protect and defend: a novel/Jack Valenti.—1st ed.
    p. cm.
I. Title
PS3572.A388P7   1992
813'.54—dc20   91-12602
CIP

ISBN 0-385-41735-7
October 1992
First Edition

10 9 8 7 6 5 4 3 2 1

Protect

Protect and Defend

To M.M.

Acknowledgments

To Jacqueline Onassis I say, "Thank you." It was she who from start to finish believed in what I was writing.

Thanks to Kirk Douglas for his encouragement and Ursula Obst for her indispensable early-on advice.

And my gratitude to:

Bill Safire for his wise counsel. Also Judge William Webster, Judge William Sessions, Bill Baker, all of the FBI for helpful corrections in FBI procedure as well as Ambassador Arthur Hummel and Arkady N. Shevchenko for their intimate knowledge of Asia and the U.S.S.R.

Max Allen Collins, for his editing judgments and assistance.

Beth Crable, my most valuable associate, and Quinn Cress and Tom Robertson for their valued aid.

I am grateful to my wife, Mary Margaret, for her understanding when I disappeared into my study on the weekend for hours of companionship with this book, and for her wise political insights which illuminated more than a few chapters.

I do solemnly swear that I will faithfully execute the office of President of the United States, and will, to the best of my ability, preserve, protect and defend the Constitution of the United States.

(Article II, Section 1, The Constitution)

This is the oath taken by every President since George Washington first swore to honor it on April 30, 1789.

If we wish to be just judges of all things, let us first persuade ourselves of this: that there is not one of us without faults; no man is found who can acquit himself; and he who calls himself innocent does so with reference to a witness, and not to his conscience.

—Letters of Seneca

Protect and Defend

One

"ARE YOU *sure* this information is correct?" Raymond Arledge Tunstall, the Senate Majority Leader, asked his aide, as he peered at the report just handed him. When he spoke, his eyebrows shot upward, pushing the furrows of his deeply lined forehead even tighter.

Early in his career, when cameras revealed this mannerism to him, he resolved to get rid of it. But he could not. Critics took amiable aim at what seemed to be Tunstall's surprised expression even when he was reciting dull budgetary facts.

But Tunstall's eccentricity of countenance had only served to help make him a larger-than-life figure on the American political scene. In more ways than one.

While not obese by any means, he waged a constant battle against the incessant assault of flesh; his hair, thick and gray, lay heavy over his skull, as if the work of a skillful weaver.

"Reasonably correct, Senator," Tom Auden said, "though I haven't had time to check out every possibility of error." The young man spoke vigorously, balancing a glass half full of scotch and soda, the tinkling of ice mingling with his words.

The Senator stood, walked to the fireplace, poked at a piece of charred wood. He put another strip of wood on top and stuffed rolled-up newspaper pages under the smoldering log. He disliked unnecessary waste; none of those damn artificial logs for him. He lit a match, watched the flame leap to the newsprint and curl around the log.

Once upon a time, the junior Senator from his own state had carelessly compared Raymond Tunstall to "a lion who refuses to be cornered, fights before he has to, and inflicts more damage than he ought to." The junior Senator was a Republican, which to the Majority Leader made the remark all the more unsuitable. For his young colleague of the "other party" to utter such a statement in public was a clear sign of ineptitude.

Men who aspired to power and grasped it and held onto it were, to Tunstall, those who spoke little in public about someone else's shortcomings—particularly if that someone else was himself in a position of power. He pondered this as he absorbed the report in his hand.

What had been confided to him by his aide was, by anyone's measure, a revelation: a planned Presidential action that, if made public early, would send shock waves not merely around this town, but through the country itself, and the world beyond.

But the Senator knew, as the President must have known, that any time a Chief Executive considers an enterprise so fraught with risk he must factor in the possibility of disclosure. What the Senator had just learned was definitely a challenge, and possibly an opportunity.

The Senator knew Tom Auden drank heavily. He considered each man imperfect, possessed of strengths and flaws. But, careful manager that he was, he made use of both. He judged Auden to be a professional, which was why he employed him.

But even before a trusted aide, Tunstall's face was a mask. "Who is this contact," he now asked, "and how did you get him to talk to you?"

Auden grinned. "It's just as well you don't know, Senator."

Tunstall endorsed Auden's cautionary reply. He wondered if a woman was involved. A long time ago, when his wife died and their childless marriage ended, the Senator determined that pleasures of the flesh were indulgences he could live without, even as he firmly rejected other intrusions which could cause embarrassment. He knew that few others could live by so rigorous a code, which made his own circumspect life-style an indispensable asset.

When he came to the Senate following a term as Speaker of the Michigan Legislature, Tunstall brought with him a compulsion to be right—and to be respected. His ambition flung itself against every man-made obstacle, and because he was willing to extract more from himself and from those who worked for him than the average political leader, because days blended into night without any slackening of his energy, his victories grew and his circle of critics narrowed. Nothing is more congenial to the gathering of respect from others than the consistency of political triumph.

On his very first day in the Senate, Tunstall met the Majority Leader, Lyndon Johnson. His first impression was one of distaste, not so much for the man, but the politician. Tunstall sensed the edge of a blade sharper and longer than any he had ever encountered. At the time, he thought what he felt was revulsion. Later he realized it was something else. Envy.

When Johnson had approached him about a vote on some long-forgotten issue, Tunstall was curt and remote. This only evoked a slight smile and a friendly shrug of the shoulder from the Majority Leader. Sometime later, Tunstall's amendment to build a reservoir and dam in the southern part of his state was destroyed in committee.

Johnson was invariably friendly and Tunstall never reproached the Majority Leader for his pitiless amputation of the dam/reservoir. Indeed, Tunstall became Johnson's ally. Only a stupid man would remain oblivious to such an obvious lesson in political power.

He remembered what LBJ once said about a Senator who was careless and insensitive in his handling of fellow Senators: "That fellow has got himself a bad case of the dumbass."

Once Johnson became President, Tunstall never attacked him frontally, but extracted a price for every crucial vote he gave.

When Tunstall's predecessor as Majority Leader, with immaculate timing, fell dead of a heart attack four days before his sure reelection to his post, Tunstall was ready. With his usual energy and diligence, he conferred by phone with every one of his Democratic colleagues, squeezing pledges from them before any one of his three opponents realized they had been outflanked.

Tunstall was not inspired by any notion that his colleagues loved him. Some had voted for him out of fear, others to gain a "marker" on him, and the rest out of respect for his leadership abilities. Even his worst enemy knew that Tunstall would not hesitate to let the President know of the Senate's will.

The Senator gazed expressionlessly at the report as he said, "Anything else, Tom?"

"No, sir."

"Then," he said with the faintest smile of dismissal, "I thank you."

Alone, the Senator climbed stairs carpeted in a deep heavy gold rug woven in Pakistan, given to him by that country's former finance minister. The Georgetown house on N Street was not lavishly furnished, but every piece in the downstairs study and living room was a valuable antique. Upstairs, he ambled into his bedroom, a large room dominated by a marble fireplace, unlighted at the moment.

He sat down at his antique claw-footed writing table, and once again read the typed report, savoring it. Then he rose and moved to the large window which overlooked the cobblestones of N Street, so serene, so lovely.

Information was power in Washington. The right information, applied at the right time and in the right way against a force, became in itself a more dynamic force. Tunstall had only contempt for his colleagues who confused publicity with power, who believed that influence and power meant courting the media, panting after headlines, having a spiritual orgasm every time they appeared for thirty seconds on the network evening news or were asked to submit to the querulous questioning of some so-called political pundits on a TV talk show.

The Majority Leader knew that the levers of power yielded only to a firm, authoritative touch, applied by those equipped with the right information, and the guts to use that information at the right time.

His hand moved softly over the report. He knew he now held a hammer that could—if he chose to use it—cause more than a little turmoil for the most powerful of public men.

He never allowed anyone to witness the incessant thrill that filled him when he challenged and won. Perhaps it was the sheer excitement of the game that shielded him from grosser pleasures; but he always convinced himself that what he was doing had merit and was in the interests of his country.

The effrontery of it all, the audacity of the President! It wasn't that he disliked the President. He didn't deal in "like" or "dislike." Those words were merely childish responses for childish minds.

What Tunstall cared about was policy, since policy affected power.

He was uneasy when he thought about the President and the impending election next year. He had begun some months ago to face the fact that this President might not be reelectable—and if that was so, who would replace him? The very few to whom he had confided his conclusion reacted in the same nervous, uneasy manner, yet they eventually came around to the Leader's bottom line. His presumptions might border on political betrayal, and if acted upon would be an immense rupture with political normalities, but the nation's future sometimes required such bold action.

He had already settled on the replacement candidate and if the time was ripe, Tunstall would not be afraid to act.

In his seclusion, Tunstall allowed himself a smile; such pleasure was private, but well earned. His aide's report had authenticity in every line. This news probably would have leaked sooner or later, but the Majority Leader had it first. What was required here was a fastidious sense of timing . . .

He pondered this challenge. How best to use the information? He did not have to ponder that query very long.

He knew the answer.

Two

CLEM BARKLEY woke quickly, the unwholesome ring of the clock alarm raking his inner ear. With blurred eyes he saw the time, 5:30 a.m. God, sleep had become a ragged exile. It was midnight before he got home from the White House last night.

He clambered out of bed, his long, lean frame almost creaking, got into his jogging suit, and began his warm-up exercises. When he came back from his early morning run thirty-one minutes later, he plunged into the shower, shaving in front of a clouded mirror, as the thin, razor-sharp needles of hot water bit into his chest. He wiped the mirror and said, "Ugh." His slightly puffy face stared back at him, eyes reddened, his rugged features partially marred by a crooked nose, broken when he collided with a partner's tennis racquet in his undergraduate days at Denison College in Ohio.

Today, he remembered, marked the eighth month since Andrea angrily denounced him for neglect, railed at him for his sodden attention to her needs, and accused him of loving the President and his White House duties far more than he did his wife of five years. "How can you stay down at that place night after night, not even caring what I'm doing, what I'm feeling" was the most moderately phrased of her hysterical, at least to him, recounting of his flaws and faults. "Try sleeping with political power sometime when I am no longer here" was her parting remark before she jounced out of the apartment and returned to her family in Columbus.

When they had met, Andrea, two years younger than Clem, and a newly minted producer at one of the local Columbus TV stations, was seemingly attracted to the rousing hurly-burly of local politics, and when Clem attached himself to then Governor Donald Kells, Andrea offered no objections. Clem told himself that at least he was spending a reasonable amount of time at home with Andrea. But then Kells began his run for the Presidency and Clem traded his clock for a calendar. The nights and days merged. There was none of this "I'll work on that tomorrow, meanwhile I'm heading home." The ruptures began slowly, but remorselessly.

The divorce was moving right along, as she put it in her last phone call, a conversation which Clem told others would have frozen the sands of the Sub-Sahara. At the age of thirty-six, Clem Barkley was learning about the sharper edges of life. He was well aware he never had any affection for argument, for confronting an emotional issue. Put it under some comfortable coverlet and let it rest; something will work out. He rejoiced in the daily challenges in his work and anything that collided with his duties was a messy intrusion devoutly to be avoided. God, he said, I'm doing something for the first time in my life that really counts. What can be better than that?

Clem, however, did not reveal to anyone else what he judged to be Andrea's most poisonous comment, which shocked him and shook him. "I hate the President," she said, "I hate him for stealing you, for absorbing you."

The sullen fact which he tried so desperately to disguise was that he would have made the choice without hesitancy if it were put to him: Andrea or the White House. Which is why the absence of his soon-to-be ex-wife became less bittersweet the more the days fled by. But how do you explain to others that the beckoning of the White House and its alluring embrace were more felicitous (Clem used that word often, though he knew it was pompous) than any other tug on his time and attention?

His post, Appointments Secretary to the President, was to him more seductive than marriage, more important than a wife. He could never, ever, commit this truth to anyone. By any of the assumed social normalities, it was horrifyingly wrong to harbor these feelings. But Clem, like an unredemptive alcoholic, could not do other than what he was doing. It was supremely addictive.

Clem knew the joy of being at the center of decision-making, the exultation of being by the President's side, privy to his inner judgments, being a part, however small, of the President's agenda. I love it, he said to himself, I do love it. He knew he was involved in a powerful, primitive transaction in which political power and the sense of political place were the equivalent of a huge intake of the most fiercesome drugs ever known. He was, he had to confess in his most secret moments, a political animal, now and forever.

He dried quickly, flung himself into his clothes, all the time watching the clock. The President was expecting him this morning, as the President expected him every morning. He dare not be late. He had moved to this tiny two-room apartment on K Street, overlooking the Potomac, within days after Andrea had left him. It was sparsely decorated, but Clem was unobserving. He spent little time here anyway. Often he slept on the couch in his office. He picked up the beige phone connected directly to the White House switchboard and ordered a car to be at his front door.

At 6:54 a.m., he alighted from the chauffeured black Chevrolet before it had fully come to a stop at the basement entrance to the West Wing of the White House.

Barkley strode through the West basement, vaulting up the stairs to his first-floor office, next to the President's. While Clem was the President's closest aide, he was not Chief of Staff. Following the example of Presidents Kennedy and Johnson, Kells had chosen to have no Chief Assistant. The President echoed his predecessors, saying that not one of his aides had been elected to anything, including Assistant President.

"Besides," President Kells had said to Clem, "if anyone is going to commit a blunder in my name, I want it to be me—not some aide of mine who thinks he's running the country."

Clem flicked through the file on his desk. He looked at the cordless clock on his desk: 7:05 a.m.

"Damn," he muttered.

He dumped his topcoat over the swivel chair near the desk and was about to rush out when his phone rang. "Barkley here."

In reply, a prep-school proper voice said without introduction: "The National Security Council meeting has been changed to nine o'clock."

It was John Wingate, the National Security Adviser.

"Damn," said Clem. "The Boss'll be feisty now."

"Yes," said Wingate, "but not for that reason."

"What do you mean? What happened?"

"I want to warn you before you see the President. The Willacy Hughes trip to China is blown."

"*What?*"

"Someone leaked it—or someone found out. Either way, it's blown."

"God!"

"I'm afraid He can't help you," Wingate said dryly.

Clem replaced the phone and in a half trot moved through the corridor, out onto the walkway to the Mansion. A crisis on the horizon only served to invigorate him. He was, after all, exactly where he wanted to be, doing exactly what he wanted to do.

The working offices of the White House were in the West Wing, built in 1901 and first occupied by President Theodore Roosevelt. The living quarters of the White House, as well as the public rooms which tourists view, were in what is known as the Mansion, occupied first by John and Abigail Adams and the residence of all Presidents since that time.

Clem got aboard the President's private elevator on the ground floor of the Mansion. The Secret Service agent on duty stood beside the policeman sitting at the phone box a few feet from the elevator entrance. Both nodded in greeting to Clem, the policeman dutifully noting in his log, "Barkley up at 7:09 a.m."

The elevator door opened and Clem was in the second-floor hall of the White House facing Sergeant Brian Watkins, the President's valet, who was seated at a desk next to the wall just opposite the door of the President's bedroom. These were the private living quarters of the widower President, his wife having died ten months before he took office.

The second-floor hall, separated into West Hall and East Hall, stretched from one end of the Mansion to the other. To Clem's right was the West Hall, the President's living room. To his left were the Treaty Room, the Yellow Oval Room, and at the end of the corridor, on the south side, the famous Lincoln bedroom.

The oaken sliding doors to the family West Hall were open. A pair of Monroe-period tables, bearing freshly cut flowers, were flanked by brightly covered chairs. A framed Childe Hassam, vaguely reminiscent of Renoir, hung between the doors to the family dining room and kitchen. Beneath the large oval window, affording a grand overview of the Rose Garden and the winding walk to the guardhouse, was a heavy couch covered in dark green velvet.

Clem nodded at Watkins.

"Go on in," said the Sergeant, pointing to the door of the spare bedroom. "He's been asking for you."

The main bedroom, to the right, was the President's. Kells used the spare bedroom-study when he worked late evenings. He liked its cozy, comfortable feel.

Clem tugged at his tie, then knocked at the door.

"Come in," a famous voice said.

Sitting in a large overstuffed chair, sipping a cup of coffee and wearing a blue shirt with thin white stripes, collar open, and gray herringbone trousers, was the President of the United States.

Donald Conway Kells was a political cartoonist's dream, with a firm outshoot of chin and a straight, long nose. The great cartoonists Herblock and Conrad and, to a lesser extent, Oliphant and MacNelly, had fashioned a character of enormous chin and fluted nose that was instantly recognizable.

During the campaign the future President had allowed his advisers to include such cartoons in his election ads. Columnists applauded Kells for his sense of humor, but in truth Kells had initially advised his advisers where to stick the ad layouts. He had only relented after consulting with his principal nonstaff professional and close friend, Willacy Hughes, the Cleveland attorney who had served Governor Kells when in Ohio and now presided over a branch of his law firm in Washington.

It had been one of the rare times that Clem saw Kells indulging himself in the midst of a horde of advisers. The President was an insular man. He took leave of his public rostrum only when involved with the most intimate of his aides.

Clem regarded the President with an affectionate gaze. Almost to the day nineteen years younger than the fifty-five-year-old Chief Executive, Clem never failed to be struck by the physical bearing of the man, whose flat stomach, broad shoulders, and erect, slim carriage belied the fact he was two inches short of six feet, shorter than Clem by four inches. When President Kells entered a room, he inhabited it.

On long sleepless nights on the Presidential campaign trail, Donald Kells had shared with his young aide the story of the early life that had formed a future Chief Executive. Later, when he was nominated for President, in triumph's afterglow, Kells confided again to Clem.

"I've always felt that luck was never too far from my side," the nominee had said. "I have this inner instinct that when things look very black, I never panic but play for time. I just *know* a lucky break will come, and I'm always ready to take full advantage of it."

Clem knew from experience that what Kells had shared with him was based in truth.

On a cold afternoon in February nine years ago, the then Governor of Ohio was exposed on the front page of the Cleveland *Plain Dealer* as having involved himself, through his brother-in-law and a dummy corporation, in a huge land-development deal near the site of a new highway.

State Senator Donald Kells had just given a series of widely acclaimed lectures at Western Reserve University on the need for extraordinary men to take political leadership; his concluding lecture's theme: "The Public Man is Public Property."

"A leader can be neither a radical on the right nor a radical on the left," he had told his audience. "But he must be brave enough to take a position—and wise enough to explain it—with a resolve to never give up, never give in. Then, though the world falls in on him, it will find him standing there, in the ruins, undismayed."

A Cleveland *Plain Dealer* editorial, the day after the exposure of the incumbent Governor, called to the attention of the citizens of Ohio the remarkable young State Senator Donald Conway Kells, unbeaten in any political race, intense, hardworking, seemingly impervious to anything except public service.

A fledgling lawyer in Willacy Hughes' law firm at the time, Clem was pressed into service and immediately drew close to the candidate. When Kells won the governorship in a landslide victory, he took Clem with him.

The President nodded to Clem, motioning him to sit, and continued to read a piece of paper in his left hand, as he sipped his coffee. There was no greeting. Clem understood that routine formalities were not to the President's taste.

Then the President put the paper down on the small end table next to his chair and looked up.

"Clem," he said, his voice uncommonly low, "I've just talked to the Director of the FBI. He tells me that one of your people talks too much."

Clem winced.

The President continued: "We're not sure who this leak is leaking to—or just how much he knows about what we're doing."

Clem shook his head glumly.

"As a result," the President said, "my plans for Willacy's secret visit to China have been bungled."

"Who the devil is talking?"

"Terry Geer," the President said.

"Damnit . . . who's he been talking *to?*"

"The Director says only that an informant has Geer leaking information. We don't know to whom, or even exactly what information—but it poisons our entire enterprise."

Clem cursed Geer under his breath. The Willacy Hughes trip was the most closely held secret in the West Wing. Clem knew that only he and his man Terry Geer—plus John Wingate, of course—had any idea the venture was imminent. Beyond this inner circle, only Willacy himself knew, and the Secretary of State.

The President's voice was almost inaudible. It was vintage Kells. The darker the political corridor, the softer the President's voice became.

"Clem, get to the bottom of this," he said, matter-of-factly. "Find out what Geer said, and to whom."

Clem nodded.

"Do it very carefully. And do it fast."

"Yes, sir."

"Confer with Willacy after you talk to Geer."

The President rose and began putting on a navy blue tie with small red stripes. Thick shaggy hair curled over the top edge of the shirt collar. The President needed a haircut.

"We'll say nothing about this at the NSC meeting. You know I've changed the time to nine, don't you?"

Nodding again, Clem looked at his watch. It was 7:16 a.m.

"John ought to be here in a few minutes," the President continued quietly. "You can go as soon as he arrives. Find out what's going on. But be back in time for the meeting."

"No problem."

The President was snugging his tie in place, his back still to Clem. "After the NSC meeting, I'll ask MacIver and Harcourt to stay behind. We have to settle what we say about the new regime in Beijing. I've got to bring the Secretary of Defense in on this, now, you know."

Kells turned around from the mirror to face Clem, who was scribbling on a piece of notepaper he had taken from his inner coat pocket. He stopped writing and said, "Mr. President, it's tough for me to believe Terry would . . ."

"Don't bother questioning it. The Director's information seems sound to me."

Clem suffered the rebuke in silence.

There was a knock at the door.

"Come in," the President said.

A tall, slightly hunch-shouldered man entered. John Wingate, the President's National Security Adviser, wore heavy-rimmed, dark-tortoise-shell glasses. His shapeless tweed jacket might have been pressed at one time, but not this year. His hand lifted to his glasses, adjusted them, then fingered his tie, as if the hand were not certain where it ought to rest.

"Mr. President, I have the agenda," Wingate said, holding out a sheet of paper. "I believe it covers what you requested, in the order you specified."

John Wingate spoke in a manner that a merciless journalist at a recent dinner party described as "half lockjaw with some chinless braying thrown in."

The President took the agenda, read it, and handed it back.

"John, I want to move through this meeting fast. Cut out everything except the China issue. Clear?"

Wingate nodded.

The President put on his jacket and faced the mirror again.

Clem wondered if the President was going to say anything to John Wingate about the Geer leak. Wingate, after all, was stage-managing the Hughes trip. Although opposed to it when first broached, Wingate quickly got aboard when the President made his decision. Clem would say nothing to Wingate.

That goddamn fool, Geer. What could he have said, and to whom?

"Clem," said the President, "I think you ought to go on about your chore."

Dismissal it was. Clem was hesitant, though, to leave.

"Shall I check in with you later, Mr. President?" he asked.

"Not until you have it straight."

No mistaking the Presidential chill. The President was holding him responsible for Geer. The President, Clem knew too well, considered bad judgment a crime second only to treason or possibly child molesting.

As Clem left the room he heard the President say to Wingate, "Looks like we have to scrap our China trip, John, and I want to be ready with an alternative . . ."

Three

THE BEAUTIFUL nude young woman in bed next to him, sitting on her knees almost prayerfully, studied Bill Rawlins with a steady, sensual gaze.

Flat on his back, naked on top of the sheets, his wide-set gray eyes open so slightly the woman was still not sure if he was awake or asleep, he smiled. Just barely.

She returned the smile, almost grinning, and leaned forward, crouched on her knees, and her large breasts, firm and round and hard-tipped, brushed his face, swaying like tantalizing fruit. He looked up at her, stretching a hand to cup first one breast gently, then the other, guiding his fingertips down to trace a slow line to her supple stomach.

She laughed.

"Hey!" she said. "That tickles . . ."

He felt her hands behind his head, fingers digging into his thick, tousled chestnut hair. Her lips covered his and her tongue searched briefly; then she sighed dreamily as she collapsed against him. He rolled with her and was on top of her, and she moaned, and she gasped, her dark luxuriant hair streaking her face, a filigree mask over narrowed eyes.

"Love me," she said, "love me . . ."

Soon they lay quietly in each other's arms, the room slowly

brightening, curtains glowing with the early morning sun beyond. The woman stirred, folding her legs fetally for a moment. Rawlins kissed her lightly on the cheek and rose on bare feet to pick up his dressing robe. He left the bedroom and padded down the cushioned stairs to the library. He stood before a Chippendale table which served as his brother's desk.

His brother Roger had bought this house ten years earlier, purchasing at the same time two adjoining houses on P Street in Georgetown. All three had been built in 1846 by one Stuart Hazeltine, who'd made a fortune in shipping and land speculations. His brother delighted in reading the ledgers of Hazeltine's past, for numbers enticed him.

He stood before the fine table, sliding his hands across its polished surface as if it were the tanned thigh of the woman upstairs. On the table sat an ancient inkwell with a bent quill pen.

"We like our privacy, you and I," Roger told him when the property was purchased. "Did you know there's an underground tunnelway connecting all of these homes? This Hazeltine character was a farsighted old codger. There's an opening just beyond the library. You can go down to the cellar, pass unnoticed through the home next door, and on into the next one. And you leave by the back and get to the garage in the alleyway, drive your car out, and all without anyone knowing you ever left." His brother smiled. "You'll thank me for this someday."

Leaning against the table now, he looked around his favorite room, so elegantly appointed, bookcases ceiling to floor. There were two much sat-in leather chairs, a small leather sofa, a mahogany tambour secretary with delicate legs. Above the fireplace was a brown and golden Bingham landscape and between the two garden windows a Daubigny oil of a tree shadowing a placid stream beside which frolicked two gaily clothed children.

The vivid landscape, which he'd seen so often, struck him in that moment as if he were seeing it for the first time, and the painting summoned a deeply buried memory of a long-ago hunting trip he'd shared with his brother.

When Bill Rawlins was fifteen years old, he had won the state debating prize on the subject "Resolved, that the death penalty be abolished." The Houston *Chronicle* heralded the event with a story about young Rawlins: "He is the apple of Buck Rawlins' eye. The famous Texas oil wildcatter informs his friends with gusto that his son Bill will one day be President of the United States."

At fifteen, already nearing six feet, young Rawlins knew he was handsome, just as he already knew that his very wealthy father had deemed him a special person with a special destiny. It was something that had been drummed into him so hard and long it preceded memory.

He simply couldn't remember not hearing his father convey what a glistening future lay before him.

On that hunting trip, his father, his brother Roger, and he were stalking deer, trudging over the Sharnhorst Ranch that belonged to Vice President Lyndon Johnson, just outside the village of Stonewall in the hill country of Texas.

Buck Rawlins motioned his sons to sit with him under a gnarled old liveoak tree beside a wisp of stream. The day was overcast, ranchland sprawling before them, scraggy grass and squat little mesquite trees sprouting from a soil that gave up a living grudgingly to those who tried to exist here.

"Hope you boys are enjoyin' yourselfs," said Buck, biting off a thick chaw. The boys' mother abhorred the practice, so their father did his chewing when he was away from home.

Bill and his brother, Roger, were silent.

"You know," said Buck, spitting a brownish stream in a faltering arc that almost drowned a grasshopper, which skittered out of the way of the tidal wave, "this land is mighty poor, sorry as hell for farming, and there sure as hell ain't any oil up here. If there was, it would give Lyndon fits."

He grinned a mischievous grin.

"It surely would," he continued, " 'cause then he would be stuck bein' a rich oil man."

The boys looked at their father curiously.

"Oh, Lyndon would like bein' big rich well enough, but he'd rather be caught shittin' on the minister's shoes than be *oil* big rich. He once said to me the one thing he didn't own or want to, was a drop of oil."

Buck tousled the fifteen-year-old's hair as if Bill were a five-year-old, but Bill didn't mind.

"You want to know why?" Buck asked, a wide grin splitting his leathery face. The boys nodded.

"Hurts his national reputation, or so he says," Buck explained. "Can't be national and beholden to oil. Did you boys know that Sam Henry Culheen and me and George Brown, Wesley West, maybe Jim Abercrombie are the only oil men in Texas who are Johnson men? The rest of them can't abide him, truly can't."

Buck's brown face, square, heavy, was in a half shadow, shaded by his sweat-rimmed Stetson. It was a face burned by thousands of sunlit days, traversed by the after-echo of countless fifths of scotch, creased by the whiplash of untold winds that roared through the wellheads he had baby-sat, waiting for the rumble of dark oil pouring from an earth that had hidden it zealously for a million or more years.

"Senator Bob Kerr in Oklahoma, he can be oil big rich," Buck was saying, "but Lyndon says that if you are going to make a difference in the country, you got to be free of the taint of the goddamn stuff. Well, boys, that's why I don't give two buckets of warm gooseshit for running for office. I just let these bunnytails get *their* spasms from being elected. It simply ain't for me."

Buck turned his gaze on Bill; it was as warm as the sun that had turned Buck's face to cowhide.

"But for you, son," he said, touching Bill's shoulder, "that's what my money's for."

Buck kicked at a branch that had fallen off the aging oak, his back propped up against the trunk. The two boys were in a squatting position on an outcropping of limestone.

"You boys are what really counts. You truly are. I'm mighty proud of you both." His eyes seemed to glitter in the leather mask of his face as he studied Bill. "I got plans for you, Bill. Big plans. I've been aiming to talk to you and Roger about this for some time now."

The brothers exchanged glances and shrugged with their eyebrows.

With inarguable finality, their father slapped his thighs and made a pronouncement. "The deer will wait. I want to talk to you about the future."

Buck put his hand on Roger's boot toe.

"Roger . . . son. I want you and Bill to stay close." Buck's eyes narrowed, the granite jaw tight. "I want you to watch out for him. He's going to be somethin' big—mighty big. I *know* he's going to be President one day."

The old man laughed as Roger and Bill smiled nervously.

"Okay, okay . . . You boys remind me of some of them skeptics at the Bayou Club. They think I'm a candidate for the loony bin. But I'm not. I ain't any more crazy than Joe Kennedy was. Old Joe may be a lot of things, but *crazy* is not somethin' you can hang on him."

Buck pointed a thick finger, as gnarled as the oak, right at Roger.

"Roger, you and Bill, for all your lives, are gonna be as rich as a farting Croesus. You won't have to worry about nobody havin' to take up a collection for you. But," Buck continued sternly, "I don't want Bill to be fussin' around with oil or ledgers. I want him to keep his mind on somethin' more important."

"What, Daddy?" Roger asked.

"His destiny." Buck savored the melodrama for a moment, then grinned widely, large crooked teeth visible. "Yeah, I'm talking about destiny. Bill's got one of them." He looked at Bill, and the grin was gone. "And I got the money to see that you get where you're bound to go—by God and destiny and your old daddy."

Bill Rawlins wasn't smiling either, now. He watched his father intently, his own gaze steady. Roger bent his head down, drawing lazy circles in the soil with a stick.

"Roger, listen to me, you hear," Buck spoke sharply.

Roger lifted his face abruptly, dropping the stick, his eyes now on his father's, his lips trembling.

"Son, you have to manage *both* your lives, so that you'll be there to give Bill whatever help he needs, so that Bill don't have to wonder or get nervous about where you will be when he needs you."

Then his voice softened and this time he tousled Roger's hair.

"I just want to live long enough to see Bill become what he's gonna be," he said. "But if I don't, then, Roger, I expect *you* to be there . . . and by God, I never want to ever think that you cut and ran when Bill needed you. You hear me, boy?"

Roger spoke low. "Yes, Daddy, I hear you."

The old man grunted approvingly.

"You boys will make a great team. Bill, you got something that few youngsters ever have, you truly do. You got talent, god*damn*, you got talent." He shrugged his big shoulders. "I don't claim to know everything, but I know somethin' about human beings. If I size up a fella and tell you he ain't smart enough to pour piss out of a boot without a four-color map, you can bet your ass you're gonna be raking in his chips, no matter what hand you're playin'."

Bill smiled.

Buck spat a long stream of dark tobacco juice. He wiped his mouth with a coarse shirtsleeve.

"You ain't going to Austin to the University, Bill. Your mother went there and she has her mind set on you going, and Roger is going to graduate there, but you ain't. You're gonna go to Harvard or Yale and get some of that shiny-pants education.

"So," Buck continued, "when you go to Washington, those high-and-mighty crud-bags will know you ain't some flabby-assed rube, but a man with a suitcase full of the best education those ivory-tower professors can shove in you."

Buck scratched his creased neck and flailed at a noisy bee circling his shoulders.

"Besides"—he grinned—"when you get through with that eastern education, no one's gonna suspect you come from Texas except when they tangle with you and get their balls tore off with a Stillson wrench."

The old man clambered to his feet, groaning as a sore leg rebelled against the sudden movement. He held onto his walking stick, cradling his rifle in his other hand, stretched, expelling air and coughing.

"Well," he said, "let's walk a bit. Air feels nippy, and I don't aim to go back just yet."

He pointed his finger toward the northwest area of the ranging meadow.

"See that buck jumping through the brush?"

They looked.

Some two hundred yards away, a glossy brown nine-point antlered buck stood motionless against the cast-iron sky. Its head was flung upright as the animal surveyed the scene, unafraid, lean muscles taut. Then it trotted off imperiously toward a grove of trees just before the horizon.

"God, what a sight," said Buck. His voice was hushed, as if he were in church. "What a goddamn pity someone has to shoot that magnificent bastard."

Bill stood upright, hands outstretched holding onto his Winchester 306; he squinted down the barrel.

"I could've downed him with one shot," the boy said.

Buck nodded. "You could do that, son. But just remember that in politics, one shot is sometimes all you get. So you better aim right and not miss."

The old man eased his thickened body forward, settling into a long-gaited walk, his two taller sons by his side.

Rawlins' reverie ended as abruptly as it began. He thought of the woman upstairs and smiled. But his appetite had been satisfied. Now he concentrated on a single task.

Roger regularly swept the rooms and the phone for unwelcome intrusions, so Rawlins picked up the phone and dialed with no anxiety.

"Yes." The voice that answered was low, rasping, unquestioning.

Rawlins put his mouth to the phone. "Tonight. Call Luther. At ten sharp."

Then he hung up and briskly retraced his steps to the bedroom.

The girl had put on her slip, which did palpably little to conceal her full bosom. He laughed. "Either that slip is shrinking or else you have expanded beyond all normality."

Her smile widened. She knew he enjoyed the sight and she made sure it was never insufficient.

When she dressed, he took her by the arm and they descended the stairs, to the small door off the library.

"You know the way," he said. "You were glorious, as well you realize. I will call tomorrow."

She kissed him on the lips, smiled sadly, knowing he wouldn't call tomorrow, possibly not for some time, and she disappeared through the small doorway.

When he had showered and was fully clothed, he surveyed himself clinically in the mirror. The hair was combed, though there was always a hint of unruliness. Rawlins recognized it was part of his out-of-the-ordinary, and to many women, alluring good looks. To him, his handsomeness was just another political tool.

He shrugged into his jacket, smoothed down the collar, and opened the front door onto a sunny morning. He looked at his watch. Eight-ten.

At the curb were two cars. One a large Lincoln Town Car, the other a Chrysler van. The van held three men who looked at him impassively. Two other men lounged near the Chrysler. One of the two, heavy-set, medium-height, moved from the car, one hand now thrust into his light topcoat, and advanced toward Rawlins.

"Where to, sir?"

Rawlins glanced up and down the street. Two people were walking toward O Street. Several cars were parked midway toward 31st Street. Georgetown seemed strangely tranquil at this hour.

"My office, Charlie. I've got an important meeting at nine o'clock. Let's move it."

The heavy-set man nodded, and gestured toward the Lincoln.

"We're on our way, Mr. Vice President."

Four

CLEM PACED the small living room/study of his apartment, a glass of Coca-Cola sloshing in his tight right hand.

This was not a mood he often felt: anger was a luxury he didn't allow himself. His role in the White House required coolness and tact. It was not his place to be combative, nor was he naturally confrontational.

Moments ago, the President's rebuke burning in his vitals, Clem had reached for the White House phone. "Get me Terry Geer, quickly."

Soon his assistant's voice, thick with sleep, said, "This is Geer."

Clem hadn't identified himself. "Be at my apartment in ten minutes."

"Clem?" Geer said, suddenly wide awake. "Why don't I just meet you in the West Wing? We're going to talk anyway after the NSC meeting this morning . . ."

"Never mind the meeting. This isn't open for discussion. Get to my place. Now."

"What the hell's going on, Clem? I only suggested . . ."

"Now," Clem almost yelled. He slammed down the phone.

For one moment, Clem felt shame. Geer wasn't just a co-worker, but a friend, a good friend. And what if the President's information wasn't correct? Then he would *really* feel the guilt running like a roiling river inside him.

But the feeling passed. The fury returned.

There was little chance this information was false, no chance, really. Geer was talking. To whom?

Could there be a woman involved? Terry's brains didn't make him immune from this town's countless beautiful women; and in Washington, powerful men knew there was a large supply of lovely women who responded to beckonings.

Several months ago, at lunch in the White House mess, Geer had boasted of his bedroom exploits. Clem smiled at Geer, who tended to embellish even a chance meeting. Now he was troubled by Geer's attitude, storing away the anecdotes of womanizing for future reference.

"You know, they oughta canonize Kissinger," Terry had said, between sips of coffee.

"I have a feeling you aren't referring to his accomplishments in foreign diplomacy."

"I was thinking of internal affairs." Geer had grinned. Then he said, "Henry Kissinger ought to be canonized for his oft-repeated maxim: 'Political power is the supreme aphrodisiac.' "

"Maybe we can get the Congress to fund a statue of Kissinger," Clem said. "A reclining one."

Geer laughed. Then he sighed wistfully. "God, Clem, I've never had an easier time of it with women. Believe me, they're drawn to this place and the men who work here with the same dumb magnetism that sends lemmings out to sea."

Clem said nothing.

"Hear what I'm saying? Power is to passion as flesh is to carnivore."

Clem laughed. "The Geer Doctrine."

That had pleased Terry immensely. The phrase became a running gag with them.

The knock at Clem's apartment door was subdued. Clem yanked it open, startling Terry Geer, whose hand was still raised.

The fair-haired Geer's collegiately handsome face was tormented with puzzlement. Clem turned his back and waved his assistant in.

Then he turned and almost shouted in Geer's face, "Who have you been leaking to, who has been jerking you off?"

Geer recoiled as if he'd been struck a physical blow.

"What are you talking about, Clem?"

"Don't play games, Terry. You *know* what I'm talking about."

Geer seemed genuinely astonished, shaken by this uncharacteristic outburst from Clem Barkley.

"Good God, Clem, what's going on? I don't have the faintest idea what you're talking about!"

Clem sat on the footstool nearby, leaned close. He said very calmly, "I don't have a lot of time, Terry. The clock's ticking. I'm going to ask you a direct question. I want the answer fast, and brief, and make it the truth."

Geer swallowed and nodded.

"Who did you tell about the Willacy Hughes trip to China?"

Geer's eyes widened.

"*Who*, Terry?" With deadly dry sarcasm, Clem added, "By the way, the reason I'm asking is just that the President's plan for the Willacy Hughes trip has been blown."

A kind of veil dropped away from Terry's face. The expression it revealed was pale with alarm.

"Oh shit," Geer said quietly.

Clem recalled Geer telling him of a day at the Stanford Law School when Terry was accused of filching notes from a professor's office. It was a preposterous lie, but he was, as he said, impaled on his own incredulity. He couldn't answer the professor, who naturally took the hesitation as a plea of guilty.

Clem sensed that something of that kind had invaded Geer's mind now.

"Just tell me, Terry," he said, almost gently. "Tell me the truth."

Geer sighed. Shook his head. "Well, I did mention it to one person, in a roundabout way . . ."

"What do you mean, 'roundabout way'?"

Geer shrugged. "I wanted to do some research for Willacy and I turned to the one man I thought could give it to me. But let's get one thing straight, Clem. Not at any moment during my conversation with Roy Hickey—"

Clem interrupted. "Roy Hickey—that Crown Broadcasting guy?"

Geer nodded. "Fact is, I just asked him a few questions about China, with no mention of Willacy. Roy rambled on, telling me about his childhood there, told me about his father, who was a Baptist missionary and spent a lot of years in China. Matter of fact, John Wingate and I talked about this earlier, about getting an outside expert to give us information, side-bar stuff. Nothing more. When I mentioned Roy, John suggested I give him a call, without really telling him anything. So I did."

"Why'd you single out Hickey?"

Geer shrugged. "I just told you. Roy's a close personal friend, one of my closest."

"You didn't tell him why you were tapping into him for back-grounding?"

"God, no. I told him I was working on a think-piece on China for a foreign policy seminar. I kept it easy—no urgency." He shrugged again. "Roy seemed eager enough to want to help. But, Clem, I swear to you, I never made mention of a trip, never said a word about Willacy. This was strictly a bare-bones foreign policy seminar."

"That's all?"

"That's all. How could Hickey make the leap from my casual request to full-blown knowledge of Willacy's trip? I can't see it."

Clem shook his head. Odd piece of business.

He said, "I believe you. I'm sorry I went for your jugular. Sorry."

"That's all right. But will this leak seal over?"

Clem shook his head again, and fell silent.

Something *had* leaked. But how, and who, if indeed Geer's story was true? The President was convinced that the leak was in the White House. This wounded Clem—not so much the leak itself, terrible blunder though it was; what hurt was this fissure in the President's faith in him.

On occasion, the President would gather Clem and the other staff aides in the Oval Office for late evening chats, and the President would reminisce, and instruct.

"You're not being courted by the press because of your baby-blue eyes and your charming manner," Kells would say. "You're big shots not because of your fascinating talents, but because you have access to me. So every time you get buttered up by some reporter or some lobbyist, you better realize they don't give a good goddamn about any of you. They want to know what you know about what the President's thinking, or getting ready to do."

These discourses did tend, as Clem pointed out, to keep the staff from developing a bad case of hubris. It was the President's way of shoveling tablespoons full of humility through the staff's clenched teeth.

And now this disastrous leak—which the President blamed on Clem.

But why Roy Hickey? The man apparently had no real information to leak, and if he did, who would he leak it to? If he really knew about the trip, why wouldn't Roy, a journalist, use the information himself?

What possible benefits come to a newsman who has a juicy story and then passes it on to someone else?

Something was out of kilter here.

"Terry, have you talked to Hickey since you spoke to Wingate about the leak?"

"No." Geer hesitated. "I did call Roy yesterday, but he seemed like he didn't want to talk. Said he had a meeting he had to run to. I didn't think too much of it at the time, but Roy's a good friend. He told me once that our friendship meant so much to him that being a reporter would take a backseat whenever we talked."

"And you *believed* him? When are you going to learn that a newsman's only friend is the next *story?*"

Now it was Geer's turn to turn sour. "Goddamnit, Clem, there was no leak from me. Hickey was strictly a background source—if he somehow leapfrogged from there to the Willacy trip, it wasn't my doing! Anyway, how the hell do you know for sure that Roy Hickey knew anything about the damn trip?"

Clem stood. Could the FBI report be wrong?

"You call Hickey right away and find out who he talked to, because he must have talked to *somebody.*"

Geer nodded dutifully. "Want me to use your phone?"

"Yes—right after I make one call . . ."

Clem grabbed the White House phone and pushed the buttons that were the private number of the President. Only he, Willacy

Hughes, John Wingate, White House Press Secretary Mike Carson, plus the Director of Central Intelligence and the Secretaries of Defense and State, had this number. Each morning the line was swept by the Secret Service.

"Yes," the President answered.

"Sir, Clem here. I'm with the man I was supposed to talk to this morning." Secure line or not, old habits are hard to break.

"Go on."

"The leak appears to be Roy Hickey, of Crown Broadcasting. Though this may not be what the Bureau thinks it is . . ."

A few seconds of silence. Then the President's voice again, low, devoid of emotion. "Get back here. Now."

Five

ROY HICKEY smoothed out his jacket as he entered the elevator. Blue-eyed, bespectacled, with the bland good looks of so many TV newsmen, he showed no signs of the strain within him.

Two hours earlier, just as he had been leaving for work, Hickey had received a frantic call from Terry Geer and had done his best to block Geer's attempts to see him.

"Look, Terry," Hickey had said hastily, "I'm sorry as hell, but I've got to go to New York on assignment. But, hey, I'll be back tomorrow and we can talk then. Okay?"

It was not okay.

Terry's voice was tight as a vise ratcheted to the edge. He had to see Hickey—*now*. Cancel the damn trip to New York!

Reluctantly Hickey agreed.

Now his hands shook as he buttoned his jacket, but not from the cool evening wind. No question about it—he was hip-deep in dangerous waters.

Still, he had no sense he'd done anything treasonous. That was a ridiculous notion; the information he'd passed on was so trivial—even if the money he'd been paid hadn't been.

Crown Broadcasting was ready to dump him. Hickey had known that for months. And none of the other networks was showing the faintest interest in his overtures for another position. At this rate he'd be lucky to find a job in local news somewhere. He was getting to that age where if you hadn't made it in this business, you weren't going to . . .

He'd been frightened, and he desperately needed money. And all he'd had to do was pass along any tidbits of information he might garner from his old friend Terry Geer, in the White House.

It wasn't like anybody was after the designs of top-secret weapons or anything like that. His benefactors were merely interested in idle talk. What gossip, what rumors, were whispering around the White House corridors? What was being talked about, what were the subjects of concern?

That was all.

Information of the most casual sort. And passing along information was what Roy Hickey did for a living, wasn't it?

But now the small truths he'd sold to his foreign contacts, and the big lies he'd sold himself, were catching up with him. Behind his placid exterior was a shambles of a man. But that shambles of a man was finally pulling himself together . . .

Hickey knew what Terry wanted to talk to him about. There was no mistaking the urgency in Geer's voice.

And Hickey also knew, without any doubt, what he was ready to do: tell Terry everything.

Starting with the man who first approached Hickey, the charming, cultured fellow with the red guardsman's mustache.

Then Hickey would ask Geer what, if anything, the White House wanted him to do. The newsman was fully prepared to play double agent for the President, if that was what it took to crawl out of an unwholesome nest not of his choosing. Whatever the cost, whatever the risk, he had to go through with it.

And now he felt a sudden relief.

The light at the end of this tunnel was not only visible, it revealed a self-respect that might be regained. Besides which, there might be a book contract in it someday . . .

The first step was to stop by his office and leave a note for the head of programming. He didn't know how long the meeting with Geer would take, and he hadn't been lying about that New York assignment.

So Hickey walked out of the building on 2000 Pennsylvania, a new structure ingeniously designed to retain the eighteenth-century façade of the houses that had once been the outer edge of downtown Washington. Within a stroll of the White House, the old houses must have, a century ago, been home to many a high-stationed government official, not to mention the lawyers and speculators who inhabited the Capital in those early days.

Hickey turned right, walked quickly past the Gap store on the corner. He turned right again onto 20th Street. He would meet Geer at the Kennedy Center, in front of the Opera House. They could wander about and look like tourists while they spoke. In Washington, privacy could sometimes best be found in public.

He glanced at his watch; he should hurry. The wind was blustery, but not as cold as it might have been. Traffic was heavy, 20th Street emptying its stream of commuters onto Pennsylvania Avenue. The sky was mottled with rough-hewn clouds, the day turning to almost dusk. He felt serene, relaxed, as he walked along, not common emotions for him lately. The strain was easing. His decision made.

Somebody bumped him.

He turned, looking for an apology.

He found, instead, two men—a burly pair in heavy greatcoats with collars up to foil the wind.

They were at his elbows, one on either side of him, and as the two of them moved along beside him, Hickey glanced from one to the other. Their faces seemed blurred, like a grainy photograph.

One murmured, "I'm sorry," in a thick voice.

Hickey grunted in reply, thinking, *Stupid lummoxes, plowing into somebody like that, on a sidewalk wide enough to accommodate a marching band* . . .

He looked away from them, toward his car, parked in the lot some fifty yards away, when he felt both his arms in a vise.

They hurt.

He turned again, "What the hell . . . ?"

His feet left the ground—barely so. Perhaps less than an inch. But, just the same, he was floating like Peter Pan . . .

Only he wasn't suspended by pixie dust, or wires, either. Hands under his armpits propelled him easily toward the alleyway nearby. To a passerby, the three men would seem to be huddling close together. It happened so quickly, nothing much registered on

Hickey's face. Suddenly the fist in his stomach doubled him over, wind gushing from him like an off-key calliope.

Hickey felt his legs buckle, but the arms held him upright.

He almost passed out, but the hot breath of one of them, in his face, kept him awake. There was an aroma of some spice, not oppressive but biting, pungent.

"My . . . my wallet's in my hip pocket!" Hickey managed. "Take . . . take the damn thing!"

"Mr. Hickey," the other one said, "Hickey" pronounced in two long syllables, the voice low-pitched, sullen, "we apologize for rough treatment. We want only to talk with you." The voice was foreign, strangely accented, the words pronounced with odd precision.

This was no mugging, Hickey thought. Something else. He felt a chill.

The thumb on his right hand was pressed backward until the awful pain threatened to collapse him. He almost fainted.

"Make no noise. Walk with us quietly, Mr. Hickey," said the leader, even as Hickey writhed in agony, the pressure on his thumb unrelenting, "and we will not hurt you."

The words were only dimly discernible to him, but then pressure on his thumb stopped, the pain subsided.

Now they were almost to the parking area. The arms of the two heavy-coated men gripped him tightly, locked under his own armpits, his feet barely touching the sidewalk. Cars were backed up, waiting to get to Pennsylvania. A driver peered out his window. Hickey tried to signal him with a shout, but a massive hand squeezed Hickey's left side. Pain strangled him into silence.

The driver had seen nothing except three men walking close together, and one of them appeared to be drunk.

The grip on Hickey's side released.

"We know your car is in the parking lot just ahead of us, Mr. Hickey." The leader's voice was gentle, reassuring.

Hickey stumbled. He wanted to vomit. His thumb throbbed, his left side burned, and his mind whirled with confusion and fear.

"You can't get away with this," he said hoarsely, "not on the street. Tell whoever wants to talk to me to call me and we'll meet like reasonable adults . . ."

The two men, grunting, moved him to the lot, taking him directly to his dull-green Pontiac four-door. How did they know which car was his? Had he been under surveillance?

They were at the rear of the hedge-rimmed lot. No one around. Hickey began to tremble.

"All right," Hickey said, trying to summon some dignity, "this is my car. May I get in and go home now?"

If I can still their anxieties, he thought, *maybe I can put this behind me . . .*

One of the men shoved Hickey against the side of the Pontiac, pushing Hickey's face sideways against the car, the heel of a sweaty palm over Hickey's left ear, right ear mashed against the car window. The leader whispered, in some guttural foreign tongue, to his spicy-breathed companion, who glared at Hickey.

Then Hickey, surrounded by the two men but without the hands of either of them on him at the moment, thought he saw a police car's red light moving along just above the hedge line that enclosed the parking lot. Without hesitation, he tried to dive between them. For a bare second he thought he had broken free.

Then his back exploded as a huge fist plunged deep into a kidney. The pain was blinding. He tumbled forward, turned awkwardly, saw a blurred figure, grabbed at the figure's coat to keep from falling, held on, and as he did caught a fleeting glance of something silver.

Something that caught sunlight and reflected it.

Funny, he thought, *on an overcast day like today, the sun reflecting in my eyes . . . there is no sun . . .*

Only when he felt something prick, then pierce, his stomach, did it occur to him that the silver thing was a knife.

He felt another similar sensation, this time in the upper left chest, just about where his heart was.

In a fraction of a second, a pittance of time, in that lingering span between then and now, a millisecond of forever, Hickey realized he had been stabbed. As the thought leaped from his brain, sending a pulse command to nerve edges and the vessels surrounding his heart, he wondered if he could ever wake from this horrible nightmare.

One of the men extracted the knife, its blade glistening with blood. He wiped the blade on Hickey's trousers. He cursed in frustration.

The police car had long since moved along.

They both hoisted the corpse, the leader opening a car door to lay the body over the front seat, the dead man's back slumped in the gear box between the two bucket seats.

"Take his money and his wallet, anything of value on him," the leader said in the foreign language they shared. He shrugged. "People get mugged every day in this country."

His assistant laughed roughly. "Especially in this city."

He quickly searched Hickey's inside jacket pocket, ran his hands over the sides of the pants. He found the wallet where Hickey had said it was, in the hip pocket. He put Hickey's loose change, as well as a ring, which he tugged off a dead finger, in one of his own greatcoat pockets.

He took out his handkerchief, wiped the car's window carefully, as the other man turned to see if anyone else was around.

Two women suddenly appeared at the far end of the parking lot, getting out of their car, heading toward the 20th Street exit. They looked briefly toward the two men, one woman's glance lingering longer than the other, and then both moved briskly ahead.

The smaller of the two men looked questioningly at his companion, alarm in his eyes. The taller man shook his head slightly and closed the car door.

They casually walked away, turning onto H Street, two Washington executives sauntering from their workplace.

Six

AT 9:01 A.M. the President entered the Cabinet Room.

The six men around the table rose at once. The President nodded in all-encompassing greeting and sat in a brown leather chair in the middle, on the Rose Garden side of the massive octagon table. President Kells had rescued the table—presented to FDR by Jesse Jones, then Secretary of Commerce—from its Nixon-era exile.

The men seated at that table today comprised the President's National Security Council: the Vice President, the Secretaries of State, Defense, and Treasury, the Director of Central Intelligence, and the Chairman of the Joint Chiefs of Staff.

Clem and Wingate, who had been following him, took their seats, Clem behind and to the right of the President, Wingate opposite, next to the Secretary of the Treasury, one seat away from the Vice President, who sat facing Kells. The press secretary, Mike Carson, sat to Clem's right.

The President leaned back in his chair, resting his elbows on its armrests. His eyes were fastened on Wingate. He nodded to his National Security Adviser. Wingate cleared his throat and spoke.

"Mr. President—gentlemen—our sole subject of discussion this morning is our response to the coup in China."

There were nods all around, and a few exchanges of raised-eyebrow glances.

"You all have the briefing papers on the Beijing matter," Wingate continued. "The Secretary of State will begin the discussion."

Clem glanced at Winthrop MacIver, peering intently at the memorandum. The Secretary of State wore no glasses, which at age sixty no doubt pleased him greatly. MacIver and his aides would have come up with a course of action backed by long hours of research and scrutiny. The President, after all, was quick to indicate his distaste for those who spoke hastily, without factual reinforcement. And MacIver was a Secretary of State careful not to incite Presidential discomfort.

Clem shifted his gaze to the Vice President, William Booth Rawlins.

Rawlins sat directly across from the President, watching the Secretary of State impassively. Forty-seven years old, a United States Senator from Texas at thirty-one, he was reelected to a second term on a non-involvement-abroad issue.

As a passionate "peacenik," he swiftly became the darling of the left, a man the New York *Times* described as "the most erudite political knockout artist of his generation." The Washington *Post* pondered, "How can an elegant liberal like Bill Rawlins so captivate the voters of Texas?" The *Post* did not grasp the depth of Rawlins' generational roots in his native state. Whatever Rawlins was or was not, he was a Texan to the core, and he never let the voters forget that.

Clem had noticed, from the first meeting, that the Vice President had very little to say when the Cabinet or NSC gathered. To Clem, the team of Kells and Rawlins was an unnatural marriage.

But he also knew they made a classic mixture of the center and left, the mingling of two brands of toughness—not to mention the blending of two states with large electoral votes.

Still, Clem never felt comfortable with the Vice President. He was too—what was the word?—slick, a Cool Hand Luke, smiling with too much elegant calculation. But Clem never doubted that Rawlins possessed one of the brightest minds in Washington. What he did not have, in Clem's view, was loyalty to the President.

Clem glanced peripherally at Mike Carson. The young press secretary wore a thin beard, the only White House aide who dared to do so. Behind that calm, plump demeanor resided all the qualities of a professional hit man, with a slightly bulging waistline.

Despite his youth, Mike Carson was a political veteran. He had served on the staffs of two liberal U.S. Senators, always vaulting a little higher each time he changed positions. Carson knew Washington's dark political alleys very well. He knew how to protect his flanks and elevate his reputation, not an inconsiderable skill.

Though he had these mixed feelings about Carson, Clem worked with the press secretary in seeming harmony. The President would have tolerated no less.

Carson could smell out those who were on the political ascent, and took care to cultivate them. He always had a hand on, and an eye alert to, the next rung on the ladder. Which was why Bill Rawlins' wealth and ambition, Clem deduced, were so alluring to him.

But even Clem had to admire the nimble way Mike Carson could captivate, disarm, and persuade the White House press corps.

The Secretary of State cleared his throat. "As you know, nineteen days ago a coup d'état in Beijing put Chang Lianfu and his cabal in supreme command of the Chinese Government."

Since the student uprising in the late spring of 1989, and the later dissolution of Deng's aged cadre after Deng's death, there had been a tenuous political arrangement in China.

"There is little doubt," MacIver was saying, "that Chang has taken massive advantage of that hesitant leadership. We estimate that the Chang forces now control most of the provinces. And we believe the army is, in large measure, in sympathy with Chang."

The Secretary of State turned to nod in acknowledgment at the CIA chieftain, who was regarding him placidly.

"Intelligence indicates," MacIver said, "that the 371st Division, commanded by General Jin Hanyong, moved swiftly to Beijing to join with Chang. Given this quick deployment by General Jin, and the lack of any forcible outcry from other elements of the army, we believe the takeover by Chang will take hold."

Again, eyebrows around the room were raised in shared, nodding glances. Everyone here knew that Chang had asked the President for financial support and for arms.

"It is our judgment," MacIver said forcefully, "that we respond favorably to Chang, to make visible our approval of this readjustment in Chinese authority."

MacIver seemed to relish the words. Clem smiled inwardly. He guessed the Secretary of State considered that phrase less strident than "we didn't like the previous regime and we do like this one."

"We are in contact with the British at the United Nations, and they will confer with the French." MacIver looked up to survey the room. "We know that China's new government has no compunctions about displaying its animosity to the Soviets. Our recommendation for China action is, of course, hinged to the turmoil in eastern Europe, and within the Soviet Union itself."

Clem knew that MacIver did not need to educate these men about history turning upside down in the last several years. The future had turned gray, not only in eastern Europe and the Middle East, but in Germany as well.

The conference on the Palestinian issue, inflammable and unstable, had collapsed. Plans to revive it were at best unsure. There had emerged in the eastern European countries counterrevolutionary forces spurred on by the abject failure of their national economies. The American dream of a New World Order was invaded by reality.

The August 17, 1991 foiled coup against Mikhail Sergeyevich Gorbachev set in motion unforeseen events that ripped apart the soiled fabric of a seventy-four-year-old Soviet ruling class. But attempts to create independent governments in the Republics soon floundered. After a few short years of bleak famine, and a breakdown of law and order, the people of what used to be the U.S.S.R. were living in near anarchy, with crime in the Soviet streets an escalating pestilence. A new leader had appeared. He quickly forged relationships with the Republics, whose dependent status was cratering. He moved swiftly to caulk the leaky Soviet economy and renovate a creaky distribution system, and he gradually restored a central authority in Moscow. A sense of nation was once more reasserted in a Soviet state that had been flying apart at its ethnic seams.

The Executive President of the United Soviet Confederation of Republics (that was how he styled himself and the new union) reassembled a leaner, fitter KGB, focusing its once awesome power to rooting out criminals with brutish zeal. As the new Executive President said in a television address, "Disorder is worse than injustice." The people agreed. He had put bread on the table and regained control of the streets.

A new aggressive spirit had fanned out from Moscow to the Republics.

And no one in this room needed to be reminded that the current government in Germany was in a fragile state, trying to digest what had been East Germany. The Chancellor might fall any hour, or then again, he might even survive the next election. It was that thin, that unpredictable.

"Germany's Democratic Alliance Party may be more than just an annoyance to the Chancellor and to us," the President said, his tone and expression dark. "It's mostly populated by a rough group. I'm not suggesting neo-Nazi, but there is an awful squinting toward the past. I don't think any of us find it a pleasant vista when Germany starts gazing nostalgically backwards."

MacIver nodded in assent. The Vice President gazed raptly at the ceiling as if he were in the Sistine Chapel.

The President said, "If we can bring China closer to us, we add a balance to what is happening in eastern Europe." He turned his gaze on solemn, gray Andrew Collingdown, Director of Central Intelligence. "Andy, give us CIA estimates of this new China Government's capability to survive."

Collingdown's eyes, unblinking, were fastened on the sheaf of documents before him. Then he looked up at Kells.

"Mr. President, our sources indicate this coup has been in the making for some time." He shrugged. "When Fan Shijin moved to take power at Deng's death, he bruised feelings among the army commanders. Chang took advantage of that. In the nineteen months since, Chang has moved carefully—and brilliantly."

Everyone around the table listened intently to Collingdown, Clem noted, except Rawlins. Michelangelo still held his attention.

"The key to Chang's survival will be his reaction to the Soviet military force on the frontier," Collingdown continued, "and whether or not, given his anti-Soviet stance, he will take any harsh initiatives." The CIA head shrugged again. "Ever since the rapprochement between Moscow and Beijing broke down, the Soviets are nervous—as well they should be."

The President stirred in his chair. He motioned to Sam Harcourt, the Secretary of Defense, who had raised a hand. "You have a comment, Sam?"

"Yes, Mr. President."

But even as he said, "Yes," round-faced, sharp-eyed, balding Sam Harcourt shook his head, as if saying no to a naughty child.

"With all due consideration to Director Collingdown and to Secretary MacIver," Harcourt said, "even if the CIA's estimates are on the money, I do not see us flying into Chang's open arms. With relations between China and the Soviet Union so tense, any friendly move we'd make toward the Chinese would damage our relations with the Soviets."

"What do you think we should do, Sam?" the President asked. His voice was colorless.

The Secretary of Defense spoke very softly but forcefully. "I think we should wait," Harcourt said. "With all due respect, sir, and full knowledge of the apparent breakdown of democracy in eastern Europe, I cannot believe that the Soviets are going to embark on stupid adventures. Frankly, I would be more fearful of a return to an ugly past in Germany."

The President nodded slowly.

"On the other hand," Harcourt added quickly, "I am only vaguely disturbed by the Democratic Alliance Party in Germany. Are you suggesting an entente cordiale between Russia and Germany? That would surprise me."

Clem's shoulders tensed. Two days ago when Harcourt and MacIver had met with the President, and the President had outlined his own thoughts, with MacIver pleading the case for support of the new government through the UN, Harcourt had seemed silently to go along. Now, this . . .

The President sat with yellow pencil in hand, slowly tapping it on the foolscap pad in front of him. "Bill, what do *you* think?"

The President's voice was soft as he informally addressed the Vice President.

Rawlins spoke quietly, easily. "Mr. President, if we move too precipitously now, we endanger a rapport with the U.S.C.R. Anyway, shouldn't we know more about Chang's motives and plans before we rush in to embrace him?"

The CIA Director frowned. Rawlins seemed to take no notice.

"I don't think that Germany is rushing toward the past," Rawlins said, gently dismissive, "any more than I believe the Soviets are planning an invasion of Europe, or that Japan and China will bed down together. Granted the economies of eastern Europe are foundering, granted that the Chancellor has had his troubles of late, and granted that any alliance between the U.S.C.R. and Germany would be troubling, but we need to be absolutely sure about our relations with the U.S.C.R. before we slap them in the face."

The President said, "Would you describe a favorable response to the Chinese request for loans as a 'slap' to the Russians?"

Rawlins smiled. "Somewhere between slap and jostle, I think." He went on: "Of course, Mr. President, despite these views of mine, I'm prepared to support your decision."

Clem grimaced. That was a bit much. Only Bill Rawlins had the capability of revealing ease and menace at the same time.

Clem found it strange that the Defense Secretary and Rawlins should be taking similar positions. In the past, Harcourt had made little pretense at concealing his contempt for the Vice President's military judgment. Of course, Harcourt had certain political aspirations, which perhaps explained his sudden affection for the Vice President.

"May I ask General Tallant if he would care to comment?" The President nodded to the Chairman of the Joint Chiefs.

The answer was sharp, brief. "No sir, Mr. President. I would rather hold my final view."

"Very well," said the President. He turned to Wingate. "What is your judgment, John?"

Wingate pressed one forefinger to his glasses, pushing them. "I agree with the Secretary of State, Mr. President." He paused. "There is risk here, but"—his smile was thin—"then there is always risk in these matters."

Wingate had opposed the President's plans when they were broached, only coming on board when it was clear the President had no intention of backing off. John Wingate, Clem realized, was finally learning political rituals.

The President turned once more to Harcourt. "Would you want to expand your views further, Sam?"

Clem searched the President's brow, his voice for some clue to Kells' feelings, but there was none. This was the first time that the Secretary of State and Secretary of Defense had not cleared their views in advance, had not spoken as a team.

Something was clearly amiss.

Harcourt smiled tightly. "Yes, Mr. President, I can go further."

The Secretary of Defense ruffled some papers in front of him, peered closely at one page, and then put it on top of the sheaf of documents.

"I have here the CIA memorandum of four months ago to the President stating its own apprehension about U.S. intrusion on the Soviet-Sino feud. We agreed then that it was in our best interest not to get involved in that part of the world again."

"True," MacIver said, his irritation starting to show, "but with the understanding that we'd reexamine our position later."

Harcourt turned to face the President. "Mr. President, once we embrace this new regime with support and money, we have a new ball game, and one in which I am convinced we would regret playing. It's no secret in Moscow that you regard them severely."

Clem could feel the murmur around the table. This was an overt reference to the President's supposedly militant views about the U.S.C.R. The tough intervention in the Muslim republics by the Executive President was not welcomed by the President and he had seized on that police action by Moscow to talk tough. The press and others had characterized the President's stance as the roughest since the days when Ronald Reagan referred to the Soviet Union as "the evil empire."

Harcourt continued: "I stand with the Vice President in suggesting that we ought to know more about what the new leadership in China has in mind before we do *anything*."

And there it was. Harcourt and Kells. Clem trembled slightly.

The President leaned back in his chair, again tapping the pencil on the foolscap pad.

Then he stood.

"Gentlemen," Kells said, "we'll reassemble this afternoon at two o'clock sharp. Right now, I'd like to chat with the Secretary of

State and the Secretary of Defense. Come into my office, gentlemen, please."

The President nodded at Clem and Wingate, who rose also and
followed their chief from the Cabinet Room, through the Presidential secretaries' office into the Oval Office. Harcourt and Mac-
Iver picked up their papers and trailed the two. Clem thought he
caught Rawlins and the Secretary of Defense exchanging a fleeting
glance.

Rawlins seemed unperturbed he'd not been invited into the
Oval Office. His tall form moved gracefully out of the Cabinet
Room into the adjoining corridor.

Seven

THE PRESIDENT sat in his rocking chair, standard Democratic equipment since John Kennedy's time. MacIver sat to Kells' right, and Harcourt next to MacIver. Clem stood behind the couch, alongside Wingate.

"Sam," the President said, "I didn't understand you felt this way about the China situation. You were fully briefed ahead of time."

"Mr. President, I don't believe I indicated to you that I didn't."

"My memory is," Kells said, his voice gently reproving, "you had ample opportunity to express yourself to me."

Harcourt was clearly uncomfortable, but he managed a smile. "I don't mean to sound coy, Mr. President—I'm only saying that since that briefing, I've given this a good deal of thought, and my advice is as I just stated."

"Sam," MacIver said, "we talked about this just yesterday, on the phone." The Secretary of State's precise tones were edged with irritation. "And you left me with the distinct impression that you were going along with our recommendation."

Harcourt shook his head. "That's just not the case, Winthrop." He shrugged elaborately. "I can't know what you were thinking— it was apparently *wishful* thinking—but you can be certain I never agreed."

The President broke in, conciliatory and somber. "Sam, I think you should know something—something I intended to tell you anyway—because it demands your counsel, and your help."

Except for a slight tightening of his jaw and a glance at MacIver, Harcourt gave no hint of surprise. He watched the President attentively.

"About a week ago," the President said, "I began to work on a plan to contact the new Beijing government personally—to sound them out, as well as sit down with them on a number of problems we all know need settling. I asked Willacy Hughes to go to Europe ostensibly on law business, and then by some routes and procedures that John worked out, get Willacy to Beijing and see Chang Lianfu face to face."

Now Harcourt's eyes blinked. He said nothing.

"It would," Kells continued, "give me a more measurable fix on their thinking. There's risk involved, but I believed we could pull it off and get Willacy back here without anything leaking."

Harcourt nodded.

"Except," the President said with a humorless smile, "it already has leaked, apparently."

Clem had to admire Harcourt's nerves. Other than a barely perceptible hunching of his bull shoulders, the Secretary showed no outward reaction to this bombshell.

Suddenly Harcourt spoke, and there was an undercurrent of hardness in his tone. "If you will excuse me, Mr. President, I am rather astonished that you would go forward with such a plan without letting me know, or Winthrop here."

It was an obvious ploy. Harcourt wanted to know, fast, if MacIver had been privy to the President's plan, when Harcourt hadn't.

The President dismissed this with a wave. "Winthrop knew, he had to know. I needed his help getting Willacy in and out of Asia, in a low-profile manner."

"Hmmm," murmured the Secretary of Defense. "How did it leak?"

"I have information that someone in our own shop has, in some way, inadvertently or otherwise talked too much, and others now seem to know."

"What do you intend to do, Mr. President?"

Kells was silent a moment. Clem could almost hear the mental gears moving—precise, automatic, confident.

"At this point, Sam, I'm not entirely sure. My instinct is to assess the damage, and possibly go forward with the plan."

"My God, Mr. President, you'd be butchered in the press, not to mention the Senate, if it looked like you were sending your own man to make a deal with Chang, without consultation with the Congress, or our allies. My God, you can't do that."

"Nixon did it," Clem said.

Harcourt almost scowled at this remark from a mere Presidential Assistant. "Yes, Nixon did it, but that was a millennium ago!"

The President seemed vaguely amused by Harcourt's agitation. "Come now, Sam," he said, paternally patting the Secretary of Defense on the knee, "it won't be that bad . . ."

But the President, Clem knew, was already playing the chess game six moves in advance. He'd determined his plan had been badly assaulted, even if he could stanch the flow of information. Kells knew it was only a matter of time, maybe hours, before the news hit the street.

The President shifted gears again. "I just know it is vital that we look these Chinese in the face, take their measure before we come to any decisions. I am not happy about groping in the dark. I need to touch them, feel them, hear them. If I can't do it myself, I can do it through Willacy. He knows my instincts, and I can judge from what he discovers."

This tactile approach was second nature to the President; Kells needed to look the enemy or the ally in the face. It was a sensitive yet imprecise caliper, but Clem had seen it operate a hundred times before. The President would gather all the information possible and then let instinct take over.

"Mr. President," MacIver said cheerlessly, "I'm afraid what Sam says makes sense. I shudder to think what Senator Tunstall would do if your scheme came to light."

The President nodded, smiling playfully. "Our Senate Majority Leader would count his day made, wouldn't he?" He paused. "Then I take it you and Winthrop believe that we need to scuttle the whole project, right now?"

"*I* do, at least," said Harcourt.

"I concur," said MacIver with obvious reluctance.

"What's your judgment, Clem?" the President asked him.

Clem knew that the President was tossing him the ball not for an opinion, but for support. The President was keeping the debate and his options open, without overruling his two prime advisers.

Clem said, "We ought to mull this over more before we come to any conclusions. We don't even know at this point how widespread the leak is. I'd like to check it out, and then we can have another go at the basic question."

The President smacked his hand lightly against his leg. "Sound advice, don't you think? Sam? Winthrop?"

Harcourt hunched his shoulders, tugged at his earlobe, and gazed slowly at Clem. Was that contempt or admiration, Clem wondered. Or both?

Then Harcourt turned to face the President. "Yes," he said easily, "I suppose it is—though I am *not* optimistic."

The Secretary of State nodded. "It doesn't serve any useful purpose to make a final decision now. We can wait a bit."

The President smiled. He stood up, signaling that the meeting was over. "All right then, gentlemen, that's all for now. I'll be in contact with both of you this afternoon before we reassemble. We still have the matter of our announcement in the UN. No need to pursue that now, until we resolve the problem of Willacy's mission."

When the two Cabinet officers had left, the President turned to Clem. "Now, quick—give me a full report on what Terry said to this man Hickey, and what Hickey did with the information . . ."

Eight

VINCENT CANFIELD—short, thickset, preeminently self-assured—sat down to write.

The tools of the nation's most read and respected newspaper columnist and television commentator were at hand. The legal-sized pad of white ruled paper before him had been made to his own specifications, with lines more widely spaced than the norm. The paper's texture was thick and rich, the nib of his Montblanc fountain pen sinking ever so slightly into the softly yielding parchment. The ink was a vivid, glowing green. When he was in Groton so many, many years ago, his father had sent him a bottle of this specially formulated ink, and he had never considered another.

Inevitably, when he began to write, there was an excitement that the years had failed to dim—an affirmation of his skills, his insights, his continuing triumph over that noble and ingenious invention called the simple English sentence.

He sat at an ancient partner's desk, its gnarled wood scrubbed and shining, its centerpiece an inlaid writing board, its handles burnished brass. A circular window faced the desk and through it he could reflect upon the pebbled English garden beyond.

The study walls were lined with bookcases brimming with browned, leather-clad, stippled volumes. On the wall facing the entranceway was an inscribed pen sketch by Picasso set in a gold-bordered frame, announcing (in French of course) the artist's affection for "Vincent Canfield, that spacious American whose mind had fled all fenced dimensions to live in its own splendor." Roughly translated.

Canfield, ordinarily not a man to flaunt declarations of praise, had displayed Picasso's immoderate expression in a rare concession to what in others he would have derided as egoism. There were no framed portraits of the mighty who had been so often photographed with him over the years, and hundreds of celebrity autographed photos sent him unbidden reposed in dusty bins in his attic. His papers, and manuscripts of his seven books, were all reposing at his alma mater, Williams College.

In truth, there was no evidence here of attachment to any persons, living or dead.

A bachelor for all of his sixty-two years, his closest family members long since flung into a mausoleum in upstate New York, Canfield had discarded visible reminders of father, mother, family, kith and kin. Whatever affection he retained for those long-departed required no rostrums to prop up their memory.

On this bleak autumn day, in his small but elegantly furnished home on Kalorama Circle, Canfield considered what he was about to say. It was his routine to write in a flowing Spenserian script. Soon thereafter, his column would be typeset on an IBM computer by his secretary, and rushed via electronic messenger to his news syndicate and then to 141 newspapers.

From his thirty-seventh birthday until this very hour, Canfield had produced, every week, two columns of eight hundred words, Wednesday and Sunday, informing not only the American public but thousands of journalists. This was particularly the case, Canfield knew, in Washington itself, where so many found in his precise sentences the first inklings of what they themselves would soon be thinking. And writing.

But not this day.

What he was writing now would indeed appear in newspapers around the nation; but this evening, his TV audience would be the first to hear and to know.

It had been eight years since he had become a commentator for CBS, debating his old rival, Dr. Henry Kissinger, and to Canfield's view, triumphantly. After all, as Canfield had told his intimates, Kissinger was simply no longer relevant.

And to everyone's surprise, Canfield's stout figure and occasional stammer were not at all the distractions that television producers had supposed. Intellectuals were not expected to resemble film actors, and Canfield never stuttered when reading from a TelePrompTer.

Today, Canfield felt concerned.

He was, after all, about to write a commentary denouncing the President of the United States.

He would condemn Kells for his stupid intervention into a world arena in which this nation had no business.

The information came to him this morning, a telephone call from a friend—no, "friend" was not the proper description. Rather, an indefinite ally, whose troops marched with the Canfield legions only when the alliance was mutually beneficial.

Canfield believed he knew the strategy that prompted the call. He was being pulled into some grand scheme. But he went willingly, with eyes open wide. So long as he understood how the game was being played, he had no qualms about playing. Nor did he have misgivings about the accuracy of the information. What he now put to paper was ripe and timely.

He began to write: "One should never attempt to instruct a President on his duty, for it is clear that Presidents know their duty. One is also reluctant to chastise a President for error since we are all flawed, with the same possibility of failure. But knowing one's duty and not doing it, and committing an error and then failing to retrieve it, is a threat to this society, leaving an observer with no alternative but to examine, and to expose, the dereliction.

"Particularly is this true when the entire affair is conducted behind closed doors. Then when it is finally done, the action would be offered us as a fact accomplished, too late for either citizens or the Congress to stay the decision."

Canfield paused, pen raised slightly from the page, the plump forefinger nestled over the front of the pen. He was searching, not for words—as usual, they flowed abundantly—but for the lance, the pointed edge of the idea that would fly straight to the heart of the matter.

Canfield did like the President, but he counted Kells too stubborn, too suspicious of the U.S.C.R. In this changing world of turning doctrines, that kind of leadership had the anachronistic smell of cold war. He began writing again.

"The President at this moment is planning a mission to China, where the object will be to ally that nation with the United States, in order to face down the U.S.C.R. When will this President comprehend the senselessness of saber-rattling? Most Americans found that aggression unsuitable even with the cozy persuasions of Ronald Reagan.

"If we learned anything at all from our Vietnam adventure it would be that we cannot make ourselves effective in an Asia so vast, so inexhaustible in its subtleties, and so flexible in its accommodation. To set foot there is to disappear into quicksand.

"It is neither to our benefit nor to our purpose to embrace China —to commit ourselves in treasure, treaty, or blood. We have no interest, ethical, financial, or military on the landmass of Asia. How the Soviets and the Chinese deploy their troops, or their words, is none of our business. To think or act otherwise courts catastrophe. A President of the United States who fails to understand this is a dangerous man."

Canfield relaxed. He sipped the Montrachet glistening in its elegant Baccarat glass. He took one more sip, set the glass down beside the decanter.

He was pleased with his prose, of course, though he was not entirely satisfied he had properly aimed the lance. It was not yet lethal. But when he faced the TelePrompTer some hours from now, he would feel confident.

He always did.

He would find the exact shaping and shading of language he desired. It would take him a little longer this day, but he would find it, and it would be perfect.

And later this evening, the jackals of the Washington press would be livid with raw envy.

Canfield found that thought comforting.

Nine

THOUGH IT WAS near the end of a long day, a ton of memoranda was piled on Clem's desk as well as unanswered phone calls, which by Presidential order must be responded to before the day was done. It was as if he'd gotten no work done at all, and in a way he hadn't. The phone had been ringing constantly. People had been in and out of his office all day.

The press howled when Canfield went public with the Hughes China trip.

Weary, his eyes burning, Clem lounged back in his swivel chair, willing away the mountain of work on his desk. As if in mocking reply, his private line to the President buzzed, light flashing on. "Yes, Mr. President?"

"Clem, bring me the Hickey file, now. And any other papers I need to see. John still in?"

"I think so, Mr. President. He was just in here a few minutes ago."

"Bring him with you. You hungry?"

"I just ate, sir, thank you."

"Coffee, then?"

"Please," Clem said.

"It'll be ready."

The President of the United States had just taken Clem's beverage order.

Clem strode through the corridor, toward the Mansion. He glanced at the Rose Garden, which looked unreal in its after-dark illumination. He remembered stepping outside the Oval Office with the newly installed President of the United States, on the second day of the Kells Presidency. He and a confident President Kells strolled the grounds. Beyond the Rose Garden sloped the undulations of the Jefferson Mounds, indentations of groomed grass and replenishing soil constructed at Thomas Jefferson's order, to give a modicum of privacy to the occupant of the newly-built Presidential residence.

As they wandered, Kells had turned to Clem with a wide smile that made it clear he found the surroundings soothing. Clem marveled that the White House environment had been so gracefully designed. On that second day of the Kells Administration, the President had begun his love affair with the Rose Garden. He treasured his solitary strolls among the flowers, Secret Service men keeping their discreet distance.

But the comforting breeze had turned suddenly brittle, and the President became detached, as if he'd been chilled by a feeling of inadequacy, an unclear menace intruding on their stroll.

Clem had accompanied the President back into the White House, through the Diplomatic Reception Room, to the private elevator. Along the way, Kells smiled at Clem and said, "Well, from here on out, we have to earn our pay."

The Presidential aide had walked quietly back to his office; within him, elation battled confusion. Clem was where he never dreamed he would be, and the prospect of failure had been sobering.

Now, at the private elevator on the ground floor of the Mansion, Clem was joined by John Wingate. There were no Secret Service agents in the West Hall; they remained on the ground floor near the elevator and stairway.

Clem glanced at his watch as they approached the President in the Oval Office. 10:15 p.m. A tray of coffee cups and gleaming silver carafe waited on the coffee table. Clem and Wingate sat on the couch to the right of the President.

"Hickey," the President said.

The single word was both statement and question.

"I asked the FBI Director to check Hickey out thoroughly," Clem said. "The initial report from the local police and the Bureau says robbery—Toni Georgihu says it only *looks* like robbery."

"She's about the best man the Bureau has," the President said absently. "Her judgment is likely to be sound."

Clem nodded. "I'm convinced the murder's tied to the China trip—though I admit I'm hard-pressed to give you any hard data."

"Then why are you so certain?"

"Instinct."

The President said nothing. He understood.

Clem went on: "Toni's digging out the details. We do know Hickey was in financial trouble . . ."

"Don't we have *anything* else?"

"Maybe."

Clem opened the manila folder clipped with a red "Secret" tag. In red, it was labeled: FOR THE PRESIDENT—EYES ONLY.

"Mr. President, these FBI reports concern an informant's account of a meeting between Vincent Canfield and a Russian embassy official, a ranking officer of the KGB . . ."

The President's eyes narrowed.

Clem continued. "Canfield has informed the KGB official that he, and Senate Majority Leader Tunstall, are"—Clem paused to smile nastily—" 'discontented' with the President."

Kells smiled wryly at Wingate. "Hope these vulgar political matters don't bore you, John."

Wingate flushed slightly. His insistence on remaining above petty political wars was the subject of jibes in the White House mess. "I'm amused, Mr. President, but not particularly informed."

"You're lucky, John. Most of the time it's the other way around for me." The President turned back to Clem. "Go on."

"According to another informer," Clem said, "a KGB agent named Vaslansky is the Embassy official who met with Canfield. Vaslansky had knowledge of the Willacy Hughes China mission."

Clem paused so the President could absorb that bombshell.

Then he picked up again. "What we don't know is if the Russian is connected to the death of Roy Hickey, and whether or not it was Hickey who passed him the essential information."

The President nodded grimly. "The Russian could have given Canfield the information—or vice versa."

"Or not," Clem said, turning his palms up.

Kells shook his head. "Either way, the press has been eating us alive all day. Is this really espionage? Some Soviet plan unfolding? Why, with all his troubles, would the Soviet Executive President play *this* risky game? And how deep is Canfield involved? He and the Majority Leader are close, but I can't believe that Tunstall would go out on a limb like this. No matter what Raymond Tunstall thinks of me, he wouldn't climb in bed with these new Soviets. Would he?"

The President's brow was knit. He was lost in the thoughts he was sharing aloud.

Then his brow smoothed and he looked sharply Clem's way. "Tell the Attorney General and the FBI you're acting on my orders to get *personally* involved. I want you to do some bottom fishing on this one, Clem. Get on it."

"Sir, I anticipated that. I'm meeting with Toni Georgihu first thing tomorrow."

The President stroked the side of his nose. "Anything tying Hickey to Tunstall and/or Canfield?"

"Nothing indicated, sir. But the Bureau does report one other interesting item: the arrival of a high-ranking former KGB official —Filipp Federof. They're not sure why he's here, but this Russian's pretty casual about his visit. Even went to Florida for a few days."

The President smiled wryly. "A tourist?"

"Afraid he's not the tourist type, Mr. President. The Bureau says he's one very tough customer, who doesn't visit embassies unless there's a reason."

The President looked pointedly at Clem. "Tell the Attorney General and the FBI Director, in person—not by memo, damnit— that I want *no* electronic surveillance on any United States Senator. Tell the Attorney General I will hold him personally responsible for any breaches of that order."

Clem looked at his watch. He closed the folders, returned them to his thin, combination-locked briefcase.

"That's it, sir."

"Fine, Clem. But stay a bit while John and I talk."

Clem nodded.

"Now, John," the President said, "let's see what you have."

John Wingate spread out his documents. "First, Mr. President, here is the brief on the realignment of ground-to-air missiles that are still remaining in Europe."

The phone by the President's side rang. He cupped the receiver to his shoulder as he read the legal-sized papers Wingate handed him.

"Damn right I want to see them," he said into the phone. "Bring them up now."

He put down the receiver, looked up at Wingate. "Mike's on his way. He's got some polls, and you can bet the bowling alley and the drugstore, they're not good reading."

Wingate said nothing.

The President continued to read, flying through the pages.

"All right, John. This brief is fine. But I wish you'd tell Winthrop to put some sharp sticks under his African desk men. For Christ's sake, we've been dragging our feet on the African economic conference. Do I have to suggest that I want Senator Wade to have a look before we send it up?"

Wingate blinked. "I wouldn't have counseled doing anything without checking with Senator Wade."

"I want you and MacIver personally to go to Wade's office. If he thinks we're trying to slide by him in this African business, he'll spill his grits. That old son of a bitch wasn't named after Thomas Jefferson, you know—Jefferson Davis is his namesake, and he's goddamn proud of it."

Senator Homer Jefferson Wade of South Carolina, Chairman of the Senate Foreign Relations Committee, was not a man to treat casually.

"I fully agree that Senator Wade has to be informed ahead of time," Wingate said, "and, I might add, stroked a bit."

The President grinned. "John, I believe you're catching on."

The President could see the chubby face of his press secretary craning his head around the side of the entranceway to the West Hall.

"Come in, Mike."

Mike Carson quickly approached the President's chair.

The President put the papers in his lap. "Sit back a minute, John—I want to hear what Mike has to say. What's the bad news this time, Mike?"

Clem watched Mike Carson carefully.

Within the Presidential inner circle, the assistants tended to eye each other warily. The presence of the President was the coin of the realm, and the assistant with most access to that presence was anointed among lobbyists, reporters, diplomats, and Capitol Hill activists.

The trick was to convey to those who chronicled White House events that *you* were that anointed one. If to achieve that effect meant raking the flesh off a fellow assistant, then—at least to some —it was worth the game.

And no one was better at it than Mike Carson.

A veteran White House correspondent had confided to Clem last week that "Mike wants us to believe that everything the President does that makes any sense came directly from Mike, and anything we judge to be foolish was done over Mike's objections."

Carson opened up his ancient attaché. "Mr. President, Canfield's story on the supposed China trip has the press lobby going ballistic. How that pompous pundit ever came onto this leak is beyond them, and me. Vincent Canfield is not exactly your typical shoe-leather reporter. I don't believe that blimp ever did the legwork on a hard news story in his life."

Carson lunched or talked with Vincent Canfield almost every other week.

The President smiled. "Cut to the chase, Mike."

"Mr. President, I have an advance on the latest Peter Hart poll. You're down to thirty-seven percent in job approval." Carson barely referred to the papers before him. "More than sixty-six percent believe we are not doing enough about inflation and unemployment. Sixty percent feel you aren't searching out ways to find peace with the Soviets . . ."

The President held a hand out. "Let me have the summary."

Carson handed the cover page to the President, who read it quickly.

"Pretty grim, isn't it?" the President said, as if saying, "Nice day, isn't it?" He eased back in the chair. "Second lowest job rating since polling began—only Truman beat me out. Kind of a reverse honor. When's it being published?"

Clem hated giving bad news to the President, though he did it often enough. Somehow Mike Carson didn't seem to have the same hesitancy.

"Tomorrow afternoon Peter Hart releases it to the press," Carson was saying. "He agreed to hold off until I had a chance to talk to you. It's our poll, Mr. President, for godsake, taken by the National Committee. What's worse is Teeter's poll for Governor Stonehaven. According to Peter, whose people've had a peek at it, Teeter's numbers confirm Hart."

Governor Robert Stonehaven of Pennsylvania was the Republican front-runner, enormously popular in his state, and seemingly, now, in the nation.

The President rubbed his nose and spoke quietly to Clem. "Get with Willacy Hughes. Get his judgment as to how we put some kind of acceptable face on these polling miseries."

He turned to Carson.

"Any reports that I'm at odds with my economic advisers?"

"Not yet, sir."

With barely suppressed disgust, the President said, "Harlan is supposed to be my chief economic guru, but he acts as if he's divinely inspired."

Harlan Carbridge, the Chairman of the Council of Economic Advisers, did exhibit some detachment about his connections to the White House. The President had once said to Carbridge, in Clem's presence, "I'm not asking you to doctor numbers, but simply to remember I appointed you."

"What's your judgment, Mike?" the President asked. "A feeding frenzy in the press room once you offer this poll to them?"

"The press, Mr. President," Carson said, "will count this poll as just more evidence that the Administration is in deep trouble. With the primaries close at hand, the talk in the press room now isn't *if* you're going to be opposed in the primaries—just who will do it."

The President smiled. "Who will it be, Mike?"

"Well, Maureen Dowd's been nosing around the West Wing, asking questions, mostly about the Vice President."

Dowd was with the New York *Times*.

The President stirred in his chair. "What kind of questions?"

"Is the Vice President in on all the meetings? Does the Vice President ever confer with the President alone? When is the President going to announce categorically he will be a candidate for renomination, and when does he plan to enter the Iowa primary?"

The President fingered the buttons on his phone console, tapping the keys in odd rhythms. "What's she have in mind?"

"She might be trying to work up a story about the renomination process, but as I said, this is the first time she's been interested in the Vice President."

The President nodded meaninglessly. "We should talk more about these polls, Mike. See me tomorrow, first thing."

"Fine, sir. I'll be in my office for a while if you need me." He paused. "One thing more. I'm sure to get a question about the appointment to the Supreme Court. Shall I finesse?"

"Finesse. You might talk to the Attorney General. Have they finished the qualification reports from the Bar? I don't think we ought to say anything until we get those results and get a fix on what they say. Anything else?"

"No, sir."

"Let's talk again in the morning. And, Clem, stay a moment so we can go over tomorrow's schedule."

Clem fumbled in his inside jacket pocket for the schedule. He liked to believe he knew everything that was going on, in and around the town.

This time, he was very wrong.

Ten

LEONID BERISOV sagged into the spacious leather chair that flanked a glowing fireplace crackling with new-flung logs, the flames leaping up haphazardly as the U.S.C.R. Ambassador contemplated tragedy. His companion, Filipp Federof, sipped a glass of Bordeaux.

"Are we embarked on something, Filipp Vladimirovich, that we will regret?" the Ambassador said.

Federof sipped once more. "This is particularly good wine, Leonid Nikolaevich. I am pleased that whoever manages these vital functions for you has the inexpressibly good taste to include this Haut Brion in your cellar."

Federof graduated from the London School of Economics and was forgiven the odium of that education from his colleagues in Moscow only because he demonstrated a most unlikely skill for brutalities conducted with the utmost discretion. But nonetheless he prized his precise, idiomatic, patrician-toned English.

"Your question? Are we mired in something we will find regrettable? Let me put it this way. Do we want this Kells warrior to be commanding the Americans for another four years? Do we have the patience? The indignities, the dangers, the possibilities, my dear Leonid Nikolaevich, are enough to cause us to do whatever is required. I cannot lament the cost of what we do when I consider the cost for not doing it."

The Ambassador sighed. How unsettling it was to have this rather dashing saturnine KGB General deposited on his doorstep. This entire enterprise was an illusion in which he found it unsuitable to join. He sometimes wished he would not be compared with Anatolyi Dobrynin, who filled this post until some years ago. It was Dobrynin whom the Americans constantly praised and beatified as a legendary envoy. Berisov presented his credentials just eight months earlier and suffered in the shadow of his predecessors, who would doubtless have conducted themselves with more confidence than Berisov felt. He did not feel confident or comfortable.

The Ambassador licked his dry lips. He knew that Federof was the darling protégé of Viktor Zinyakin, the chief of the renovated and redesigned Komitet Gosudarstvennoi Bezopasnosti, the State Security Committee, familiarly known to Americans as the KGB. Though the KGB for some months after the failed coup in 1991 seemingly was headed for the garbage heap of history, it was revived under the leadership of the Executive President, who promptly installed Zinyakin, his close collaborator, as its boss.

Berisov also knew that this man Federof had asserted a reputation that won him the approval of most of the leaders of the U.S.C.R. The KGB Chairman had dispatched him, with the consent of the Executive President, to Washington. Berisov was not cheered by untidy political strategies and their emissary in the person of a handsome assassin.

Thus it was when Filipp Federof arrived with certifiable credentials naming him as the Deputy Ambassador to the United States, Berisov was stunned. Not only was there a lingering odor of savagery about Federof, not only did Federof cause him anxiety, but the General outranked him! Though the outside world would think Berisov still in charge, Berisov would suffer mutely. He had to. There would be comment in the American press as to how on earth this fast-rising star in the Soviet firmament suddenly emerges as the deputy to Berisov, and none of these reports would accurately report that Federof was back again in KGB harness. There would be ample speculation and then it would melt away. Of course, the FBI and its brothers-in-arms would dissect this radical transfer with their usual diligence and probably find out no more than Federof wanted them to know. But one truth Berisov would know is who is in charge at the Embassy.

Berisov decided to take a mild offensive. That killing of Hickey. Stupid, clumsy business. This would be his gambit.

"So tell me, Filipp Vladimirovich, who is managing this affair? I wonder if the Americans will discover the whole truth about this unnecessary Hickey matter. How do we allow ourselves to be so," the Ambassador searched for the right word, "so bumbling? For that is what it was."

"Perhaps you are right, it was bumbling." Federof was amazingly cheerful. "But it will not happen again. When we resort to employing mercenaries we risk unanticipated intrusions." Federof filled his wineglass, sipped the red liquid, and leaned lazily against a large upright chair. His tanned face, recently upturned to the Florida sun, regarded Berisov with intensity.

The room in which they talked was deep inside the U.S.C.R. main Embassy building in the Northwest quadrant on Tunlaw Street, atop Mount Alto, the highest hill in Washington. The roof of the Soviet Embassy bristled with electronic gear, and the room itself was made proof against the daily probings of the FBI, given increased energy since Donald Kells became President. The most agile-minded scientists Moscow could find had cemented the room insofar as they were able to warrant it from any FBI sensitive equipment. But Berisov was never quite sure. He knew, as did Federof, that the FBI knew the KGB General was in the United States. Indeed, Federof had brazenly traveled to Florida on what Federof called "a rest period" solely to suggest to the American agents that his business here was not at all pressing.

Federof said: "I have had communications with our friends here to find out just how vulnerable they are, stupid though they are. We are in no danger for the time being. However, there is always Nightingale to alert us if I am wrong. Consider too it was Nightingale who suggested the encounter."

Berisov shivered. He had pointlessly wandered into deep, cold waters. He knew very definitely it was not safe to know this most closely held of all Soviet secrets, a live, working agent in the bowels of the U.S. Government.

There was a knock at the door. Berisov frowned. He pressed a button on the side of the stunt-legged coffee table.

"Who is there?" he asked.

A muffled voice replied, a soft feminine voice.

"It is Irina, Excellency. I have the food you wanted."

"Ah." Berisov smiled. He pressed a second button and the huge, heavy steel door, overlaid with lead, gradually opened. A short, dark-haired woman in a gray maid's uniform entered holding a tray of biscuits, cheese, fruit, and caramel-colored wafers. The drab shirt blouse failed to hide her full figure, and the skirt was unable to conceal the curving form of her leg. Federof gazed assertively at the maid, nodding to her provocatively as she managed a demure smile. The servants in the Embassy had spoken of nothing today other than the presence of the dazzling General from Moscow. Irina could not wait to confirm to Misha and to Erika that the General was as handsome as they had imagined.

"Put the tray here, Irina," Berisov gestured. She bent over to put the tray on the coffee table, the skirt, heavily starched, curling upward, revealing to the persistent gaze of Federof a most appealing upper thigh.

"Thank you very much, my dear," he said, handing her the empty wineglass. "Please fill that for me." She curtsied, held the wine bottle firmly and poured. She handed the glass to him, feeling the touch of his fingers on hers, held there for a second, and then released.

"Is that all, Excellency?"

"Yes, yes," said the Ambassador, unaware of the sensual tension that Federof was emitting.

When the heavy door had closed, Federof's manner changed. He moved closer to the Ambassador.

"Leonid, my business will be done shortly, but I do not intend to return to Moscow quickly."

Berisov groaned inwardly.

"You will arrange, as we have previously planned, a meeting for me with the Deputy Secretary of State. I will pass on to him some thoughts of our President, not officially, merely as my assumption of what our leader feels so firmly."

"Yes, of course," said Berisov, though the General had not yet confided to him precisely what it was the Executive President firmly believed. What Federof did not convey to the Ambassador was that the views he would present to the State Department were not specific instructions from the Executive President of the U.S.C.R., but what the KGB Chairman had instructed him to offer as the Executive President's views. To Federof, however, there was no doubt they were one and the same. The KGB Chairman had put it bluntly: "You will follow my orders and report to no one but me. Is that clear?" To Federof it was very clear.

Federof moved to the door. "I will take a little walk, Leonid, I need some fresh air. Meanwhile, ask that charming maid, Irina, to bring some hot tea to my apartment, say at ten-thirty this evening. Would you manage that?"

Berisov nodded resignedly.

Federof strode down the dimly lit hall, his two security aides following him. "There is no need to stay with me," said Federof to the heavier of the men. "Stay here, and go to bed when you are ready. I will need you no further tonight. I will go to my quarters after I walk a bit and read for a while."

The two men shook their heads apprehensively. It was their duty to stay with their General at all times. But he had ordered them not to follow him and they obeyed unquestioningly.

Federof nodded to the guards at the main gate, waved to them as the gate opened. The air was mild, the sky was clear. Federof loved to be alone when he walked. He felt good. The Executive President reposed great trust in him, as did the KGB Chairman by whose orders he was here. He would not stain their beliefs nor corrode his own fidelity.

Fifty yards to his right he saw the always-there U.S. Protective Service officer leaning against the building. A few feet from the officer was the blue van of the Protective Service. Harmless, though he knew at this instant the van was alive with the crackle of messages back to the control center.

Federof walked across Tunlaw Street. In front of him was an undistinguished apartment building. It would not have astonished him to know that the third-story apartment facing the Embassy was inhabited twenty-four hours a day by FBI agents with cameras at the ready and sensitive listening gear always turned on and tuned in. He turned left and strode quickly down Tunlaw. He passed a whitewashed apartment, crossed the street, and continued ahead, past small banistered houses on his right. Federof always found the wide disparity of income amazing in the U.S.A., but he found even stranger the ownership of homes.

The houses were mostly dark. The overhanging trees discolored the pavement. Without lights, the street turned dour. He abruptly turned to his left, crossed Tunlaw to reach 37th Street so that he would find himself eventually on Wisconsin Avenue and then back to the Embassy. He thought about his mission, and about Berisov, the bungling ass that he was. Perhaps it was better to deal with ineptitude than some cunning younger Ambassador energetically aiming at a higher star.

He heard footsteps, and by instinct glanced behind him. Two men were walking faster than he. He slowed. They were dark-skinned, one about his height and the other round and much shorter. The taller one was wearing a gray sweatshirt, with the sleeves expertly cut off at the shoulder, revealing arms rippling with thick muscle enclosing ranging, granite-like veins. The other had on a black jacket, half-zipped over a putty-colored shirt.

Suddenly the taller one was in front of Federof, the shorter one holding back.

A blade flashed.

"This here's my introducer, man, and it is sayin' to you, hello there and why don't you show me all the dead presidents you got on you, man." The voice was slurred but understandable. The shorter man was now behind Federof, holding what looked like a policeman's night stick in his hand.

"Dead presidents—I do not understand," said Federof, not so much afraid as he was confused.

"Dead presidents, man, heavy green, man, you never heard of presidents' pictures on money paper, you dumb, or somethin'," the muscular one said, even as he wondered why this well-dressed dude was so calm. Sure wasn't a cop, even looked foreign, though you couldn't tell in Washington, so many foreign-type mothers wandering all over. "And we might as well have all the jingle jangles you got there on your wrist," pointing to Federof's Rolex gold watch and the half-inch-wide gold wrist bracelet he wore.

Federof nodded slowly as if to corroborate his understanding. He wanted no trouble, not now. He was beginning to be very angry. He would have detached one of his balls before he would give away the Rolex and the gold chain. They were gifts from the ethereally beautiful wife of a British peer with whom he had, as the Americans would say, a "relationship." He found that word unsuitable, for it bespoke in a flaccid fashion the gymnastic exertions of Lady Elisa Burndall which had illuminated those months he spent in London. Because Federof was not casual about such memories, this interruption was most vexing. These stupid young men. He began to unlatch the watch and the bracelet and held out his arms as he fiddled with the watch clasp. Then he held up his left arm, the watch dangling. The tall man flipped his knife to his left hand and reached with his right to grab the watch and the bracelet. It was an ill-informed movement by the taller man. Within a half blink of an eye, Federof's right hand, fingers and thumb outstretched, tautly held together to form a lethal chisel, struck with blurring speed at the lobbing Adam's apple. The chiseled fingers flying faster than the eye and the mind could comprehend collided with the man's throat, thrusting the Adam's apple deep into the rear of the throat, shutting off the flow of air, and causing in that instant a burst of blood to course from the esophagus, until it leapt out in a flood from the man's mouth. The tall man tried to scream but no sound came as his large frame wilted and collapsed.

Without a second's hesitation, Federof in a graceful arc flung his body around to his left, his right leg ascending from the ground to the upper chest of the shorter man, the leg jackknifing at the knee, and in a millisecond catapulting forward, like a projectile being hurled from a slingshot. It was a perfect example of Tae Kwan Do, the classic Korean karate movement, velocity and balance coinciding in flawless unity, culminating in an explosive force, a human bludgeon. The short man's body imploded, a great "whoosh" rushing from his throat as he crumpled in a heap.

Federof turned back to the tall man now groveling on the sidewalk, inert, barely breathing, and, with the same right foot that had so abruptly felled the short man, kicked the tall man in the face, the front teeth crackling and spilling. A river of blood, unrestrained, cascaded from the tall man's face, now frozen in a grisly rictus. Another kick, this time to the forehead, indenting the forehead, rupturing the outer rim of the skull.

Federof, breathing a little heavily now, returned his attention to the shorter man. He was patently unconscious, the chest collision apparently more serious than Federof contemplated. Federof surveyed him for a few seconds, then once more propelled his right foot with its pointed shoe toward the cheek of the shorter man, an escalating movement which tore the skin from the cheekbone, shredding the jaw and shattering the inner cavity of the nose.

He stepped over the shorter man, adjusted his tie, brushed his sleeves, and walked firmly and regally back to the Embassy. It was a messy piece of business. He almost regretted the unleashing of his temper. But they were about to disconnect him from his Rolex and gold chain. It was an obscenity which he deemed worthy of the response.

Upstairs in his bedroom on 37th Street, an elderly man getting ready for bed just happened to look out his window and gasped in surprise as he watched a tall man kick the living beejesus out of two prone men on the sidewalk across the street. "What the hell," he murmured, peering closer at the scene below him. The tall man was mighty cool, he thought. As he watched, he reached for the phone beside his bed. He had never dialed 911 before. This was going to be the first time.

In his Embassy apartment, Federof removed his clothing, showered, put on a paisley dressing gown he had purchased some years before in London at Turnbull & Asser. He snuggled into a pair of velvet slippers, ran his hands along the side of his head, patting down the hair, still faintly moist. He looked at his watch, and smiled reassuredly as he heard the discreet knock at his door.

He strode across the room, opened the door. Irina stood outside, a tray in one hand with tea and milk and some small biscuits on a linen coverlet. She was now wearing a white softly-clinging dress, fully outlining her body so recently and unhappily disguised, her hair out of its severe bun, hanging loosely to her shoulders.

"Your tea, Excellency, as you requested," she said softly.

"Yes, Irina, so it is. Come inside."

She placed the tray on the night table next to his bed, the

bedspread already removed and the white sheet pulled back diago-
nally.

"Is there anything more you would like, Excellency?" she said,
face upturned and a bit flushed.

"As a matter of fact, Irina," he said, his left hand reaching ever
so slowly toward her, touching her right hand, and holding it
gently, "there is."

Eleven

THE LAMBERT MANSION sat in bulky grace some two hundred yards from the northwestern slope of Foxhall Road. The mammoth Georgian structure was self-defaced by an ungainly wing where the late Horace Lambert had once housed his celebrated collection of toy soldiers.

Lambert had come to Washington in the early Eisenhower years and purchased every available piece of real estate that his father's considerable fortune would allow. He bought in the District's downtown area, two blocks from the venerable Willard Hotel, and on a vast acreage erected what was the largest twelve-story hotel in the United States, the James Monroe Capital Inn. The night after its grand opening—attended by Senators, Congressmen, and even the President himself—Horace Lambert frolicked, naked and jubilant, in the Bridal Suite, with a friskily nubile secretary he had recently employed. As he contemplated to his immense astonishment and gratitude an engorged erection, he was assaulted with an earthquake of a coronary. It was one of the few times in Horace Lambert's life when his timing was really bad.

For his widow, Christine Jones Lambert, however, the timing was excellent.

She was rid of an unfaithful, corpulent husband and was sole executor of an estate estimated, conservatively, at $175 million.

As much as Christine loathed the grungy odors of the business world, she relished its rewards. She could indulge her one passion —to be on the "inside" with the politically elite.

At least twice a year, Mrs. Lambert was hostess to a lavish evening for the proconsuls of the Capital. They came for two reasons. First, they would meet their own kind, with no press around to soil intimate political conversations; deals could be cut, information shared. Second, the food, the service, the ambiance were everything an unrestricted purse could provide.

Reporters canonized Mrs. Lambert and her parties as the essence of inside Washington. Mrs. Lambert joyously concurred and persisted in barring her door to them.

Tonight, as on so many nights, Mrs. Christine Jones Lambert stood in the foyer of her marbled entry hall and greeted her distinguished guests.

To her right was the massive dining room, to her left the endless living room. Parquet steps led down to a lush off-white wool carpet. French doors opened onto a stone terrace that flowed into a contoured lawn which, on this cool fall evening, was canopied, guarded by stanchions with softly burning wicks.

"Ah," said Christine, "how good to see you, Mr. Secretary."

Sam Harcourt, the Secretary of Defense, his bulky form clad in a tailored tuxedo, smiled brightly. Nodding to the matronly woman at his side, he said, "Lois and I just took a vote, and we agree that you're the most generous hostess in town."

Christine smiled. How lovely life was tonight—a guest list of the most powerful, delightful weather, and a chef who had previously presided over a two-star restaurant in Paris.

"Mrs. Lambert, what a joy to be here with you."

She turned to greet the newly appointed Librarian of Congress. "Dr. Warren, I'm so pleased you've arrived! I'm sure you'll lift the intellectual level of our little group."

Dr. Worthington Warren, fresh to the ways of Washington, actually believed her.

Less than half an hour ago, the President had come abruptly into Clem's office as his aide was changing into his tux.

"Going to a fancy-dress ball, Clem?" was the President's casual query.

"Yes, sir—on my way to Mrs. Lambert's. Thought I might wander around and listen to what's being said."

The President grinned wryly. "Be sure to remember everything, to tell me tomorrow." Then with dry sarcasm, Kells added, "If you run into the Majority Leader, give him my warmest regards."

Clem grinned back. "You mean, if I run into him with my car, don't you?"

"Be sure to stop and offer first aid," the President said, and with a wave was gone.

Now Clem was face to face with the formidable Christine Lambert. "Mrs. Lambert, the President asked me to tell you that he would have enjoyed being here himself but you never invited him," said Clem merrily.

Mrs. Lambert tapped him lightly on the shoulder. "Dear boy, I always invite the President, whoever he is."

Clem knew the Washington doyenne was pleased by his presence. Mrs. Lambert would have felt the omission, had the White House been totally absent.

In the library, under high exposed beams, near a towering, glowing fireplace, the Majority Leader, Senator Tunstall, held Vincent Canfield's forearm.

"I am not really sure what you mean, Vincent," he said.

The imperially pear-shaped form of Vincent Canfield stirred slightly. Canfield was never comfortable in settings like this, but he had some minor affection for Christine Lambert. She had, after all, responded with outrageous munificence to the recent fund drive to endow the Vincent Canfield Chair of Comparative Literature at Williams College.

"My dear Raymond," Canfield intoned, "I am simply saying that our President, while a decent-enough man, has failed to fill the role of leader. I cannot s-s-s-surmise what prompts him to entertain such shoddy thinking, or, what is worse, to suffer such f-f-fools as advisers."

"And you think we ought to do something to cure those ailments, eh, Vincent?"

"I am saying precisely that."

Senator Tunstall bent closer to Canfield. "Perhaps you ought to come to my office tomorrow afternoon, around three. Let's say you are gathering information for your television show."

"Yes, I would f-f-f-find that useful."

Senator Max Baucus of Montana and Senator William Cohen of Maine smiled at each other as they greeted Clem. "I see you are heading toward the summit," said Baucus, pointing toward Canfield and the Majority Leader. Clem understood that Senator Baucus, Democrat, and Senator Cohen, Republican, accounted Canfield to be a pretentious ass. Actually, Clem joined them in this view. He sometimes wondered why there was such a lingering appeal for Canfield in both officeholder and public. Baucus and Cohen, in unison, walked slowly out of the library into the living room and onto the tented lawn.

Senator Louise Kimmel of Iowa, the Senate Republican Whip, and Senator Karl Overlujd of North Dakota, Chairman of the Senate Commerce Committee, moved into the library, both smiling at Tunstall and Canfield.

"Ah," said Tunstall, "Karl—you missed Vincent's gloomy assessment of our world. Louise, perhaps Vincent will confide more in you, since you are the only Republican Senator who truly understands him."

Louise Kimmel laughed. "I read Mr. Canfield, Raymond, but I'm not sure I understand him."

Canfield twitched a frown. He knew that Senator Kimmel held him in minimum high regard. And as much as he valued Tunstall as an ally, he became annoyed when Raymond persisted in trying to be cute with him.

"I think I know what Vincent was telling you," Senator Overlujd said, sipping his drink. "That the President ought to head for the hills?"

Canfield was about to reply, but Tunstall touched his forearm again.

"Careful," Tunstall whispered to Canfield. "Here comes the President's ambassador to our evening."

Clem approached the little group near the fireplace—which he'd already heard referred to as the evening's "summit meeting" by Senator Max Baucus of Montana.

"Clem!" the Majority Leader said. "You look fit, my boy. I trust the President's in fine fettle these days."

Clem shook Tunstall's hand and greeted the others warmly.

"He is, Senator. Just a few minutes ago, he asked to be remembered to you."

"Well, please return the compliment," Tunstall said. "Clem, you do know Vincent Canfield, don't you?"

"I watch Mr. Canfield on television."

Canfield granted Clem a slow nod in the manner of a landed baron to a vassal in the field.

There was a stir in the living room. Eyes turned toward the library doorway, where appeared the tall, slim figure of the Vice President.

Overlujd said, "Bill! I didn't think you'd make it tonight!"

As the Vice President approached, Canfield bowed slightly, and smiled. Such deference from Canfield would have surprised Clem, had he not known that Canfield's commentaries often paid tribute to Rawlins.

Senator Overlujd shook hands vigorously with the Vice President. Rawlins touched Tunstall on the upper arm and reached out to clasp hands with Canfield. He bent to kiss Senator Kimmel on the cheek. She glowed at him.

"Clem," the Vice President said with a disarming grin. "Good to see you here! Business slack back at the ranch? Or do you really want to consort with us revelers tonight?"

Clem smiled politely in response.

Canfield said, "I was r-r-r-recounting before you arrived, Bill, the problems Don Kells is facing, and why he ought to reconsider his options. Sorry to offer these odious remarks in front of you, Mr. Barkley."

Clem said nothing.

Rawlins smiled. "It's hard to talk politics so early in the evening, particularly when I'm waiting for my first drink to turn up."

Kimmel said, "Perhaps the Majority Leader would offer his thinking."

"Who said I was thinking?" Tunstall said, which got a laugh from the little group.

From everyone except Overlujd, that is, who flicked his cigarette ash into a small tray. "I'm always amused by the Majority Leader. When he says he's thinking, he's usually just rearranging his prejudices."

"Karl," Tunstall said, with a big grin, "I don't think that was ever put better—even when Adlai Stevenson first said it."

"Come now, Raymond," the Vice President said, "a good song can be sung by anybody, not just the guy who wrote it."

Clem had to silently approve the Vice President's gentle rejoinder.

Tunstall turned, tapped the Vice President on the shoulder, and bowed to greet Mrs. Lambert, who appeared on the library threshold.

"All of you must come into the drawing room," she said, coming over to the gathering around the Vice President. "You're greatly missed."

Just behind her stood a tall, black-sheathed woman. She was, in Clem's considered opinion, exquisite. Her figure was fully formed. The dark strapless gown, expensive as well as revelatory, set off her soft blond hair.

"I'd like you to meet my house guest, Laura Hurley," Mrs. Lambert said. "Her father is a business partner of Lambert Properties."

Mrs. Lambert turned to the Vice President, her jowls moving slightly.

"I've given you a wonderful gift tonight, Mr. Vice President. Laura will be sitting to your right, so I urge you to be at your most charming as a courtesy to me."

Rawlins stared at Laura Hurley, fixing his eyes so steadily onto hers she looked away. Clem was staring too, but she didn't seem to notice.

Laura Hurley said to Tunstall, "I have always wanted to meet you, Senator. My father speaks highly of you."

"I'm pleased your father thinks as well of me," Tunstall said, "as do I of him."

What Tunstall did not express, Clem noted, was his gratitude for the funds Malcolm Kent provided to the Senator's political action committee, Leaders for America.

Senator Overlujd shook Laura Hurley's hand, as did Senator Kimmel. Clem smiled with as much grace as he could summon when this lovely woman acknowledged his presence. Canfield nodded his head respectfully; Malcolm Kent was too important, too powerful not to pay deference to his daughter.

Rawlins stepped forward, took Laura Hurley by the arm. "May I escort you to the dining room, Mrs. Hurley?" he asked, his tone low and friendly. Clem shook his head in admiration and mounting envy. The Vice President never missed an emotional beat.

Laura Hurley looked up at Rawlins and smiled. "Yes, I'd like that—if you promise to be as charming as Mrs. Lambert requested."

"I never refuse Christine, and especially this time," he said.

Christine Lambert had to suppress a huge, self-satisfied smile.

The Chief Justice sat to her left, and to her right was the Vice President of the United States, that delicious man. The ten round tables for twelve people were buzzing with conversation; it was a tribute to the time she'd spent planning the seating arrangement.

She had put the Secretary of State next to that lovely Faith Hendricks, whose husband was the chairman of some profitable conglomerate whose name Christine could never remember; Faith was a graduate of Radcliffe and could match Secretary MacIver in erudition. Jane Seymour, the beautiful British film star, was seated on the other side of the Secretary, and next to her was the Majority Leader. Tunstall would be enchanted with Jane. Senator Louise Kimmel was seated next to the Chief Executive Officer of General Mills. Since Louise was on the Agriculture Committee, they would have much to talk about.

Clem Barkley had been placed next to the prima ballerina whose ballet was opening in two days at the Kennedy Center. That tall, rather handsome Presidential aide was just right for her.

And Laura Hurley and Bill Rawlins made an exquisite couple . . .

Basking in self-admiration, Christine turned to talk to the Chief Justice.

. . . .

"Where is your husband, Mrs. Hurley?" Rawlins asked.

She smiled. "Where is your wife, Mr. Vice President?"

"Home in Texas. Her father's been seriously ill for some time and she's taking care of him. But you knew that, didn't you?"

Laura toyed with the veal, which swam in some mysterious, delectable sauce. She felt the Vice President's knee against her thigh for a fleeting second. She shivered with reluctant delight. She had determined to resist this man about whom she had heard so much. She was almost frightened, and she didn't know precisely why.

Rawlins leaned near. "Be honest—doesn't all this rather lavish evening seem a bit much to you?"

She laughed, a deep, hearty laugh.

"Mr. Vice President, if I told you this evening was a bore, wouldn't you find that answer inappropriate, since you're the center of my universe here?"

He let the question pass, saying, "If we're to survive a most non-intimate Washington evening together, perhaps you'd rather start calling me Bill. Mr. Vice President is a bit heavy, don't you agree?"

"Yes, I do. It doesn't have quite the ring that Mr. President does, don't you agree?"

Rawlins looked at her with mounting admiration.

"Yes," he said with amusement, "I was thinking the very same thing."

She laughed again, a melodious laugh that Rawlins found more than a little attractive. She felt his hand on hers, lightly, like a hummingbird lingering effortlessly over a flower, and then it was gone.

Christine Lambert turned to the couple.

"I can see you two are thoroughly enjoying each other, so why don't you come to lunch tomorrow, Mr. Vice President? Laura will be here for two more days and we'd love to see you again."

"Ah, Christine, I would love to, but I've already gotten Mrs. Hurley to say she'll have lunch with me at my Capitol office tomorrow."

Christine's disappointment was clear, but Rawlins assuaged it with a glorious smile.

Laura whispered to Rawlins, "That wasn't fair. I couldn't publicly contradict the Vice President!"

He leaned toward her. "So lunch is on?"

She smiled. "Lunch is on, even if it was unfairly gained."

He chuckled. "You have a wonderful presence of mind. Ever thought of running for political office?"

Again the hand was on hers, and again withdrawn, though this time it stayed longer.

Could others recognize the flush of blood rushing to her cheeks? She was being courted by a powerful, dominant, very attractive *married* man. She had the distinct feeling he was toying with her, and yet all her good, common sense had fled.

She knew she was beautiful. She knew her body was a magnet for male eyes. And she also knew her husband, dear, sweet, good man that he was, had no sense of the passionate woman he had married. Arthur believed the daughter of one of America's richest and most patrician of men could not possibly be the sensual creature that she was. Laura had suffered through so many of Arthur's fumbling attempts to please her. Before long she realized, to her horror, that Arthur, handsome, blond, willowy, and so very intelligent, was caught in a shadow land between genders. Her father detested divorce; so did she. But what about alternatives?

She had stayed with the marriage, agonizing over what her life was about, always knowing that she was unfulfilled, and yet not willing to settle for momentary affairs.

Now, on this evening with this man Bill Rawlins, she was being tested.

The dessert came, a delicious, delicate flan.

"No dessert for you?" she asked Rawlins.

"I'm too busy wondering how you manage to stay so slim, eating as much as you do. I am abstaining because I don't think there's much of a market for fat Vice Presidents."

Laura laughed. "I'm not going to eat again for two days. I'm a regular camel." With a spoon of flan near her lips, she said, "I take on provisions when I can, and then I'm ready to trek long distances with no further need of fuel."

"Then tonight's snack ought to get you through the night."

"I think it might."

"Do camels ever get . . . lonely . . . on a long night?" His face was near hers.

She hesitated. "Some camels don't. Does that surprise you?"

"It doesn't surprise me. It does disappoint me." He laid his hand lightly over hers. "Is it possible, before this caravan departs, that you and I might find time to have one small nightcap?"

She didn't withdraw her hand, though she was terrified by her excitement.

But she managed to face him, trying to look cool, hot though she might feel.

"Come now, Mr. Vice President . . . Bill . . . this has really gone a little too far. I don't think a nightcap would be wise for either of us. I'm staying in the guest cottage, and . . ."

"All right," said Rawlins, his disappointment obvious. "But it would only be courteous if I walked you to your door . . ."

Clem tried not to stare at Laura Hurley, one table away. She and the Vice President made quite a cozy couple, he thought, still envious.

Christine rose at her table, striking an empty glass with a small knife, gently. The assembly turned to face her.

Her voice trilled throughout the room.

"In this home, we always have but one toast. Ladies and gentlemen, to the President of the United States."

The crowd in unison echoed: "To the President," and then with glasses raised, and a scattering of "Hear, Hear," all sipped their Dom Perignon.

Conversation resumed as Christine rose again, and, escorted by the Vice President, moved to the large drawing room, where coffee and cognac were served by white-jacketed waiters.

Tunstall appeared at their side. "Glorious evening, Christine. Unhappily, we poor public servants need our rest if we're to serve the national interest in the morning."

The Chief Justice nodded approvingly.

"Why must Washington be an eleven-o'clock city?" asked Christine.

Vincent Canfield approached to say, "Christine, I fully intend to have coffee with you and if I am the last one here, so be it."

Clem, overhearing this, had to smile. Vincent Canfield loathed social evenings with unhidden scorn. Mrs. Lambert must have given more to the Canfield Chair at Williams than Clem had prudently estimated.

As the assorted power elite of Washington began to take their leave, the string quintet played Mozart soothingly. Clem stood near the garden doorway talking to the prima ballerina, who'd been most gracious to him all evening. He watched the Vice President and Laura Hurley as they walked through the exit beside the rear bay windows, and then they were lost to his sight.

Laura Hurley and Bill Rawlins strolled down the pebbled path to a serenely lovely one-story cottage. The night was cool, the sky glittering; a half moon rode the heavens. Laura stood with her back to the door. She held out her hand.

"You've been a gentleman, and you have been charming, as you pledged you would be," she said.

Rawlins grinned. "You know, as Vice President, in the Senate, I can vote to break a tie. Which is what we have right now."

"What do you mean?"

"One vote for shaking hands—one vote for a kiss. I vote to break the tie."

"You're voting *twice* . . ."

"That's called rising on a point of personal privilege."

He held her very close, kissing her tenderly, and then with more intensity. Her back was against the door and she felt the full length of his body on hers.

He was kissing her more urgently, his hands on the small of her back, drawing her nearer. And she felt her own back arching, pressing against him. Resistance was now abandoned, gone in a blurred and indistinct time span. She felt him reach around her, turn the doorknob and, still with his lips on hers, push the door open. She was gripped with an exaltation she had not felt for years. Every barrier she had erected crumbled, all the resolve she had banked inside her collapsed, like a levee so carefully constructed breaking under a mighty tidal wave, all her entreaties to herself now vaguely mute. The door shut behind them.

Inside, the living room was dark, streaks of the fall half-moon night glancing through the large front window.

She felt the zipper sliding down her back, her gown slowly falling to the deeply woven carpet. She was naked and free and he was looking at her approvingly, eager to hold her. In the shrouded light she sensed more than saw his eyes, and she shivered under the touch of his hands. She could no longer hear the string quartet whose Mozart was so comforting.

Twelve

CLEM BARKLEY rocked slowly sideways in his swivel chair in his sparsely furnished office, next to the Oval Office of the President, facing Toni Georgihu, a woman he found both disconcertingly attractive and professionally competent.

When Donald Kells became President, he had asked that a top official of the Federal Bureau of Investigation serve as liaison with the White House. Toni Georgihu was vouched for by the Director of the FBI as one of the ablest agents in the Bureau. Her parents had emigrated from Romania before she was born. She entered the Bureau as a young woman, right out of New York University, and rose rapidly in the hierarchy. When her husband and young son were killed in an automobile accident, she poured her energies and life into her Bureau work. Seven months earlier, she was promoted to Deputy Associate Director for Investigations, making her the highest-ranking woman in the FBI.

When he first met her, Clem was instantly aware of and rather put off by her formidable size, within a bare half inch as tall as he. And that professional demeanor, no smiles, no small talk, always sternly attentive to business. The thought struck Clem that she was quite capable with a few turns of arms and hands to do harmful things to any foolish man who chose to intrude on her. Nonetheless, he found himself stirred by her. Her large, finely-formed body moved gracefully, easily, her dark blond hair always carefully framed. When he took her by the arm to escort her out of his office two days ago, he almost blushed at the spice of the emotion that ran through him. She had turned to him and, for the first time, smiled at him, a most nonprofessional smile. He thoughtfully surveyed her now. Suddenly he wanted to ask her to dinner.

Instead he said, "There's something terribly wrong here, Toni. Terry Geer asks Hickey for background on China for a foreign policy seminar. No great cosmic event. Terry gives no details, no specifics of the trip. Hickey has financial problems. He obviously tells someone what he knows, who in turn passes it on to some Russian characters. Then, someone silences Hickey just before he's to see Terry Geer. Now the President's trip has leaked, he's had to cancel. At the same time, a high-ranking KGB general, somebody named Federof, arrives in Washington. That's what we have. The large question is, where is the connection, what does it mean?"

"First, it probably means this was not your usual mugging," she said, "nor was Roy Hickey your usual muggee. And then if you were going to mug someone would you choose 20th and Pennsylvania?"

Clem stirred in his chair. "In this town, any place is a usual spot for mugging."

Toni went on: "Moreover, if you really were bent on mugging, would you accompany your victim to his car?"

Clem shook his head. "Not likely. What have you found? The DC police got anything?"

"The DC police have been most cooperative with us since you called me. No prints on any part of the body or the car or any part of it. Every part of the car had been wiped clean. Professionals do that sort of thing."

"What about the weapon?"

"A knife, probably a six-inch blade. Not the kind that the local muggers usually carry. It wasn't a switchblade. Too large for that. He was stabbed twice, in the stomach and in the heart, and a bull's-eye insofar as accuracy is concerned. It pierced the large aorta. Death was quick."

"Which is why you label them professional. The police find anything?"

"Almost nothing. We did find a button, probably torn from the coat of the assailant, and a thread hanging onto it."

"That's all you have?"

She smiled, a teasing smile, he thought.

"Not quite," she said. "A woman walked into the parking lot and saw two men walking away. Maybe they had nothing to do with it, but we think they could have been the assassins."

"Assassins? So you have come to that word? You think those two guys are the"—he hesitated—"the assassins. Why?"

"If the lady is correct, it was about the time we place the death. The two men were also wearing large greatcoats, which, the woman remarked, didn't seem "the usual garment." The button could have come from one of them. It is too large to be a jacket button."

"How the devil did you find the lady who gave you the description?"

"I had our agents check every car on that lot and then seek out their owners. We figured that the same people park their cars every day on a contract basis, and we interviewed every one of them. We hit a bingo with a lady who works in the same building where Hickey was employed."

"Did she see their faces?" Clem leaned forward.

"No, she didn't, at least not well. The only reason she remembered at all is the greatcoat business. It wasn't that cold. Cool enough to wear a light topcoat, but not something that heavy, or at least something that looked that heavy. The lady in question has an eye for such things."

"Do you think she would recognize them again?"

"Not likely, but you never know. She's not terribly sure of what they looked like, except for the clothing. She might be more forthcoming if she saw them in a lineup."

Clem slid a letter opener up and down his thumb.

"Something is giving off an odor, Toni. Something I can't put my hand on. Even if we knew who killed Hickey, there is still the 'why.' What did he know? Did it have to do with more than the China leak? And if it did, why was it necessary to kill him?"

She said, "What we cannot link up is a motive and the nature of the assailants. The only jot of evidence we have now is the great-coat threading and the button. Our lab is trying to check on the threading, a small little sliver, really tiny, and the button itself, to see if we can make something of it. It's not much, but it's something. We're doing a thorough backgrounding of Hickey to see if there is some connective tissue we can analyze with friends of his, or acquaintances or whoever."

Georgihu examined closely the little notebook she had extracted from her jacket pocket.

"The puzzling thing is the motive. Who stands to gain the most from the leaking of the trip, regardless of Hickey's role in it?"

Barkley frowned. "Good question. The Soviets because they don't relish any approaches by us to the new Chinese Government. Anyone who wants to see the President hurt politically, because it did hurt. That includes a lot of people. Some of the folks in the Congress who would like to watch the President wallow in quicksand. Republicans who are eager to wound the President just before the election. And maybe a few members of the press who dislike Donald Kells because he doesn't toady up to the Russians or anyone else he believes to be moving around in ways that aren't in our national interest. That's about the sum of it."

Georgihu busily inscribed some notes on the small notepad. She replaced it in her large purse, which hung on a dark strap over her shoulder.

"Nice small group, isn't it?" she said. "Although the real nerve edge of this whole affair might rest on the connection between the leak and the people who benefit from the leak, and Hickey's strange connection to this entire puzzle. That's a tough one. Right now, Clem, we're going to try to zero in on the killers. If we get close to them, we might have answers to the riddle."

"Tell the Director this is high priority. The President has instructed me to tell you that we want you to be the field commander. We trust you, and we know you will keep the engines going on this until you come up with something. Inform the Director of the President's instructions."

Georgihu rose to her feet. "I will tell the Director. And so far as I know, I can stay on top of this for the Bureau. Our Washington agent-in-charge would normally be in command. But this is not a Bureau homicide. This belongs to the District police."

Clem leaned over to shake Georgihu's hand. "No waffling on this, Toni. Tell the Director no Washington office agent-in-charge crap, no police crap. Have the Director talk to the Mayor and the Chief of Police. They'll be cooperative. Tell him the President wants you in charge."

Georgihu smiled. "We don't disobey the President, do we?"

Clem fumbled with his tie, gazing on it as if it had some monstrous stain on it. He looked back up at Toni, speaking hastily, chewing on his words: "Look, if you don't have any plans for tonight, could we have dinner?"

Toni Georgihu stared at Clem. "I'm not too sure about this, Clem."

"Sure about what?"

"You and I. We have important work to do together. I have a heavy responsibility. So do you. I'm not sure we ought to mix that up with something else."

"Look, I can't see why we can't have dinner together. We need to meet and talk about this very messy problem. Why can't we do it over dinner? Or are you opposed to eating?" Clem was amazed at his own insistency.

"Let's not make it tonight. We'll have dinner some other time." Her voice and manner were, to him, unsuitably equable.

Clem was furious at himself for the disappointment that lodged in his throat. Rejection by this towering, definitely attractive woman, who doubtless had a large revolver in the large purse she carried, was not pleasant. Actually, at that moment, he envied anyone who dealt with situations like this in a confident, plausible manner.

Toni stopped at the door. She turned and said, "Ask me again."

When the door closed behind the FBI agent, Barkley settled back in his chair. He gazed at the ceiling, stirred by her parting remark. He felt a nice anticipatory feeling circling around inside him.

He suddenly sat up straight. The President knew nothing of this meeting. Donald Kells would be off the wall if he knew what Clem was up to without being informed. Few people understood the power of the three magic words, "the President wants." If they were uttered by someone close to the Oval Office, the entire country shook with the energy of people trying to carry out that bidding. It was scary. Events were moving fast and no doubt the Director would not allow his ass to hang bare in the wind. He would be calling the President to sort of check up on things. Clem bounced out of his chair. He pushed down the intercom.

"Mr. President, may I see you? It's rather important."

Thirteen

"GENTLEMEN," the Vice President said matter-of-factly, "I believe this country is on the threshold of war."

Bill Rawlins lifted his glass of cognac and sipped while two of his three guests exchanged puzzled glances.

Senator Gifford Gray sat before Rawlins in the rustic study of the Rawlins farmhouse. The Senator from Tennessee was the single most respected, admired, and influential member of the United States Senate. For more than forty years he granted counsel and wisdom to his fellow Senators. Republicans and Democrats alike well knew that when Gifford Gray gave his word, no force on earth could sever him from that pledge. Small, compact, he cut a commanding figure in the corridors of the Russell Building and on the Senate floor with his gleaming bald head, oarsman's back, and patrician manner. In Washington, Presidents, Congressmen, and press, in turn, learned long ago that the Senate was his life, its institutional durability and its parliamentary process two divinities he worshiped and sustained. The few times he betrayed his genetic courtesies were when he was confronted by a novice to the Senate or a presumptuous journalist who viewed casually the Senate's institutional heritage or its procedures.

Next to Senator Gray was the only black Senator in that chamber, Wilfred Matthews of Massachusetts. Six feet seven, a Rhodes

Scholar, Matthews was the most dramatic orator in the Senate, his rolling baritone blessed with a rhythm and cadence in keeping with his family's long tradition of preaching the Protestant gospel. The great source of Senator Matthews' electoral strength was, his Protestant creed notwithstanding, a strong personal appeal to large segments of Catholic voters in Massachusetts. Will Matthews spoke infrequently on the Senate floor, but when he rose to address his colleagues, the floor usually filled up quickly.

The fourth man in the room was a most unlikely-looking Texan: gaunt, bony Hoyle Henderson, the state Democratic chairman of Texas, regarded as the most Machiavellian of contemporary politicians. But even his enemies conceded the man's intuitive gifts. Henderson had what Bill Rawlins, quoting Churchill, called "the seeing eye."

Gray, Matthews, and Henderson had arrived an hour earlier by charter helicopter, courtesy of Roger Rawlins, whose Empire State Enterprises manufactured the same model chopper in its upstate New York factory. Later the trio would return to Dulles Airport, and it would be as if they'd never left. The ungainly-looking chopper squatted on the meadow pad where it had landed, some two hundred yards from the main Rawlins house.

"Come now, Bill," said the huge black Senator, "this talk of war is a touch apocalyptic, isn't it? We're hardly mobilizing—unless you're privy to information I don't have."

Rawlins leaned forward. "I can confirm what Vincent Canfield revealed on TV the other night: the President was indeed planning to send Willacy Hughes to China to make common cause with Chang."

Gray—as Chairman of the Armed Services Committee, the most important man in the Senate in matters of national defense, though his writ ran through all issues, foreign and domestic—said calmly, "I can't believe the President would embark on this kind of adventure without consultation. He's not an impulsive man."

Rawlins said nothing.

Matthews seemed thoughtful. "It's no secret the President takes a pretty harsh view of the Soviets, particularly since they've gotten their act together under this new Executive President."

Senator Gray, nodding, said, "The President does have a kind of foreboding about the Kremlin and its new leader. But if what you say is true, it would be a breach of his usual caution."

The Vice President gestured with an open hand. "Gifford—Will —believe me, that mission was on until it leaked. The President intends to aid the Chinese in every way he can, short of sending troops and invoking the War Powers Resolution."

Rawlins rose, lifting his tumbler of cognac, swirling it in his tapered fingers. He felt serene. He relished the large room—its high-beamed ceiling, the rough-plank floor that groaned underfoot, the vast arched fireplace, the semicircular immense sofa, the flickering flames of hurricane oil lamps. The Vice President came often to this family farm in Middleburg, to this rambling two-story house, built by his father, sitting in the middle of eighty-two fenced acres.

He stood directly over Senator Gray.

"Gifford, two months ago when we dedicated the new Trident Mark II, you said that unless we make an agreement once and forever reducing the threat of another war, we are destined for extinction. You said that we need rapport with these new Soviets *now*. You were eloquent. You were believable. And you were right."

The old Senator's gaze never wavered. "I have no reason to believe Don Kells doesn't agree with my view. Granted, the President has been sluggish in his response to domestic problems; that does worry me. But what is it you're proposing, specifically?"

Rawlins strode back to his heavy wing-backed chair. He looked at the large oil painting of his father by the huge fireplace. In front of a blackened oil derrick, the old wildcatter stood regally, confidently, in well-worn jeans, leather jacket, and mud-caked boots, a battered Stetson in one hand-on-hip. Every wrinkle and crease in his dark brown face was starkly visible. "Don't show me like some jackass matinee idol, paint me with the bark off," Buck Rawlins had told the artist, Gordon Willis. When Buck Rawlins died sixteen months ago, it was Bill Rawlins' darkest hour.

"Well, Bill," he heard Matthews ask, "what's on your mind?"

Rawlins sprawled back in his chair.

"I'm going to challenge the President in the primaries," he said casually.

Gray's eyes tightened. Matthews' mouth curved downward.

"I intend," Rawlins said, "to go to the voters in the primaries with my opposition to the President's policies, domestic and foreign."

Silence hung heavily in the air like thick strands of Spanish moss.

Finally, Hoyle Henderson spoke.

"He's tellin' it for real, Senators," Henderson said in a gravelly drawl. "He can beat this President, who has the lowest job rating since Truman in '52. Hell—*lower* than Truman."

Gray straightened his back, his hand brushing aside some invisible lint on his coat lapel. His hand's skin looked toasted, the thin furrows of aged skin creased by tiny lines visible in the light from the lamp at his elbow.

"Bill, you know I have affection and respect for you. The very first day you came to the Senate, I remember you came to my office and asked my counsel. I gave it then. I give it now."

"I was grateful then, and I will be grateful now," said Rawlins.

"Perhaps you won't be when you hear me out. I tell you this is madness. You would destroy the party and you would forfeit the election. It would be a shameful failure. You, the Vice President, taking on your President? I would say it is crazy, but then because it has never been done before, the only way I can describe it is to say, as calmly as I can, this is mad."

Will joined in. "I share Gifford's concern, Bill. This is a terrible idea. It can't work and it would collapse the party's chances to hold onto our majorities in the House and Senate."

Rawlins seemed almost amused, as if he had anticipated every word he had heard. His manner reflective and relaxed, he leaned his head back farther, almost glancing at the ceiling.

"What if I told you I believed, strongly believed, that if I win the primaries, I can deal with the Russians, I can win over the Germans when their government falls, as it surely will. And I can deal with the Japanese. Moreover, I know I can get a handle on inflation, now going out of sight. I can certify what I have just conveyed to you."

"Bill, in a way, what you propose stops just short of treason," said Matthews, very quietly.

"Treason, my dear Will, is merely a matter of dates. Treason can't be a proper description for a course of action which relaxes the possibility of war and relieves the people of their anxiety. Don't you agree?"

Matthews turned to Gray. "What do you say, Gifford?" He knew that Gifford Gray's opposition or support was crucial to the Senate's reaction, if and when it was possible to communicate Rawlins' plans.

The old Senator's right hand rubbed the armchair's outer covering, a slight movement back and forth.

"Please tell me," he said, "what you mean by 'I believe I can deal with the Russians, and with the Germans when their government falls?' Have you talked to them? Do you truly know?"

Rawlins stood up, walked to the large bay window next to the fireplace. The vast stretch of greenery was vividly bright under the scrutiny of powerful illumination fed by six high-candlepower lights hanging over the roof of the house. A Secret Service man walked slowly across the pebbled driveway, and a second agent lounged by the front fender of a black Lincoln.

Senator Matthews watched Rawlins closely, giving no evidence of the slight tremor he felt coursing through his stomach. He felt the vague stirrings of a thin hesitancy as he observed the Vice President, a strange and almost illicit feeling as if he had passed an open window on a cold and bitter day.

"When the time comes," said Rawlins, "the Soviets will respond favorably to my suggestions for a total treaty on nuclear weapons reductions. Why shouldn't they? They know I am not as nervous as the President. The new Germans who will govern their country know that I don't see the world as our noble leader does." Rawlins leaned against the wall, shoulder pressed against the paneling. "Gifford, I don't have to talk to Germans and Russians to know how they will react to a reasonable leadership in this country. They don't trust us any more than the President trusts them."

Gray said nothing. He was immobile. The large face, worn with age and work, glowed in the soft light. He stirred slightly in his chair. "Are you saying, Bill, that you are committed to this action?"

"That is exactly what I am saying, Senator." Rawlins' voice turned stern. Senator Gray was unperturbed.

Matthews said quickly, "We are not saying the President is not vulnerable. He is. The polls confirm that. With Governor Stonehaven the likely Republican nominee, I do personally doubt that Don Kells could win the election."

"I agree, Will," said Rawlins. "I agree that as of this moment Governor Stonehaven will devastate the President in the election. Anxiety, unemployment, no rosy outlook for the future, it is all there. We are talking pocketbook, home-and-family issues. Does any one of us want to run and try to support a President who is dragging such an unwholesome burden? Now, you add to that drab catalogue one more sour ingredient and you have, dear colleagues, an indigestible political menu. I am, of course, talking about belligerency, I am talking about anger, I am talking about a political saber-rattling blunder by the President."

Gray rose.

The old Senator walked slowly across the room, stood before the taller Rawlins, whose slim figure seemed no sturdier than the ramrod soldier's stance of the smaller Gifford Gray.

"I like you, Bill, very much. Your father was for most of my public life a longtime friend as well as a very generous supporter. I admire your intellect and, I must say, until this moment, your political judgment. But I am bound to say to you that I am not happy with what you are saying. I only know I am ill at ease with this conversation and with what it seems to forecast." He laid a hand gently on the forearm of the Vice President. "I don't want to publicly quarrel with you. I will not be your enemy unless you force me to. But in this enterprise, I cannot be your friend, either. I am sorry, Bill, I can only counsel you to think clearly, think deeply about this. What we are talking about tonight is the seedbed of a tragedy."

The old Senator fell silent, held out his hand to Rawlins, who shook it vigorously.

"Shall we head back home, Will?" Gray said.

Matthews unreeled his frame from his seat. "I'm ready, Gifford." He looked sadly at the Vice President. "Good night, Bill," he said.

Rawlins put his arm around the shoulders of Senator Gray. Affectionately, he said, "Gifford, you are a rare man and I care about you. Will, I thank you too." His smile now disappeared. "But this enterprise, as you call it, is already in motion. And when a heavy body starts down a hill, it increases its velocity. No one can stop it. Hoyle, will you see that the Senators get aboard the chopper? A car will be waiting for you all at Dulles."

As the threesome drove off into the night to the chopper pad, Rawlins watched them from the window. He moved to a small desk at the back of the spacious room. He picked up the phone, dialed a number. It rang twice.

A voice said, "Wilson Transport."

Rawlins held the phone close to his mouth. "I am sorry, perhaps I have the wrong number. I was trying to reach 338-0005."

The voice said, "You have the wrong number."

Rawlins hung up. The link was intact.

Everything was on course.

Fourteen

AT 9:25 THE NEXT MORNING, Hoyle Henderson was one of fourteen men and two women sitting around a conference-room table at 1700 K Street, the office of Brackenfield, Wyland and Magee, one of Washington's premier lawyer-lobbying firms.

Everyone present in this richly furnished room wore on his or her calling card the nameplate of some prestigious law firm that practiced more lobbying than law.

Those assembled were more than lawyers, more than lobbyists. They were what Hoyle called the "herd bulls" of the Washington Beltway, chief custodians of political money and guardians of political stability, as they measured it.

B. J. Brackenfield glared morosely at Sid Welling, whose jaws were clamped over a monstrous cigar.

"Goddamnit, Sid," B.J. said, in his heavy Arkansas drawl, jowls shaking, "your exhaust is putting out more fumes than my daddy's old Hudson."

Welling grinned. He shook the ashes from his Montecristo Number One, and returned it to his mouth. Welling, an early supporter of Ronald Reagan, had served the first two years of that administration as Deputy Solicitor General before inserting his name in the venerable firm of Wistern, Hightower, Middleton and (now) Welling.

"B.J.," Welling said, "the richer you get, the more delicate your nose gets. If you can't enjoy the scent of the finest cigar in the known world, I pity you."

Hoyle Henderson, sitting next to B.J., didn't smile. He checked his notes, looked up at his colleagues, cleared his throat.

"We're here," Henderson said, "to figure out how the hell to win the election next year. If Bobby Stonehaven wins, we lose the Senate, maybe the House. If the Senate goes, we got big trouble. I don't have to tell you what happens if we switch Chairmen of Finance, Appropriations, Banking, and Commerce. Tunstall's ass is out, and Harvey Blake is the new Senate Majority Leader. You'd *love* that, wouldn't you, Maggie?"

Dark-haired, petite Maggie Carothers, chief lobbyist for the housing industry, frowned. She'd had to call in every marker to beat back the tenacious Senate Minority Leader. Senator Blake's attempt to hamstring her pet project to create the largest low-cost housing program in America was well known to her colleagues. That the program went through at all, even at radically reduced levels, was considered a triumph for Maggie.

Henderson continued. "Mitch, what's the verdict on the PACs next year?"

The Political Action Committee was a contrivance that allowed corporations and unions to extract hard-earned money from their employees and members to convey to favored candidates, mostly incumbents. In the campaign contribution zoo, PACs were the big gorillas.

Mitchell Joyner and B. J. Brackenfield were, by anybody's yardstick, the best fund-raisers in town. The New York *Times* described them as "first-class vacuum cleaners sucking up every stray dollar in sight." Joyner, once Deputy Secretary for the Treasury, had a blue-chip client list. Twenty-some *Fortune* 500 corporations retained him to look after their interests with the House Ways and Means Committee and the Senate Finance Committee. Brackenfield's client list was just as impressive.

"If the President runs again," Joyner said, "and if the polls stay hostile—if inflation and unemployment continue—Stonehaven would have his pick of the PACs."

B.J. concurred: "All Kells will get is the minimum. Stonehaven will get the family jewels. We got big problems in the country. There is, as the peanut man from Georgia used to say, 'One large fucking malaise out there.' "

"It's that bad, Mitch?" asked Stanley Weisgarten, whose law firm represented major investment bankers.

"B.J.'s right, Stan," Joyner said. "The President is deep in the briar patch right now."

Willa Hammond spoke up. She was a tall, solemn, handsome woman, formerly Deputy Secretary of Health and Human Services under Carter. She had returned to the practice of law and was now leader of the insurance industry's lobby. Her political acumen was common knowledge. It was she who constructed the ingenious plan of improving on the Business Roundtable that summoned chief executive officers to Congress when a comprehensive business issue arose. Willa Hammond organized business roundtables in each district and state, and deployed these local constituent businessmen to the Congressmen in whose district they resided and in the state where the Senator knew of their origins. It is difficult for any public servant to dwell too heavily on the merit of a cause when so many of his constituents, armed with political contributions and garmented in local political power, clamour loudly and insistently for his attention, and his vote. There is nothing so compelling or so frightening to a Congressman or Senator up for reelection than the angry buzz of the local multitude.

"Our principal concern," Willa said, "shouldn't be how to give mouth-to-mouth resuscitation to the President, but who to fall in behind, to win next November. No sense pouring money down a Kells rathole. We've got Stonehaven on one side. We need a world-class candidate on the other."

What Willa Hammond could leave unspoken was that her clients' PACs, and all the others, were curiously and cruelly nonpartisan.

If the company's CEO had a personal repugnance for Democrats, his political scouts and professional consultants were cheerfully immune to party preferences. This assembly of political power barons had a casual memory of party loyalty or even friendship. Incumbency was the name of the game. PACs picked up the spoor of whoever had power, poured funds to him or her. If you had a chairman or key member who was sensitive to your needs, which party that friend belonged to was irrelevant.

The men and women in this room believed their concerns would be better served if the current chairmen stayed in power. Willa Hammond knew, better than the press that reported the "evils" of money-giving, that contributing to a Senator or Congressman never guaranteed you a vote. But, because the average Senator has to raise about $15,000 every week of his tenure if he or she hoped to be reelected, the bottom line was that contributors got listened to.

Last month Willa met with some of her clients, telling them, "Campaign reform is an idea whose time has not come. It's beguiling to editorial writers, those pundits prancing around on TV news shows, Ralph Nader, Common Cause, and some lonely Congressmen and Senators. But most, not all, incumbents are terrified of federal financing, and challengers don't want to be hitched to some kind of spending ceiling."

B.J. leaned back in his heavy leather chair. "I second Willa's motion. None of us is looking at the President's hole card. But all of us are seeing the same cards on the table that Kells is seeing. Even if he has aces wired, he can't beat Stonehaven's full house. What Stonehaven has going for him is the economic mess that Kells has created and the messy fix the world is in. All right, maybe he didn't create it, but who gives a shit?"

The assembled lobbyists nodded in agreement.

"So even if the poor bastard Kells didn't do it," B.J. said, "there just ain't anybody else to blame. Fact is, hardly nobody in this town or elsewhere knows what the hell is going on in the world and what to do about it. Every panty-hosed think tank in these parts is working overtime trying to come up with answers and they don't know cowshit from chateaubriand."

B.J. continued: "Look, I got plenty affection for the President. I'm not gonna yield to any man in my admiration for him and I paid my dues to him four years ago. I think it's fair to say that Mitch and I were out front with money-raising that the White House crowd damn sure was grateful for. But times are different now. Do we want to change the Congressional leadership? No sirree. Do we want to win the White House in November? Well, if we do, we have to have another horse. Can't beat a slick thorough-bred with a spavined old mule.''

"Who do you suggest, B.J.?'' Welling asked, his Montecristo riding the corner of his mouth.

B.J. raised an eyebrow. He spoke slowly. "The only man I know who can do it is Bill Rawlins.''

The group digested B.J.'s suggestion in silence, surprised not so much by the knowledge that the President had to go, but by the revelation that the Vice President's name was out in the open.

Willa looked curiously at Hoyle Henderson. His face was grim, no outward response to B.J. Did Hoyle prompt B.J.? Perhaps, she thought, but B.J. has no personal animosities, he has no personal gods—he goes with the winner, and if the winner is someone who causes nostrils to twitch in distaste, B.J. always finds some way to cure nostril-twitching. No, Willa felt, B.J. is on his own here. No way Hoyle could convince him to go in a direction that B.J. thought was either foolish or fruitless.

"What about it, Hoyle?'' Willa finally asked. "What B.J.'s sug-gesting bears the faint aroma of Benedict Arnold. Does that bother you?''

Hoyle displayed his crooked teeth in a smile, but said nothing.

"Well,'' said Willa, "I like the idea. Bill Rawlins may be about the most attractive political figure on the horizon right now, in either party. Stonehaven is effective enough, but alongside Bill Rawlins, he'd look pretty stodgy.''

Now Hoyle shrugged, his hands, palms up, before him. "I got nothing to hide. I believe the Vice President is the single most powerful force in the Democratic Party today. Question is, what'll the President do? Go quietly, or fight? Would he and Rawlins chew each other up till Stonehaven orders an ambulance and goes his merry way? Friends, Bill Rawlins can win this election when no-body else in the Party can. It's as clear and as simple as that. And someone in this room has got to be smart enough to figure out how to get the President to withdraw without nuclear war in the prima-ries.''

Henry Bastion spoke up. The old warrior had worked as a newly-minted lawyer for Harry Truman in his last year in office and was the last living original partner of O'Rourke, Bastion, Whalen and Magruder.

"Perhaps I'm old-fashioned," he said, "but somehow the idea that the Vice President can just move in and challenge the President, the man who put him in office, smacks of low-down dirty pool, not to mention putting a knife in the President's back."

"For godsakes, Henry," B.J. said, "we're not talking morality. We got no frigging nunnery here. We're talking about how in the cherry-striped chambers of hell we're going to beat Stonehaven!"

Bastion said, "I say stick with the President and see if we can help him out of the morass."

"For Chrissakes, Henry," Welling snorted. "You of all people can't be so naive. I think B.J. is right—don't you, Willa?"

Willa Hammond carefully surveyed her fingernails. "Henry, I join you in your distaste for this suggestion. But Bill Rawlins can make a race of it—he's good-looking, he's the best speaker in the Party, and he can galvanize this campaign. Besides, his father was richer than the Rockefellers and Kennedys put together. Rawlins could damn near finance the campaign out of petty cash."

Hoyle sat mute during this exchange. He had predicted to the Vice President how the meeting would go. He had surmised that Henry Bastion would take the high ground, and had primed B.J. in advance, though he didn't have to prime that hard.

B. J. Brackenfield was no purist. He had to be with a winner, simple as that. Hoyle knew the others smelled defeat and that was anathema. They, like B.J., would ride with a winner, even if it meant deserting the President. Their own mothers would not be safe if the alternatives were losing the election or throwing Momma off the train.

These people were harbingers. When these professionals made their decision, the drumbeats would be communicated to all those they represented, inserted into the entrails of the hundreds of PACs whose purses financed the election and whose clients' "soft money" fattened "get out the vote" projects, as well as a clandestine funding of campaign staff. It was all a rowdy adventure, a political game whose rules everyone knew and systematically violated.

This meeting was the first step in an electoral chain that would

alert business proconsuls as well as tweak the thousands of political antennae in clubs, boardrooms, and labor unions, within court-
houses, city halls, and state houses in every district and state in the
country. It would seep to the press, which would go public with
the choice, and then the battle would begin.

An hour and a gallon of coffee later, the meeting concluded.
Willa Hammond was last to leave.

She said to B.J. and Hoyle, "Kells is a proud man. He won't go
easy even if he knows he'll get slaughtered at the polls."

Hoyle's lopsided grin was at odds with his bony face. "Don't
forget LBJ called it quits when the war got too messy to win, too
bloody to stop and no way to parley. There's a time in draw poker
when a player looks at his hand and says to himself no matter how
many cards I draw I can't win the pot. So I'm throwin' in my
hand."

Willa stopped at the door. "Maybe so, Hoyle. I wish you luck.
I'm ready to put up my ante, anyway."

She waved over her shoulder as she headed for the elevator.

B.J. and Hoyle were alone.

"The first shot's been fired," B.J. said. "Figuring your next
move?"

Hoyle lifted himself to his feet. "Right now I got another meeting to attend, to spread some more gospel."

"You're going to leak to the press yourself, aren't you? Damn!"

"I didn't say that, B.J. Speaking of gospel, why don't you have a
talk with Jimmy Winger, that cousin of yours, and see if that intimate of the Lord, that TV-preaching sumbitch finds our plan suitable."

"Jimmy aims to help out, Hoyle—trust me."

"I trust you, B.J. It's somebody who talks to God and thinks he
hears somebody talking back that gets me nervous. Still, we could
use that wallet-lifting preacher to work the born-again crowd."

"Jimmy's got a lot on his mind now," B.J. said, "what with all
those investments he's making."

"Let's put it this way, B.J.—the Reverend Jimmy will know that
the Lord endorses our plans once he understands you're going to
be a large benefactor to his God's Condominiums project. Maybe

that Arkansas bank of yours can find its way clear to make a nice loan. With God building those condos, least you can do is feed the collection plate."

B.J.'s laughter bellowed through the room. "Goddamnit, Hoyle, you're right. Hell, it's the only Christian thing to do."

Fifteen

ROGER RAWLINS sat in his library in the house on 31st Street in Georgetown. With him was his brother, the Vice President, who had joined him via the secret pathway, and now sat on the leather sofa, a cup of tea in hand.

Roger Rawlins, Jr., was drinking coffee. A bulky man with out-croppings of gray in his brown hair, his chin fleshy, Roger had been since childhood the son his father had never appreciated. Bill, on the other hand, had been the golden boy from the start, good-looking, nimble, a natural athlete, and possessed of winning ways that always brought others to his side.

But Roger Rawlins, Jr., had never resented his younger brother. He was proud of him, though in rare moments he wondered why Fate had made him the elder son, and the stodgy one.

"How was the party at Christine Lambert's?"

Bill sipped his tea. "Tolerable. Though it did have some high moments."

"Luther has lit the fire?"

"It's lit, Roger—burning bright. Tomorrow morning it'll be on the front pages and the lead story on every TV news show."

"You have never really explained why you think you can get the President not to run. Granted, he's in trouble, but so was Truman . . ."

"Roger, Truman lived in another world, about a hundred light-years away. In one TV broadcast, I can reach more people in one hour than all the people Truman and Dewey spoke to in their entire campaign. Nineteen forty-eight might as well be the sixteenth century."

The older brother sighed. "Somehow this all has a funny smell, Bill . . ."

"Remember what Dad used to say? 'Them that can't defend themselves are ripe for the taking.' "

"Sure, I remember. But I also remember Dad never went back on his word. That was the one thing he truly cared about."

Bill glared at his brother.

Roger raised his hands, palms up, contrite. "Yes, yes, whatever you do, I'll be there to back you. You know that. But damnit, Bill, Kells is a good man. Fact is, when you ran with him, you told me he was 'the right man at the right time'!"

"And I meant it. But this is *not* the right time for Donald Kells. Stonehaven will blow him away. But I can whip Stonehaven. Can anything be more simple?"

"I just keep remembering how Dad got his start—and it wasn't because he reneged on a pledge."

Bill frowned. He rose, jaws clenched, as if he were going to strike Roger, then turned to the small bar and poured himself a tumbler of scotch.

Roger almost said, "Little early for that, isn't it, Bill?" but stopped himself. No need to irritate his brother further.

Roger knew his brother was reflecting on a story they had both heard a hundred times from family and friends—everyone except their father.

When Roger Rawlins, Sr.—Buck to his friends—was thirty years old, newly married, struggling in the oil business, he rode in a Packard sedan, south from Houston toward Corpus Christi, to a piece of Texas soil called the Bill Beckett ranch. The driver was his partner and longtime friend, Sam Henry Culheen, older than Buck by four years and already modestly rich through his discovery of the Shrimp Hill field near Matagorda. Buck, an oil broker, was barely staying out in front of the Second National Bank of Houston, which held too many of his notes.

"Got a proposition for you, Sam Henry."

Eyes not straying from the two-lane road, Sam Henry grunted, "What's the deal, Buck?"

"I need $250,000, Sam Henry, and I need it today. I got a deed in my pocket turning over to you my quarter stake in the Bill Beckett well for that amount. That strike you as fair?"

Sam Henry slowed the car, turned to Buck. "That strikes me as lousy—for you. If this well comes in, and I know in my bones it will, your share in this field will be worth—what?—fifty million minimum? This is our big one, Buck—we're goin' to be on top of the hill, when that well gushes. You want to toss it all away for a paltry quarter million? Bad deal, Buck, bad deal."

"If that well's a duster, I'm broke, I truly am. I need the two-fifty today. I need it now."

Sam Henry cursed.

"You dumb, stubborn jackass. Aw right, I'll take the deed and I write out the check. But you'll regret it to the last hour you live. God, I'd just as soon hold a horse in the rain without a slicker on than argue with a dimwit dunce."

At nightfall, they turned off onto a pitted trail winding through an open field, past a grove of scraggly trees, and four miles from the highway, they saw the rig, a rickety-looking wooden affair, and could hear the bit grinding into the earth. A man in blackened overalls waved, and shouted, "Sam Henry! You come at just the right time."

Sam Henry said, "Good ole Bobby Pitfield. Best damn rough-neck around. He can smell oil when everybody else is sniffing dust."

Pitfield shambled over to the Packard. "We're down to eight thousand and ought to be deep in that sand sometime evening. I tole Ed"—pointing to the other roughneck—"if he misses that crevice I'll kick the limeback dirty out of him. You can turn in, and I'll let you know when we hit."

"If we hit," said Sam Henry.

Bobby let loose a wide tobacco-stained, cavity-blotched grin. "Hellfire, Sam Henry, I heard Governor Jimmy Allred say just the other day that Texans don't know nothing about can't do. All we know is can do. Right, Buck?"

Buck grinned. "Sure as hell hope so, Bobby."

Sam Henry looked morose. "Me and Buck here are going to sashay to the cabin and lie down a while . . ."

Two hours later, a black-stained Bobby Pitfield was jostling Sam Henry awake; Bobby's whooping woke Buck as well. A pungent smell was in the air.

It was the smell of money. Big money.

"Sam Henry," Bobby was bubbling, "you done brought in a whopper, gonna be bigger than Tomoconnor and Spindletop combined!"

Now Sam Henry yelled, and Buck lifted his arms in triumph. "You did it, Sam Henry, just like you said you would!"

"Bobby, get your ass back on that rig! Let's get her under control—and we're goin' to the bank tomorrow and get ready to dig some more holes!" Sam Henry shouted.

Bobby ran out of the cabin, his glee echoing through the night.

Sam Henry turned to Buck. "Buck—I'm about to take that deed of yours and tear it right in two. You were my partner, and you still are my partner."

Buck's face grew stern. "No matter what you do with that deed, Sam Henry, you bought me out. I never cut and run from a deal and I don't aim to start here."

"Are you crazy? Your interest's going to be worth—what?—fifty million, maybe seventy-five, maybe even a hundred if we do our digging right. A hundred million, Buck! You going to throw that away on some fool kind of pride? Goddamn, man, you're my partner, you're my friend, my best friend—"

"I truly am that, Sam Henry—but one day you'd think about this and say that old Buck done broke his word. You gave me $250,000 for my share, which I sorely need. So let's you and me draw on our britches and get our asses out on that rig and watch you become a pissant multimillionaire."

Sam Henry grabbed Buck and hugged him. "All right, but when I get back home every jackleg oilman in Houston is goin' to know about what you did today. I'm goin' to make it known that when Buck says it's a deal, it's a deal, you can bank on it. When Buck Rawlins says a rooster can pull a boxcar, by God, you just hitch him up."

Buck's friend kept his promise. Sam Henry was like an evangelist, declaring that Buck Rawlins was that special breed of Texan whose word was worth more than precious metal; precious metal fluctuated in value, but Buck Rawlins' word was stable—it never wavered or broke.

Within four years, Buck was the recipient of a dozen brokering deals and equity positions, and his net worth far exceeded the $50 million minimum that he "threw away" on the Bill Beckett field. Within ten years Buck was the second richest man in Texas. Only Sam Henry Culheen was wealthier.

Bill Rawlins stared at the glowing fireplace.

Finally he said, "Roger—what I'm doing has nothing to do with Buck Rawlins and any pledges he made. I didn't give my word I'd stand helplessly by and watch a slaughter at the polls. It's simply not the same, and Dad would be the first one to tell you so."

Roger shook his head, sadly.

Bill said, "First, let us settle some crucial issues."

He sat, thumbed through papers in the manila folder on the coffee table. "I want Hoyle to have carte blanche up to two million of my funds. No questions asked. If he needs more than that, I'll authorize it."

Roger said nothing, then nodded glumly.

Bill needled his dour brother with a grin. "Dad wouldn't want me to go short just when we're about to bet the ranch, now, would he?"

Sixteen

THE FRONT-PAGE HEADLINE of the Washington *Post* burned the eyes of every professional lobbyist and government bureaucrat on Capitol Hill: RAWLINS TO KELLS: I'M IN THE RACE.

The New York *Times* offered a two-tiered front-page headline and a story by Maureen Dowd: VICE PRESIDENT IN SURPRISE MOVE CHALLENGES PRESIDENT FOR PARTY NOMINATION.

Nibbling a doughnut for breakfast, Clem Barkley read the Washington *Post* in his apartment without surprise. The story had broken first on the late evening TV news, the anchor describing Washington as "like a city after an earthquake."

He picked up the White House phone as he glanced at the clock. It was 6:15 a.m.

"Yes, Clem," the President said.

"I'm looking at the *Post*."

"Mike Carson called me last night to alert me. He got a call from the *Times*. I told him to finesse all the questions that came in late last night."

There was a slight pause, then the President said, "Obviously, Mike was right about the questions Maureen Dowd was asking. I suggest you talk to Mike right away. I think we should say up front that the Vice President's action took us by surprise, that he gave me no notice of his plans, and that if he wants to run, fine. We'll do what we have to do."

"I agree, sir. I never really did trust Rawlins."

"No time for that, Clem. We have a fight on our hands. I don't intend to go quietly. I suggest you get down here as quickly as you can."

Clem hung up and then rang Toni Georgihu. Her voice seemed vibrant.

"Do you always sound so 'up' so early?" he asked.

"I've already run three miles," she answered. "Anything wrong?"

Last night they had dined at I Ricci. She kept the conversation on the Hickey matter, and when Clem had tried, vainly, to steer her toward something more personal, she brought him back to the murder. But when he said good night at her door, she did give him a very warm smile—or had his imagination run rampant.

"Nothing," he said, "except the Vice President is loading up his AK-47, and we're putting on our flak vests. You see the morning papers?"

"Yes, I did. I also got a call from my office late last night with transcripts of TV newscasts. Does this have anything to do with what we're working on?"

"Not that I'm aware of," he said. "But it does make it all the more urgent that we clear up this Hickey killing. You never know *what* will surface in a bitter political fight."

"You're the expert in that field," she said.

He hesitated, then he said, "I enjoyed being with you last night. I hope we can do that again, soon."

"It was a good evening," she said.

He liked the way she said it.

He raced to the shower and began to sing. Funny, he never sang in the shower before.

Filipp Federof nodded to himself as he read the story in the New York *Times*. He had finished reading the *Post* story thirty minutes earlier. He was smiling.

At his home on N Street, Ben Bradlee, though retired as Executive Editor, retained his zest for the political town he knew so intimately. Bradlee slapped his leg and said to the *Post*'s political writer, David Broder, and Paul Taylor, who covered the White House, "That bastard Rawlins has got some heavyweight cojones, all right."

Broder nodded. "What's puzzling is why Rawlins made his move now. He's young—he's got time to wait it out."

"Sure," Taylor said, "but he's probably figuring that if the President's a goner, the Republicans'll come in and he has to wait eight more years."

"True," Broder said, "but even in eight years he'd still be one of the younger candidates."

"You guys are missing the point," Bradlee said.

"Yeah?" Broder said.

"Yeah. This town's swarming with ambitious men, but to Rawlins, ambition's like religion. My instinct tells me running for President means more to Rawlins than money or sex or power. It's like a tribal rite. So long as that rite is unfulfilled, he can't function. The very idea of waiting eight years, out of office and out of sorts, is unacceptable. So, he says, to hell with it, I go now, even though it means shafting Don Kells, whose Vice Presidential creature he is."

"Could be, Ben," Broder said.

Paul Taylor shook his head. "Anyway, the news won't be dull for a while."

Bradlee grinned. "That's what keeps us in business."

"What the hell you talking about, Peter?" Senator Flag Foster demanded.

Around a new table in the spacious living room of the Vice President's Middleburg residence were seven men: the Vice President; his brother, Roger Rawlins; Hoyle Henderson; Peter Weymouth, Chief Executive Officer of Weymouth, Williams, Inc., advertising agency and the Vice President's Harvard roommate; two paid pollsters; and Senator William Flagler Foster of Illinois, winner of the Congressional Medal of Honor in Korea, at the cost of his left arm and left eye. He wore a colorful paisley eye patch that made him look like a benign pirate.

"What I'm talking about," Peter Weymouth said, "is the issue of Mrs. Rawlins."

The men at the table stirred.

Weymouth sighed. "Look—we're all here because we believe in Bill. We want him to win. But we should play moot court with ourselves, and be brutally, unsparingly honest. Kells' people won't hesitate to shove hot spears up our collective ass, I assure you."

Everyone looked toward the Vice President. He was seemingly unmoved.

"I think Peter is on course," he said. "Keep going."

Relieved, Weymouth leaned forward. "Sooner or later, probably sooner, the other side will charge that the Vice President is not a dutiful husband."

The uneasiness in the room was palpable.

But Weymouth pressed on. "Why isn't his wife with him? Is she with her father in Texas, or in a hospital for depression? If so, why does the Vice President's office continue to say she's tending her sick father? Is it true the Vice President has liaisons with other women?"

Weymouth paused to light a cigarette in an ivory holder.

Foster erupted. "For God's sake, Peter, we're mounting a political race, not a goddamn letter-writing campaign to Dear frigging Abby."

Weymouth was unmoved. "If we can't answer those questions here, we'll find them answered in Conrad and Herblock cartoons, in whispered gossip over America's back fences, and in every press conference as well."

Foster frowned and turned to Rawlins. "Should we have to answer this garbage, Bill?"

"Yes," said the Vice President, "I think we do."

Roger Rawlins bowed his head to study the gnarled wood decorating the thin rectangular table.

"First," Rawlins said, "my wife *is* ill, *and* she's tending her father in Dallas. Second, she has had some problems that could be diagnosed as depression. And third, I am not a womanizer." He grinned. "Or does that sound too much like 'I am not a crook'?"

He held up his hand as Weymouth rose to protest.

"There's talk, I know," Rawlins said, "but talk will go on no matter how much we say or do."

"Bill," Weymouth persisted, "we can't dance around this.

Kells'll run on the integrity issue, he hasn't got much else to go on, and—"

Rawlins was on his feet, staring hard at Weymouth.

"Integrity?" His voice began to rise, uncharacteristically. "Integrity is what Jay Rockefeller has because his great-grandfather was the most gifted monopolist ever born. Integrity is what Ted Kennedy has because his daddy kicked the balls off Jewish movie moguls and lifted the wallets off assorted stock broker scumbags. Don't tell me integrity. That's pure bullshit. Just because our dear smart rich dads snookered some poor dumb bastards doesn't give us integrity—it gives us money to run campaigns with."

There was stunned silence.

Roger continued to map the table. Peter Weymouth had never witnessed the normally cool Vice President in such a mood. Weymouth extracted his cigarette from its holder and pressed it against the ashtray mainly to stay his trembling fingers. Senator Foster glared at Weymouth, while Hoyle Henderson rose and went to the bar.

Then Rawlins laughed and spread his arms. "Wasn't *that* a spirited reading! Right out of *Hasty Pudding*, Peter, wasn't it?"

He smiled languidly and patted Weymouth's shoulder.

"Peter," Rawlins said, almost gently, "leave this issue to me. I'll wager in the polling booth Mr. and Mrs. America will find far more compelling the rotten state of the economy, and President Kells' predilection for armed adventures in faraway places, than personal gossip."

Rawlins spoke evenly, his resonant voice now at its normal level.

"Oh, they'll listen to gossip. It's irresistible. We all love it. But when they pull the lever, it won't matter."

"All right," Weymouth said quietly. He cleared his throat, still trying to expunge from his mind the brawling tirade to which he had been witness. Odd, it was. "We all know the issues. I say we streamline the campaign, attack those points in the line where Kells is clearly vulnerable, hit them again and again." He turned to one of the pollsters. "You're on, Mack."

Mack Horowitz, the polling expert, absently patted his thinning hair.

Peter Weymouth remained uneasy. Since their undergraduate

days at Harvard he remained close to Rawlins, visiting him often in Texas and in Middleburg. And yet, he always found himself a hairline away from intimacy. In spite of Rawlins' seeming warmth, Weymouth felt a glacially guarded privacy.

The pollster spread open his folder. "According to our studies from focus groups you are immensely well liked. To quote from a woman in her sixties, who lives outside Omaha, 'The Vice President is so good-looking, even my husband said Mr. Rawlins reminded him of Clark Gable in one of those old movies—you know, a man's man.' That is a general theme throughout our interviews, women and men alike—that they find the Vice President movie-star attractive. On substantive issues, they like his confident attitude, because it's casually expressed, not coming off as arrogance but as a quiet belief in his own abilities, without lording it over others who may not be so gifted."

Horowitz paused to sip a glass of wine, turned the page, and looked up at the Vice President. "Our best weapon is that Kells is in power, and that Rawlins is not being held accountable for the Administration's lack of success. Finally, Kells is perceived as unable to cope with the economic mess, but also as not merely a hawk but a fellow who honestly believes that power is meant to be used."

Senator Foster said, "Godalmighty, how much faith can you put in those damn interviews?"

"This is not a scientific survey, admittedly," Horowitz allowed. "But we feel these focus groups indicate a thread that runs through the national conscience."

"Agreed," Hoyle Henderson said with a mischievous grin. "My people tell me that Kells' poll takers are picking up the same smell. He is up to his eyeballs in owlshit right now, and they know it—and so do we. Hell, that's why we're taking the run!"

Peter Weymouth said nothing. He knew Hoyle's position with Rawlins and he never encroached on it. He often wondered what the rapport between Rawlins and Henderson truly was, other than Hoyle's loyalty, and ability to wield a billy club. He was a little frightened of Hoyle Henderson. He wondered if Rawlins ever felt the same way.

· · · ·

Later that morning, Hoyle Henderson flung a foot over the armrest of the thickly cushioned wing chair he sat in. B. J. Brackenfield's library was quite cozy. He pressed the remote control unit and the TV set flicked on.

"It was on Channel 20," said B. J. Brackenfield. "This was taped just before Bill Rawlins threw his hat in the ring. Jimmy Winger had his big soul-saving in Little Rock. Sumbitch had them in his hip pocket. I really don't know how the bastard does it. We're in the wrong damn business, Hoyle. If I could talk like that Jimmy, I'd have me a little old tabernacle, get me a fine microphone and a good-looking choir and, shit, I'd pour the Lord to them out of the biggest ladle I could find. How much you reckon Jimmy takes in a year?"

"Would you believe one hundred million?"

"Shit, that's better than IBM, because they pay all their taxes. And knowing Jimmy as I do, the little fart is probably skimming a bunch. I told him once that if he hadn't gone into the God business he would have made one fine Las Vegas casino owner."

The screen displayed a massive auditorium, not one seat empty. Hoyle guessed it housed about fifteen thousand people and every one of them at white heat, eager for the Reverend Jimmy Winger to make his appearance.

"Brothers and sisters in Christ, here is God's witness and your friend, the Reverend Jimmy Winger," intoned the announcer.

From stage right strode the brisk, small figure of Jimmy Winger, outfitted in a black suit, white shirt, and blue tie with tiny replicas of Christ on the cross implanted in the design. He wore a black cape, tied loosely at the neck with a white halter. He stretched his arms upward, a huge, rolling smile on his face, enormous white teeth held firmly in place with a double dollop of Polygrip, glistening against the bright hard spotlights. Behind him one hundred and twenty-five white-robed choir members lifted their voices in "God Believes in You, Believe in Him," written by Jimmy Winger and his wife, Lucy Ruth. The organ thundered and the voices soared, laser lights blurred, cascading over the stage so that Winger was bathed in alternating blues and whites. His arms still upraised, Jimmy joined the chorus as he approached the rostrum pulpit, his thin reedy voice assaulting the melodic ascent of the Winger hymn. "God believes in you, believe. God receives your prayer, believe. Cast your vote for Jesus, and he will vote for you."

Jimmy Winger began to wave his arms as if he were enticing the heavens to take up a collection from the full amphitheater that very moment.

"Amen, amen," he roared. "Amen, amen," came the roar from the crowd. "Hallelujah, praise Jesus," bellowed Jimmy Winger. "Hallelujah, praise Jesus," responded fifteen thousand voices in clamorous conjoining.

Jimmy Winger held the cordless mike in hand and began his now trademarked stride from stage left to stage right and back again, a stiff-legged replica of a frenetic Mick Jagger, an incessant pacing that infected the audience with its raw animal energy. His left hand held his black leather Bible without which, Jimmy Winger once declared, he would be naked.

"I carry the Lord with me, in His book and in my heart," was Jimmy Winger's teary advocacy of always having the True Word at hand.

A leatherette replica of that same bible was available by mail for a donation of $19.95, postage extra, and contained Jimmy Winger's free-flowing autograph inscribed inside: "God believes in you, Jimmy Winger believes in you." Jimmy always gave God top billing in just about everything he wrote and said. The Winger warehouses shipped an average of two million Bibles each year. Jimmy's printing presses were able to print on offset type and bind, as well as insert the autograph at a laid-down cost of $4.75. Price Waterhouse calculated in its audit that the Bibles netted the Jimmy Winger God Believes in You Tabernacle an undisputed $26 million annually. It was, as Price Waterhouse declared in its latest report to Jimmy, his most attractive profit center, though his newest real estate project in northern Arkansas, God's Condominiums, had the potential of a vast bottom line.

There was only one disconcerting warning. The accountants reported that God's Condominiums required enormous sums of capital, including a bridge loan of $50 million. The entire project had an estimated budget of $200 million. There had to be available, admonished the accountants, access to some kind of solid loan, else God's Condominiums would be in, as Jimmy Winger's old boyhood friend and first cousin, B. J. Brackenfield, suggested to him, "deep shit trouble."

"Brothers and sisters, God speaks to us all. Hear His voice, hear Him and follow Him." Jimmy Winger's voice had a strange, mesmerizing sound, much as if he were speaking with Willie Nelson's voice and Moses' rock-solid convictions, the kind of conviction that Charlton Heston demonstrated so vividly on screen. Jimmy Winger had seen Cecil B. DeMille's epic *The Ten Commandments* at least twenty times.

"What is God saying? Oh, Lord, I am listening, speak to me." Jimmy peered into a faraway distance toward stage right, each eye in the audience tracking his gaze.

B.J. leaned toward the TV screen. "Hot damn, Hoyle, lookit that Jimmy. You reckon the Lord's listening to him? Maybe ole Jimmy's got a special unlisted phone number, kind of a celestial MCI, or would God just want AT&T?"

Hoyle, unsmiling, said, "If he's got a heavenly credit card, you can bet the sumbitch is stiffing the Lord."

Jimmy's eyes closed as if he were praying.

"Y'know, Hoyle," said B.J., "he closes his eyes to pray because those TV lights burn hell out of his retina and he won't wear tinted glasses. Says he don't want to look like some candy-assed Hollywood boob-tube star."

"I hear you, Jesus," Jimmy wailed. "Yes, God's Condominiums are as you wanted them to be, a refuge from the stinking vile profane cesspool of a secular world that is spilling its refuse on us. It is madness and abomination out there and as Proverbs has told us, 'as a dog returneth to his vomit, so a fool returneth to his folly.' Yes, Lord, God's Condominiums must be filled with God-fearing Christian people who have seen the Lord and heard His plea. You want these condominiums to be filled with Your folks, don't You, Lord?" There was a rising hum of urgency from the audience, transfixed by this querying of the Lord.

"I have here," he reached into the innards of his voluminous cape and hauled out a piece of paper, "here, my brothers and sisters, is a check for ten thousand dollars from the Vice President of the United States. He has heard me tell you that God's Condominiums are for loving, fearing, praying, church-going Christians.

The Vice President knows that some of you might have problems raising funds. So he has asked that this money be the beginning of others who will want to join in his offering of pledges to help those who can't help themselves. Oh yes, 'he that giveth to the poor shall not lack.' God has spoken to me and He has made it known that those who live in His way and in His house, in God's Condominiums, will find the tomorrow filled with all that you have ever prayed for. Give and God will give back to you. Oh, praise that wonderful, loving Vice President, the Honorable William Booth Rawlins.''

Tears began to stream down Jimmy Winger's cheeks, and he began to sob.

B.J. said, "Goddamnit, Hoyle, I never really understood how the little shithead does it, but I swear on my Grandma's grave, those are real tears. Lucy Ruth told me it was for real. I wouldn't believe Jimmy if he pissed green apples, but Lucy Ruth is a good woman. How do you figure he does it?''

Hoyle peeled a banana very carefully. He took a small bite. "It's his business, B.J. He's a pro. If you are going to be a professional TV preacher and you want to shake down folks when they can't even afford to pay the mortgage on their home, you got to learn to cry real tears, and on command. You want to be a star in a porno movie, you got to rise on command. That's what being a professional is all about. It's as simple as that.''

B.J. nodded approvingly. "Sumbitch is good, ain't he?''

Jimmy wept. A murmur, growing steadily, lifted from the audience. Women began to wail, and in the middle of the hall two full rows of men and women rose hesitantly to their feet and began to roil and shake, their voices shrill and unintelligible, mouthing undecipherable shrieks.

"My daddy used to take me to what they called brush arbor revivals in Mena, Arkansas,'' said B.J., "and I remember the first time I heard Arkansas folks speaking in tongues. Goddamnedest thing I ever heard. Never could do it myself, until I came to Washington and got the hang of it spending so much time at Ways and Means committee meetings.'' B.J.'s stomach shook with laughter.

Hoyle grinned. "Have another drink, B.J. You deserve it.''

"Don't mind if I do.''

Hoyle pointed the remote control device at the TV set and clicked. The picture blinked off.

"Good work, B.J.," said Hoyle. "First-class performance. The Vice President will be pleased. One small item. I thought, fact is, I am sure, that the cash we gave you was twenty thousand."

"It was, Hoyle, but Jimmy figured that twenty K was a bit much. He told me he'd make up a fake check to use in the hall with ten K on it."

"And the rest of the money?"

"Well, Hoyle, Jimmy does have heavy expenses. It was a donation. I figure Bill would understand." B.J. started to laugh. "I'm not sure the IRS will, but then, that's Jimmy's problem. Maybe one of those psalms will give him specific instructions on how to screw those revenue agents."

B.J. bellowed with laughter.

Seventeen

CLEM BARKLEY gazed out the Cabinet Room window. Gardeners sprayed the carpet of grass with green dye in wintertime, so even under today's surly clouds, the Rose Garden looked comforting. Only not so comforting to Clem, who faced a cheerless Saturday afternoon meeting convened at the President's request.

At the oblong table sat National Security Adviser John Wingate, and to his left, Press Secretary Mike Carson.

On the other side of the table, next to the President's empty chair, was Willacy Hughes. Imposingly tall, silver hair combed in faint waves, features finely sculptured, jaw still firm at sixty-one, Hughes wore an expensively tailored double-breasted chalk stripe suit with boxy shoulders. He'd worn the same model suit for twenty-five years.

Next to Hughes was the President's pollster, bald, bespectacled, deceptively bland Hickam Greene, who had probed the national spirit for Kells in his first race for the Presidency.

Clem sat. "I suggest we take stock before the President arrives." He lifted a sheet of buff paper. "Hick's report here is the result of an overnight search. Error probability of plus or minus five percent. Let's have a look . . . Hick, clarify when necessary."

Hickam Greene nodded.

Clem twitched a frown. "No question the President's approval rating is about as low as you can get—two percentage points beneath Jimmy Carter's abysmal score. Most disturbing is the slow but regular descent over the last eighteen months."

"And without something to halt the slide," Greene said, "it's going lower."

Clem nodded glumly. "The President's in for some bleak days ahead. A campaign conducted by a tough, smart opponent would keep him constantly on the defensive."

"Granted the President is in a tight political spot," Willacy said, "but what do these respondents have to say about our esteemed and loyal Vice President?"

"I was coming to that," Clem said. "Before I begin, let's get something straight. Not one piece of paper leaves this room, not one shred of information. And what you don't need to know, don't ask. Each of you is here for a specific reason. We have to counsel the President, and each of you has a piece of the puzzle."

Mike Carson broke in. "Why isn't Tommy here?"

Tom Freebairn was the Chairman of the Democratic National Committee.

"He's not here, Mike, because I don't trust him anymore." Clem's voice was flat.

Tommy Freebairn was a college chum of Mike Carson's and it was Carson who brought Freebairn to the President's attention.

Astounded, his chubby face turning a touch red under his beard, Carson asked, "Why in hell?"

"Simple. He's a Rawlins man. Over the past year Rawlins and Hoyle Henderson have courted him. He wants to run for the Senate back home in Wisconsin and my guess is Rawlins will empty the burlap sack of cash for him."

Carson smiled politely. It almost hid the cold rim around his lips. "Am I to understand that you're working the guillotine? Deciding who lives and who dies?"

The room grew very still.

"Anybody who is not a hundred-percent Kells man has no business being involved in this campaign," Clem said. "That's straight from the President. Any questions?"

"No," Carson said, and shrugged.

"All right," Clem said. "Willacy, give us your assessment."

Willacy glanced at his notes. "We're not going to beat Rawlins unless we go for his gut and bust him wide open. One, he's vulnerable on personal issues. We can't cringe about exposing them. Two, he must be branded a traitor. And we have to make it stick. Three, we have to dig deep, with the best investigators we can find. Follow the money, someone once said. Rawlins must be brought to his knees as soon as possible. If we do that, he'll get out and not run. Perhaps we can suggest to him that the election after this one is more suited to his time frame."

A few eyebrows were raised at that.

"Rawlins has a reputation for quick intelligence," Willacy continued. "He's highly regarded in the Senate. Women are more favorably drawn to him than men; college-educated like him more than less-educated, yet because of the Texas connection, rural voters find him attractive. In short, Rawlins' negatives are lower by half than Kells', and his favorables are much higher. Conclusion, we must hack away at his image. We simply have to put a face on Mr. Rawlins that isn't so goddamn handsome."

Clem spoke quietly, his gaze on the National Security Adviser. "John, you're here not because the President believes in your political acumen, but for your foreign policy judgment. If this campaign gets dirty, how will it affect us abroad?"

Wingate stirred in his chair. His lips pursed and a throbbing just above his left ear pulsated like a bubble on a bellows.

"There would be some compassion on the part of western European leaders," Wingate said, "who would identify with the President getting tough with a subordinate who betrayed him." Wingate pressed a handkerchief to his mouth, faintly coughed. "But I must caution you—if this gets truly nasty, it could be damaging in the long run."

"Come to the point, John," Clem said edgily.

"I would recommend resisting the Vice President with all the force we can muster, but not in a bitter, personal way."

"I value your foreign policy judgment," Clem said coldly, "but not your political views."

"Why in hell don't we force Rawlins to resign?" Willacy's voice was gravelly. "How, damnit, can he remain as Vice President, come to Cabinet meetings, when he is now pledged to destroy the President?"

"According to the Attorney General," Clem said, "there's nothing in the Constitution or in the law that offers an answer to your question. Actually, it comes down to a political decision. How will this play with the people? Does Rawlins become a predator if he assaults the President and persists in remaining on his team?"

"Then what *do* we do?" Willacy asked, almost irritably.

Clem shrugged. "Let that question be asked by the press—and by the voters."

"What do you think, Mike?" Willacy asked.

Carson was nodding. "This is one blow we don't have to strike. Someone else will wield the axe for us."

The door opened.

President Kells strode to his chair, nodding to the group. He wore an open-necked checked shirt under a denim jacket, and looked fit and hearty, if pale. No sun for the President in the last month, unlike Bill Rawlins, who either slept in the sun or had the best tanning salon in Washington.

The President grinned at Clem. "Well, Mr. Chairman, what resolutions do I abide by? Am I correct in assuming you have a plan? You and Willacy look pleased with yourselves."

Clem smiled wanly. "Not exactly a plan, Mr. President—more a series of alternatives. Shall we lay them out?"

The President nodded again. "Clem, fill me in."

Clem briskly and briefly outlined the plan.

The President leaned back in his chair, his left hand drumming on the table. "I've always believed that, in politics, nothing lasts forever. If you're down, chances are you can go up; and if you're up, chances are you'll be heading down. No doubt we're in some despair now but, I assure you, it will get better."

Willacy started to speak up, but the President raised a hand.

"If I can lay out to the American people precisely what this Administration is about—not only our domestic plans for handling the slump we are in, but also how we're going to operate in the world—this slide will stop."

Clem bowed his head. He desperately wished he could be excited by the prospect of the campaign. But he felt at this moment a terrible slackness, as if he had been wandering about in a hall of mirrors.

The President said, "You all truly believe that I have to go for Bill's groin. But I don't play that game. Frankly, I was surprised that Bill determined to make his run now. Hell, I know his ambition. That late father of his preached his son's destiny since he was a kid. But Bill switched his timing on us. So."

He clapped his hands, once.

"Let's get to work—but no hits to Rawlins' balls. We have to set a tone. Keep in mind that Governor Bobby Stonehaven is ready in the wings to take me on once I handle Rawlins. I may win the primary battle but lose the election war."

The door to the Cabinet Room opened and Clem's secretary peeked in. "Please forgive me, Mr. President," the business-like brunette said. "I have an emergency call for Mr. Barkley."

The President smiled. "Clem, if that's the *Times*, tell them I'm alive and well and itching for a fight."

Clem rose quickly. "I'll be right back, Mr. President."

In his office, he yanked the phone off the hook. "Clem Barkley here."

"Clem, I need to see you," Toni Georgihu said.

"Now?"

"Now. It's best you come to *my* office. I'll meet you in the garage. How soon can you get here?"

Clem paused. "It's that important?"

"Yes."

"Fifteen minutes."

He slammed the phone in its cradle and told his secretary to get him a car. Then he scribbled a note to the President: "I have to leave. Important. Will report back ASAP."

He stuffed it into a White House envelope, wrote on it "President's Eyes Only," and handed it to his secretary. "Get in there with this now. If anyone asks you, you don't know where I am."

She blinked. "I don't know."

"Good," he said, and went.

Mike Carson, walking down 16th Street, looked casually over his shoulder. The sidewalk behind him was deserted. He glanced across the street at the Capital Hilton Hotel. Cabs were disgorging passengers, but he saw nothing to cause him anxiety.

He crossed M Street and turned left into the Jefferson Hotel, nodded to the bellman, and strode through the empty lobby to the elevator. He got off at the third floor, glanced to his left and right, and walked swiftly to Room 306.

He knocked.

The door opened. "You're a punctual man, Mike," said Hoyle Henderson. "Drink?"

Carson shook his head as he stepped inside. "Why don't we get to it? This isn't exactly a safe haven for me."

"Nobody's going to leak this visit, Mike. Not me, not you. But my friend thought we ought to talk."

"So talk."

Hoyle Henderson plopped down in a deep-cushioned chair. "Damn fine little hostelry this Jefferson, even if my ass does disappear into these goddamn cushions."

"You doing a commercial for straight-backed chairs, Hoyle? Get on with it."

Hoyle's expression changed abruptly. "We're goin' to cut your boss a new asshole, Mike. He's about to become an ex-President, who's going to be spending full time on his Library, to keep him out of mischief. Unless you want to become one of them overpaid, fat-bellied lobbyists, you may have to trundle back up to the Hill and find yourself a new niche. Unless . . ."

"Unless what?"

Hoyle lit a Marlboro, inhaled slowly. "Unless you decide your friend Bill Rawlins' is the side you ought to be on."

Carson rose, wandered slowly around the hotel room. He stopped at the TV and turned it on. Errol Flynn, resplendent in the uniform of the 27th Lancers, was telling the Commander of the Light Brigade of his orders to immediately take Balaclava. The screen filled with cavalry units ready to take the field.

Carson turned up the volume, loud.

"You a movie buff, Mike?"

"Yeah, I always liked Errol Flynn."

Hoyle grinned. "Mike, you're a suspicious sumbitch. Jesus, you think I got this room bugged?"

Carson grinned back. "An honorable fellow like you, Hoyle? What a dastardly thought."

Hoyle came close to Carson. He put his mouth near Carson's ear. "What I'm saying, Mr. Press Secretary, is how would you like to be a Cabinet officer at age thirty-six?"

"You bribing me, Hoyle?"

"Who, me? Hell no, I'm merely suggesting you dream a little. Doesn't every man in this town dream about where good American lads might wind up if they work hard, think fast, and get on the winning side of a Presidential election?"

Carson turned back to the screen, tugging at his expanding paunch. Errol Flynn was leading the charge, galloping at full speed, saber and arm outstretched toward the enemy.

"Tell you what, Hoyle. Why don't I hear this dream recited to me by your 'friend,' personally? If that happened, I might want it to come true. Otherwise, I would be afraid of nightmares."

"If that's what you want," Hoyle said, "no problem. In fact, I like your style, Mr. Press Secretary. What's your private home number?"

Eighteen

THE J. EDGAR HOOVER BUILDING was a grim edifice, as squat as a Washington Redskin linebacker, and, some wags suggested, the architect's revenge on the long-dead leader of the FBI whose name the building bore. Around the corner from the main entrance on Pennsylvania Avenue, Clem's car rolled down the 10th Street ramp into the FBI building garage.

Toni Georgihu called to him as he alighted from the White House car.

"Why the cops and robbers routine?" Clem asked. "Why couldn't you come to my office?"

"I wanted you to hear this firsthand," she said. "Then the Director wants to see you."

They took the elevator to the third floor of the FBI building.

"I didn't even get you a visitor's badge," she said. "I didn't think it wise for you to be logged in."

They walked swiftly through the spare, winding corridors. He followed her into a rabbit warren of small enclosures, each jammed with computers and scientific gear, largely unfamiliar to him. Shelves were stacked with glass vials, books, files and papers. It was not untidy, just crowded.

Soon they were greeted by an amiable young man with horn-rimmed glasses and a pleasant smile.

"This is Al Wallach," Toni said. "Al, Clem Barkley."

"A pleasure," Wallach said. "We're expecting you."

The trio stood in a well-organized cubicle with a small desk and several scientific instruments, including a computer.

"We are in what is known as Hairs and Fibers. This unit is headed by Al here and his group. They can do magic you would not believe. It was this unit that cracked the Atlanta child murder case some years back. Do you remember?" Clem nodded.

"We inspect ropes, strings, tape, threads, buttons, feathers, you name it, and we can trace them, match them, and identify them. We took the button and thread we found clutched in Roy Hickey's hand and we have been analyzing them most carefully. Al, would you now take it and tell Mr. Barkley what we have found?"

Al Wallach took off his glasses, wiped them carefully with a handkerchief, put them back on and smiled again at Barkley with bright, intelligent eyes.

"Mr. Barkley, my associates and I have examined the button and thread. We have specialized equipment that gives us a kind of X-ray result, with layers of the fiber exposed to us. This gives us a cross section of the fiber, just as if a surgeon slices through your body with a scalpel, uncovering layers of your flesh and muscle. If the structure is unique, we can trace it. We can, with total accuracy, match it up with a similar fiber found on either the victim or the accused. Here we are not dealing with match-ups, so we had to determine if this fiber was so unique that we could find its ancestry and then pinpoint its origin." He punched a button and the screen lit up with squiggly lines.

"This is your sample. And we were lucky. It was unique. Now, we don't possess in-house the fingerprint, as it were, of all the fibers in the world, but we have first-class sources, people in the fiber business whose expertise allows them to know, to the millimeter, where plants are located that manufacture that particular, unique fiber. We tracked it down. We know exactly where it came from."

Al Wallach picked up an object lying on a fresh piece of paper to the left of the table. He held it up for Barkley to see. "This is your button. We put this button through several tests. One was to immerse it in an epoxy-like substance to get a cross section of its structure. Then, with other specialized devices, we explore the trace elements present in the material. We can actually lay bare the particles, in this case, laid with mica and a form of titanium dioxide. The way light interferes with this particle gives off a luster that is identifiable, a type of reflectivity that can be traced. The trick, and the luck, is to come up with a particle that is different from all the others, else too many manufacturers would be handling them and tracing would be well nigh impossible. All we could do would be match-ups, which at this time is useless to us since we have nothing to match up."

Al Wallach was warming to his subject, and Barkley was visibly impressed with his cogent and unhesitating recital of a visible expertise, but he was itching to say "Okay, you told me how, now tell me what."

"We were lucky again," Al Wallach said. "We determined the base of the button, a highly reflective particulate, which we were able to describe in detail to our sources in the button business. They, like the folks who make fibers, know the world of buttons as you and I know our bathrooms and offices. We traced it clearly and, we believe, accurately." Wallach smiled widely. It was obvious he was proud of the speed with which he and his colleagues had performed their task. Barkley turned to Georgihu.

"All right, Toni, bottom line."

"Bottom line, Clem, is Sofia."

Barkley said, "Sofia, Bulgaria?"

"Bingo. Both the fiber and the button are unique. That is, they are manufactured in two plants, both in Sofia, whose equipment is some years behind the times. They are the only plants in the world who use the fiber composition method we found. Likewise, the factory making the buttons uses a highly reflective particulate found nowhere else but in that Sofia location. The sources we consulted were positive. No doubts of any kind. Therefore, the fellow who murdered Roy Hickey was wearing a coat that was constructed in Sofia, and we are not leaping to conclusions to confirm that he came from Bulgaria. The coat surely did. Our sources tell us that greatcoats of this kind with these fibers and buttons aren't exported from Bulgaria to the U.S. They go to the eastern European countries."

Barkley clapped Georgihu on the shoulder and nodded to Al Wallach. "I'm so pleased. Very good work, Mr. Wallach. Have you ever thought of taking this magic act on the road?"

"I'm afraid David Copperfield has better stage presence than I," Wallach said, with a shy but grateful smile.

"That's not all, Clem," Toni said.

"Oh?"

She took his arm. "I'll tell you on the way to the Director's office."

They took their leave of Wallach. Toni spoke in hushed tones as they again wandered the cold corridors.

"When we IDed the fiber and button," Toni said, "we worked with the DC police force and staked out every East European embassy in the city. Within twenty-four hours we got lucky."

"Lucky?"

She laughed. "Embarrassingly lucky. One of our agents spotted, by chance, two characters walking into the Hardee's restaurant in Farragut Square. The only reason he gave them any notice was the greatcoat worn by one of them. It was a thick, heavy garment, matching the description given by the woman who saw the suspicious pair in the parking lot off 20th Street, where Hickey was killed."

Their footsteps echoing in the corridor were louder than Toni's voice; Clem had to strain to hear.

"Our agent casually followed them into Hardee's, stood behind them when they ordered hamburgers, in an accent he couldn't make. He sat behind them at a table, and one of the two slung his greatcoat over a chair, hanging with the button side of the coat easily visible to the agent. Guess what? A button was missing, second from the top."

"Lucky is right," Clem said.

"Our agent alerted the Bureau quickly. Then he followed the suspects to a small hotel, the Woodfire, just off 15th Street. They're registered under what we consider to be assumed names."

"Have you made an arrest?"

"Not yet. They're under twenty-four-hour surveillance. We've got them covered from all angles, with little chance of detection. We're trying to find out who they report to."

Moments later, the Director of the FBI was rising behind his desk to greet them.

Like his predecessor, the new Director was a former federal judge, of medium height and build, with a square, open face, hair flecked with gray, eyes blue and penetrating. His handshake confirmed his reputation as a physical fitness fan.

"Thank you for coming, Mr. Barkley," he said.

The Director's face tightened; down to business. "If we assume that the two men we've located are indeed the murderers, the central question becomes crucial: who would want Hickey killed?"

"And," Toni added, "is there any connection between the murder and the China leak, and if so, do our reports on Vincent Canfield and the Majority Leader's aide have any relevance?"

Clem blinked. "Surely you're not suggesting that the Majority Leader and his aide are involved in a murder?"

"No," she said. "I think Canfield and Tunstall are bit players in this little mystery-melodrama."

Clem turned to the Director. "Have you discussed this with the Attorney General?"

"Yes, I have," the Director said. "We both feel the President should be kept up to date on every detail of the case."

"I agree," Clem said, nodding. "We'll work through Toni."

"Excellent." The Director rose, extended his hand again. "Please inform the President I'm available to him at a moment's notice."

When Clem got back to his car, he touched Toni lightly on the forearm. "I'm glad you're on this, Toni. The President has faith in you." He hesitated. "I do too."

Toni smiled. She stood close to him. "I'll keep in touch," she said ambiguously.

Back at the White House, in his office, he asked his secretary, "Are they still in the Cabinet Room?"

"No, sir, the meeting broke up just after you left."

Clem punched the button marked "Pres."

The President's voice was clear and even. "Clem, come right in. I've been waiting for you to call."

Clem buttoned his jacket and raced to the Oval Office.

Nineteen

SENATOR RAYMOND ARLEDGE TUNSTALL sat comfortably in his spacious office on the second floor of the Capitol off the Senate Chamber entrance. Once the baronial fiefdom of earlier Senate Majority Leaders, it was now Tunstall's preserve.

The Majority Leader was enjoying the statesmanship period of his seventh term, the first year of his new six-year tenure. The Leader never took reelection for granted, which was why, said both his critics and friends, he was always reelected.

At the mahogany table, gleaming from the polishing of one of Tunstall's aides morning and evening, sat the Chairman of the Senate Foreign Relations Committee, Senator Homer Jefferson Wade of South Carolina; the Chairman of the Commerce Committee, Senator Karl Overlujd of North Dakota; Gifford Gray, Chairman of the Senate Armed Services Committee; and the oversize figure of columnist Vincent Canfield.

"Gifford," Tunstall said to his venerable colleague, "you're looking extremely well."

Senator Gray's face creased with a smile. "Why, thank you, Raymond. But am I at that stage of life when looking well is so surprising?"

"Hell, Gifford," Senator Wade said, jowls quivering, "at our age, just bein' ambulatory is surprisin'."

Canfield frowned, his ample cheeks a bit flushed. "Come now, gentlemen—we didn't gather in the office of the Majority Leader to discuss our health. We're here to discuss the President and the Vice President, and how we might avoid a holocaust within a few months."

Karl Overlujd's contempt for Canfield was barely disguised by a smile as he said, "Vincent, our Leader may be surprised to find Gifford looking so fit, but I'm more surprised to find you taking part in a political discussion among Democratic Senators. Isn't that a breach of journalistic ethics, or is that a contradiction of terms?"

Canfield's patrician tones reeked with sullen, graceless annoyance. "I was invited here by Senator Tunstall and saw no reason to d-d-decline. I care as much for my country as you do, sir."

"Oh, Vincent," Overlujd said, "you can prattle on in your column and on television when you and Henry Kissinger are experts on everything but sewer bonds if you like, but spare us the patriotic gloss behind closed doors."

"Gentlemen, please," Tunstall said, patting the air with his palms in a peace-making gesture. He looked deferentially toward Senator Gray. "Gifford, you wanted to chat with me, and I suggested these others join us. What do you have in mind?"

Gray's eyes glistened and hardened. "You all know very well what I have in mind," Gray said. "We are set forth on what is, in my judgment, a catastrophic course. The Vice President has damaged, in a serious and perhaps irresponsible way, both his own office and the institution of the Presidency."

"Senator Gray," Canfield said, before anyone else could respond, "the damage to the Presidency is being committed by the current occupant of the White House, whose lack of leadership is confirmed by countless national surveys."

"As Lyndon used to say," Gray said, "this country could be run by a part-time committee of manure-kickers if all one had to do was read the polls each morning."

Canfield scowled.

Gray continued: "There are larger concerns here, having to do with the institutional roots of the Presidency and the country. Are we to set ourselves up as judges before the people have voted, and exile whoever is in the White House simply because, at a given moment, all is not going right? I find that unacceptable."

Gray had spoken so softly that Senator Wade had leaned forward to cup his right ear.

Tunstall said, "Gifford, there is no one who holds the respect of his colleagues more than you. I've often said that my chair belongs to you, and the only reason you're not in it is because you chose not to sit there."

Gray sat immobile.

"But," Tunstall continued, "we currently have a President who, instead of trying to find rapport with the Soviet Union, goes to battle station. We should be using a new treaty with the Russians as a bridge to dealing with these horrible budget problems, particularly in defense!"

"Gifford," Senator Wade said, "ah think ah have to back Raymond up on this one. Ah grant you ah never cottoned to Kells. Ah have always said that a man who didn't serve in the Congress ought never be President, and Jimmy Carter and Ronald Reagan only proved mah point. But leavin' aside mah personal feelings, Kells sure as hell is in the tar pit in mah state and across the South. We ain't goin' to vote for him."

"Gifford, I have no personal feeling, pro or con about the President," Overlujd said. "His first year and a half in office, he did a competent-enough job. But his paranoia about the Russians baffles me. As does his apparent lack of concern for our economic mess."

Overlujd leaned forward in his chair.

He continued: "I think Bill Rawlins can win and ought to win. When was the last time you witnessed the leader of the Senate and several influential committee chairmen in the Senate banding together to oppose a second term for their own party's President?"

Gray was motionless; he might not have been breathing. His bald head glistened under the ceiling light.

"I came here not to praise Donald Kells nor to denigrate Bill Rawlins," he said. "His father, Buck Rawlins, was my friend. I admire Bill, and I have affection for him. I simply state again that there are covenants, some signed and some unspoken, that must be respected. Nations and families are bound by them and societies cannot exist without them."

Tunstall said quietly, "No one quarrels with that, Gifford, but . . ."

"Those aren't sentiments that can be qualified with a 'but,' Raymond." Gray stood upright. "I don't know how this will turn out. I don't choose to forecast the election. I only know that we lose something of immense worth if we, for whatever reason, collapse a set of political values that have stood the test of time."

Gray looked hard at Tunstall.

"There are words, Raymond, like loyalty and fidelity that are not as old-fashioned as some would have you believe." He waved his hand absently. "I have one vote in the Senate, one vote, that's all. But I always cast that vote, because my vote counts, if for no other reason than it counts with me. Good day to you all."

The old Senator walked, back straight and firm, the step unhesitant, opened the door and, without turning, closed it behind him.

"Well," Canfield said, "wasn't *that* a p-p-p-pompous performance!"

Tunstall faced Canfield. "With all due respect, Vincent, you are out of line, and out of touch."

Canfield flinched.

"Vincent," Overlujd said tightly, "Gifford Gray is a thoroughly honest man who cares more for his country than himself. There's not a single man or woman in the entire Congress, or any state house or courthouse, fit to carry his file folders. That I disagree with him doesn't make me right and him wrong; it only shows I have a mind of my own. *Gifford Gray* ought to be President. Funny thing, Vincent—he never wanted to be."

Canfield's face was flushed, his body shaking. "I don't appreciate the lecture. I too have my own mind to g-g-g-guide me."

Tunstall grinned and slapped the columnist on the back. "Vincent, you just made the mistake of taking out after the one man every one of us respects. Otherwise, your remarks are welcome. Meanwhile, gentlemen, the issue remains. How do we persuade Kells to back off and retire gracefully?"

Twenty

FILIPP FEDEROF cursed under his breath. He sat alone next to
an empty seat in the twelve-seat first-class cabin of Aeroflot flight
number 318. There were two other passengers in first class, sitting
one row forward and to the right of Federof, a corpulent fellow
with thick glasses next to what obviously was his wife, a wide-set
woman with massed gray hair and a pair of glasses dangling from a
black strap around her neck. The woman's jaw hung slack as she
gently snored while her husband fondled a tumbler of vodka as he
read a book.

He had departed Dulles International Airport in the Virginia
countryside at 3:40 p.m., landing in Gander at 8:35 p.m. At Gander,
he had peered out of the window at murky, uninviting dark clouds.
Now they were aloft again, hurtling through the air on the way to
Moscow. He knew the flying time was a total of eleven hours and
forty minutes, but they had been delayed for some stupid reason
in Gander for over an hour.

The message was clear and precise and it came from Viktor
Zinyakin, the KGB Chairman. Federof knew Zinyakin all too well.
He had carried out several missions for the KGB chief when
Federof was his third in command.

Federof was fond of assuring all those with whom he worked
that fear was not part of his being. "If you feel fear, you encourage
defeat," he admonished his young colleagues.

But in those deepest crevices where he hid even from himself his own hesitations Filipp would have to confess a sliver of distaste. He would never admit the tiniest jot of fear, but in fact that is what he felt around the KGB chieftain. Viktor was unpredictable. When Viktor hurled his full gaze on an enemy, what Federof saw was the unlovely image of a poisonous serpent living just below the hairline, a discolored, shifting menace, ready to strike without warning. At that moment, Zinyakin was to be viewed and handled with utmost caution.

"Return to Moscow. Leave tomorrow. You will be met. I will see you as soon as you arrive."

Curt, but clear. Filipp ranged over the possibilities. The Presidential matter in the U.S. was now boiling. The Vice President and the President would soon be at each other's throat. Kells was to Zinyakin, as Federof knew so well, a threat, more than that, an unacceptable leader of the Americans.

Zinyakin had never met President Kells, but Federof recalled Zinyakin's low-voiced comment to him recently: "I don't like him. He is not with us." Federof expressed no visible surprise, though he found it amusing that Zinyakin felt rancor because the President of the United States seemingly concealed his affection for the KGB Chairman. He never responded to Zinyakin's remark, because he understood Zinyakin's brutish nature. Filipp had an appreciation for brutality, but he placed no value on indiscretion. He knew that ordering an assassination was not beyond Zinyakin, for Federof had been his instrument on a number of occasions. But there were some perimeters beyond which sensible men did not go. Not because of morality, not at all, for neither Federof nor Zinyakin chose to define the word, since they considered morality to be an awkwardly conceived reliquary, stupidly cherished by a hypocritical U.S., but because retribution can be a nasty, untidy boomerang. So there must be limits, concluded Federof, surgical limits, and wise, bold men always mapped those outer boundaries. There are so many innovative ways to achieve one's objective without disturbing the core principle which secret police of most countries honored, which is never to kill another nation's leader, else your own leader is in danger. This does leave you considerable leeway with those lesser mortals around the leader. They're fair game.

Federof had to admit to one nagging intrusion. Why, in the midst of the efforts of the Executive President to renovate the Soviet Union's political and economic framework, why when the so-called fledgling democracies of eastern Europe were flapping about like harpooned dolphins, why in the middle of unrest in the Soviet Union did Zinyakin persist as if the Cold War was in full, undiluted fury? He had to admit that, publicly, Zinyakin was not perceived as such. The KGB chieftain was invariably supportive of the Executive President's policy, but Federof was still perplexed. It is true that what Zinyakin had predicted, the collapse of the democratic movements in the eastern bloc countries, was confirmed by the erratic economic struggles of those nations and the ascending success level of counterrevolutionists inside their borders. Still, the KGB Chairman's private aggression was not at all decipherable.

Federof felt a touch on his shoulder.

"General," the stewardess said softly, "the Captain asked me to notify you we'll be landing in Moscow in twenty minutes."

Federof nodded and smiled. The girl was only moderately attractive, but he'd gotten her address nonetheless. "Thank you, my dear. Convey my compliments to the Captain."

He looked out the window at the expansive countryside outside Moscow. He would visit his wife and children later. He would not have much time with them, nor his mother. But they understood.

The plane, descending more rapidly, began its wide, arcing turn to Sheremetyevo International Airport. They flew the downwind leg and headed toward the runway. The landing was bumpy but Federof barely noticed. He could already see the long black Chaika limousine sitting on the tarmac as the huge plane rolled to a stop.

He clopped down the metal steps and was soon inside the limousine. The car started forward the instant the back door was closed. Lev Ryzinsin slapped him on the leg. "Filipp Vladimirovich! It is good to see you."

Federof replied coolly, "It is good to visit with you again, Lev Panfilovich."

"You look well. You have prospered in the United States."
Ryzinsin laughed. "You found lovely women there to take to bed,
no? But beware, they have tape in strange places."

Lev Ryzinsin was one of the six trusted deputies who reported
directly to KGB head Viktor Zinyakin. Therefore Federof suffered
the boorish Lev with resignation.

"Do I go directly to the Chairman's office?" Federof asked.

"Immediately."

"What draws me back to Moscow so soon?"

Ryzinsin leaned forward to pour a tumbler of vodka from the
limousine's portable bar.

"I have no knowledge why you are being brought back."

Federof believed him only because he knew the KGB Chairman
would not loosely disclose anything of spacious importance and he
would not have been summoned to Moscow for some whimsical
reason. "I have much work to complete in Washington."

"And what is that work?"

Federof turned. Lev's thick jowls trembled as the car bounced
over an undulating street surface. Lev had small capacity for in-
trigue. He lacked that edge of lethal delicacy which provisioned
every disciple of Machiavelli and his Russian acolytes. No, Lev
was not burrowing. He had a simple appetite. He just wanted to
know.

"You know better than I that Viktor will tell you what he
chooses you to know, and the same with me. What you have not
been told by Viktor is probably best you not know."

Two blocks from the Kremlin, they approached their destination. The Center, as the KGB complex is called, used to occupy a
collection of drab unmarked buildings. The central building was
garmented in yellowish cast brick and used to resemble worn shel-
lac that refuses to glisten in the sunlight. But after the advance to
power of the Executive President, the façades of all the buildings
were refurbished in a handsome brown which reflected brightly
the rays of the sun. It is a bit ironic that within a short walking
distance is the Bolshoi Theater, centerpiece of Russian cultural
dominance in the world of the dance. Soviet historians, with a
mordant sense of humor, enjoy recalling that the KGB headquar-

ters was once the main office of the All-Russian Insurance Company before the Revolution.

In front of the KGB complex is a small little island carpeted with grass. In its center used to reside a commanding statue of the most resolute of all Russian enforcers, Feliks Dzerzhinsky, the first Soviet policeman, the one who outfitted the KGB in all its coarse and surly garments. Encased in bronze, he brooded everlastingly over the adventures of his progeny, until that sunlit day in August 1991, when a restless, jubilant mob hauled down the statue and smashed the likeness of Feliks forever. Or at least they thought so.

Their car stopped at the guardhouse. A tall uniformed sentry leaned down, peered inside, saw Lev, saluted and waved them on. The limo rumbled forward as Ryzinsin fumed.

He turned to Federof. "This is bad security. What if you had a Makarov in my ribs? That fool saw me and assumed all was well."

They alighted from the car. Two more uniformed guards flanked them as they were escorted via elevator to the KGB Director's offices on the third floor.

Unlike other corridors here, whose wooden floors were bare, the third floor was thickly, softly carpeted a dark green. Two guards, lounging outside the office of the Chairman of the KGB, snapped to attention at Ryzinsin and Federof's approach. The two men entered an anteroom where a gray-haired, unsmiling woman sat behind an aged desk. She stood as they came forward. Her dress was a heavy black affair that was not the work of a French designer.

"He is waiting for you," she said gravely and guided them to a large mahogany door, which she opened.

The squat man in a tailored brown suit held out his arms affectionately. His thick gray hair was like a cheap toupee on his large head; his eyes glistened behind tortoise-shell glasses. He moved with surprising agility across the heavy Persian rug.

"Filipp Vladimirovich—I am pleased to see you."

"And I, you, my Leader."

The Chairman laughed. "Ah, your Leader . . . I will not inform the Executive President of your title for me."

The large office was paneled in rich, dark mahogany, with four levels of bookshelves. The ceiling was high and tall windows allowed the Moscow sun, unhappily absent today, to stream in. Beyond the windows was a view of the square on Marx Prospekt.

In front of the windows was the Chairman's oversize desk. An array of Soviet telephones spread over the left side of the desk. One, the Kremleyvlca, dispatched the KGB Chairman's voice to the Kremlin's offices. Other phones connected the KGB Chairman to key KGB offices throughout the Soviet Union, and still others connected the KGB Chairman to his six deputies.

Zinyakin held up a vodka bottle ceremonially. He passed them tumblers, filled his and theirs. "To the glory of the Executive President and the Motherland."

They drank silently.

Zinyakin motioned to Lev. "Filipp and I have much to discuss."

It was a curt dismissal.

With Ryzinsin gone, Zinyakin pointed to a large leather chair in front of his desk. Federof sat.

"Our plan, Filipp, must succeed. To rid ourselves of this threat in the White House and replace him with someone . . . compatible . . . with our long-range views is a rare opportunity."

Federof nodded.

"How would you forecast our chances?" Zinyakin asked. "Kells seems determined to run again. Even the senior members of his own party in the Congress are opposed to him. Only the elder statesman Gray stands with him."

The KGB Chairman was extremely well informed and Federof had not supplied the data. Could it have been Nightingale, the highly-placed mole in the U.S. Government?

Zinyakin's unblinking eyes were fastened on Federof. "We are not making the progress I had hoped we would," he said.

"But we *have* made progress," Federof said. "Rawlins has made a move unprecedented in American history. No Vice President has ever dared do what Rawlins has done."

The KGB Chairman walked around the desk to stand close to Federof. He leaned down. Federof could smell the acrid breath of the second most powerful man in the Soviet Union, as well as his spicy after-shave.

"It is clear," Zinyakin said, "that the aggressor Kells will not voluntarily resign. Even the opposition of the most important senior Senators, the most influential journalistic voice in the United States, and the opinions of the American public are making no impression. What then is needed to make this warmongering President desist?''

Federof knew he was not being asked to respond. Zinyakin doubtless had some plan in mind and would unveil it at a melodramatic moment of his choice.

"What is needed is a thunderbolt," Zinyakin said, hands flailing. "Something that will make people gasp."

Federof believed that silence was wisdom.

Zinyakin paced. "I have an idea, Filipp Vladimirovich, that requires your seasoned and experienced hand."

"Yes, Comrade Chairman?"

"The Americans have strange and sometimes silly rules by which they play their stupid political games. Why not exploit those silly rules?"

Federof knew all too well that Viktor adored to wander about in this dialectic manner, which his subordinates had to endure and from which only the Executive President was immune.

"Our goal," Zinyakin said, "is to leave the field free for Vice President Rawlins. Whatever is required to readjust this warrior Kells' thinking, we must do."

Zinyakin laughed, a deep rumble starting in the lower part of his ample belly.

"You are a loyal and efficient servant of the state, Filipp Vladimirovich. Listen carefully and remember all that I tell you."

The squat Chairman leaned down, his mouth only inches from Federof's right ear. He spoke clearly and distinctly and unemotionally.

Federof listened, first with mounting curiosity, then with surprise, and then with admiration.

"What is your counsel, Filipp Vladimirovich, now that you have heard my idea?"

"It is quite in tune with human nature," Federof said, impressed with the Chairman's innovative mind. "I like it very much."

The Chairman was obviously pleased. He clapped Federof on

the knee, a reverberating slap. "You like it, eh? We thought you would."

We? So, this plan was something the Executive President and the Chairman had devised together.

"You will report directly to me, no one else. In America or here." The Chairman's eyes were stern, his mouth a straight line. "You will leave Moscow tomorrow for your first stop. Every forty-eight hours you will send by confidential code whatever you think I should know, and I want to know. Is that pig Berisov suitable to you?"

"He is a stupid man, Comrade Chairman, but he will serve me as I desire. Perhaps it is best that he is not more intelligent, for that would only incite his curiosity."

"It is settled then. You will choose whatever support you need. You have blanket authority to command this operation. If anyone doubts you or challenges you, refer them to me, and me alone. Understand? Me alone."

Federof's eyes narrowed at this relentless secrecy. Who else would he report to? The Executive President?

"There is one other instruction." The KGB Chairman's voice grew lower. "There is someone you will visit when you go to Berlin. You will listen to him, as if I were speaking to you."

"May I ask his name, Comrade Chairman?"

Zinyakin managed a tight smile. Federof almost winced. He knew the mannerism. The last time he saw it Zinyakin had slapped the face of a Soviet Embassy official in Paris.

"I will tell you all you need to know." He scribbled on a piece of paper. "Here is his name, his address. Memorize it, then shred the paper. He is very important in the German Government structure, and his view of the future is mine."

Zinyakin spread his arms, laughing. "We are too serious, Filipp Vladimirovich. Be on your way now to see your family—you have only a short time here."

The KGB Chairman embraced Federof and guided him to the exit. As Zinyakin opened the massive doors, he said, "Good luck, Filipp Vladimirovich. Do not fail. And remember—report to no one but me. What we speak of can never be revealed to another."

Federof stepped into the anteroom. "You can rely on me, Comrade Chairman."

The doors closed.

Federof moved quickly through the corridors, down the elevator, guided by two armed guards, and then walked into the brisk Moscow air. Immediately he was approached by a slender man of indeterminate age, with a large black mustache.

The man bowed slightly.

"General Federof, Kirsanov—Danil Kirsanov, aide to the Executive President. My credentials." He handed Federof a leather wallet with an identification card.

Federof looked at him keenly. "I know you."

Kirsanov smiled. "Four years ago I worked with you on the Armenian problem."

"I recall you handled yourself with great skill." What Federof didn't mention was his estimate then of this young fellow, Kirsanov. Ambitious, with a willingness to do whatever was necessary. Federof had found Kirsanov much like himself.

"The Executive President requests your presence." The thin emissary pointed to a black Zil four-door sedan.

Federof gazed at the Zil affectionately. It confirmed the rank and the purpose of Kirsanov. Only a handful were available in the Soviet Union, each literally handmade, the Soviet equivalent of a Rolls-Royce. Behind the driver's wheel was a stone-faced uniformed soldier, and to the driver's right sat another unsmiling soldier, a captain.

Federof settled back in the cushioned seat in the back of the automobile. He looked through the rear window. Was the Comrade Chairman watching? This was an astonishing turn of events. He had not asked to see the Executive President, nor had he considered for a moment that the Executive President would ask to see him.

He admired the Executive President. He knew of the struggle the Executive President had embarked on when he succeeded to the leadership of the Soviet Union. Yet, there were more than casual murmurings of discontent. What Gorbachev had stirred was still in motion, but the renaissance of a patriotic Soviet spirit had come with the Executive President's own policies.

Not so long ago, the Soviet Union was dismantling itself. And then the Executive President had begun a new revolution. The productivity of agriculture had been the first segment of the society to slowly turn upward, forging a new distribution system that worked, and managing to instill hopes that the ruble would soon be convertible, a goal that several years ago would have been unthinkable.

Indeed, while the rest of the world was stumbling in its own economic discomfort, today there was reason to believe in a leaner, more powerful U.S.C.R.

There was seemingly no one now to challenge the leader, no one on the horizon who had the strength, resolve, or toughness to provide an alternative. Zinyakin might qualify for that role, but he was on the Executive President's team. The Executive President had defied the odds. He was winning. Only this stubborn, cold-war-style American President seemed to stand in his way.

They sped through the streets of Moscow, heading for what used to be the office of the Central Committee of the Communist Party. Federof recalled that the back of the Handicraft Museum sat serenely across from the front of the old main Central Committee building. As a young lad growing up in Moscow, he knew the area well, for his father took him there often. The Zil slowed carefully as they neared Staraya Ploshchad 4, the address of the Executive President's headquarters. The car picked its way through a guarded entry point to the courtyard of the building complex which only the highest-stationed officials of the country were allowed to use.

Kirsanov mutely led the way to the corridors to the office of the Executive President. A long greenish carpet streaked with red stripes flowed down the center of the final hallway. Two guards, standing at attention, saluted Kirsanov.

"Follow me, General," Kirsanov said.

Federof trailed Kirsanov through a large anteroom, where a guard-receptionist snapped to attention, and then another anteroom, occupied by an empty desk.

Kirsanov knocked at a massive door.

Then Federof found himself in the office of the Executive President and the leader of the new U.S.C.R.

Kirsanov quietly disappeared.

A flat oaken table, neatly stacked with papers, served as a desk. Another long oaken table perpendicular to the main desk table, cushioned chairs on either side, could accommodate at least ten people. Alongside the desk was a round table with the inevitable array of telephones. A vast window behind the oaken desk offered a listless view of the courtyard. Fitted in the walls on either side of the desk were bookshelves, five levels high.

Behind the oaken desk a stocky, balding man stood calmly. He smiled at Federof and confidently walked around to greet him.

"My dear General—I am pleased to see you."

The Executive President's voice was resonant; he had an air of energy about him.

"Sit down, General—sit here." The Executive President pointed to a straight-backed chair near the table. He in turn sat in a similar chair in front of Federof.

"Thank you, Comrade Executive President," Federof said. "You do me great honor."

The Executive President waved expansively with a strong, sturdy hand. "I am curious to know how you see what is happening in America. Ah, yes, we are constantly briefed by those around us, but I count more valuable the judgment of those who are actually in the United States. Do you think that Vice President Rawlins will be victorious over President Kells?"

"I believe that Vice President Rawlins will win, but it will not be easy. The central issue is whether or not the President will stay in the race. He is low in the polls and my belief is that the weight of public opinion will force him out."

The Executive President nodded, his brown, observant eyes fixed on Federof. "But even if President Kells seems, for the moment, to have lost the favor of the voters, is it not possible for such events to be overcome?"

"Possible, but not probable. Seldom has a President been so low in the esteem of his fellow citizens as this one. It is generally believed that the opposition party candidate, presumably the Governor of Pennsylvania, would easily win against Kells."

"This man Rawlins—what is your feeling about him? Comrade

Zinyakin tells me he is suited to friendship with us, and that it is in our long-term interest that Rawlins win."

"I agree, Comrade Executive President. Rawlins is a very attractive man, and very knowledgeable. He has large support within the Party of the Democrats. It is simply that the President is a proud, stubborn man. It will not be easy, but"—Federof smiled meaningfully—"I am *sure* he will withdraw."

The Executive President pursed his lips, brushed his finger against his cheek. "That is good to hear. But how can you know this?"

Federof was instantly alert. "May I ask, Comrade Executive President, what you mean by that?"

He must move very carefully here. It was unthinkable that Zinyakin had not revealed everything to his boss . . .

The Soviet leader fixed his gaze on Federof. "For example, what do we really know about this man Rawlins? What is it that convinces you that he will be, as you said, agreeable?"

Filipp said calmly, "There has been contact with the entourage of the Vice President. I am confident that these contacts have produced verifiable information."

The Executive President shook his head slowly, absorbing what Federof had said. He absently ran a forefinger slowly up and down the right lapel of his suit. "Contact, you say. Does that seem wise? May I inquire as to who made these contacts?"

Federof chose his words carefully. "My colleague in the Embassy and in the KGB, Boris Vaslansky. He handled these approaches with much skill."

"I worry, General," said the Soviet leader, "that we might get so involved in this contest that it may rebound against us. What would you say if the Americans inserted themselves in efforts to defrock me and put someone else in my place?"

"But we are discreet. Our soundings have been made in deep cover."

"Filipp Vladimirovich, I am not suggesting you have not used extreme discretion. But I have little faith that anything is really secure from public view. Would our own people feel comfortable if the Americans were engaged in a similar activity here? I think not. May I suggest that you continue to observe, keeping us informed, but restraining yourself and those who serve you so that if this struggle becomes heated, we will not become culprits."

Federof felt a chill spread through him.

"Pardon me, Comrade Executive President—but are you instructing me not to be involved in this fight between the President and the Vice President? To stay neutral?"

"Precisely. You have served me with fidelity, as you have the Party and your country. I am relieved that the KGB Chairman asked you to be in Washington to observe for our personal benefit the antics of the American political system. But I am sure he also suggested to you the embarrassment that would follow if it became known that, through you, I was trying to influence the election. That would be counterproductive. It would undo the policy I am pursuing, not only in the United States but in western Europe."

Federof prided himself on his detachment, but at the moment he was nearly trembling.

The fact was there, unobscured, indisputable: the Executive President, the preeminent leader of the U.S.C.R., did not know what his chief policeman was doing and planning!

He heard the voice of his leader.

"You understand, do you not, what I am ordering you to do?"

Federof struggled to retrieve his calm. "Comrade Executive President, I will continue to observe but not allow myself or anyone near me to become involved in this political contest."

The Executive President smiled hospitably. "Good. Now . . . why don't we let you enjoy some time with your family . . ."

When Federof got back to the car, he was consumed by puzzlement mixed with anxiety. But one ominous and poisonous fact kept intruding: the Executive President was not aware of the existence of Nightingale!

Twenty-one

WHEN FEDEROF'S Aeroflot plane landed at Schönefeld Airport in what used to be East Berlin, Vlady Miektor was waiting.

Miektor flung Federof's bags in the trunk of the large Mercedes, attending Federof with genuine affection.

"Vlady Aleksandrovich, my old friend, all is on schedule?" Federof asked.

"All is on schedule, Filipp Vladimirovich. She will be waiting at the designated place."

Soon Miektor was guiding his prized Mercedes west toward the central city.

"What does she understand?"

Miektor shrugged. "The general assignment, but no details."

"Do you trust the choice of this woman?"

"According to the Germans, as well as one can trust any woman. The Germans say she has been successful in other tasks."

Federof gazed out the window. It was best not to confide in Vlady the disturbance inside him, though Miektor was his longtime, loyal friend. He peered out the window. What a dreary city. Slightly more appealing than his last visit four years ago, but still a thickset landscape of blocky, colorless buildings. Throwing out a communist government was not going to refurbish this dingy environment.

Miektor turned right onto Unter der Linden, the broad boulevard—once bisected by a green, flowery esplanade—now grown
seedy and worn. They passed the large hulk of a building that
housed the U.S.C.R. Embassy staff.

"You want to stop?" said Miektor.

"No."

In the hazy, windy distance, Federof could make out the Munic-
ipal Town Hall. To his left, he saw the Unter der Linden Hotel,
and to his right, the beguilingly beautiful new Grand Hotel, built
by the Japanese in imitation of a fine European or American hotel.

Soon they were passing the bulky statue of Frederick the Great,
mounted imperiously atop a stallion. The stupid Germans, in their
persistent fit of guilt, had hidden the statue until several years ago,
finally repositioning it in its once-traditional spot.

Miektor turned off the boulevard onto a small plaza where the
Nazis once staged book burnings. The Opera House was in front.
Now Miektor eased the car to the left and parked just beyond the
wide marble steps of St. Hedwig's Cathedral.

"She will be on the left on the upper level," Miektor said, "in
the back pew. She knows what you look like. Carry this in your left
hand for corroboration." He handed Federof a booklet: "The Pergamon Museum."

"Why this game, Vlady?"

"Because she has been tutored by the Germans. She has been
instructed to meet General Federof, whose mission is unknown to
them."

"When will she be here?"

"In two hours."

"Good. Then let us go find that German I've been ordered to
meet. Do you know him?"

"I met him last year. A very serious man, this German. Very
much to himself. And strange."

"Strange?"

Miektor shrugged. "He kept looking over his shoulder, as if he
were being watched."

Federof grunted. "Maybe he was right."

The Mercedes turned down Hannoverstrasse, past dingy beige

buildings, and a few shops. A man in front of a furniture shop was sweeping the sidewalk.

"Turn right—he's somewhere on Friedrichstrasse—a dark brown door, with a small lantern."

Miektor guided the car right, slowed to find the right address.

"There," Federof said, pointing to a four-story, dull yellow building. An old wrought-iron lantern hung over a heavy brown door.

"Stay in the car."

Federof climbed the narrow dark stairway to a second-floor landing, and a door with a tarnished plaque engraved "12." He knocked. A heavyset woman, fiftyish, with slack hanging hair and thick black eyebrows, answered.

"I am Herr Federof," he said in flawless German.

She motioned him inside.

The room was about fourteen feet square, windowless, an aged air-conditioner sitting in a hole cut in the wall. Behind a bare metal desk sat a man with a close-cropped reddish beard. His blue eyes peered at Federof. He remained seated.

"I am Filipp Federof." Federof held out his hand, but the man waved it off, pointing to a metal-backed chair.

"Let us speak Russian," he said, in a thickly Germanic-accented Russian, his voice surprisingly deep for his slight frame. "I want everything I say to be clearly understood. Sit down."

Federof wanted to say his German was far superior to the miserable Russian lurching from the red-beard's mouth. He said nothing, and glanced about the room. On one wall was a large map of western Europe. On another was a detailed map of the United States, and on the third, a blackboard.

"You are Werner Haffenstorn?"

The red-bearded man nodded. "Viktor Zinyakin reposes great trust in you. I pray he is not incorrect in his estimate." The tone was without inflection.

Federof said nothing.

"Do you know why you are here?"

"Only that Viktor Zinyakin ordered me to visit you."

The German surveyed Federof carefully. His eyes never faltered. "We are in the midst of a great enterprise. Today's appointment at St. Hedwig's Cathedral is merely one step in that journey."

The red-bearded man rose and moved to the blackboard, picked up a piece of chalk. Had he been a professor? He certainly appeared comfortable in front of that blackboard, idly turning the chalk in his hands.

Haffenstorn drew a square on the board. A foot away, he drew another square, and beneath both, a third square. Then he connected each square with a line.

"What you see here is an alliance. Germany is now united. But despite what the Chancellor may believe, Germany is not yet unified." He pointed to the first square. "Germany . . . The dominant state in the European Community, almost twice the size of any other—productive, innovative—but our pride and ambition are buried beneath ridiculous guilt. These emotions need reviving. And the time is at hand. By the next election, this irrelevant Chancellor will depart. The Democratic Alliance Party will govern Germany."

There was an odd presumptive assurance to the red-bearded man, a violence under harness. Federof knew the signs too well. This Haffenstorn was a high official in the East German intelligence service, distantly related through his mother's family to the legendary Reinhard Gehlin who had been Hitler's chief intelligence officer.

Haffenstorn pointed to the next square. "The U.S.C.R. . . . Your country and ours will be allied again, only this time there will be no duplicity. The Reichsführer was blind to fate, and his destiny collapsed because of that omission. Together, we will determine the course of Europe."

He traced the line connecting the bottom third square. "Japan . . . We will ally ourselves with Japan and exert dominion over Asia as well."

He drew a fourth square, larger than the other three. Then he marked a huge "X" over the square.

"The U.S.A. . . . No longer will it function as a world power. It will be isolated. Already it is turning lame and feeble. Fractured by divided ethnic groups and squabbling politicians, it will soon be no better than a collection of Balkan states, unable to act decisively. And we will make certain all its infections have no cure."

Federof narrowed his eyes and nodded, thinking, *What a patronizing prick!* He resented the professorial manner, as if Federof were some wide-eyed innocent, fresh out of KGB Training School.

"This first step you will take," Haffenstorn said, "lays the groundwork for the defeat of Kells."

"I presume," Federof said, "the Executive President and Comrade Zinyakin are in agreement on this?"

The red-bearded man placed the chalk on the ledge of the blackboard. He wiped chalk dust from his hands with a rag. Without looking at Federof, he returned to the desk and his chair.

"I am told," he said coldly, "that you are an obedient servant of the KGB. That you are capable of carrying out your assignments, however difficult; that you do not question orders, nor hesitate to fulfill them. Yes?"

Federof nodded.

"Then let us concentrate on your task."

He stood and went to a small rectangular table and picked up a file.

"Here are the details of what Viktor mentioned to you."

He beckoned to Federof and they both bent over the file.

"You will meet the woman. You have your instructions about how to handle her. You may improvise so long as what you do furthers our design. You may need to go beyond what you have been ordered to do."

Federof said, "I understand." But he did not. What was unfolding before him was beyond his capacities to absorb. In this room hung the odor of long-laid plans and secretly arranged covenants.

"You must have no contact with Rawlins and his entourage unless absolutely necessary. This Canfield journalist is susceptible to us, though he has no knowledge of the scope of our designs. If you think it wise, use him."

Federof would have relished jamming a fist into this red-bearded Nazi's balls. But he only smiled and said, "Perhaps I should take my leave now, and prepare to meet the woman. Is there anything else I must know?"

"No," Haffenstorn said.

He rose quickly, almost coming to attention.

Without shaking hands, or even offering his, Haffenstorn bowed slightly. "Good journey."

Class, apparently, had been dismissed. Federof bowed and walked out the door.

Federof, Pergamon Museum pamphlet in his left hand, drew his coat closer to him and moved out of the car. The wind chilled him to the marrow, despite his warm apparel.

He entered St. Hedwig's. The church was starkly modern, with a surprisingly small number of circular pews. In the middle, a wide stairway led to a lower landing where a figure resided in the black marble enclosure, right hand upraised in a blessing, left hand holding two large keys. About a dozen people were milling down there, and a like number on the upper church floor. He looked to his left.

She was sitting, staring toward the altar. Glossy chestnut hair hung to her shoulders from under a brown fur hat; she wore a long brown fur coat.

He walked to her. She looked, saw the Pergamon Museum booklet in his left hand. He nodded. She nodded back, and he sat beside her. She watched him carefully, but with no apparent anxiety.

In German he said, "You know why you are here?"

"I know I'm to meet you, but I do not know why." Her voice was low, modulated, but her German was predictably from Leipzig.

"Once you leave here, you will only speak English. Clear?"

She nodded. "Yes, if that is what you want." She answered in English. She had an accent, but Federof estimated that in America lovely women with accents were counted to be charming, so long as they were intelligible.

"It is not only what I want, it is what you must do. To anyone with a knowledge of German it will be painfully clear you are not from Switzerland but from Leipzig. You are from Leipzig?"

She seemed to blush as if she had awkwardly committed an inexcusable blunder. "Yes, that is true."

"I want you to walk to the right, slowly, go to the table at the top of the landing and pick up two of the booklets that are lying there, and return here to me. First, remove your coat, lay it on the pew in front of you, quietly, easily, and then proceed."

She stared quizzically, as if she had not heard him clearly. "Walk to the table"—she pointed—"there?"

"You need not point. Simply do as I have asked."

She stood up, hesitated, removed her coat, casually flung it over the metal back of the pew, walked as he had ordered, around the pews, to the small wooden table which held piles of postcards and papers and booklets. She picked up a copy of each, surveyed them briefly, and then, glancing back to Federof, strode purposefully to where he waited.

She was tall, but not excessively so. Her figure was formed quite nicely, he thought, the legs slim, the ankles in proportion to the curve of the calf. It was not a slatternly walk, not at all, but confident, assured, neither provocative nor halting. He liked her eyes. They were dark blue, flanked by high cheekbones. She was not a strikingly beautiful woman, but she would be noticed because there was a silken elegance to her. He would describe her as pretty in a way that other women would not find threatening, graceful, almost patrician, a woman of some quality, and, yes, sensuality, without its being too overt. That was good.

She sat down again, moving to her seat as a model would do, leaning slightly backward, weight on the feet until the body had found its resting place, smoothing out her dress with a casual brush of her hands. Yes, he thought, the Germans chose well.

He reached in his inside coat pocket for a packet. "Your passport, confirming you as a citizen of Switzerland; your birth certificate, giving your age as thirty; your driver's license, obtained in Zürich. A ticket aboard TWA's flight leaving Zürich day after tomorrow. Your name is Greta Hulved. Until you have permission, respond to no other name. You are a free-lance journalist. You will be met at JFK Airport in New York, outside the customs area, by Mr. Wayne Malloy. He has a red mustache and will greet you as his dear cousin Greta, whom he's not seen since your twentieth birthday. You will answer, 'How lovely of you to remember, cousin Wayne. How are Meg and the children?' Put yourself in his hands. He will see that you arrive in Washington and he will give you any information you need about your apartment there. The day you arrive you will open a bank account with Riggs National Bank in Washington. In a safe-deposit box there, you will find all the other background data you might need."

She read over the papers as Federof glanced around the church. All was well. No one had entered since he arrived.

She stowed the papers in her large sharkskin purse. Federof liked the way she moved. The more he regarded her, the more attractive she became.

He held onto her arm and drew her closer. Her shoulder touched his.

"When I am done," he said, "you will repeat my instructions, exactly."

Her chestnut hair glistened in the half light streaming from the stained windows.

Federof put his lips close to her ear. It would be, to anyone who happened to watch, a scene of love and contentment.

He told her exactly what to do. He gave her the lines of communication open to her. He advised her to be relaxed, but ever vigilant. When he was done, he said, "Now repeat."

Any misgivings Federof had about entrusting a crucial mission to an unknown operative disappeared as she reeled off his instructions perfectly.

"Now we'll walk outside, across the boulevard to the Memorial. You'll go inside and I'll pause to light a cigarette. Stay inside for three minutes. Then leave, and accept instructions from the man who brought you to me. You will be on that TWA flight day after tomorrow. When I see you next, you will neither acknowledge me nor even note my presence by a glance or a nod. Clear?"

"Clear," she replied huskily. She was impressed with Federof and he knew it. And he was filled with a desire to hold her.

They rose, his hand resting lightly on the back of her arm as he guided her to the door. Wind sliced into them, her hair whipping about her face.

In front of the Memorial, he paused, extracted a cigarette, brushed his lips across her cheek. "Remember what I have told you, Greta Hulved. You are embarking on a mission of grave importance."

"I will remember. And when I see you next, I will not even know you." She laughed, for the first time. "But perhaps some day I will . . ."

Federof allowed himself a tiny smile. "Perhaps, Greta Hulved."

He looked over his shoulder. Vlady was in the Mercedes on the street in front of the barracks that housed the young soldiers who still guarded the Memorial in a bitterly freezing wind.

He slammed the door and Vlady gunned the engine.

"Yes?" queried Vlady.

"She will do, Vlady, she will do. The Germans chose well."

Vlady grinned with pleasure. "And if she fails you will not have to pick up the pieces. I will do that, my old friend."

Federof did not answer; he could not confide in his friend. He kept remembering the Executive President's face, and the shock that coursed through his own body when it hit him that what he was engaged in was not known to the leader of the Soviet Union. Now this Haffenstorn linked to Zinyakin—a tricky, hazardous business. Haffenstorn was high-placed in the German Government, and he was, as Federof dared to think, perusing the same game as Zinyakin. This was no minor excursion, modestly formed, nonlethal; it was menacing in the surliest way. He was unsure of what he was doing, and why he was doing it. He was now the shuttlecock in a deadly badminton game. It was more than dangerous, and it possessed all the ingredients of a gigantic confusion. For one of the few times in his life, Filipp had no alternatives. He would draw the endless, fatal wrath of Zinyakin if he disobeyed him in order to obey the Executive President. However, the Executive President had the potential for absolution; Zinyakin did not. With Haffenstorn's revelations about the outer boundaries of Zinyakin's scheme, there came to him a deep discomfort that invaded every cell within him. The enterprise was now in motion, and like some out-of-control heavy body rolling down a steep hill there was no way to stop.

Federof sighed and leaned back against the headrest. It was not a common gesture with him. Vlady looked at him quizzically.

Twenty-two

ON THE SECOND FLOOR of the Mansion, the living quarters of the President, Willacy Hughes and Clem Barkley sat in the President's bedroom.

The TV screen illuminated the logo of "This Week with David Brinkley," and with it the famous face of TV's senior correspondent.

"This is David Brinkley. We're doing something a bit different today. We are in New York. First time we've broadcast from here. With me in the studio at ABC headquarters is the usual group, George Will, Sam Donaldson, and joining us today for some free-wheeling discussion later on in the program we'll have ABC correspondent Cokie Roberts. We are here in New York with our special guest, the Vice President of the United States, William Booth Rawlins, who has declared himself a candidate for President. Since the Vice President couldn't make it to Washington, we've come to New York. Never before in this century has any sitting Vice President determined he would take on the incumbent President in the primaries. Never been done before. But it has now. And we will talk with the Vice President, and try to find out how all this came about.

"Good morning, Mr. Vice President," said Brinkley. "Glad you could be with us. There are a number of questions we would like to ask you, questions a good many Americans might be keen to ask themselves. The fact that you are here tells me you are ready to answer them. Sam?"

Sam Donaldson peered beneath floating eyebrows at the Vice President, who seemed to lounge back in his chair, almost eerily relaxed.

"You have done something, Mr. Vice President, that is really unprecedented. You turned on the man who made you Vice President. Isn't that disloyal?"

"Yes, it is, Mr. Donaldson. Disloyalty to my President as friend and leader. Yes, I think it is a fair way to describe it. But I am also being loyal to my party and, most of all, to my country. It is crucial to make that distinction. I have affection and respect for President Kells. He is a good man. But the truth, harsh as it is, must be stated. The President has forfeited the authority to govern. The people are demonstrating they have lost faith in him as a leader. No man can lay claim to leadership when those who confer power on him are no longer willing to extend their mandate. Rather than have this election won by default by a Republican candidate who I do not believe is capable of restoring confidence in the Presidency, I am asking the American people to choose me to represent them."

Rawlins' voice was lustrous, calm.

"Ye Gods," said Willacy Hughes. "Can any sane citizen believe this drivel?"

Clem said, "I disagree, Willacy. He's very composed, and very believable."

"Hogwash, it's all posture, and, I might add, blatantly so."

The President waved gently at Willacy. "I think Clem's right. Bill's pretty good in this kind of environment. I've always admired the way he handles himself before an audience. It's not easy to do this on television." He grinned. "As you know, I'm still working at it."

George Will was saying, "But do you not consider your action as an aberration? Not since Aaron Burr and Thomas Jefferson has a sitting Vice President got into a row with the President."

Rawlins smiled widely. "Please feel relieved, Mr. Will, I have no intention of shooting any modern-day equivalent of Alexander

Hamilton, as Aaron Burr did the original Hamilton. But I caution you not to judge a man of one age by the standards of another. What happened yesterday or a hundred years ago has no grip on today. Times change. They require different responses. Challenges appear in different forms. And that which can do damage to the spirit of the country and the stability of the Government has to be confronted in ways that Mr. Burr or even Mr. Jefferson would find unimaginable. Your question then—or was it a declaration?—is really irrelevant."

"If I may continue, sir," said Will, "you are indulging in political ricochet. The fact is, you are displaying a casual regard for your party, your President, and possibly your country by inciting a political bloodbath for no visible benefit to anyone, least of all the country you have pledged to serve."

"I disagree, Mr. Will. The art of governance is not forever the sole province of any one man. Today the times are in radical upheaval. That's why it's most assuredly in the public's best interest for the guidance of the nation to be entrusted to someone who can capture the affection and the confidence of the vast majority of unfrightened Americans who are proud of their country. President Kells, good man that he is, has forfeited both the affection and respect of the country. I will try to recapture that for our party. And when this election is done, the nation will be set on a compass course so as to reassemble the economy and to expel from the land all these anxieties about the possibility of armed conflict. A retrieval of the economy so that Americans can be secure, in their jobs, in their homes, without the overhang of someone doing something foolish and starting a war that nobody wants. I can set us on that course. Sadly, unhappily, regrettably, President Kells cannot. There is nothing personal about this. But friendship and debts owed to the President are of small value when the nation stirs uneasily."

Brinkley said, "Why you, Mr. Vice President? Why not someone else? How did you come to the conclusion that you, and only you, ought to do whatever you think needs to be done?"

"The fact he is President makes it mighty hard for a Senator or Congressman or Governor, or anyone else for that matter, to challenge him. The one man who might do it is the man who is Vice

President, the only person other than the President who was elected by all the people. That's why I have come forward to ask the American people to consider something that is, as Mr. Donaldson suggested, not at all usual."

Donaldson stirred in his chair. "You would agree, I think, Mr. Vice President, that the rules of the political game have changed rapidly, not necessarily for the better, but change they have. So, I put to you this delicate question. It has been reported that you and your wife are not living together and there have been rumors about your personal conduct in your private life."

The President, watching, frowned. "Didn't take them long to get the knife out, did it?"

Willacy grinned wickedly. "Frankly, I wondered why they waited so long."

Odd, thought Clem, this line of questioning might be the President's blessing. But his distaste was real.

Donaldson's voice came hurtling out of the TV screen. "Would you comment on whether or not these rumors of other women are true, or not true?"

Rawlins brushed at his ear, a negligent touch of his forefinger. "Mr. Donaldson, your question is discourteous and a bit crude. It is also stupid. I never answer stupid questions but I do from time to time engage in conversation with stupid questioners. Let's go to the next question."

Brinkley's durable calm served him well at this moment. He raised his hand as if to ask for silence. "Perhaps we will go on to another question. Sam, George?"

Clem was transfixed. It was a gutsy question by Donaldson, who, to Clem's eye, was not at all disconcerted. Donaldson was a veteran professional, Clem mused, who expects rough replies to rough questions. Clem knew as Donaldson doubtless did that Rawlins was not about to confess all. Clem had expected some kind of outburst from Rawlins, though not as harsh or as elegantly delivered as the one just visited on Sam Donaldson, but he suspected that it didn't faze Donaldson at all, and that in fact Donaldson had foreseen the answer.

Donaldson calmly pressed on. "Another question, Mr. Vice President. Do you intend to continue on in your duties as Vice

President? Will it not be awkward to sit in meetings now with the man you are challenging in the primaries? How do you intend to handle that?"

"Very easily, Mr. Donaldson. Tomorrow morning I will deliver a letter resigning as Vice President."

Clem watched admiringly. The Vice President was in control.

The President smiled wanly. "Good shot, Bill."

There was an audible gasp in the TV studio control room. The associate producer of the show almost shouted for joy. She could hear the stampede of a hundred newsmen clambering to file their stories. Tomorrow, "This Week with David Brinkley" would be quoted on every TV newscast and on every front page of every newspaper in America. The dream of every Sunday political talk show is to ignite the headline news story for the next day. And this was a barn-burner. Brinkley understood the impact of this revelation, and Donaldson smiled triumphantly. George Will gazed at the Vice President with a hint of a smile.

Brinkley said quickly, "You will resign tomorrow?"

"That is correct," said Rawlins.

"And you will contest the President in the primaries in February and thereafter?"

"Again, correct."

On the second floor of the Mansion, the President surveyed the Brinkley show with exquisite repose. Willacy Hughes was solemn. The President pressed the remote control and the TV set went dark.

"What do you think, Willacy?" said the President.

"He was good, very good. I think he blew Donaldson away with that retort." As he spoke, Willacy stirred his drink. Clem watched Willacy closely. Clem knew that Willacy loathed Rawlins, always had. Clem's emotion was not hate, but he did resent any suggestion that Rawlins was in any way a superior man. Clem would have counseled the President against choosing him as the Vice Presidential candidate, had he been asked. Rawlins was too good on the surface. Beneath that radiant exterior was, to Clem, the picture of Dorian Gray.

Clem looked sharply at the President. He was devoted to Don Kells. He possibly loved him. Clem was devastated by Rawlins' performance. It was graceful, tough, and most horrifyingly believable. It was also very smooth. He knew that Willacy counted Rawlins to be a malignancy, a man of viral ambitions whose amorality was a menace to the nation. But Clem had to confess, to his terrible sorrow, that Rawlins was a consummate performer. In the serrated and politically illusionary world of television, Rawlins was a master craftsman of the game.

"Mr. President," said Clem, "we are in trouble, deep trouble. We simply have to confront a most unhandsome problem. Yes, I thought Bill Rawlins was terrific. He took the offensive on his private life which, as we damn well know but can't prove, is a piece of lies and deceit."

"Let me pose a question to you both," the President said. "Is Bill right? Have I really forfeited the right to govern? Is the economy so bad it can't be redeemed?" He rubbed his chin absently. "Am I wrong to want to keep this nation secure and not believe, like some lost innocent, that the Soviets are simple shepherds for peace? Is it an error to want to shore up our allies and keep the balance of power from tilting away from us? Is that so wrong?"

It was as near to a confession of indecision as Don Kells ever got with his old friends. Clem said, "No, Mr. President, you're not wrong. We're in a descending curve right now, that's pretty clear, but curves go up as well as down. You've said that a hundred times."

The President smiled. "True. But we don't have a lot of time available to nudge this one upward, do we? But we do have some time. What we can't do is sit around and grouse about bad luck, or what we might have done. I have done the best I could do. But I will not sit idly by in a trance and let Bill Rawlins strip me of this office. We have work to do, my good and loyal friends, and work is what we will begin."

In his Georgetown home this Sunday morning, Ben Bradlee watched the David Brinkley show, with David Broder.

"That Rawlins is one charming pisser," said Bradlee. "Tying a bell to his tail isn't going to be easy. But I have this little elf somewhere in my gut that keeps whispering something's not kosher. What the hell is it, Dave?"

Broder nodded. "I can't put my finger on it, Ben. But your instincts are right. Query: What do we do?"

Bradlee leaped to his feet. "We find out, you find out if this fucker is for real. Meanwhile, the President is skidding on an oily street, and that little Republican Bobby Stonehaven is probably snickering that the Democrats can't count to two without having a dogfight."

Laura Hurley hugged her knees to her chest, her chin resting on her kneecaps as she viewed the show. That her heart leaped wildly, beating so furiously she was angry at herself, was not so surprising. She had read the note earlier, typed on plain white paper addressed to "Christine's guest" and signed "Dinner companion." It read simply: "8 E. 65th, apartment 701, 8:00 p.m. Today. Call 857-8601 and say 'yes.' "

She trembled again. She had struggled with herself ever since the note arrived. She sighed, picked up the phone, dialed the number. "Hello," she said, when a man answered with a curt "Yes?" "Are you the proper person to respond to a note I received this morning?"

"Yes."

"Then I will be there at 8:00 p.m."

"Thank you." The click sounded in her ear.

Bill Rawlins came out of ABC studios in Manhattan flanked by four Secret Service men. Charlie Embaugh, head of the detail, nodded to the driver of the Chrysler limo and motioned to another agent, who walked swiftly to the car and opened the rear door. The Vice President bent his head as he eased into the rear seat, saying, "Charlie, the Waldorf Towers."

They sped through almost empty streets, without sirens or flashing lights.

"Later this evening, Charlie, I'll be at the Rawlins Oil apartment. I'll leave at nine tomorrow morning. I need to be at the publishers' meeting by nine-thirty, no later. Keep the detail small tonight, will you?"

At the Waldorf Towers, Embaugh and the other Secret Service agents led the way. Soon the Vice President was inserting a key in the lock of 34F, his brother Roger's permanent two-room suite, where a group of well-wishers waited.

Rawlins had insisted on going to the interview alone. No aides, no staff, just Bill Rawlins, by himself, saying to Donaldson, Will, and whomever, you boys don't scare me, and I don't need handlers to shove papers at me when asked a question.

Peter Weymouth saw him first, and raised a glass of bourbon to him. "Bill, you were just terrific!"

Senator Flag Foster, Weymouth, and Henderson crowded round him. Rawlins was in fine humor, among his loyal lieutenants. He was pleased but not surprised by this fidelity. Since his youth, he'd found it simple to win loyalty and friendship. His father had cautioned him, "Choose your friends carefully, but once you've chosen them, don't forget them, and never betray them."

Rawlins beckoned to Henderson and drew him aside in the adjoining bedroom.

"Activate Luther everywhere, Hoyle. We now pull out all the stops."

"Luther's already in motion, Bill. We'll have a minimum of eight, maybe ten, fund-raisers in the next two months. Day after tomorrow, we announce eleven state Party chairmen for Rawlins. Figure we'll add three to five more shortly. Jimmy Winger has about twelve evangelists ready to stand with you. All of this will hit Kells right in the balls. Flag tells me that Senator Tunstall'll deliver at least twenty Senators to the Rawlins for President Committee. More defectors than a Russian ballet troupe. Three weeks from now, we'll have organizations in Iowa, New Hampshire, and South Dakota twice as big as any Kells and his folks can muster."

Rawlins laughed. "Hoyle, you caught the bastards bathing and you stole their clothes."

Hoyle nodded. "And left 'em clown costumes."

At five minutes after eight p.m., Laura Hurley stepped from her car on East 65th Street. She murmured to the driver, "Go back to the apartment, Robert. I'll call you there." The driver held the door for her, tipped his cap.

The Rawlins Oil Company's office was at 6 East 65th Street. Next door was 8 East 65th, owned by a real estate company quietly controlled by Rawlins Oil. To all but trusted Rawlins people, they were separate buildings. But in the latter building was the private apartment of Bill Rawlins, constructed so that he had a connecting link to the company's building through the rear of his own apartment. To outsiders, there were simply two buildings, next to each other, not related at all.

Laura approached the security guard in the lobby of 8 East 65th. He gave her a glance and motioned her to the elevator bank. She punched the seventh-floor button, and when the elevator door opened, she walked down the corridor to its end to a door marked 701. Trembling, she gripped her handbag and pressed the buzzer.

The door seemed to open instantaneously.

There the Vice President stood, in a blue blazer with an open-neck sport shirt, an amused look in his gray eyes.

He held out his hand.

"You came. I'm relieved."

"Did you think I'd stand you up?"

"In politics I never believe anything until it actually happens. With you, however, I did hope you would be here."

"Well, here I am."

She laughed a little, as Bill Rawlins took her hand, squeezed it, and drew her inside.

The lighting was subdued, the glowing fireplace muting the understated elegance of the decor. On a low-slung coffee table an ice-laden silver cask embraced a cold bottle of Montrachet. Rawlins poured the wine into two thin, fragile glasses.

He gave her one, lifted his and said, "To charming company."

She smiled. "My father says it takes him two glasses of wine to reach 'charming.'"

"Maybe I should drink this quickly and get on with my second glass . . ."

She laughed again. "Do you ever mind that your father made all the money, and you didn't?" she asked impulsively. "As one spoiled rich kid to another?"

Now it was his turn to laugh. "Not at all." In an arch tone, he said, "Churchill once said that Balfour, freed by family wealth from the vulgar necessities of earning a living, was able to expend his considerable talents for his country and not his selfish interests." He swirled his wine. "Who else do you know that would tell you these historical bon mots?"

"You're saying that you want to give your talent to your country."

Rawlins gently rubbed her hand. "I guess so."

"You were good on television today."

"Thanks. Maybe you'd like to help me compose my letter to the Secretary of State."

"What on earth will you say? Mr. Secretary, I quit because I want to be President?"

Rawlins leaned back on the soft cushions of the sofa. "I'll simply say, 'I resign.' "

"How will you feel? I mean—deep inside. Any regrets, about going up against the President?"

"I really am fond of the President. He's a good man. Do you believe me?"

"I believe you. But you think you're better."

"Not better—better-suited."

She watched his profile—the strong, straight nose, thick, tousled hair. She was pleasantly surprised by her own self-confidence tonight. She had worried she would be tongue-tied, but she felt so comfortable with him. She found him fascinating. Yet, there was that pinprick of anxiety. A married woman with a married man, a powerful leader who might, in such a short time, be President, and where would she fit in, if she fit in anyplace at all?

He turned to her. She felt his hand tugging her closer to him. His arm went around her and his mouth was on hers, softly. He drew back a moment, then kissed her again, a deep, longing kiss. She felt his arms tighten around her and she grasped his neck, pulling him closer.

His hands were on her, moving all over her. Then he rose, lifted her in his arms, kissing her as he brought her to the bedroom. It was as if they were reenacting a silent-movie scene, where the Sheik, nostrils flaring, brings the maiden to his tent, to have his way with her. She almost giggled, and would have, except he was unfastening the hook at the back of her dress.

She helped him.

Twenty-three

THE NEXT MORNING, in Rawlins' campaign headquarters, Peter Weymouth sat across from Senator Flag Foster, who had been designated Campaign Director, though in truth he was no such thing.

"Got to hand it to that little peckerwood," Foster said, referring to the *real* campaign director, Hoyle Henderson. "Five fund-raisers set, Iowa, Texas, California, New York—and right in my own Illinois backyard! And I didn't even know he was doing it."

Weymouth nodded. "We have the storyboards for the TV spots ready for you and the Vice President to approve. We ought to have 'em on the air within two weeks."

Hoyle and Rawlins, of course, would provide the real yea or nay on the commercials.

"What about the advance men and the phone banks?" Foster asked.

"Done," said Weymouth. Hoyle had assigned veteran personnel to the key tasks. "Direct mail begins in ten days. We're setting up storefronts in damn near every city in every primary state. And if a car isn't sporting a Rawlins bumper sticker, it'll be an oversight or a Republican."

"Got a budget yet, Peter?"

Weymouth picked up a yellow pencil and scrawled on a pad the words: *Whatever the hell it takes.*

Foster laughed. "I heard Bill say if this election's lost it won't be for lack of spending every dollar his old man ever made."

Weymouth grinned. "Here's the tentative schedule for the Vice President. First, Iowa—four events set there, and three crucial meetings with folks ready to come aboard once they get to smell and touch the candidate."

"Wouldn't want to sign on myself unless I had a face-to-face with the man I was working for. What'd you think about the reaction to Bill's resignation?"

"Good, very good. The public will tolerate a lot so long as they think the candidate isn't playing games with them."

The TV news shows and newspapers, editorials, op-ed pieces and columns were filled with favorable commentary on the Vice President's surprise resignation. The press seemed to feel unsubstantiated assaults on Rawlins' private life were off-base. Weymouth knew this would change as the campaign heated up. No one around Rawlins believed for one minute that Clem Barkley and Willacy Hughes were not going to go for Rawlins' jugular.

Willacy Hughes, Mike Carson, and Clem Barkley were in a smallish room in a newly rented building on K Street. Also on hand was Hickam Greene, the President's polling expert. The building was owned by a friend of Willacy Hughes' and was in the process of being renovated when Willacy called and suggested that, though it was unfinished, the Reelect Kells Committee should be installed there.

"Our opponent has come out of the blocks awful fast," said Hickam Greene. "I've gotten a quick readout on the last twenty-four hours and it's pretty bad for us. Most people believe Rawlins did the right thing when he resigned quickly. Right now, this poll shows that Rawlins would win thirty-six to thirty, but there are some thirty-four percent undecided. I don't have to tell you that when any incumbent, President or not, starts a reelection campaign that far behind, with that many undecideds, it is serious bad."

"And how do you interpret that?" said Willacy.

"We'll see over the next several weeks how the undecides shake out. But that's not the key. The key is going to be, is Rawlins moving up or down? Is he starting a trend, or is this just a reaction to the resignation, and the President's terrible showing in job approval ratings? I don't know right now. I will tell you this, if Rawlins picks up some statistically significant strength in the next couple of weeks, we may be in quicksand faster than we thought."

Willacy stared at Hickam Greene. "Bullshit. The reason he is up and we are down is that we have been getting the shit kicked out of us in the press the last six months and Bill Rawlins has been bowing, smiling, and spending his daddy's money in every goddamn state in the Union. And that bony-faced treacherous fart named Hoyle Henderson has been greasing skids and palms in every one of our bases."

He pointed a long finger at the pollster. "We're going to take this bastard down, as they say in his home state, just a tad. I have retained a group of ex-FBI agents who have their own security firm to do a swab job on Rawlins. We are going to find out what he has for breakfast, lunch, and dinner and I am not talking about food, I am talking about women. Then we are going to give it a public airing and let the folks decide if they want a Janus-faced adulterer in the White House."

"Come on, Willacy," said Clem soothingly. "We ought to spend more time and energy trying to fix what is wrong with our campaign rather than sling mud at Rawlins. This can backfire and we can't suffer any more erosions in the polls, as you can plainly tell."

"Backfire, you say, backfire?" asked Willacy. "I don't intend to publish this ourselves. We will find suitable companions within the press who would like to ram a baseball bat right up Bill Rawlins' classic nostrils. No, our fingerprints won't be on it, and even if they are, we are merely suggesting full disclosure for all the candidates, a pants-off survey we are willing to participate in as well. At least Don Kells is a widower."

Clem turned away, stared at the wall.

Willacy scowled at Barkley. "I believe we have to turn the heat up on Rawlins. If we do nothing but distract him for a time until we can turn around this damn economy, get some favorable indicator figures for a change, we will have gained a triumph."

"You know, Willacy, you remind me of that old political story," said Barkley. "This old sheriff in the boondocks of the South had been in office for thirty years, never contested. Until one day some young chief of police in a small nearby town challenged him in the election. The old sheriff was beside himself with anger that some whippersnapper was taking him on. So he gathered his aides and said, 'Now, boys, I want you to hit the streets and spread the rumor that this young punk has been screwing a sheep.' 'Migod, Sheriff,' one of his aides said, 'that ain't so and we know it.' The old sheriff hung a wicked smile on them and said, 'Yeah, you know it and I know it, but let's make the sumbitch deny it.' "

The group broke up in laughter. Even Willacy managed a mild grin.

"No," said Willacy, now dead serious, "Rawlins won't be able to deny it because we will have him nailed. I got some information for you." Willacy turned to the others and said, "This is Top Secret, for your ears only, and if it leaks, well, let's just say you will all be deported to Bill Rawlins' ranch and never heard from again." It was the nearest that Willacy wanted to get to humor this day.

Willacy leaned forward. "We had him under surveillance the night of the Brinkley show. We figured the bastard wouldn't let an evening in New York go untended by a little screwing. We staked out the Waldorf as well as the Rawlins office on Fifth Avenue. We also put a team on the Rawlins Oil apartment at East 65th. They got two entrances to that place, one on Fifth and the other at 6 East 65th."

"Well," said Mike Carson, "don't leave us in suspense. What did you find?"

"Nothing, nothing at all," said Willacy. "We traced him to the old man's place on Fifth. Our guys were there until about three in the morning. They figured if anyone was going to be there, they would have arrived by that time."

"But how would you know who was going to see Rawlins? Are there not other people living in that building?" said Alvin.

"Correct, and we got a good picture of everyone going in who was female, good-looking, and unattached. We even photographed those who weren't by themselves, figuring they might be bearded. But not a single candidate really looks like they might be the target. Well, that's not exactly right. We got two pictures of two women with escorts. We checked them out and they live there.

One is divorced and the guy was her new boyfriend, and the other was with her husband. I don't count husbands as being 'beards.' "

Barkley found this momentarily amusing.

Willacy went on: "We did get a shot of a terrific woman, great legs, beautiful, blond, and alone. She got out of a chauffeured limo but she went in next door to the 8 East 65th address. I am going to check it out just as a precaution, but I don't think it will turn up anything. Oh yes, the ex-FBI guys didn't get a full license plate make on the limo so we may have some trouble finding out who she is. But no matter. Sooner or later, we'll nail him, we will."

Hickam Greene thumped his fingers on the table. "Frankly, I think Willacy is right. It's the only crack in Rawlins' shield, if it is a provable crack."

Clem Barkley stood up, leaning over the table. He said, "I don't like any part of this. Shouldn't we all be a little ashamed? Here we are staking out the Vice President, taking photographs of women with terrific legs, blond and beautiful, jotting down license numbers. For God's sake, you sound like you're doing a story for *Playboy* or the *National Enquirer*. Let's start acting like professionals."

Willacy's face darkened with anger.

Clem was not yet done: "Come on, Willacy, if the *Post* got hold of this story they would make you look so ridiculous, and the President even more so. You'd be banished from the campaign. The President would have to disown you."

Willacy spoke very quietly. "Perhaps, Mr. Presidential Assistant, you might like to offer some specifics about how you would attempt to bring Rawlins down to size. Would you suggest publishing some of Hick Greene's studies, showing the President struggling to keep breathing politically, or would you press a button and get employment up next week? Just what would you, in all your political wisdom, put on the table today?"

Clem Barkley raised a hand in mild protest. "Willacy, I am on your side, on the President's side, remember? Are we to have strategy sessions with our tongues tied and our mouths gagged? May I not offer some other views without you exiling me from the room? It's not your style, Willacy, not worthy of you." Barkley's voice never wavered nor did it rise in temper. He was very calm.

"You're right, Clem." Willacy was quickly contrite. He knew

Clem Barkley lived and died for Don Kells. He didn't want to bruise him any further. "We have to move swiftly to counter Rawlins. Unlike an ordinary candidate, he doesn't have to gas up. He's got all the money he will ever need. He can spend fifty million of his own money and never miss it. I am simply saying that we cannot run this campaign in the traditional fashion, else one of the finest men of this generation is going back to Ohio sacked by the people he tried, goddamnit, to serve."

Carson raised a hand toward Willacy. "I know this will sound traitorous, but ought we not be a little bit sensible? Is it worth the run to have the President humiliated in these primaries, or having gotten through them, crippled and worn, to be torn apart by the Republicans? Don't we want the President—"

Clem and Willacy exploded at the same moment. Willacy was louder. "If all you can offer are defeat lyrics, for Chrissakes, Mike, shut up. We are not going to surrender, we are not going to quit. Understand?"

"Okay, okay." The press secretary seemed unmoved by the violent reaction. "I am merely putting on the table an option that intelligent people ought to consider."

Clem said savagely, "Consider us dumb, Mike."

Mike waved his arms in the air. "Okay, Pearl Harbor is being rerun here. That's all I am saying."

The group began to stir, pushing chairs back. The meeting was over.

Clem suddenly had a vagrant thought. He sat still for a moment. Terrific legs, blond, beautiful. Who was that woman at the Lambert dinner party, the one Clem found extraordinarily appealing? Didn't the Vice President pay special attention to her? At one moment in the dinner, Clem stared at them, the blond woman and Rawlins, their heads tilted toward each other, Rawlins on point, in action, charm pushed to the firewall. Could she be . . . ? Clem pushed his chair back. God, Willacy was making him feel like a gumshoe. God.

Federof, sitting pensively at the small desk in his apartment in the Soviet Embassy in Washington, started at the sound of his ringing phone. But when he heard the chief of security say that Comrade

Miektor had arrived, he smiled. Eighteen hours ago—just a few hours after he'd gotten back—he had sent a cable which he himself coded, forbidding anyone else to be present in the code room. He had cabled Zinyakin, requesting that Vlady Miektor come immediately to Washington.

Miektor entered and embraced him. "Ah, Filipp Vladimirovich, I am so glad you called for me."

"Come, Vlady Aleksandrovich. Let us walk about the grounds."

They strolled in the compound. Federof turned on a little buzzing instrument in his coat pocket, to deflect any electronic surveillance.

"I have a terrible problem, old friend. What I am going to tell you is for your ears only—should others know, both our lives are in peril."

Federof told Miektor of the murder of Hickey, and that the two Bulgarian assassins were in a downtown hotel, under constant FBI surveillance. But he did not tell his trusted friend of the Executive President's unambiguous order to him, and the KGB Chairman's opposite command. Even Miektor could not handle that kind of dilemma.

Miektor looked down at his shoes as they walked. "What must be done, Filipp Vladimirovich?"

Federof spoke to Miektor slowly, and Vlady nodded, his weathered face impassive.

"Let us go inside now, Vlady. Perhaps we should have some vodka and talk of less serious things. Perhaps we will have Irina serve us."

"Irina?" asked Miektor.

"Ah, old comrade, it is so lonely here in Washington," Federof said, a knowing smile on his face.

The request for a meeting came to the President through Clem Barkley and not the Congressional liaison office as ordinarily it would have. The President's secretary came into the Oval Office and said, "Mr. Barkley said the Majority Leader is hopeful you can see him today, at a time that would be convenient to you."

The President smiled grimly. "What is an open time?"

She looked at the notebook in her hand. "Mr. Barkley thinks

that 1:00 p.m. would be a good time. He believes that you ought to see him as quickly as possible."

The President glanced at his watch. 9:10 a.m. "Call the Majority Leader. Tell him that one o'clock would be just fine."

He pressed a button on the phone console. His press secretary answered: "Yes, sir."

"Mike, Tunstall is asking to see me. Anything registering on your gossip meter in the press room?"

"No, sir. I've heard nothing about that. What we do know is Senator Tunstall is tight with the Vice President. My guess is the Senator will soon be going public with his support. But he may not. Hard to say how that wily rascal will turn," said Carson.

The President said, "Right now, keep a lid on this meeting. We'll let the press know in due time." He pressed his console button connecting him with Clem Barkley. When Clem answered, he said, "Get in here fast."

The President leaned back in his chair when Clem arrived. "I'm seeing Tunstall at 1:00 p.m. as you suggested. What do you feel, what do you think?"

Clem answered quickly, "He'll probably recite a long list of reasons why you ought not run, and why the stand he may take is in the public interest. I figure Tunstall has some kind of deal or he's going to confide his preference for Rawlins with the usual disclaimers of any animus for the President. Maybe he's having second thoughts."

"You know the script, don't you, Clem," said the President. "Call Willacy and tell him to stand by. I may want to talk with him. And tell the Secretary of State to be in his office if I need him. Not that it's likely—not bloody likely. On the other hand, there are no precedents for what's going on. Raymond could offer some surprise."

Clem nodded his head. He knew that Senator Tunstall was not impulsive. The Senator from Michigan would not commit unless he had inspected every alleyway for possible ambush.

"All right, Clem. Be available when Raymond comes in to see me."

.   .   .   .

The Majority Leader looked fresh and fit as he entered the Oval Office, his brown chalk-striped suit complementing his ample frame. He smiled hospitably, hand outstretched. He nodded to Clem.

"Mr. President, you were most kind to see me on such short notice."

"Raymond, you're always welcome here," the President said, coming from round his desk. He motioned Tunstall to a seat on the couch flanking the fireplace. The President sat easily in his rocking chair.

"Coffee, Raymond?"

"No, thank you, sir."

"Raymond, I've been wanting to thank you for helping out on that transportation measure. We're checking it out with some of your midwestern colleagues. I don't want either of us to be caught napping."

"That's wise, Mr. President. I believe the objective is sound. By the way, who will the Senate be addressing as Vice President? Do you have someone in mind?"

"Vice President is a worthy title, or so I've always believed. Lately though, Raymond, it seems a bit biodegradable."

Tunstall laughed, not heartily, but graciously. "But as we both know, the country's interests come first, no matter what path any one of us chooses to take."

The President offered a slight wave of his hand.

Tunstall leaned forward, eyebrows ascending, thick furrows appearing on his forehead. "Mr. President, I come on a difficult mission. I would prefer, frankly, not to bear these tidings, but I see no reasonable alternative."

So that's it, Clem thought to himself. Raymond Tunstall is going to make the break final.

President Kells drummed his fingers lightly on the arm of the rocking chair. "That's why we're both here in Washington, Raymond. Alternatives are seldom reasonable, and often not very accommodating."

"Yes, Mr. President. But some alternatives are even less reasonable than others. Do you think a fratricidal war between you and the Vice President will produce anything other than an electoral disaster for us all?"

The President fixed his gaze squarely on Tunstall, his face open, but with no hint of any emotion. "Before I go to the mat, Raymond, are you suggesting you want to broker some kind of arrangement whereby Bill Rawlins changes his mind and withdraws? Is that what you are saying?"

Ah, thought Clem. You, dear Raymond, are an old fox in the woods, sniffing the scent of the hounds. The President is going to force you into the open.

As if reading Clem's thoughts, the Majority Leader smiled ruefully. "Not precisely, Mr. President. I am really here to try with all the passion I can summon to try to convince you that even if no one contests you in the primaries, Governor Stonehaven will be very formidable in the general election. We will have to fight the war on his turf—the economy, foreign policy. You have done your very best, sir, and with all due respect, your best is not good enough. Events have taken a dismal toll of your Presidency. Why invite a war in which we cannot count the wounded, there will be so many?"

The President stood up, walking slowly to the windowed door that led to the Rose Garden. He stared out, hands in his pockets. He turned to face the Majority Leader.

"Raymond, I understand this is not easy for you. You have come to tell me what you truly believe. I think you are trying to be helpful, as you see the future. I owe you an answer, and it is this: I will go for renomination, and I will win. I will beat whomever the Republicans put up in the summer." He came close to Tunstall and leaned over the seated Senator, until their faces were only inches apart. "I will go to the country, Raymond, and I will make it clear in great detail what the alternatives are. I will make it clear that I can govern this country with more skill than those who want my job. I don't intend to cavil or hesitate. I thank you for coming by."

It was a signal that the meeting was over. Tunstall rose wearily, his thick brows dancing again. "I hear you, Mr. President, I hear you. But I am saddened by your response. This will be a war of the most violent kind. There will be no winners in our party. And I daresay some of your friends and mine in the Senate who are up next year will find the election results most lamentable. As will I." He turned to Clem, smiling wanly. His smile now turned to the President. "I thank you, sir, for your time."

The President grasped Tunstall by the elbow and walked him to the door. He smiled. "It's not as bad as you may think, Raymond."

Twenty-four

THE CORCORAN GALLERY glowed with fresh flowers and was filled with the bustling of some two hundred of Washington's elite who either controlled political power or were the cliff dwellers, the natives who held commercial influence in the town as the transients grabbed hold of everything else. Waiters offered drinks to the guests, who were all black-tied and designer-gowned, crowding the lower level, mingling among the elegantly decorated tables later to be occupied for dinner. The dark-coated Strolling Strings of the U.S. Air Force played softly in one corner of the upper level.

Guests moved up the splendidly carpeted wide stairway. Many guests were gazing with varying degrees of expertise upon the new exhibition of American painters.

Clem Barkley was trying to shroud his exuberance. Toni Georgihu's arm was slipped inside his, the two of them equal in height. She leaned toward Clem. "This is really quite a nice idea of yours. Do you know I had to buy an evening gown?"

Clem laughed, squeezed her hand. "The gown is superior. As are you."

He waved across the room.

Terry Geer, standing beside a preoccupied John Wingate, waved back.

Geer, slim and rather handsome in his Neiman Marcus tux,

smoothed his sheened lapels. Terry was delighted with the cut of the jacket. He turned to John Wingate, who was attired in what Terry would have described as a tux in permanent need of renovation, with a recent food stain on the left lapel. Harvard, thought Terry, is no guarantee of tidiness.

"Did you see Clem over there with that giant of an FBI agent?"

Wingate nodded appreciatively. "If you like Amazon cops," he said, "she's not too bad."

"Hey, John, you're noticing something other than these dull paintings. Terrific."

"Bierstadt is anything but dull," Wingate said, viewing the huge canvas by Albert Bierstadt, a magnificent panorama of a vast mountainside, populated by a camp of Indians.

There was a small crowd building up around the Bierstadt picture, but Terry felt sure they were attracted by the proximity of two very powerful White House aides. Terry found this political adulation not to his dissatisfaction. He hoped Clem would not saunter over. He wanted to bask in this attention without more Presidential assistants dividing the glow.

He felt an arm collide with his left side and could feel the splash of liquid on his sleeve dripping to his hand. He looked down. It was wine, cascading down the sleeve of his brand-new tuxedo. He looked up at the horrified face of a remarkably attractive woman, whose dark blue eyes were filled with embarrassment.

"Oh, please, please, I am so sorry. I was so terribly clumsy. How unforgivable." Her husky voice was vaguely European.

"Don't fret yourself, it was really nothing." Terry brushed at his sleeve with his handkerchief. She was superbly gowned, in dark scarlet, bare shoulders gleaming white, and Terry's eyes strayed ravenously, against his will, to her breasts, enticing over the rim of her dress. She looked up at him expectantly.

"Can you truly forgive me?" she said warmly.

John Wingate said to her, "My dear, Terry simply wouldn't dare to say anything else except you are forgiven. My name is John Wingate and this young fellow whom you have just christened with very good wine is Terry Geer."

Terry was impressed with Wingate. He handled that with more than his usual grace. The woman seemed grateful to Wingate.

"That is so cordial of you. My name is Greta Hulved. I am so pleased to meet you both." The language was formal, English was clearly not her first language.

"Please, it's all right. It is difficult to move through this crowd trying to balance a drink at the same time."

"You are so kind. I just want you to know that I do not try to make this a habit, this dropping of wine on strangers."

"You said your name was Greta Hulved?"

She nodded.

"Is there a Mr. Hulved with you?" said Terry unabashed.

"A Mr. Hulved . . . You mean my father?"

"Well, is he here? Though I meant your husband."

"I have no husband, but I do have a father in Zürich."

"Then you are by yourself?"

"Yes."

John Wingate leaned close to Terry, whispering, "Find out where she is sitting, and get next to her."

Terry laughed. Turning back to Greta Hulved, he said, "Please forgive the whispers, but every now and then, my friend John is struck with brilliance. Not often, but right now. Will you wait here, please, for just a moment? John, guard Miss Hulved with your life. I will be right back." With that, he bolted from them and almost ran toward the lower level.

Greta Hulved stared after him with puzzlement. "Is something wrong?" she said.

Within minutes Terry was back at her side, and her place card was now next to his.

As they descended the carpeted steps with the rest of the crowd, a frail-looking man, sporting wispy red hair trailing over his ears and an incongruously large mustache, appeared beside her and glanced briefly at her. She nodded, a barely noticeable nod, faintly smiled, and redirected her attention to Terry Geer.

The frail-looking man walked to the door of the Corcoran and beckoned to one of the chauffeurs waiting in attendance. The chauffeur hastily came to the door. The frail-looking man gave the chauffeur a note. "Take this to our guest." The chauffeur departed instantly and in less than a minute was in a large Cadillac speeding off.

Clem and Toni Georgihu sat down at their table. Clem observed the room. "Who is that woman over there, three tables over, the one seated next to Terry? He's turning on the charm to her, as you can plainly see."

Toni didn't look up. She was being greeted by the Chairman of the Riggs Bank, who asked her congenially as to the health of the FBI Director.

Terry, modestly ecstatic, leaned toward Greta Hulved, totally oblivious to the others at his table, who included the Deputy Director of the CIA, a senior member of the House Foreign Affairs Committee, the owner of the largest Honda dealership in the Washington area, and Mrs. Christine Lambert.

Terry Geer stirred in his sleep, flopped on his side and then came awake, slowly, haltingly. His mouth still tasted of what he now vaguely remembered to be about three bottles of Jordan cabernet sauvignon. His throat felt a bit raw. He slowly turned to his left. The imprint of a body was still there, but she was gone.

He sat upright. Where had she gone? He tumbled out of bed, reaching for his bathrobe dangling over a chair. Then he turned.

She stood nude in the doorway, a faint light piercing the bedroom window. The light gave her a burnished cast, full breasts, small waist, flat stomach, long, graceful legs. Jesus, she was lovely.

At first she had resisted his invitation to join him at his apartment for a nightcap. It was late, and she was a journalist, with deadlines to meet. But finally he had worn down her resistance. He dismissed his White House car and they drove in her car to his apartment in Old Alexandria on Duke Street. She had seemed distant, as they came into his living room, but when he turned on the stereo and the pure clean voice of Streisand flowed through the room, she warmed up. He uncorked the first bottle of the Jordan cabernet, and they sipped and talked.

He told her about his boyhood in Michigan and his college days at the University of Michigan and his tenure at Yale Law School, where he'd met Clem Barkley, who had introduced him to Willacy Hughes. He'd become an acolyte of Donald Kells, and now he was in the White House, a trusted aide to a great President. It was more exhilarating than anything he'd known or would ever know.

She'd listened intently, talking little about herself. She seemed nonpolitical—her journalistic world was the arts. She asked a few questions about his work, but she was interested in the President as a man, she said. What was he really like?

Terry was falling for this sophisticated, enchanting woman, and she appeared to at least find him attractive. But when he had tried to kiss her, she drew away. His disappointment must have shown, because she looked at him and gently laughed.

"Terry, you look as if you lost your best friend. If I kiss you, will you be happy again?"

"Try ecstatic," he said, and she kissed him, and suddenly the world was his private candy store . . .

"Couldn't sleep?" he called to her.

"I've only been up a few minutes," she said.

She came slowly to him, her naked body a walking vision. God, he wanted her. She began to pick up her undergarments. She reached down, as he sat on the edge of the bed, and kissed him lightly, then more lovingly. He reached out for her, and she danced away.

"It was such a lovely evening, so unexpected, so spontaneous," she said. "I won't deny how good you made me feel. But can we not, how do you say this, go slow?" She laughed again, lightly. "You look sad again, but it won't work this time. We need to get to know each other so much better, do you not agree?"

As she drove away, Terry stood in the doorway, hands thrust into his robe, watching her car disappear in the early morning dawn. He stumbled back into the living room. He put the empty wine bottles away, and then determined not to worry about tidying up. His shoes were near the coffee table. What the hell were his shoes doing here? God, he must have started undressing in the goddamn living room. Never in all his life had he made love to a woman who urged him on with such vitality and passion. He picked up his shoes and walked into the bedroom.

Time to shave and shower and get on with running the country again.

Later that evening, the East Room of the White House was jammed to capacity. In eleven minutes, at precisely 8:00 p.m.,

Eastern Standard Time, the President of the United States would hold his first live nationally televised press conference since the resignation of Vice President Rawlins. Helen Thomas, senior member of the press corps, was in her usual front row center seat, Brit Hume of ABC one row behind her. Joe Develin of *Time* was seated next to Paul Taylor of the *Post*, who was in turn next to Andrea Mitchell of NBC. One row back of them sat Lesley Stahl of CBS and Judy Woodruff of PBS in intimate conversation. There was an incessant buzz in the famous old room. Large paintings of George Washington and Dolly Madison flanked the walls.

A voice over the microphone bellowed: "Ladies and gentlemen, the President of the United States."

President Kells strode into the East Room, beaming, shoulders thrust back, right hand in the air waving in recognition to several of the newsmen now on their feet. The President motioned them to their seats.

Myles Hall of Gannett murmured to Priscilla Beekman of the Los Angeles *Times*, "Looks mighty fit for a fellow in a battle for his life, doesn't he?"

Beekman nodded, and said, "What can he say today that will bring him out of this slump?"

"Don't know, but he had better give it his best shot."

The President gazed crisply at his audience and then said, "I have no prepared statement. Let us begin the conference."

Helen Thomas stood. "Mr. President, what is your personal reaction to the recent move by Vice President Rawlins? And how do you feel deep inside about this unusual act by a man you chose to be Vice President?"

The President grinned. "Deep inside, Helen? How deep?" Laughter from the group. The President tugged at his right earlobe.

"Vice President Rawlins is a friend of mine, and I count his abilities to be considerable. If I hadn't, I would never have asked him to be my running mate. Was I surprised at his decision? Not entirely. Was I disappointed? Yes, I was. Did he ever discuss this with me at any time? No, he didn't, though I believe I can understand why. It is not easy for someone who has been given high office to confront the one who made that possible and say, 'I want your job.' "

Lesley Stahl leaned to Judy Woodruff. "Ouch, he shoved the dagger in a little bit."

Judy Woodruff nodded appreciatively.

"But it is surely within the rules of the game. The Vice President believes he can offer the American people something that I cannot. I don't share that judgment. This campaign will be the ground on which the American voter will determine who is right. I have strong and even profound views about the direction this nation should take to build for the next generation. And I will express those views as clearly and as passionately as I can."

Brit Hume was on his feet, as the President gestured to recognize him.

"Mr. President, the Vice President claims that you have lost the confidence of the American people, that you can no longer govern. Since you obviously disagree, will you tell us what you are planning to do over the next few months to restore faith in your Administration that the polls are indicating you have lost?"

"Polls, as we all know, pinpoint a specific moment in time. They do not forecast and they do not and cannot tell you what the mood of the country will be next week. I read a poll as one reads a billboard on the highway, knowing the next billboard will have a different message. What are my plans? First, I am convening an emergency economic assembly next Wednesday. I am asking the Chairman of the Federal Reserve, the Treasury Secretary, the Chairman of my economic advisers, and twelve other men and women of confirmed distinction to meet with me and hear my ideas for a swift attack on the economic virus that plagues us. I hope the Chairman of the Federal Reserve will find my ideas suitable to him, so that he can implement what I think ought to be done."

Murmurings grew louder in the room.

"Moreover," the President continued, "I have today sent a private note to the Executive President of the U.S.C.R. asking him to consider a meeting with me somewhere in Europe in sixty days to identify and collaborate in ways to soften the tensions that exist between us, and to see how each of us can soothe out the controversies and the problems that are now infecting countries in eastern Europe. I will await his answer."

Joe Develin scribbled on his notepad: "Pres. striking back. Surprise announce. Cutting off Rawlins' charge. Inflation and Russkies, hit the enemies head to head."

Andrea Mitchell, on her feet quickly, asked, "Isn't this merely your way of responding to Vice President Rawlins contesting with you for the nomination?"

"I am just doing my job, Andrea. A President's task is to try to find ways to give opportunity and hope to the country that he has pledged to lead. We have problems, we know what they are. My responsibility, my task, is to design solutions to them. That is what my announcements mean, no more, no less. So long as I am President, that is the path I will take. I will report to the American people what progress we are making. The people will make their own choices as to which leader they feel comfortable with, whose judgment they most trust."

Clem nodded in silent approval. The President had delivered that summation almost precisely word for word as Clem had written it, and the President had rehearsed it. Clem resisted the smug feeling that ached to gain entry into his mind.

Federof watched the President's news conference in the Embassy. He sat with Berisov and Vlady in the Ambassador's study, all eyes and ears glued to the fifty-inch Mitsubishi TV set.

Federof pondered the screen. He sipped his glass of wine slowly. "It is a smart political move. The Executive President will be pleased, I think. The President has come to him, not the other way around, and yet both stand to gain."

Vlady nodded vigorously. "Yes, it is a good move."

Berisov said nothing. He disliked having to share intimate political conversation with this KGB person in the room. Though Vlady was obviously trusted by Federof, Berisov did not know him. It was not right for Federof to inflict such indignities on him this way.

Federof considered what was happening. This was all becoming very complicated. He turned over the alternatives in his mind very carefully. Neither Berisov nor Vlady had any inkling of the racing thoughts in his brain. He could not stop what was now in progress but he must protect his flanks. Now, from here on, every move must be carefully plotted. He must examine each possible action as one plays chess, assessing the board five moves in advance. He must think clearly.

He rose to his feet. "Come, Vlady, join me in my apartment," he said, abruptly striding from the study without even a gesture to the Ambassador, whose gloomy countenance betrayed his humiliation.

Inside the apartment, Federof beckoned Vlady to a chair near the shortwave radio. Federof flicked it on. He turned up the volume. "I have inspected the entrails of this radio. It is clean. Now, give me your ear. Let us talk."

Vlady leaned down, his face a few inches from Federof, in front of the radio speaker.

Federof spoke, his voice very low.

"The Bulgarians are a source of risk. They must not be allowed to exist any longer. I will have Vaslansky up here shortly to be your guide in this enterprise. They are in the hotel on 15th Street. They have been there for a good while. The surveillance continues, and it will not be easy to terminate them. But it must be done, and it must be done so that the FBI has no inkling of who managed to get inside. They will know the Bulgarians had to be silenced, but they will not know the reason why.

"Here," Federof pointed to a blueprint he extracted from his briefcase, "is the layout of the hotel. I was able to get it from the District of Columbia archives. The two Bulgarians are staying on this floor in this room"—he circled the room on the blueprint—"and here is the fire escape and the stairs. Study it carefully tonight, and form in your mind how it will be done."

Toni Georgihu sighed with fatigue. It was much too late at night. She had been at her desk since seven o'clock this morning, and now as the night blew away the daylight, she was reading the report of Special Agent Maxwell on the surveillance of the Bulgarians at the Woodfire Hotel.

"Memorandum: SA Richard Maxwell to Associate Director, FBI. Bulgarian suspects. Bureau File 65-08624.

"Current investigation in instant matter is being conducted by round-the-clock surveillance of subject suspects. At present they are confined in Room 706 of Woodfire Hotel.

"Subjects venture out of the hotel only one at a time during the day at various hours, usually in the morning. Only one subject is visible outside the hotel at any one of these sightings. In every instance, they walk briskly around the block of the hotel. Suspects are in constant view during these sojourns. Suspects visit, singly, a small grocery store a block and a half away, purchase food articles, and walk back to the hotel. They have twice used two pay telephones on the back side of the hotel. We have received court authority to tap each phone used thus far, though none of them has ever been used the second time.

"Reliable informant in the hotel asserts no incoming phone calls. No outgoing calls. All their calls, if made, will be monitored by our informant.

"Surveillance continuing as ordered."

It appeared to Georgihu that stalemate had set in. They hadn't moved, that was clear. What did that mean? Who were they calling? They weren't running, which meant either that there were other chores for them to perform, or they were on ice until a propitious moment when they could flee. She knew they knew they were under the watchful eye of the Bureau. That is why they had been so careful about their calls. Should the Bureau move in and arrest them? What hard evidence did she have? What she didn't know was whether they had diplomatic immunity. If they did, she would lose them before she had a chance to interrogate them. On the other hand, if they left the hotel, there was the possibility they would lead the Bureau to whoever was controlling them.

She slowly read the report again.

Georgihu had an uneasy feeling. She had received Clem's judgment about Hickey's death with discomfort because she felt she had no substance to counter his instincts. Was there more to this than a killing of one unimportant player? Clem strenuously believed there was meaning to the murder, that it had an international taint. Bulgarians were not hired assassins in the sense that one orders a killer from a catalogue. She agreed with that. They moved lethally when they were under orders of a government, if not theirs, then this new Soviet Union, using Bulgarian hit men as the old U.S.S.R. once did. She was absolutely certain of that. But beyond that she had no heft to her certainty.

She got up wearily. She put Maxwell's report back in the file folder. She was ready to go home. Nothing was going to happen tonight. She would talk to Clem after she conferred with the Director.

The author of that report, Special Agent Dick Maxwell, sat with Agent Leland Fries in a dingy gray Buick suitably located across the street from the entrance to the Woodfire Hotel. Two other agents were on either side of the hotel on the side streets. He alone knew what the Bulgarians looked like and had, through an artist's sketch, provided the Bureau and his colleagues with their likenesses. It was Maxwell who had spotted the greatcoat at the Hardee's restaurant on Farragut Square.

He stirred in the front passenger's seat. He fixed his eye on the entrance to the Woodfire. His notebook was open before him. It contained a log of everyone who entered the hotel, and a brief description of anyone who had the faintest reason to cause some suspicion. The Woodfire was a relic, one of those modestly-priced hotels that fell somewhere between a Holiday Inn for businessmen on a stringent budget and the flea-bag rooms that used to dot the Washington downtown landscape. It was eight stories high, and dated back to the Second World War. It was only a matter of time, thought Maxwell, before it was toppled and some new office building took its place. Air-conditioning units ornamented each room window on the top three floors, indicating that the money had run out for finishing central air-conditioning before it reached those upper levels. Their informant on the desk had revealed to the Bureau that the two Bulgarians, registered under the names of Wysak and Normyle, were ensconced on the seventh floor, in the corner room.

"What time is it?" asked Fries.

Maxwell grinned. "You don't want to know."

"Yes, you do have great insight, Dick."

"Did you ever think when you were so enthusiastic about becoming a member of the Bureau that you'd be part of some enchanted evening like this—I mean, having fun at the Woodfire with that devilishly charming fellow, Richard Maxwell?"

"I fantasized about it, Dick, but I never thought my dream would ever come true." Fries leaned back and sighed. He was tired.

Six minutes later a small, swaying-hipped black woman, good-looking but hard-looking, approached the hotel from the opposite side. She stopped at the entrance, fluffed her hair, smoothed the side of her tight-fitting dress, and continued on through the entrance. Maxwell jotted on his notepad, "small black woman, attractive, probably prostie," and wrote down the time.

Three minutes later, Maxwell saw an old man navigate across the street, his crutches reaching out like a long stride. His right foot was in a cast but he was rather adept on his new-found locomotion. The old man, or at least he looked old, maybe sixty or so, was wearing a battered hat, an ancient fedora. He moved through the entrance of the hotel and disappeared.

Maxwell wrote down the time and a cryptic "old man on crutches, large, heavy, cast on right foot."

Fries said, "I'm going to do a turn around the building. I'll check in with the rest of the team."

"Why not check with them on the radio?"

"Hell, I want to stretch my legs."

Maxwell understood. He glanced up at the room on the seventh floor. The lights were out but there was a glow through the curtain. Probably the TV set was on.

He lit a cigarette, almost with anguish. He was going to stop smoking and had tried. It was the long stake-out chores that enticed him to light up. He chided himself on his lack of firmness.

The room on the seventh floor suddenly was illuminated. Maxwell sat up. He watched the window intently. He thought it might have been no more than one, two minutes when the lights were extinguished again. He made note of that. Probably piss-time, he thought, and saw Fries leisurely approach the car. Fries opened the driver's door.

"All's well, I am sorry to report," Fries said. "What we need around here is a little break in this unbelievable excitement."

Maxwell didn't answer. He watched the old man with the

crutches reemerge. The old man, this time with less awkwardness, moved across the street and disappeared around the corner. Maxwell flung open his door. He started across the street toward the hotel.

"What's up?" said Fries.

"You stay with the car, Leland," said Maxwell, "I have a funny feeling . . ." He walked slowly toward the entrance, his hand on his radio. The lobby was empty, its marble floors showing the strains of four decades of use. He ambled easily to the front desk where the clerk was leaning over some papers. The clerk looked up. Maxwell flipped his wallet exhibiting his FBI credentials. The clerk's chin went up sharply and his eyes flitted back and forth about the lobby.

"Yes, what can I do for you?" Nervously, wonderingly. He did his tasks for the Bureau but he never enjoyed any face-to-face meetings. He did his talking via the phone.

"That fellow with the crutches. He came in about ten, fifteen minutes ago, and just left. Where did he go when he came in?"

The clerk frowned. "I don't rightly know. I saw him. He took the elevator." The clerk motioned to the single elevator to the right of the desk, some fifteen feet away. "Then he came down again just a couple of minutes ago and left, when you saw him."

"Don't you find that a bit strange?"

The clerk managed a knowing grin. "Around here, man, nothing's strange, like having an FBI agent at my desk at midnight."

"Are your guests still in 706?"

"Yes, as far as I know."

"Why don't you call up there and say noises were reported on the seventh floor, and find out if they know anything about it."

"Now?"

"Now."

The clerk picked up the phone. The phone system operated through a PBX just behind the desk. He thumped out the number, and listened, his eyes wavering off Maxwell. He waited. He looked up at Maxwell. "No one answering."

Maxwell tensed. "You stay here. Give me a key to the room." He flicked on the radio. "Fries, this is Dick. Get in here fast.

Tenser, Mirelli, hold your positions and be alert, Leland and I are going to the suspects' room."

Within seconds, Leland Fries was at his side. Maxwell motioned to him. They got off the elevator at the seventh floor and, in a noiseless trot, moved down the worn carpet to Room 706. Maxwell hand-signaled Fries to move on the other side of the door. Maxwell unholstered his service weapon, a Sig Sauer Model P-226, a 9mm, 16-shot double-action automatic. Maxwell gripped his own automatic, a Heckler & Koch 9mm. Holding the Sig Sauer in his right hand, Maxwell slowly inserted the key with his left, and turned it as quietly as he could. The door opened easily.

They darted inside, weapons at the ready. Maxwell flipped the switch. The light was garish. It was as if it had intruded on something that was not yet ready to receive guests. It was a large room. To the left was the bathroom, and against the wall were twin beds. In each of them was what used to be a live human being.

The one on the left, a pale-complexioned man, about forty, with thick hair, lay on his left side, two holes in his head, one just below the right temple and the other at the top of his nose. The other sprawled, bald head against the bedboard, one gaping hole in the center of his left eye; a second shot had shattered his upper teeth and roared undeterred into the back of his brain.

Maxwell cursed. "Silencer," he said. He examined the damage in the first man. "Nine-millimeter, I'd say."

Fries picked up the phone. "Shall I call it in?"

"Yes. Get the Bureau first, try to find Toni Georgihu, then call the locals. Ask for Captain Hodges in Homicide, and then call Chief Wiggins. He's been involved in this case. He should be told. They won't be on duty, so get them at home."

Maxwell looked out the window. He flipped on the radio again. "Tenser, Mirelli. Maxwell here. Tenser, get moving down H Street. Bobby, go with him. We're looking for a man, about sixty, wearing a felt hat, on crutches, white cast on the right foot. My guess is it is a sham, but move anyway. If you spot him, which I doubt, he's armed and very dangerous. Apprehend him, but be careful. We need him alive. Move it."

He flipped off his radio.

While Fries was murmuring into the phone, Maxwell prowled

the room. Across from the beds and against the wall was a Zenith TV set atop a skinny-legged platform. There was a hot plate on a round small table next to the chest of drawers. An assortment of canned food was stacked on the chest of drawers, and on the small table as well. On the floor next to the chest of drawers was a pile of magazines in a foreign language—Bulgarian, Maxwell surmised. He started rifling through the chest of drawers. Soiled clothing filled the bottom drawer, with some clean shirts, shorts, some thick socks in the other two. Underneath a pile of what looked like T-shirts was a brown folder. The clasp was open. Maxwell peered inside, turned it upside down. Papers flew out, including six passports. Two were Swiss, two were Angolan, and two were U.S. "Don't leave home without them," said Maxwell under his breath.

Maxwell examined the papers. Most of them were in what Maxwell assumed to be Bulgarian. He slid those in his inside coat pocket. A small notepaper fluttered to the floor. It had obviously been tucked away inside the other papers. He leaned down and picked it up. There was a series of numbers: "293-0601."

He turned to Fries, still on the phone. Fries cupped his hand over the mouthpiece. "I'm waiting for Captain Hodges."

"Get the Bureau back after you talk to the Captain and have them check out a phone number, 293-0601."

Fries nodded and began talking to Captain Hodges.

Maxwell turned to face the two dead men in the twin beds. It was eerie. Here before him were these two Bulgarians, pawns in some as yet obscure game.

"Jesus," he whispered.

Twenty-five

B. J. BRACKENFIELD swirled the scotch and soda in his tall glass and gazed out the third-floor window. He saw a wide expanse of thick verdant grass. Beyond enclosing hedges was a lovely little pond, sun shimmering off its calm surface.

Evangelist Jimmy Winger's home sat in the middle of twenty-two acres just outside the little town of Mena, Arkansas, a three-story clapboard house, built some forty-five years earlier by his father, who had moved here from Little Rock. It had the look of a nice little farmhouse, bigger than most, but unobtrusive. Two new wings had been built since Jimmy took it over, but they looked no more modern than the rest. "Want the new ones to look just like the old ones. Want nobody to say Jimmy Winger's putting on airs," was how Jimmy put it.

Inside, the front parlor was pretty much in the same decorative spirit of Albert and Sadie Winger, a piano in one corner and chintz sofas flanking the windows. The dining room's long oak table shone with wax, long-backed wooden chairs on all sides. A sideboard against the wall held the china that Sadie's mother had given her and which now belonged to Lucy Ruth and Jimmy Winger. The kitchen was an old-fashioned one, with a large butcher's block in the middle, an ancient Franklin stove at the far end. The one concession to a modern sin-filled world was state-of-the-art gas-breathing cooking equipment.

On the third floor, however, no visitor's presence was requested unless he or she was a vintage Winger ally or intimate. The master bedroom had a fieldstone fireplace, with an enormous king-sized bed, canopied and draped in flowing white. Off the bedroom were two giant dressing rooms, each with large bathtubs. Sprouting out of Jimmy's bath were the nozzles of the latest innovations of the Jacuzzi family. Behind Jimmy's dressing room was another enormous room, a sun room, equipped with pool table, massage table, a fifty-inch television set, with Bang & Olufsen stereo equipment that B.J. said cost more than the annual Mena city budget. Jimmy Winger called this haven his "Healing Room."

B.J. stood beside the huge bay window on the third floor, still eyeing the pond.

"I always admired the work of the Lord, Jimmy," said B.J. "Damn, he does move in wondrous ways, don't he? Now take that little pond you got. Wasn't there fifteen years ago and, what do you know, God just said, 'Jimmy, you been such a good servant to me, you got to have a little pond, and I'm going to make you one.' "

Jimmy Winger, lounging indolently in his motorized leather swivel-backed "hugging chair," as he called it, smiled beatifically. "B.J., you getting religion? How come you know so much about God?"

"Where's Lucy Ruth?" B.J. said.

"Gone to Little Rock to see her sister. She's going to stay there while I'm out for the next three weeks, saving souls and kicking shit out of the Devil."

"And stirring the masses for Bill Rawlins, ain't that so?"

"That's so, B.J. How about some more of that ambrosia?"

"Don't mind at all."

"Martha," yelled Jimmy.

The door to the sun room opened. A tall stoutish woman with a large, seemingly firm bust and dark hair flecked with the beginnings of gray entered, carrying a tray on which was an ice bucket, Perrier, two glasses, and a bottle of Chivas Regal.

"This what you want, Jimmy?" she said.

Jimmy patted her on her voluptuous backside. "You just minister to my needs, Martha, and especially to my rich lobbyist friend and cousin from the sinful capital city of your country."

Martha grinned tolerantly at him, put the tray on the coffee table, and vanished.

"You know, Martha is the kind of help I admire. She's got an ass that is world-class, tits bigger than Dolly Parton's, has no gumption for talking to the press, and has hands and fingers that were born to massage. You know what I mean, B.J.?"

B.J. mixed himself a fresh drink.

"Let's talk about saving souls and getting votes," B.J. said. "Since we are in this healing room of yours, lay your hands on me and help me get rid of these feelings I have that we are not doing so well among the masses."

"Your trouble, B.J., you can't hear the Lord when he talks to me. I can hear him right now, if you truly want the truth."

"That ain't the Lord you just heard, I was farting in Old Testament cadence and you didn't know the difference."

B.J. put his drink down.

"Let's cut the bullshit, Jimmy. What's going on? What do you hear about this campaign?"

Jimmy scratched his thigh calmly. "Bill Rawlins is doing just fine because my people are hurting. Crops ain't selling, costs are too high, interest rates gone out of sight. Frigging A-rabs mucking around with the price of oil. It's scary out there. Bill Rawlins keep oozing that line about Kells being a decent fellow who can't find his butt with both hands and he'll sail in."

"How you doing with those fellow sin-busters of yours?"

"I got the majority of the preachers on our side, excepting those two airheads in Fort Worth and Birmingham. But they don't take sides either way, so they don't hurt as much as they could. I do have to say one thing, B.J. Folks out there don't cotton to foreigners buying up our country, don't like commies even if they suddenly got religion, and most of all they don't care much for a married man poking his pecker in women not his wife. Tell Bill to zip up his fly and not to cozy up too much with the japans and the russkies. The President says he wants to talk to them, but folks know that Kells washes his hands after he shakes hands with that foreign trash."

"Come on, Jimmy, we ain't in bed with anybody, including women. And you are five furlongs out of touch since communism is as dead as a dead dog's dick. President's got a hard on to start a war and Bill finds that stupid. You want bodybags stacked up on the Little Rock airport baggage carousel? You want to preach over funeral services at the Mena church?"

"Not saying that, B.J. Talk to them russkies, okay, but don't let them get their hand in his fly. Can't help it, B.J. I been flogging the balls off commies, abortion, pornography, and heathens too long to go short on any of them. The kind of folks I talk to got set ideas on such things. And what's good for my people is good enough for me. By the way, your banker friends in Little Rock are getting edgy again about God's Condominiums. Any chance you can talk to them, honey them up?"

B.J. said, "You buggering me, Jimmy, aren't you? You're stirring up some doubts here in order to get your goddamn loans in order?"

Jimmy Winger held up his hands in mock horror. "Would I lie to you, cousin?"

B.J. snorted. "In a New York minute."

Jimmy settled back in his lounge chair. He gulped down his drink. "I get good responses when I thank the Vice President for his attention to the needs of the Lord. That always gets a thundering 'amen and hallelujah.' But my folks're a little uneasy at times. Kells' folks moving across my territory slurring Bill about his commie leanings, the way he's approving of foreigners buying up the whole damn country, as well as trying to lay on him stories about his getting too much pussy on the side. Hell, any pussy is too much pussy for a fellow who is supposed to be married and wants to be President." Jimmy held up his hand. "All right, I hear you. I'm not saying anything except tell him to take one of them monk's vows until twenty minutes after the polls close next November."

Jimmy leaned forward, grinning. "Now, you're a big, high-paid lobbyist and you can get away with it because folks believe you lobbyists are mostly tubs of lard with no more idea of morality than a randy rhino. And I get away with it 'cause the Lord is my guide. But Bill can't get away with it because he's supposed to be lifting the quality of life in the country, and that bugshit can't stand anything except the pure, clean light of Jesus, family, and tithing.

You hear me, B.J.? Keep away from commies, japans, and pussy, and not necessarily in that order."

B.J. belched. "I hear you, Jimmy." Inside, B.J. was thinking, thinking hard. Jimmy was about as opaque to scruples as a choir-screwing preacher could ever get, but no one ever accused him of being dense. He had a sixth sense about people.

He remembered Willa Hammond and some of the other custodians of the PACs in Washington shooting the breeze at Duke Zeibert's restaurant a couple of weeks ago. And Willa had mused about how incestuous was the lobbyist's life in Washington. Willa had said that "inside this Beltway, we think we know it all, when most likely we are just xeroxing what someone said at some dinner party, something that passed for ultimate truth or what some Senator had said to some underpaid, overworked legislative assistant, or, what is worse, listening to those TV political talk shows where experts were dishing out pap and calling it pure wisdom. Then, B.J., you and I and the rest of our crowd attach all that to our so-called fund of knowledge. Does anybody ever wonder why the folks never listen to us back home; that is, if any of us have a back home anymore?" Smart lady, that Willa.

Meanwhile, he was here in Mena and wouldn't leave until tomorrow at noon. Might as well enjoy himself.

"Jimmy," he said, "how about getting Martha in here and telling her a most renowned public figure who will become even more powerful after the election would like to have himself a first-class massage."

Federof heard the knock at his bedroom door.

"Who's there?" he said.

A muffled voice replied, "It is Boris Andreevich. I have a message."

Federof knew that Vaslansky would not disturb him if it were not of more than casual importance.

He opened the door.

The large, heavy figure of Boris Vaslansky loomed before him. "Yes?"

"The weather forecast is good."

Federof absorbed that news quietly. He stood silent for a moment. "Pass that message as per procedures. When is the next drop time?"

"Tomorrow at 7:30 p.m.," answered Vaslansky.

"Make the drop," said Federof. He turned away and then turned back. "Careful, Boris Andreevich, careful."

"I will be careful, Filipp Vladimirovich."

Vaslansky entered the Safeway store at the corner of MacArthur Boulevard and 28th Street at 7:25 p.m. He picked up a red plastic basket next to the vegetable row and moved briskly across the store. A portly man pushing a cart bulging with canned goods, cartons of milk, and packages of frozen food almost ran into Vaslansky.

"Excuse me," he said to Vaslansky, and the Russian nodded. Several people stood in line with food-laden carts at the checkout counter. Only two counters were operating, one for express customers.

Vaslansky moved past the bathroom products and turned left at the last aisle. He examined some Jewish rye bread, kneading it in his hands, as he absently ran his gaze down the end of the aisle toward the refrigerated meat section.

No one was in the aisle.

He glanced left, replaced the rye bread, and swiftly attached a small strip of paper on the upper edge of the highest bread shelf, invisible to any passerby. He turned and walked slowly to the open refrigerators of packaged meat. He hefted a plastic-wrapped package of frankfurters. He retraced his footsteps to the express counter. He smiled at the cashier, a tall, thin woman with graying hair, who smiled back, took his ten-dollar bill, returned the change, smiled again and said, "Have a nice day," to which Vaslansky flashed his finest smile.

Within minutes after Vaslansky departed via the 28th Street exit, a man entered the same way. He pulled out a cart, rolled it past the magazine stand, where he paused, picked up an issue of *People*, thumbed through it, replaced it, and then walked slowly down the last aisle, stopping for a moment at the bread section. He picked up a loaf of Wonder bread, and simultaneously retrieved the tiny paper taped to the upper shelf.

He casually walked down the aisle, picking up packets of knockwurst and bologna, examining some chicken legs, placing them in the cart with the other products. He paid the cashier at the express counter and, with her "Have a nice day" trailing after him, exited through the same door he had entered.

Hoyle Henderson sat across the table from Loretta Wigham and Bruce Gustafson. It was a cold, windy day in Des Moines. Hoyle had flown in just two hours earlier, with little sleep the night before. Now he was closeted a second time with folks who had been described to him several months ago as "the two wizards of Iowa." He watched them intently. It was a new kind of political warfare these days. Here he was flattening his ass in a hard-cushioned chair, listening to two experts whose names were totally unknown to anybody outside the claque of bored reporters covering the Iowa primaries and the new pack of political consultants whose computer printouts bulged with like kind in every primary state.

These two were the new breed, the Praetorian Guard of primaries, locals who relished the smell of political combat, who each Presidential primary were in the trenches, alert and energetic. They were committed, and tenacious as a wild boar whose teeth were clamped on your boot. They knew all the alleyways and polling precincts, they were alive with the knowledge that was grist for the candidates. Who was leaning which way, and why, and how to reach them, and only the Druid priests of Iowa politics knew the answers. It was the readers of indecipherable precinct lore like Wigham and Gustafson to whom the candidates in the primary were attracted. They were more than priests, more like first draft choices, sought after, valued for the same reason: they were professionals whose yeast rose at the first clap of primary thunder, and without whose aid a questing primary candidate was disadvantaged.

Hoyle had long ago conceded that one couldn't change what was, but he plainly yearned for smoke-filled rooms once again. At least one understood the lingua franca of the back room and, more important, had no doubt that the small group in the room knew what the hell they were doing and why. They were going to pick a winner. None of this "cause" crap, no lonely, forlorn reaches for some squishy unformed crusade which was certain to collapse in polling booths around the country. But Hoyle never clung to what was, he always dealt in what is. And "what is" to Hoyle were the two people sitting across from him right now.

These two were firmly in Bill Rawlins' camp. Hoyle had lassoed them two weeks earlier, this time with sugarplums dancing in their heads. Hoyle had pledged Loretta that if Rawlins won she would no longer be living in Grinnell, Iowa, but in Washington. He was careful not to be too specific, but enough so that he saw the light dancing in her shrewd blue eyes. Loretta had a room full of crates holding a multitude of Rolodexes containing the names, phone numbers, and addresses of local contacts, county by county, a goddamn treasure trove, worth more than a sunken galleon bulging with salt-crusted Spanish doubloons. Loretta warranted his attention and Hoyle aimed to lavish it on her. For his part, Gustafson had his own reasons. He didn't want to move from Des Moines. He was like the fellow who jumped out of airplanes. When someone asked him if he really liked doing that, he said, "No." Then someone said, "Why do you do it?" And the fellow answered, "I don't like jumping out of airplanes, but I like to be around people who like to jump out of airplanes." Gustafson was a political junkie, with no known cure in sight. Frankly, Hoyle liked this kind better than any other. They never really presented any markers to you after it was over.

Yet Hoyle resented almost fiercely that one half of one percent of the voting populace in the nation would affect so mightily the question of who was going to run the country.

"The way I figure it, Hoyle," said Loretta in her Debra Winger hoarse voice, "is that Bill Rawlins has a very good chance to win this. It's not that our people are mad at the President, it's just that they feel he has let them down, on all fronts. They are hurt and puzzled. Bruce, living in Des Moines, has been spending his time cajoling the main elements in Kells' organization here. Oh, we don't have them all by any means, but we have—at least Bruce has —picked off the key leaders." Loretta still had her rural twang, which betrayed her origins at the University of Oklahoma before she married an Iowa-born internist, from whom she was now separated, which may have explained her obvious delight at the prospect of a move to Washington.

Hoyle turned to Bruce. "I agree, Hoyle," Gustafson said. "Loretta and I have made some very good progress. My guess is when Rawlins visits here day after tomorrow, we can move him around the state without having to make cold calls."

Bruce plopped down in front of Hoyle a thick packet of documents. "There's every possible delegate to the caucus, with a skinny on each of them. Loretta has checked it all out, and she agrees."

Looking through the document, Hoyle was mutely impressed: These sonsofbitches are real pros; they know their business. He stopped on a page. "What do these stars mean beside some of these names?"

Loretta said, "It means that delegate needs further work. That's why we are having small klatches in each city we'll be in, to give the Vice President time to work on the starred ones with some face-to-face charm."

"We suggest," said Bruce, "that the Vice President not get too specific about what he's going to do. What he needs to do is sort of muse about what has gone wrong, without clobbering the President, and suggest in his own way that we need to have a fresh new leader in order to get things sorted out the way they ought to be. He has to be really briefed on the farm problems, I mean really briefed. Nothing so pisses off our folks than some fellow out of state trying to talk about agriculture when he doesn't know a cabbage from a saxophone. He's got ranches, so he ought to know about the land."

It was really a stupid way to elect a President, thought Hoyle. In Iowa you didn't give a cow's pinkeye for what the state population cared or thought. You just zeroed in on a few appointed and anointed who had got their jollies "being involved" as delegates, or as Loretta had told him, "the caucuses get the blood flowing with a lot of folks down here." Hoyle reminded himself you could damn near paw every delegate to the caucus, one on one, feel up their leg and turn them on. Same thing in New Hampshire. Hoyle used to find it amusing if not downright pathetic that by the time the primaries got to California, the largest godfriggingdamn state in the Union, a few farmers and storekeepers in Iowa and New Hampshire had already cast the die. And then South Dakota got in its lick next. After that, the press declared "winners" and "momentum" and catalogued the losers, who may have gotten about three hundred votes less than the winners but were losers anyway. No matter, the press elite had anointed the victor. This was about as sensible as playing grabass in a downpour.

"Well, what do you say, Hoyle?" asked Loretta.

"He'll be well briefed," said Hoyle. "Wherever he goes he will be briefed, count on it, whether it's tugging at some milk cow's soggy teat in Iowa or kicking that Loeb paper's ass in New Hampshire."

Twenty-six

THE MAJORITY LEADER'S "hideaway" was on the second floor of the Capitol around the corridor from his main office. "Hideaways" were the provinces of the senior members of the Senate, off limits to all except those who were invited, and absolutely impervious to the prying eyes of the unwanted and the unknown and most of all to tourists or inquisitive constituents.

The Majority Leader was comforted by his hideaway. Above a lowboy was a James Bard sea scene; on the floor a late-eighteenth-century French Aubusson carpet of muted floral design. Two fine leather couches were separated by a long coffee table; bookshelves housed hundreds of volumes. A twenty-six-inch TV set glowed in a modular unit, which included compact disc player, FM and AM radio, and VCR. On the screen Senator Millard Hatchford of Florida, on the Senate floor, was declaiming the odious intrusions of an amendment curtailing the U.S. Navy in combating Caribbean drug traffic. No one in the room seemed to find this of even meager interest.

Raymond Tunstall poured himself a scotch and soda from the bookcase bar. Gifford Gray rubbed his bald head absently. Senator Homer Jefferson Wade, the Chairman of the Senate Foreign Relations Committee, puffed on his gnarled meerschaum pipe, the aromatic flavor filtering through the room. Vincent Canfield sat heavily on one of the couches, looking at the editorial page of the New York *Times*. Seated across from Canfield was General Thomas Tallant, Chairman of the Joint Chiefs of Staff.

"Care for anything, General?" Tunstall asked.

"No, sir," Tallant said.

Gifford Gray turned to face the General. "You were kind, General, to respond so quickly. Incidentally, Mr. Canfield understands everything said here is off the record."

The General nodded. Everyone knew that he was here only because of a request from Senator Gifford Gray, Chairman of the Senate Armed Services Committee.

Tunstall sat next to Canfield, and Gifford Gray next to Tallant.

"General," Gray said, "as I understand it, you feel that there is currently no visible restlessness in the Russian armed forces that would justify any anxiety on our part?"

"That's correct, sir."

"But surely, General," Canfield said, "the President's unfortunate gesture toward the new Chang government is viewed as a hostile act by the Soviets!"

"Sir, that is a matter for intelligence sources to surmise and for political leaders to judge," answered General Tallant. "But we have detected no extraordinary movement by the Soviet Union—perhaps because they already have a sizable force arrayed along their southern flank, and suitable air power as well. Our intelligence, cross-checked with the CIA, confirms this."

Gifford Gray turned to Tunstall, with a nod to Wade. "Any so-called 'crisis' with the Soviets over China is clearly nonexistent—though there's no guarantee there won't be one in the near future."

The General nodded.

Gray continued: "But a more pressing concern, it seems to me, is the tearing of this nation's spirit. If the President is to make a summit meeting with the Soviets a reality, if he is to begin repairing the economic damage, he's going to need assistance from the Majority Leader, from the Chairman of the Foreign Relations Committee—and some easing of damnation from the press."

Canfield flushed.

"I'm not unhappy with the President's press conference," Tunstall admitted. "But, Gifford—once a President loses public confidence, it's damn hard to retrieve it."

Wade nodded, jowls flapping.

Gifford Gray said, "Raymond, unless we preserve the integrity of the Senate, unless we resist whimsically deposing our own party's sitting President, we're letting loose political dogs of war that will stain this land, perhaps permanently."

Gray's voice grew lower. "I worry that Bill Rawlins has gone beyond what is right, to fulfill ambitions stirring inside him too long. Ambition, Raymond, raw, unbridled ambition is greed—and ego gone berserk. Unsuitable for a leader who ought to be cool-headed and wise. And I say this about a young man whose father was for many years my friend and supporter."

"Senator Gray," Canfield intoned, "what if General Tallant is wrong? He's not in possession of all that goes on inside the minds of the Soviet leaders. If Rawlins is elected, he's likely to nail down a firm agreement with the Soviets, and at the same time tackle the economy in ways that Kells, good man though he may be, has not."

Gifford Gray observed Canfield impassively, a scientist examining the results of a minor experiment. "Then the ends justify the means, Mr. Canfield? I suggest you reread Tacitus. In A.D. 69, four Roman emperors ascended, and three were brought down by the mob. He who wears a crown ripped rudely from his predecessor is himself vulnerable to the next would-be emperor."

Canfield began to respond, but Tunstall frowned at him. The columnist was clearly annoyed that Senator Gray would instruct him in the classics.

Gray stood. "Raymond, I will speak my mind in the Senate next week before adjournment. I will put on the record what I have expressed to you, my dear friend, and to all of you here."

Tunstall gathered himself to his feet. "The floor is yours whenever you want it, Gifford. I hesitate to counsel you, since I have looked to you so many times for counsel."

Gray's hand grazed Tunstall's shoulder affectionately.

Turning to General Tallant, Gray said softly, "General, thank you for joining us."

"Yes, General," Tunstall said. "You're always welcome here."

Canfield and Wade bowed slightly to the Chairman of the Joint Chiefs, and Tallant returned the gesture.

With Tallant gone, Tunstall turned to Wade and Canfield. "Would you mind, Homer, Vincent, if I had a private word with Gifford?"

Wade waved his hand. "Not at all, Leader. Always good to be with you, Gifford. Come along, Vincent—ah'll show you out of this rabbit warren."

Canfield sullenly trailed Wade out the door.

"Sit down, Gifford, please," Tunstall said.

Gray sat.

"I want to tell you something I should have spoken to you about sooner. Just before Bill announced his candidacy, I visited with a man close to the Soviet Ambassador—Vaslansky, his name is. Definitely KGB, but also a senior official at the Embassy. As you know, Berisov is a bit of a bungler, not nearly in Dobrynin's league, or even Dubinin's. Vaslansky said, in words not even couched in diplomatese, that if Rawlins were to be a candidate, the Kremlin would immediately come forward with positive proposals and back them up with quick implementation. Easing of controversy, cooperative ventures, and possibly a confirmable end to these nagging shots across each other's bow . . ."

"Did they seek you out?" Gray asked.

"As a matter of fact, yes."

"Why, do you suppose?"

Tunstall shrugged. "Probably because they don't trust Kells and those hawks around him. Probably because they think that with Rawlins in they could secure their U.S. flank and get on with getting their own country in order."

"Raymond, if they sought you out before Rawlins announced, maybe they approached Rawlins beforehand, too—to solicit his cooperation!"

"Gifford—"

"Consider this. The Soviets play a trump card we've never seen: encouraging a contender for the Presidency to make his move, promising that as soon as the election is over, he can close a deal with the Soviets redeeming his peace pledge to the people. At what price to the contender? What does Rawlins give up in return?"

Tunstall pursed his lips, sipped his drink thoughtfully.

Gray continued: "The FBI says a very important official with the KGB, named Federof, has been in Washington for some time. What is his role? He's superior to Vaslansky."

"Good God, Gifford, are you suggesting Bill Rawlins is in the employ of the Russians?"

"Of course not. He is—ambition aside—a patriot. But if you are as intelligent as Bill, and as confident of your own abilities, and are offered a Faustian bargain, and you believe you can handle the devil, even *use* him, why not take it? Remember, Bill Rawlins yields to no man in the assessment of his own capabilities."

"You mean, Bill is consorting with this Federof?" Tunstall fretted that he lacked the knowledge Gray had so readily. He made a mental note to query the FBI Director, as well as talk to Senator Francis Burgholtz, the Chairman of the Senate Intelligence Committee. He would fill in these gaps.

"I can't say that, Raymond," Gray said. "But Federof is no small fry. He's the power in the Embassy—Berisov's a nonperson there. And Federof has just gone back to the Soviet Union and recently returned."

Tunstall's inner feathers were ruffled. Gray had pulled the rug out from under him with his clearly superior access to facts that Tunstall, despite his vaunted network, simply didn't have.

"Things are going on, Raymond, things that you and I, who ought to be aware, are not aware of." The old Senator thrust his hands in trouser pockets. He rocked gently on his heels. "I am troubled, Raymond. There is some odd, dark vision at work here. It bothers me."

Tunstall nodded, then raised his glass. "To my best intelligence source."

Gifford Gray smiled faintly, nodded, opened the door and was gone.

Raymond Tunstall put his glass on the table. He stood silently for a long minute before he turned to the phone.

. . . .

In his room at the Jefferson Hotel, Hoyle Henderson handed a diet cola to Mike Carson while Bill Rawlins sat quietly, looking on.

"Can't stay long, Bill," Carson said.

"Mike, the President's dead in the water. I'm not suggesting you denounce him, or resign in despair or anything. I count you one of the rising stars of our country. When I'm President, I just want you to know I want you in my Cabinet, heading Health and Human Resources or Education, whichever you want. Of course, I also think you'd make a fine Secretary of State."

Mike Carson took care not to reveal his heart leaping inside him. He took a slow drink of the cola. "That's quite an offer, Bill. But what can I offer you in return? You said no denunciation, no resignation, and I agree with you—I find both those options unwise."

"Just know that when I win this election, you'll be in power, far beyond what you have now. And if you get restless in the Cabinet, keep in mind my brother Roger's looking into the purchase of a major daily newspaper, maybe a large entertainment enterprise. You'll have the option of the Cabinet or going with Roger. What I'm saying to you, Mike, is you have alternatives with me."

Hoyle knew that Carson was mesmerized by the wealth, the personal force of Rawlins. He was caving fast. But, Hoyle reminded himself, you never really knew about this slippery Presidential press secretary.

Carson spoke slowly. "Let's leave it this way. I think you ought to be President. My boss is going off track on too many issues. I think you'd set things right. And let's say that I find what you say to be attractive. Maybe I'll be able to help you from the inside. Does that sound reasonable?"

Bill Rawlins clapped his hands noiselessly. "Sounds reasonable. Let's leave it the way you say."

When Mike Carson closed the door behind him, Hoyle said, "He's hooked, Bill. When you mentioned Secretary of State, I thought he was going to piss in his pants."

There was an odd look in Rawlins' eyes. "He's hooked all right. And do you know why? Because he's a bit like me. He's impatient. He wants it *all*, right now. You see, I know that about myself. But young Mr. Carson doesn't. He'll destroy himself. Sooner, maybe later, but surely."

"What the hell are you getting at, Bill?"

Rawlins cocked an amused gaze at Henderson. "Hoyle, you're so used to kicking a guy in the balls, you don't realize you can kill him with anticipation."

With Toni Georgihu at his side, Clem fished nervously in his pocket for the key to his apartment. Tomorrow morning he would accompany the President on the trip to Los Angeles, so this evening had to be fitted into a very tight schedule.

"I'm having second thoughts about inviting you for a drink. This place doesn't win any *House Beautiful* awards."

Toni touched him on the arm. "Why should it? You live at the White House anyway, don't you?"

"Yeah," said Clem. "Maybe that's the reason."

They stepped into the K Street apartment, a nondescript couch against one wall, a large unpainted bookcase filled to overflowing, a bargain-basement coffee table on whose brownish top were magazines and newspapers. A large window. The sky was open, clear, fresh.

Toni surveyed the room. "No, your home did not make the cut in the *House Beautiful* awards. But it did win the Most Possibilities for Improvement laurel."

Clem put on the coffee table a bottle of wine he extracted from his bookcase, a corked, half-full bottle of Mondavi cabernet sauvignon. He poured into two small plastic containers. "I'm sorry I don't have wineglasses. I'm not Washington's most honored host."

She picked up one of the plastic containers. "Clem, you may start a trend here, though the environmentalists would frown."

They drank slowly, silently.

Clem put his glass down on the coffee table. She did the same. He moved closer to her, his eyes fixed straight on hers, at the same level. He put his arms around her, feeling a slight resistance at first, then she seemed to relax, ever so slightly. He felt her back, her waist, firm, no vagrant flesh, taut, yet smoothly pliable. He kissed her lightly, then harder, more fervently. Her mouth was slightly open. He held her closer.

She broke away abruptly.

"Clem, we're moving fast. I know that sounds silly, almost

childish. But it's been a long time for me, a long time since I have felt what I'm feeling now."

"What we're both feeling now," said Clem, still holding onto her hand.

"All right, what we're both feeling. But you and I are deeply involved in something terribly important. We need to be very professional, and I am tonight about to lose all my professionalism—among other things."

He came closer, very close, stretching his body next to hers. She withdrew slightly, and then she pressed against him. She saw his eyes, alight, fervent. "Oh, Clem, I feel exactly what you feel. It's just going faster than I thought it would. I may sound like a schoolgirl, but I am not young anymore, as well we both know.

"Who's counting," murmured Clem.

"How on earth can you and I think through the mean problem we both face when we are"—she stopped for a second—"when we are causing each other a lot of emotion? Though I have to confess it's a nice, most inviting emotion."

"What do you suggest?" said Clem, voice slightly ragged.

"Oh, to hell with it," she said wantonly. She kissed him passionately. They held each other, Clem's arms wandering up and down her back.

"What I suggest," he said softly, "is that we talk this over more comfortably."

He moved her in the manner of a couple stiffly dancing with slow mincing steps, until she collided against the bed and fell across it, Clem on top of her, murmuring into her ear.

She giggled. "Do you know that in all my Bureau training they never instructed me in the proper defense for this kind of move."

Clem's hand was inside her blouse.

"Toni, dear Toni, if you'll hold still, and if we do this right, maybe they'll put it in the Bureau training manual."

Clem was rather amazed at his poise.

Twenty-seven

AIR FORCE ONE sailed majestically through the sky, skimming gracefully through a blurred morning haze.

The wide-bodied 747 offered accommodations of quiet, uncrowded luxury to the Chief Executive, including a master bedroom, spacious toilet facilities, a roomy shower with sufficient closet space to house the President's and the First Lady's traveling wardrobe, as well as a grand Presidential office. Aft of the Presidential bedroom and sprawling gracefully from the front entry to midship was the airborne paneled Presidential office, and aft of the office was seating for staff and press.

On the top deck of the huge plane was a galaxy of communication gadgetry enabling the President to exercise his authority swiftly and securely no matter his pinpointed locale in the sky.

The President lounged back in his thickly cushioned chair. Clem Barkley sat before him, as well as John Wingate and Willacy Hughes. Clem mused at the electrifying effect *Air Force One* produced in whatever audience was in attendance when it landed. They would be setting down in a half hour at Los Angeles International Airport, where all air traffic would be restricted until the President's craft had squished to its usual feathery landing. President Kells always regretted the torment of interrupting air flow into the airfield of *Air Force One*'s destination. "It is not calculated to win friends and votes when passengers find out they are being relegated to a holding pattern while the President lands," he said.

But Clem Barkley was not fretting. Whenever the silver-bodied Presidential plane with stately blue lettering UNITED STATES OF AMERICA marching across the flanks of the aircraft came into view, onlookers were recipients of a palpable thrill. Barkley once remarked that the picture of *Air Force One* landing, taxiing confidently from the runway to its positioned space at the airfield, coming to a stop so that the President could stand in the exit way, poised for a moment, hand outstretched in warm and friendly greeting, was worth five thousand votes each memorable moment. Whatever the cost to the Reelect the President Committee, it was surely worth it.

Willacy shuffled papers in front of him. He peered over his reading glasses at the President.

"The polls managed to get worse, somehow," Willacy said. "Rawlins' early movement has had its effect." He thumbed through papers. "We can't shake the inflation rise, the high interest rise . . ."

The President gazed out the window at the wisp of thin clouds marring an otherwise unblemished day. "It's not going to be easy to remedy the economy. That takes time. What disturbs me is public opinion on our Soviet policy." He turned to Wingate. "What we're trying to do is to preserve our sense of balance. If we disturb one part of the arena, the other part will also be shaken."

Clem said, "The CIA notes possible internal wrangling inside the U.S.C.R. The new leader is not yet fully in command, though outwardly he seems to be."

"If there's any kind of new direction from the Soviets to try to take advantage of eastern European turmoil," the President said solemnly, "we will certainly be at risk—even if Raymond Tunstall and Homer Wade can't see it."

"I know that, Mr. President," Willacy said. "Everybody around you knows that, but Bill Rawlins and his crowd have the press in their pocket. Let me nail Rawlins to the wall! He's a dangerous man, malignantly ambitious, too rich to bother about little items like funding. Let me strip him of his pretenses and show him to the country for the rogue he is."

Clem laughed. "Any minute now, Willacy, you'll call him a 'knave.' Or maybe a 'cad.'"

The President smiled, then the smile disappeared. "Willacy, I'm not comfortable with that kind of campaign. I chose Bill Rawlins because he has a first-rate mind. Ambitious, yes, and a bit of a demagogue, perhaps, but a superior public man. I chose him, so I must bear the brunt of whatever faults he may have."

A steward quietly entered the Presidential compartment and bent near Clem's ear.

"Excuse me, Mr. President," Clem said, standing. "Toni Georgihu's on the phone. She says it's urgent."

The President, frowning thoughtfully, nodded.

At the communications console, Clem said to the staff sergeant manning it, "Secure line, please."

The technician flipped a switch, turned a knob, and handed a bulky phone set to Clem. "You're secure, sir."

"Can you hear me, Toni?"

"Loud and clear, Clem," she said. Her voice sounded metallic.

"What's so urgent?"

"Bad news, Clem. Very bad."

Clem gripped the phone, his throat constricting.

"What is it?"

"The two Bulgarians we had under surveillance have been assassinated. Messy piece of business."

"Christ!"

"It gets worse. The District police picked up Terry Geer two hours ago on an anonymous tip."

"Picked him up? What the hell for?"

"The tip said Terry was stealing top-secret government papers. Also that he was dealing drugs."

"What? That's absolutely crazy, totally insane!"

"Tell me about it. But the police got a search warrant and headed for Terry's home. Someone had the good sense to alert Chief Wiggins of the impending search of the apartment of a key Presidential aide. The Chief called me immediately. I got out to the house about ten minutes after the District cops arrived."

He hated to ask. "What did they find?"

"Pasted to the upper shelf of the bookcase in his living room, a thin folder. Inside . . . top-secret memorandum on Zeus missiles for deployment on the Trident Mark II."

Clem felt a monstrous tightening in his chest. "God, I remember that meeting! Only one copy of that memorandum was in existence. The President wanted no copies made. John Wingate saw it. I read it. And of course, the Secretary of State, the Secretary of Defense."

"Was Terry privy to it?"

"Yes. Terry and I were the only staff present. Toni, this has got to be a setup!"

"The officers also brought along a dope-sniffing dog. It prowled the house. Started howling and carrying on when the cops put all of Terry's kitchen containers on the floor. In the sugar jar was about a kilo of cocaine in neat plastic bags."

Clem wanted to scream. "Toni—who the hell hides coke in a sugar container? That's the first place to look."

Toni's voice was calm. "You're right, Clem. But the document appears authentic, and the coke sure as hell is real. Damn near undiluted."

"What's Terry's status now?"

"He's in jail. Been there since they searched his apartment. What do you want done?"

"Play it by the book, Toni. The President wouldn't want it to appear Terry's getting any special treatment. Willacy'll call you in a few minutes. He'll get someone down to the jail and bail Terry out, as well as counsel him." He sighed. "I'll tell the President."

"Clem, I don't think I should talk to Willacy Hughes. The FBI has to be open on this one, so when the Director's asked, we can say we *did* play this one by the book."

"I agree and I understand, but please, Toni—find out what the hell is *really* going on. My money says someone in Rawlins' camp has thrown a time bomb into Terry's apartment set to go off in the President's face."

"Clem—I saved the worst for last."

"Oh, Christ. What now? Drugs and secret papers in *my* apartment?"

"Close. We found Terry Geer's phone number in a bureau drawer in the hotel room where the two Bulgarians were killed."

Twenty-eight

THE ARREST of Terence Geer assaulted Washington as a massive thunderclap violates the serenity of a neighborhood.

Dan Rather on "CBS News" called Geer's alleged felonies "a bizarre, unexplainable act." The New York *Times* in its lead editorial lamented that "this bewildering event has intruded on an Administration already battered." David Broder, on the front page of the Washington *Post*, posed the cheerless question, "Why and how did this happen?"

The subject of the Capital's and the nation's scrutiny was sunk in a stupor in the study of Willacy Hughes' home on Kalorama Road in the northwest quadrant of Washington. Clem Barkley and Willacy sat in front of him. Clem and Willacy had just arrived after a commercial flight from Los Angeles to Washington.

The shell-shocked Geer had already described his humiliation to them, his arrest, the snap of manacles on his wrists behind him, the booking, fingerprinting, mug shots, a dozen policemen surrounding him at the station house, the clanging of the jail door after he was flung into a cell. Now Terry would have to run a gauntlet of every camera crew in North America; already the media were hammering away at the grotesque political event. Geer did not look up now as Willacy and Clem questioned him.

"Terry," Willacy said, "listen to me, and look at me."

Geer only shook his head, cradling it in his hands, fingers digging into his temples. His breath came in short jerks.

Willacy Hughes grabbed him by the shoulders and shook him. "Goddamnit, look at me! How can I get to the bottom of this frame-up unless you cooperate?"

Geer slowly raised his face, a face suddenly grown old.

"Did you," Willacy asked, "bring those documents home? And if you didn't, can you remember anyone who might have? Could you have been drunk, and someone brought you home?"

"Goddamnit, Willacy, I don't get drunk at the White House, or any fucking where!"

Clem was relieved to see Terry reacting with some spine. He asked, "Have you had any meetings with anyone outside work that might have some bearing on this? Does anyone else have a key to your apartment?"

Geer shook his head again. "Nobody else has a key."

"Any strange calls lately," Willacy asked, "either at the White House, or at home?"

"None."

"Did you mention the documents to anyone in the West Wing or anyone in the government?"

Geer seemed on the verge of tears. "No."

Willacy sat. He jotted a note on the yellow legal-sized foolscap paper in his lap. "Terry, someone you know or don't know managed, somehow, to get into your apartment, and more impressively, spend enough time there to find a hiding place for those documents, and drugs . . . Any guests . . ."

Geer's eyes widened. "Jesus—a few nights ago, I did have a guest, a woman." His eyes narrowed. "Greta— God, I don't want to believe that . . ."

"Who the hell is Greta?" Clem demanded.

Geer stood, his legs trembling. He paced, then stopped before Willacy.

And he recounted, in as much detail as he could summon, his recent evening which had begun at the Corcoran Gallery; Willacy took hurried notes.

"I tried to call her the next day," Geer said, "but the number she gave me didn't answer. No answering machine, either."

"Address?"

"All I got was the phone number. She said she was going out of town for a day or two, but then we'd have dinner again."

"I'll check the phone number," Clem said. "The FBI can trace her address from that. You know, I remember her, vaguely, from the gallery—a real traffic-stopper."

"When she stumbled into you," Willacy said to Geer, "spilling that glass of wine, it may have been deliberate."

Geer shrugged helplessly. "I was just standing there with John Wingate and suddenly she appeared . . ."

Clem said, "I'll follow up with John. Maybe he remembers something you don't. Are you *sure* there was no one else with the same accessibility to your apartment as she had?"

"No—no one else. I've had no one at my apartment for over two weeks. I have a maid who comes in but she does a lot of apartments in my building. You can check her out."

"Damn straight," Willacy said. "What about your office staff, your secretary, anyone you work with at the White House?"

"God no, Willacy. My secretary is a professional, she's been there since the Carter Administration."

"We'll check her anyway," Clem said, knowing Geer was right. The secretaries to Presidential aides had withstood the most thorough security checks.

Willacy turned to Clem. "I think you better call Toni Georgihu right away."

Clem nodded, picked up the phone, dialed Toni, and got her at once. He quickly filled her in.

"Switzerland, free-lance journalist," she said, taking notes. "Okay. Does Terry know when and where she arrived in the U.S.?"

Clem turned and asked him.

"She didn't say, and I didn't ask." Geer smiled humorlessly. "I guess I did most of the talking that night."

"Hear that, Toni?" Clem asked.

"I heard. Ask Terry to write down a detailed description of the woman."

"We'll also get John Wingate to do the same," Clem said.

"Good. How was she able to attend the Corcoran evening? Was it a fund-raiser, or invitation only?"

Clem beckoned to Geer. "Get on the other phone, so you can answer Toni's questions."

Geer took the hallway phone and told her, "Invitation, Toni. The evening was underwritten by Occidental Petroleum and IBM. It's no big deal getting an invitation to something like that in Washington, if you really want to go."

Clem broke in. "Terry's right—my invitation came to me from a Senator who couldn't go and gave me his tickets."

"I'll check it tomorrow," Toni said. "In the meantime, I'll track her address from the phone number and we'll pay her a visit."

"If she hasn't already flown the coop," Clem said.

"But if she has," Toni said, "that tells us something in and of itself."

They made hasty good-byes and hung up.

Geer came back into the study, sighing. "God, what a mess. What . . . what did the President say about all this?"

"Terry," Willacy said, "you're to stay away from the White House. The President has asked that you either stay with me and my family here, or at your place. I am going to have some protection for you if you go back home."

"I'll go to my place. But how the hell did I get elected fall guy in this farce?"

Clem shrugged. "You're single, and could take a girl back to your place. This was a well-conceived and professionally-designed trap."

"And I was the mouse they sprung it on," Geer said bitterly.

"Well, I can't blame you," Clem said. "I *saw* the cheese . . ."

They were having sandwiches in the kitchen, eating slowly and enjoying the silence when the phone rang. Willacy picked it up and it was Toni; she wanted Clem.

Clem took the phone. "Got something already?"

"Not much. I dispatched two agents to Greta Hulved's apartment. She's not at home and hasn't been there for two days. I've put out an alert; we're flagging her passport. An FBI artist will be with you in a few minutes to work with Terry on a sketch which we'll distribute to the bus stations and airports . . ."

. . . .

A slightly dumpy, gray-haired woman in a dark cloth coat, a dingy carryall over her shoulder, held out her ticket at the Delta ticket counter in Newark International Airport.

The petite young black woman behind the counter looked at the tourist-class ticket, flight 467, bound for Dallas/Ft. Worth, and then on to Mexico City, departing in one hour.

"May I see your passport?"

The thick-waisted woman fished about in her carryall and produced a German passport identifying her as Hilda Mertz.

"Where would you like to sit?" asked the clerk.

"Any window seat," the woman said in a guttural accent.

"I have you in 18A. That's nonsmoking. Is that all right?"

The woman nodded. She put her ticket and her passport in the cloth bag and walked unsteadily to the passenger area where she sat and waited quietly for the departure announcement.

The press briefing was taking place in the small ballroom of the Century Plaza Hotel in Los Angeles, the same hotel in which the President and his party were staying. Immediately on landing in Los Angeles, the President had instructed Mike Carson to conduct the briefing. Inside the ballroom over a hundred reporters had crammed into the seats available.

The din was growing, a bustle of voices in a room redolent with anxiety. Mike Carson stood behind a makeshift lectern.

He held up his hand to try to slacken the racket that was growing deafening to him.

"Now, here is what we have." The buzzing in the room subsided. "Terence Geer, Special Assistant to the President, is now on bail pending a hearing on possession of classified Defense Department documents and possession of an illegal substance. That is all we know. Except Willacy Hughes, the lawyer representing Mr. Geer, has issued a statement saying that it is so gross a frame-up it can hardly pass even the simplest inspection."

Andrea Mitchell of NBC was on her feet. "Frame-up? Who is doing the framing, Mike? You have any evidence of that? We understand that a secret document, highly classified, was found in his library and that cocaine was found in his apartment. Now, who is framing whom, and why?"

Carson coughed. "I have no evidence, Andrea, I am only reporting what Terry's lawyer has said. He said it was a tank job because there is no motive of any kind, no prior experience that would lead even the functionally illiterate to suspect Terry Geer is a goddamn spy and drug dealer. Hell, he doesn't even smoke."

"What's smoking got to do with dealing?" cried a voice from the rear of the room.

Paul Taylor of the *Post* spoke up: "What is the President's reaction, Mike?"

"The President has put Terry on leave of absence without pay, and if he is indicted, Terry will resign from the White House. The President has faith in Terry's innocence and once this misadventure has been resolved, Terry will be back on the White House staff."

"Then he is sacked for now, right?" said Marvin Drayle of the Cox newspapers.

"Sacked? For Chrissake, Marvin, give us a break. Terry is off the payroll while this plays out. The President, I repeat, has confidence that Terry will be vindicated, no question about that."

"What about others on the staff? Has there been any evidence of drug-taking by staff members?"

Carson's jaw tightened. "What a pissy question. Of course not. No drugs of any kind have ever been detected around here and if it had been, you characters would have been all over me like a rash, which, I might add, is what you are giving me right now."

"No need to lose your cool, Mike," said Drayle.

"Losing cool—who the hell is losing cool?"

"Will the President issue any personal statement about this?"

"No," said Carson, "I just told you his reaction. But the President believes, along with Mr. Hughes, that someone, for whatever motive, has deliberately used Mr. Geer as a setup for political reasons."

Wesley Wanger of *Newsweek* spoke up: "Mike, unless you tell us who is setting Geer up, or who you think is setting him up, how can we absorb this frame-up story you are telling? Are you saying this is a dirty trick by the Rawlins' people, and if not them, who would want to poison the well?"

"No comment on that, Wes, just write it down that it is a frame, from start to finish. You don't work with a man like Terry Geer as long as I have and as long as the President has and not know that this is a sleazoid setup of the rankest kind."

"Mike, tell us about the highly classified document," said Winona Crider of CNN. "Why would Terry Geer keep it in his home, and is there any evidence of any kind that contact with foreign powers was made to peddle the document or whatever he intended to do with it?"

"The document is highly classified, as you just said, which means I cannot tell you what it is. It is definitely top secret and it is definitely something we would not want to fall in foreign hands. But to answer your question, why would Terry Geer want to have it in his home . . . Well, why would he? The answer is that someone put it there, and Terry is totally innocent."

"Top secret, you say," Andrea Mitchell said, "yet it is found in Terry Geer's apartment. If he didn't take it, how on earth could a top-secret paper find its way there, and who would leave it there, if Terry didn't? Mike, this isn't Twenty Questions time, but we are getting off into goofy territory."

Mike threw up his hands. "Goofy, who's goofy? The only thing that's goofy is how otherwise intelligent people can't see the absurdity of all this."

Pete Wissanski of the Chicago *Sun Times* yelled, "Mike, would you like a Valium?" The crowd laughed uproariously. Carson scowled. Then the questioning began again.

"When will the President have something to say personally about this?"

"No precise time on that, but you can be sure he will not be silent."

After the briefing, Rick Gleason of the Los Angeles *Times* closeted with Mike Carson. "Mike, let's roll back the cover on this. What's going on? Is the White House in such disarray that Terry Geer can feel free to do all this shit?"

Mike leaned back in his chair. "Off the record?"

"Sure."

"It's scary. Obviously Rawlins and his camp are not involved. It's too obvious for that. But I have to honestly tell you, I cannot confirm that Terry is innocent, just as I can't tell you he is guilty."

Gleason smelled the odor of crucial information. "What you are saying, off the record of course, is that the White House cannot categorically deny Terry was dealing, and they cannot confirm he wasn't. Is that the size of it? And the reason is, nobody in the White House knows what the hell is going on? Who's running the rebuttal in the White House—Barkley, Willacy Hughes, who?"

Carson turned in his swivel chair to face the wall. "Willacy's not really calling the shots."

Gleason stared at him.

"We're deep off the record, Rick," Carson said. "You know the rules."

Gleason looked properly somber and nodded. "Mike, I know the rules. Trust me. Can't confirm innocence, Clem Barkley steering the charade. Right?"

Mike rose to his feet. "I didn't say that, Rick, now did I?"

Gleason grinned malevolently. "Of course, you didn't, Mike, of course you didn't."

Twenty-nine

THE DUMPY gray-haired woman peered out the taxi window onto a narrow, dimly-lit street just off Reforma Boulevard in Mexico City. The turnoff was a mile and a half from Chapultepec Palace. She frowned as she searched out the street numbers, then she said in halting Spanish to the driver, "Aquí, aquí. Esta casa a la izquierda. Muchas gracias."

The driver half-turned, and fumbled to give her change for the large peso note, but she waved it off and sent him on his way.

She rummaged through her handbag for a silver key, which she used in the door of an apartment on the ground floor of a mostly unkempt complex. Inside, she snapped on the overhead light. The place was small, drably furnished, but seemed clean.

She threw down her carryall, discarded the cloth coat, and clawed off the dress and the thick padding held in place around her hips by Velcro. She whipped off the wig, and shook free glowing chestnut hair.

Greta Hulved fetched from the carryall a thin cashmere robe, which she shrugged on. She ran a hot bath, checked for towels, and, when the tub was almost full, removed her robe and slipped into the comforting warmth of the water. She scrubbed herself with a fresh bar of soap, then stretched out languorously.

She was to wait here one day, at least. She would be contacted within that time with new instructions. She prayed it would be back home to Leipzig. She'd performed well. There would be no lamentable postmortems about where she failed or how she could have achieved more. That pleasant young man, Geer, figured only fleetingly in her thoughts as she stirred and stretched in the water.

Then she sat erect, splashing the floor.

Had she heard something? She looked toward the bathroom door. Yes, she heard a noise, the sound of footsteps.

And now he was in the doorway, a bulky man with heavy features, half-smiling as he gazed down on her nudity.

Startled, without thinking, she slid down in the tub again, as if the water would hide or protect her.

"Madame Mertz—Wayne asked me to call on you. I have news about your brother. May I chat with you?"

It was the prescribed greeting.

Her jangled nerves began to reassemble. She reached down to the floor for the large towel, drew it to her and, dripping more water on the bare floor, wrapped it around her as she stood up.

"I hardly expected you to enter while I was bathing."

The large man gestured absently. "We all do our job, Madame Mertz. You must do yours, and I must do mine."

He turned casually and walked into the bedroom.

Clutching the towel around her, she followed. "Are you to give me my instructions as to when and how I leave here? Do I go back to Leipzig?"

The large man, standing at the foot of the bed, turned slightly and held out a sheet of paper. She walked toward him to read it. As she did, she felt his hand on her neck.

The breath froze inside her and she was stricken with woozy, indescribable pain. She was thrown on the bed, towel flapping loose, leaving her naked and wet. The man withdrew a long, thin knife, its blade shimmering from the bathroom light. He leaned over her and put its razor-sharp point at the left side of her throat.

"If you move one inch, Madame Mertz, you will die."

She wanted to scream, but obeyed. She didn't move. Was this brute an impostor? How could he have a key, how could he have known the coded greeting, unless he was her real contact?

The large man, still holding the knife, his eyes solemnly fastened on her, began to remove his trousers with his left hand. My God, she thought, this foolish man wants to rape me! She almost lost her fear and only just managed to restrain a smile. Stupid idiot, didn't he know that she could, if she chose, find ways to report this fatuous behavior? But for now, she would simply lie there and let this cretin pump her a while. Perhaps she ought to help him speed up the process.

"You don't need a knife," she said softly, trying not to betray her fear. "Here let me help you," and she reached out to pull his boxer shorts off him. The large man, still solemn, said nothing, though still holding the knife upright at his side. She gently removed the shorts. He stood there, clad in his jacket and shirt, but naked from the waist down.

He was ready for her, turgid, throbbing. Without a word he fell heavily upon her, the knife still in his right hand, emitting a rough groan as he thrust into her, the back of his right fist squarely on the bed, the blade upright. She held the back of his head, pulled him closer and moaned with him, though she felt nothing except a mounting revulsion and the urgent need to get this boor off her stomach and out of her and then get from him her new instructions.

He was huge, deep inside her. There was nothing but grating, guttural noises spilling from his mouth, so near her face, sputtering, heavy lips in motion against her neck. He groaned louder this time, his body in a momentary spasm, and she could feel him spewing inside her, seemingly without end. She lay quite still now, waiting for him to rise off her.

He lay there, an elephant of a man, inert, heaving with quick breaths. Then he slowly moved off her. She rose to a squat on the bed. "Can you tell me . . ." she started to say, but the blow was blinding, too fast for her to evade, too swift and too heavy to feel pain. His fist hit her with such brutish impact she felt nothing at all as she was hurled back by the velocity of the blow.

The large man wiped himself on the towel, drew on his shorts and trousers, moving slowly but efficiently. He picked up the towel where he had flung it on the floor, and wrapped her in it as neatly as he could. He put the knife back in his belt. He took a paper bag out of his jacket pocket and moved about the room, picking up her purse and clothing and stuffing it in the paper bag. He bent over and, with apparent ease, picked up the towel-clad woman, slung her over his shoulder like a sack of grain. He opened the door. He looked to his right and his left in the hazy darkness. No one was to be seen. With an agility that belied his bulk, he moved across the walk, opened the back door of the car and flung her inside.

He did a U-turn in the narrow street, backing up and then going forward. He turned right on Reforma and drove slowly, attracting no attention. He turned right again, this time down another narrow street, which debouched into a deadend where there appeared a half-built concrete structure glowering in the darkness. It was some building that had given up the construction ghost, lying there, half erect and half skeleton. He stopped. He turned and looked around him. Again, no one in sight.

He opened the back door quickly, picked up the woman and disappeared through a patch of bare ground into the half-finished structure. He could feel her faintly breathing. Good.

Yesterday he had surveyed this place carefully. He knew exactly where he wanted to go, an open room, no roof, only bare walls, with a worn canvas on the ground where some weeks earlier stonemasons had labored.

He put the woman on the canvas, carefully removed the towel. Then he reached inside his jacket and extracted the long thin knife, and put the large paper sack beside the woman. He leaned over her. The woman was still unconscious, but beginning to stir slightly, a low moan slipping through her lips. He slowly put the knife edge to her throat and, as her eyelids fluttered, rammed it in. The knife punctured the artery as if it were guided by lasers. The blood spurted. He drew the whetted steel across and deep into her neck, slicing through what had once been so slenderly sculptured. He had carefully moved to his left, and the cascading blood, its trajectory a dark crimson stream in a drooping arc, puddled at the edge of the canvas.

He withdrew the knife, pulled some paper tissues from his

jacket pocket, thoroughly cleaned the blade before reinserting it in a thin holster attached to his belt. He fished in his pocket for a metal-jacketed lighter, flicked it to flame, and stoically burned the tissue. He rubbed the ashes into the stony dirt, smoothing it out with his hands, then wiping them on his trouser leg.

She lay there, her nude, beautiful frame deprived of all life now, the breasts still full and only slightly flattened against her chest. Her long legs, now carelessly slack, were wide and invitingly apart. He opened the paper bag. He drew out the dress she had worn and tore it down the side. He opened the purse and left it beside the dress, the clasp still open, all of its contents gone. He carefully let her undergarments float to the dirty canvas.

He stood over her. When someone found her, the police would come and they would stand over her as he did now. The legs would still be apart, beckoning to the detectives' assumption that someone had earlier penetrated her; there in the thick, reddish hair where her legs parted, a vile man had buried himself. They would make their investigations. They would search the fingerprint files, and connect nothing. After a while, they would mark the file as still open but the body unidentifiable. Terrible, the authorities would say, but it happens too often to be called bizarre. When they burrowed further they would be told by the medical examiner that there was indeed evidence of sperm in her vagina. They would furiously scribble in their notepads that this was clearly a violent and vicious rape, that this lovely woman either lived in Mexico City or arrived here as a visitor, address unknown.

The large man stood silent, still gazing at her, her head now lolling at an awkward angle. He looked carefully about him. He put her passport in his pocket. He would later burn it. He efficiently folded the white towel, tucked it under his arm, along with the empty paper sack, and walked slowly through the open skeletal archway, peered again at the street, waited patiently for fully five minutes, then walked slowly to his car. He would park it near the safe house, walk into that apartment once more to tidy it up, and dispose of whatever she might have left behind. He would destroy the towel and paper sack, and return the car to the rental agency where he had paid cash for its use. Only then would he board a plane to Rio and, after one day, fly to Lisbon and catch a flight to Washington.

Having considered all this quite thoroughly, Vlady Miektor slowly accelerated his car back to Reforma Boulevard. It might be several days before Greta Hulved's first and only visit to Mexico City would be discovered.

Thirty

CLEM BARKLEY clasped his head with his hands and leaned back in his chair.

Willacy Hughes fished through the stack of papers in front of him and lifted out a sheet. They'd been meeting in Clem's office for over thirty minutes.

Willacy gave Clem a xerox of the front page of the Los Angeles *Times*. "This story is all over the country and it's poison for you, and, I might add, for the President as well. It blames you for botching the President's campaign. Our friend at the Los Angeles *Times* didn't just dream it. Who's leaking, Clem?"

Clem threw the xeroxed clip at the wastebasket. "I'm trying to figure that out even as we speak, though I've got to tell you I think I know."

"Well, you better caulk that hole, my young Presidential Assistant, else we'll be looking like a shuttlecock in a badminton game faster than you think."

"Willacy, I got the message," said Clem.

"The Washington *Post,* as I need not inform you, is following up on Gleason's LA *Times* diatribe." Willacy held up another xerox. "This asshole at the *Post* says flatly that the President can't deny anything about Terry because we have no knowledge whatsoever that he was or was not dealing. They claim the White House is a house of mirrors, out of control, sloppily managed. How the hell do they come up with that kind of story?"

"Come on, Willacy, get off my case."

The President's trip to Los Angeles had tottered and wobbled as the questions about Terry persisted. The President was equable in public, as television reports of his California visit confirmed, but Clem, watching him closely on the screen, saw the gray fatigue that had begun to etch his face. The President had arrived back at the White House several hours ago, and Willacy and Clem awaited his presence.

"Look," said Clem, "it could be worse, though I have to say I am not sure how. I suggested to the President that we just simply put a lid on answering any more questions. Mike Carson says we can't. We have to get up front with this story, he claims, and do the best we can, which, by the way, is precious little right now. Can we manage any rebellions in Latin America or maybe a coup in eastern Europe in the next twenty-four hours?"

"You're a real hoot today, Clem. I've sent the President a memorandum. Here's a copy of it. I'm on your side of this one." He flipped a two-page document to Barkley.

"What it says," said Willacy, "is that the President must get this behind him, quick. Best way to do that is simply have the same answer to every question, and that is, 'I am sorry, ladies and gentlemen, but this matter is in the hands of the authorities. I am confident it will be suitably answered for everyone. Next question.' Anything more than that, and we keep the prosecution alive for the rest of the campaign. You agree? Do you believe our dear beloved friends in the press will let him get away with that?"

"We have to try," said Clem. "Mike may have other ideas. But there's no law, either civil or canon, that requires all questions by the press to be answered. Your advice to the President is sound."

The door to Clem's office opened. The President walked in. They both stood up, and he gestured to them to sit.

"I have read your memo, Willacy, and as usual it is on the mark." He turned to Clem. "I've asked Mike to step in. Go over Willacy's paper with him. This is the way we will handle it. By the way, any late news about Terry's status? Have you talked to the FBI?"

"No, sir, we don't have any later news," said Clem. "I'll be talking to Toni Georgihu before the night is done."

Mike Carson entered the office, nodding to everyone, a casual smile across his bearded face. The President gazed absently at Barkley. "Clem, don't feel too bad about those stories now churning out. Just remember, it's not your hide they want to nail to the wall, it's mine."

Clem smiled wanly.

"Oh yes, Clem," the President said in a casual tone as if he were conveying the weather forecast, "you, Mike, and Willacy should know I am asking the Secretary of Transportation if he will accept the Vice Presidency. I want to present his nomination to the Senate this week before they adjourn. We dare not leave that spot vacant too long. I appreciated your memoranda to me about that appointment."

Clem Barkley nodded, not entirely surprised but a bit disappointed. "Peter Roncalli is a good choice, Mr. President. He's loyal, and he's a decent man and a former Senator, so he ought to be an easy confirm."

Carson nodded. "He's as good as anyone, Mr. President."

"And," said Willacy, "he's not going to push you down any tall stairs. You can trust him."

"You have a skeptical mind, Willacy. That's the danger of living in this city too long," said the President.

He waved warmly at them and closed the door behind him.

Willacy turned to Mike Carson. "Can we handle the press as I have suggested?"

"Not sure, Willacy. This Geer thing smells to high heaven. If we just say, 'It's in the hands of the authorities,' it sounds too much like a fellow caught in the act who says he can't talk about it because it's part of litigation and in the courts. Won't sell, Willacy."

"Come on, Mike," said Clem. "You know Terry Geer. You know this is bald bullshit, from start to finish."

"You know it, I know it, but I am saying to you, we have nothing, absolutely nothing to counter that the drugs were there, that the document was there. Do we say, 'Don't believe your eyes,

believe us'?" Mike stood up. "I'm going to do the best that I can."
He walked out of the room.

Clem fought back a fury he had to contain. "I suspect the best is
not going to be good enough."

Willacy nodded gravely.

In the dimly lit, elegant bar of the Hay-Adams Hotel, one block
from the White House, Willa Hammond sipped her margarita and
B. J. Brackenfield swirled his scotch and water while Mitchell
Joyner surveyed them both. It was five o'clock in the afternoon
and the bar was unusually empty, except for the lobbyists, and one
lone couple under the archway across the room.

"What in Christ's name is going on with this Geer thing?"
Joyner asked.

"How the hell should I know?" B.J. replied.

"You're joined at the hip with Hoyle Henderson," Willa said
flatly, bleakly, "and word is, Hoyle's the architect of this tank job."

B.J. was solemn. "Jesus H. Christ, Willa, that's crazy. If it was a
setup, don't you think that Hoyle would know that everyone
would be pointing a finger at him? He wouldn't be caught dead
with his fingerprints on a jerk-off deal like this."

"So you say, B.J., so you say," Joyner said skeptically. "*I* say,
what does *Hoyle* say?" He looked at his watch. "Where is that
sneaky bastard, anyway? He's late!"

"Sneaking up behind you, son," Hoyle said, appearing behind
Joyner, who turned to grin. Hoyle grinned back cadaverously.

Hoyle took the empty chair, snapping his finger at the waiter,
who scurried to his side. "J&B on the rocks." He turned to Joyner.
"No, I did not pull any scam on Geer, and you know why? It was
A, old hat, and B, too slick. Old as Moses, but requiring some
logistical planning. Too damn risky. By the way, Bill Rawlins had
the same thought as you good people, and he put me on the rack
until I convinced him I'm clean. At least, I am on this one."

Willa stared at Hoyle. She was prepared to believe almost anything about this dwarfish schemer. But she had to believe that
Hoyle was not lying now. Who would have hustled this real dirty
trick? Maybe the old Nixon gang grew nostalgic and wanted to
keep their hand in, maybe Stonehaven's folks were getting a bit

giddy. But she also retreated from that line of thought. It was to Stonehaven's advantage to take on the President. Kells is vulnerable. Rawlins is an unknown quantity, too attractive for the Stonehaven crowd to really want to take him on in the election. No, she believed Hoyle. She voiced the question that now invaded her. "Okay, Hoyle, I believe you. But I put it to you, and to you two, if Hoyle wasn't the architect, and if Terry was fixed, who put him in the tank?"

Joyner shook his head. "Goddamn good question, only I haven't got an answer. Who would want the President's head, when the sonofabitch is draining from a hundred wounds right now? Hell, if they just let him alone, he'll bleed to death."

"That, my rich lawyer, lobbyist, ally, and friend, is sure as hell the 'Wheel of Fortune' question," said Hoyle. "I have been pondering that same wiggly little query myself. Who? Why? What the hell is going on, unless we old pros are so frigging quick to suspect all but the obvious, and that is that Terry was a stupid fuck-up. Anyone want to play with that a while?"

B.J. said, "Hoyle, I think maybe you got it wrong. The President is in the barbed wire right now, but he is no dummy and he doesn't have dummies around him. All his inner circle are first-class pols and first-class intellects. Their elevators stop on all floors, right, Willa?"

"Yes, B.J. I count you right. So we are back to basics. I am convinced now that whatever happened, it was a frame, performed by some talented people. I mean serious talent. And, gentlemen, if you will pardon an aging old lady's proclivity for the disturbing phrase, that scares the living crap out of me."

Bill Rawlins smiled as Loretta Wigham, flanked by Bruce Gustafson, led him through the throng around the Des Moines mansion of Warren Holman, whose six-bedroom home, sitting on a five-acre estate twenty minutes from downtown Des Moines, was built with a small portion of the revenues that flowed to the Holman land development and farming empire. In Rawlins' pocket were three telephone messages from Laura Hurley. She was calling too often. But he would handle that later.

Some two hundred men and women were swarming over the

Holman home, invited by Gustafson and Wigham, in Holman's name. Holman, small, plump, graying, was making his first foray into big-league politics, recruited by Gustafson with visions of invitations to the White House as President Rawlins' personal guest.

"What a great honor to have you here, Mr. Vice President," Holman gurgled.

Rawlins took him by the shoulder. "Mr. Holman—may I call you Warren?—I'm only a former Vice President. Big difference."

Holman, now incurably infected, laughed loudly. "Makes no difference to me, sir."

Rawlins squeezed the man's shoulder. "Call me Bill."

Holman, joyous, turned to his wife, a tiny, firm-featured woman who gazed on her husband's delight approvingly. More in control than her husband, she bowed slightly to Rawlins. "You're always welcome in our home, Senator Rawlins."

Loretta's arm was inside Rawlins' elbow, moving him on, steering him into the enormous living room, with Gustafson on the other side. As they slowly walked, Gustafson introduced Rawlins to each group that crowded round. Waiters moved through the gathering with drinks and food. Conversation always subsided as Rawlins neared. Within an hour, Loretta and Gustafson had moved the candidate through the entire assemblage, both of them pleased, even marveling, at the ease with which Rawlins punctuated each brief encounter with small talk.

Eleanor Brinkman and Mary Ellen Gates, wives of the leading wheat grower in the state and the head of the Agricultural Cooperative, respectively, murmured to each other.

"God, he's handsome, isn't he?" Eleanor said.

Mary Ellen, a tall, comely redhead, nodded appreciatively and said, "Do you believe those stories are true?"

Eleanor Brinkman smiled faintly. "I hope so." She started to laugh, cupping her mouth with her hands.

"Eleanor," said Mary Ellen, leaning toward her friend, "you surprise me only because I was thinking the same thing. I suspect, though, that Bill Rawlins really doesn't think that Iowa women think about those things, or does he?"

Bruce Gustafson clapped sharply as he stood on the makeshift little platform in the Holman living room. "May I have your attention, please!"

The crowd fell silent, but for the clinking of errant ice against glass. Rawlins stood motionless next to Gustafson, hands folded serenely in front of him, gazing brazenly at the faces turned toward him. His eyes lit for a moment on Mary Ellen Gates, who seemed to blush. She turned slightly to her husband next to her, but his eyes, too, were fastened on the slim and elegant frame of the now ex-Vice President. Eleanor Brinkman frowned, until she noted Rawlins' eyes were now leveled at her. She was glued to Rawlins until she finally looked away, furious with herself for being so nervous.

"We are privileged that Vice President Rawlins is here with us," Gustafson was saying, "and we are so very grateful to Gladys and Warren Holman, two of Des Moines' most prominent citizens, for being so hospitable today."

The two prominent citizens widened their smiles in suitable gratitude. Holman tugged at his tie, hands trembling.

Gustafson continued: "We are privy to a great moment in American history. Years from now you can tell your children and grandchildren that on this day you were in the presence of the next President of the United States." Loretta started clapping, it was such a dream applause line, but she didn't have to. Others in the room were pounding their palms even before Gustafson finished the sentence.

Gustafson beamed. "I present to you the former Vice President, and soon to be President of the United States, Bill Rawlins of Texas." Gustafson's voice was now booming and reverberating through the massive living room.

Rawlins approached the lectern that had been set up, but he waved it away and picked up the small microphone on a wire stem. He stood in front of the lectern to face the group.

"There are enough barriers between a candidate and the people without adding more."

Appreciative smiles blossomed in the audience.

"I would like to stand here, close to you, and chat with you very briefly. Indeed, I am convinced the best counsel any speaker can take is to be brief, be bright, and be gone."

Laughter sparkled through the crowd.

Rawlins smiled warmly. "I cannot certify I will fulfill the middle part of that advice, but the 'brief' part and the 'be gone' part I can surely handle."

More smiles of intimate delight.

"You all made sacrifices to be here, and for that I am deeply in your debt." The reference to the $1,000 per couple tariff for this event at the Holman home was readily absorbed by those in attendance. The usual fund-raiser in Des Moines had a tab of three figures, not four.

Loretta Wigham was swelling with pride. She had picked a winner. Rawlins was easy-mannered, comfortable to be with, not stuffy, and he was incredibly good-looking, in a way that men would not find threatening. He was thoroughly masculine. She had the word "macho" on the edge of her mind but discarded it quickly.

"I am here because I believe this nation has been going down the wrong path to the future. It is wrong to live with a debacle in the farm country. It is wrong to endure inflation at risky and hazardous levels, blighting the family farm's future. It is wrong to accept interest rates that frustrate families who have for generations tended the land of their grandfathers and their great-grandfathers and now they are bewildered because they cannot afford to borrow what is required to keep them alive. It is wrong to rattle sabers in the world, frightening our allies and angering those whom this Administration calls our enemies. It is wrong to tolerate mismanagement in every nook and cranny of this Government, which in turn disturbs and confuses businessmen, farmers, professionals, owners of small enterprises, and mothers and fathers trying so desperately to give their children some glimpse of the hope that was part of their own childhood."

As he spoke, Rawlins slowly turned to face each side of the room, not overtly, but casually, as if he were in intimate conversation with each of them. His eyes, like an expert fly-caster, flew to and gripped the eyes of a single person for a second or two, then moved gracefully to those of the next person. His gestures were bold but not awkward. His voice, soft, then rising, gave a rhythmic cadence to each repetition of the phrase "It is wrong." The voice was unblurred, resonant, and unmarred by any sense that the words were memorized—which they were.

Loretta knew that Rawlins knew he had this group in the palm of his hand.

"If," he went on, "we can establish even a minor accord with the new U.S.C.R., not naively, but with clear eye and firm purpose, we might be able to dismiss the blight of mistrust. Don't you think it's worth the effort?"

He paused, half-smiling. There were nods of appreciation from the group in front of him, though none of them would bet the farm and the homestead on their knowledge of the Soviet mind and purpose, nor did they truly understand why "democracy" in the U.S.C.R. and eastern Europe was on the ropes.

Mrs. Holman thought that this wonderful Senator or whatever title he had was the right man to lead. Nobody wants a war, and besides, we are spending too much on those awful bombs when we could be helping people buy homes and keep their farms. Mrs. Holman nodded to herself in some awe of her wisdom.

Then Rawlins said, "I entered this race reluctantly. Of course I did. How could it be otherwise, when I am forced to take the field in opposition to a friend, a man who brought me to the Vice Presidency, and a man I respect both as leader and friend? But that respect just has to take second place to what I believe to be my duty. I can no longer conduct my public tasks when I no longer have faith in the compass course to which our leader has committed us. President Kells is a good and decent man. But he has lost his ability to lead. That doesn't make him a bad man. Not at all. It does make him a bad leader. The worth and durability of the nation's agenda are far more important than the fulfillment of one man's reelection ambitions."

He leaned slightly forward, his voice now rising.

"And so I come to you here in Iowa, I come to ask you to join me. I come to ask you to support me, to help me, to give me the incentive to continue. I come not to ask you to depreciate the President. But I come to suggest to you that what was right to do some four years ago, has been radically changed by events none of us imagined when you and I believed in this Administration. So, come join me, stand near me, be with me, let us, you and I, all who think like you, try to set right what is so clearly wrong. Let us, you and I, and all who believe as you do, redeem the American promise. Let us, you and I, and all who care as you do, work together. Let's make America great again."

Rawlins' voice rose in ascending emphasis, and as he concluded, the crowd broke into applause, a long crescendo of applause.

Mary Ellen Gates and Eleanor Brinkman furiously clapped their hands, their husbands joining them in sincere tribute. Mary Ellen looked cautiously out of the corner of her eye toward her husband as she continued to applaud. It was as if she were overtly displaying the rousing emotions she felt inside her. God, he was absolutely riveting, irresistible; she had never been so affected by any public man before. She glanced at her friend and realized intuitively that Eleanor was experiencing the same cascading thoughts. What was even stranger was that, in other ways, Mike Gates seemed to be caught up in the same tremors. God, she thought, Rawlins wasn't bisexual, was he? Goodness, no, no man could invade her emotions as quickly as Rawlins did and not be heterosexual. Satisfied with her sociological soundings, she smiled happily as the applause continued.

Gustafson turned to Loretta. "Hello, there, White House, here we come." Loretta giggled, an uncommon admission on her part. "Yup, Bruce, this is what is called a bandwagon, and guess what, we're driving it!"

Hoyle Henderson, in a shadowed corner of the room, giving him a full-frame picture of the assembled crowd, stood quiet, unobtrusive. This was all on film. Hoyle had allowed the press camera pool to be inside the room. It was a gamble, but Hoyle knew he had won.

Now there was the necessity of getting out among the "peepul," as Hoyle was wont to say. That meant you mushed all over the state trying to enchant a few thousand folks in a godawful expenditure of time and energy. Hoyle had small patience with academics staggering under the burden of their idiotic ideals. Don't tell me what the issues are. Tell me who's going to vote, and don't forget they vote with their hearts and not their minds. Most voters choose a President with the same imprecision with which they pick a husband or a wife. Jesus, thought Hoyle, here in a state with almost three million souls, you had to crap around with a tiny minority who called all the shots. Hoyle didn't like farmers to begin with, couldn't understand parity and all the gobbletalk that infected agricultural political dialogue. He barely withheld his contempt for cattle, an inner secret that he guarded with more zeal than the Curia in the Vatican protected whatever the hell those Eye-talian cardinals strove to secure. In Texas, had he made public his nose-holding animus for stinking Hereford white-faces and Santa Gertrudis, he would have been targeted for assassination.

Now, he groaned, it was on to Council Bluffs, a visit to some goddamn farm, and some pulling away at heifers' teats in some stupid barn, as well as slopping around in a field full of cow turds. Thank God, it was going to be friskily cool. In the summertime, cow turds in a field got soggier than Hoyle counted to be reasonable. He always remembered Harry Truman's sensible advice that the one thing a man should never do was kick a cow turd in a field on a hot August afternoon. However, Hoyle had to admit Rawlins could handle the teat-tugging in good form. Rawlins always did his homework, even if it meant spending a few hours learning the right squeezing techniques. But, Jesus, what a man had to do to become President. Thank the good loving Lord, as Jimmy Winger would say, that campaign commanders for candidates don't have to put up with any of that electioneering crapola.

Thirty-one

JEAN-FRANÇOIS DUVAL picked up the memorandum and its attachment with a weary gesture. It was late in Paris and the Assistant Chief Inspector of the French National Police was hungry. He glanced at the paper, a message to him from FBI Deputy Associate Director Toni Georgihu. Such a difficult name to pronounce in English, even more difficult to spell. Duval was not casual about such precisions.

The message was in English and Duval, who prided himself on his understanding of that barbaric language, read very slowly. This Georgihu was seeking information about a woman, around thirty, whose name was Greta Hulved, with a passport, country unknown, though it was thought to be Switzerland. Attached was an artist's sketch of the woman in question.

He would send a message in return tomorrow. He jotted a note to his assistant, asking him to swiftly search whatever files were required so that Duval could make his answer specific. The woman in the artist's sketch was quite attractive. Perhaps she was here in France. How in the name of God was one going to find her if indeed her name was not Greta Hulved, which the memorandum pointed out as a potential hazard to a quick discovery? Ah, well, it was late, and his wife was not the most understanding spouse in the Republic. He flung the memo with his notation into his "out" basket. Henri, his aide, would do something about it tomorrow.

In Rome, at his cluttered desk, Carmine Ferro wiped his mouth to erase the remnants of the heavy soup he was eating. Being the deputy of the terrorist section was more work than it was glory. The Government had changed today, the fifty-third time—or was it the forty-third?—since the end of the War in 1945. Ferro never kept accurate count.

He picked up the memorandum from the American FBI with its artist's sketch of a magnificent-looking woman. "Che bella ragazza," murmured Ferro. To find such a woman would not be unpleasant. Ferro's marriage was not—how would he put it?—in a blissful state at this moment. But he had other, more pressing matters. The riot in Naples by some stupid strikers who ought to be working was grinding him down. He flipped the memorandum to the side of his cluttered desk where he kept nonpriority items. It would wait.

In Mexico City, Manuel Reguerro Oñez gazed meditatively at the pile of documents in front of him. On top was a memorandum from the FBI in Washington. It would never have been there except for two things. First, it was in Spanish, a notable exception from the Americans who had the imperial notion that everyone south of Brownsville spoke English, and second, it was from one of the few American police he found trustworthy, the woman agent, Toni Georgihu. This American FBI agent always treated Reguerro with respect whenever they met, which was seldom, but enough to solidify Reguerro's judgment that she warranted some special treatment. He pushed aside the thoughts that squirmed inside him when he first met Georgihu. He had explored the possibility of taking the clothes off this tall woman and indulging his passion, but he hesitated when she rebuffed his overtures and made it clear if he made a move she would kick his cock off with a well-placed pointed toe, without even a second thought. A fine officer, this Toni Georgihu.

He read it carefully. Ah, what a pity he could not help. It would be almost impossible to trace any such woman in Mexico City. Reguerro sighed, for he knew the record-keeping was not so good. Finding a specific woman with a specific name would not be easy.

He rose to his feet, put on his hat, shuffled the papers gently. He looked once more at the artist's sketch. He flipped it back on the desk and moved toward the door.

He stopped. His eyes narrowed as he searched for the source of that niggling thought that halted him. He picked up the phone. "Ricardo, bring me the photograph of that woman you showed me yesterday, the one you told the joke about, the one with the wide-spread legs of a harlot and the face of a Madonna."

Within minutes his deputy was in his office with a file. He handed the photo to Reguerro. The Chief of Police gazed at it steadily. He picked up the artist's sketch and said, "Does this sketch resemble the corpse?"

Ricardo looked quickly at both pictures. He turned to his superior. "But, of course, it is the same."

Reguerro nodded. "Get on the phone. Call the FBI in Washington. Ask for Deputy Associate Director Georgihu. Now."

Federof held the message with trembling fingers. It had just arrived, like a sealed but active bacillus; he had decoded it personally . . .

An earlier cable from the Executive President's office had merely stated that the Executive President had agreed to the summit meeting with President Kells. Federof had been annoyed and alarmed that there'd been lack of any word from Zinyakin. Should he halt any more covert activity, until Zinyakin conveyed some message to him?

The Washington *Post* had told him more about the meeting than the cable: President Kells would meet with the Executive President in six weeks in Geneva. There would be no specific agenda, no requirement to sign any agreements. An opportunity—said Press Secretary Mike Carson—for a thoughtful exchange of views to see if tensions could be lessened and a discussion of the turmoil in eastern Europe.

Now this: a second cable, a *personal* message to Federof from the Executive President himself. Nothing, the message had said in the plainest of terms, must soil the planned summit.

Did the KGB monitor the Executive President's messages? Did Zinyakin know the contents of this paper? Federof had survived in the aberrant world of the U.S.C.R. because he never surmised the best and always assumed the very worst.

Slowly, Federof got to his feet. The end game was near. He must be prepared. Preparation was a requisite of survival.

The President rose from his desk in the Oval Office and motioned the Majority Leader of the Senate and the Chairman of the Senate Armed Services Committee to seats on the sofa near the fireplace. John Wingate, Secretary of State Winthrop MacIver, and Clem Barkley flanked him.

"Gifford, Raymond, I am pleased you came so quickly. I want to brief you on the meeting we'll have in Geneva with the Executive President."

Tunstall smiled broadly. "Mr. President, I cannot tell you adequately how cheering this forthcoming meeting in Geneva is to me and most of my colleagues. I feel so very good about it all."

The Majority Leader did not fully reveal all that he felt since he had forty minutes earlier concluded a phone conversation with the former Vice President, who accused Tunstall of instigating the meeting in Geneva and even blasted the Soviets for their acceptance. The Vice President was also, to frame it broadly, thought Tunstall, highly pissed at the reception Tunstall had received in his personal visit with the President.

Vincent Canfield had reinforced Rawlins' discomfort with his call on the Majority Leader. "Raymond," Canfield had told Tunstall, "President Kells is not honest about this trip to Geneva. This is political hypnosis, plain and clear." Tunstall said little in response to either Rawlins or Canfield. He had determined that Kells' move was shrewdly designed. Tunstall did not act imprudently, no matter his personal feelings.

Gifford Gray shook his head appreciatively. "It is a splendid move, Mr. President. Even if it comes to naught, I do believe that you and the Executive President will find some mutually agreeable moments. You both have much to discuss. The unruly business in the eastern European countries affects him as it does us. Perhaps he will take more comfort from this unrest than you, but it is nonetheless important to talk. In any case, I congratulate you, sir."

The President clasped Gray's hand in his own. "I want you there with me, Gifford."

The old Senator looked mildly astonished.

Tunstall turned to the President. "Great idea, Mr. President, truly a great idea. I can assure you that if Gifford is by your side, the Senate will be there in spirit."

Gifford Gray reflected a moment. "That's very thoughtful of you, Mr. President." He bowed his head slightly.

Clem studied the President admiringly. Good move, it was. No President in his memory had ever had a sitting United States Senator by his side at any important summit meeting.

Clem's hand began to tremble ever so slightly. Now was coming the trump that no one in the Oval Office suspected would ever be played. Clem had suggested this idea in a memo three days ago to the President, and the President was plainly taken with it. Clem knew that now was the time to lay the card on the table.

The President looked firmly at Senator Tunstall. "I am also asking you and Homer Wade to join me in Geneva, at the summit meeting." Clem saw the perceptible movement in the Majority Leader's jaw as he heard what he never expected to hear ". . . as well as the Minority Leaders of the House and Senate, the Speaker, and the ranking member of the Senate Foreign Relations Committee."

Tunstall was speechless. Four Democrats, three Republicans. Two from the House, five from the Senate. Clem glowed. God, it was a masterful stroke. The joy of a triumphant political move was, to Clem, the supreme excitement.

"Moreover, I know we have severe economic problems, and we will tend to them as best we can. I use 'we' because I expect, Raymond, cooperation from the Senate on some of my plans." The President smiled easily. "I want to meet with you and the Finance Committee people, along with the Speaker and Ways and Means. We can't avoid hitting this head-on, don't you agree?"

Only four days ago Tunstall had said to Canfield and Overlujd, "Never underestimate anyone who has climbed to the top of the greasy pole."

"I agree, Mr. President, I most heartily agree," said a still-amazed Tunstall.

. . . .

Toni Georgihu spoke calmly to the Director of the FBI, but her heart beat faster than she revealed. Clem Barkley, by her side, watched her intently.

"Identification is complete, sir. I had someone in Mexico City yesterday examining all the photographs and talking to the Mexican officers who found the woman, violated, and her throat cut brutally. My agent just returned several hours ago. The woman was still in the Mexico City morgue. In another two or three days she would have been buried. We have several dozen photographs of her, which my agent took, and they have been carefully gone over by both John Wingate and Terry Geer, as well as Clem Barkley."

She looked at Clem. "It's the woman they knew as Greta Hulved." Clem nodded.

The Director gazed carefully at the file in front of him. "What's the next move?"

"We have interviewed everyone at the Corcoran Ball, as well as the people who handled the logistics for the evening. We have determined that a man named Wayne Malloy, with a rather huge red mustache, may have instigated the invitation for Greta Hulved. This fellow is a business consultant whose major clients have been American companies doing business in eastern Europe. Malloy has been picked up. He is, we believe, the link between"—Georgihu paused—"the KGB here in Washington and Greta Hulved."

"Do you know this, Toni, really know it?" said the Director.

"I believe I do. But I don't know if we will have enough to indict the red-mustached fellow or, if we did, if we could prosecute him successfully."

"Then, the next question. Why? What is the motive, what is the aim? Why involve Geer in this? To what purpose? In short, what the hell is this all about?"

"That I cannot answer, sir," said Georgihu. "I am convinced that the KGB is involved in the Geer matter, the Hickey murder, and the Bulgarian assassins."

Clem broke in. "I suggested to Toni that we deal with Vaslansky. He's the senior KGB official in the Embassy, and his tracks are all over our files on those screwy goings-on with some high public officials. I hope you will agree to put a twenty-four-hour cover on him. Then there is the matter of this man Federof. Toni's got a file on him that certainly confirms the fact he is a civilized killer. He is not here on a Frequent Flyer vacation. Why are the Soviets engaging in this heavy stuff when they have so many other things to occupy their minds? Why?"

"Maybe that's a question the State Department ought to answer," said Toni. "They're the foreign policy experts. We are merely the police."

The Director turned in his swivel chair and gazed at the wall. He turned back to Clem and Georgihu.

"Clem, I assume you will inform the President. I will do exactly as you suggest. I'll visit with the Attorney General today. Toni, run all the traps you have in the field. Get back to me this afternoon."

The eagle swooped low over the scrubby terrain. Its talons were outstretched. It soared high and then, wings swept back, dived steeply. It leveled out above the outcropping of the granite slab and dug its talons deep into the back of the man fleeing the eagle's seeking claws. The man screamed again and again as he felt himself lifted off the ground, his shoulders and back imprisoned by a vise-like grip. He could feel the warm river of blood that erupted from his back. He closed his eyes and screamed again. He opened his eyes dizzily.

Bill Rawlins woke, his hand grazing his sweating forehead. He sat up in bed. The room was dark. The morning had not yet come. He got slowly to his feet. Where was he? In the darkness at this hour the bedroom in his brother's house was unfamiliar to him. He stumbled to the bathroom and splashed his face with cold water.

He was not a superstitious man. He placed no faith in mind-reading, extrasensory perception, thousand-year-old gurus, or conjurers who peddled such nonsense. But he felt strangely unsettled. This was the second time he had envisioned this grotesque scene, which invaded his sleep with such rudeness.

He reached for the phone and dialed quickly.

"Hoyle, did I wake you?"

The voice at the end of the line managed a slight laugh. "No, no, Mr. Vice President. I was lying here at three in the morning just hopin' you would call."

Rawlins ignored the retort. "When can we go over the schedule?"

"Same time we agreed on yesterday, nine o'clock this morning. We are meeting at the headquarters, just like we planned. We got the big mo going, Bill—momentum like you never dreamed."

"What about the summit Kells is planning?"

"Not good for us, but I got the media guys preparing some counter stuff. How come the President got off his ass just now? Is he playing politics with our future? Can he be tough for three and a half years, and suddenly get lovesick for the Soviets? Why doesn't he do something for the folks hurting in this country? Is he just trying to forage for votes? Can we trust him? Isn't this the action of a desperate man? Desperate men do funny things. We'll pepper his ass. I've got five key reporters ready to accept this spin."

"When do I leave for New Hampshire?"

"Six days from now. First we go to Chicago, and then New Hampshire. We have a platoon of state legislators coming out for you the day before you arrive in Manchester. They're in deep economic shit up there and we can belt the President pretty good. He's going to think that some condor bit him on the ass, lifted him by the nape of the neck, and dropped him on hard pavement from ten stories up."

"Condor? Drop him from ten stories up?"

Hoyle Henderson's voice lowered. "Turn of phrase, Bill. Why, what's the matter? You sound kind of funny."

Rawlins didn't answer. He replaced the phone in its cradle.

Thirty-two

RAYMOND TUNSTALL sat upright in his chair. Facing him in the Senator's hideaway was Senator Homer Jefferson Wade, South Carolina's longtime Senator and Chairman of the Senate Foreign Relations Committee.

Tunstall was silent for a few seconds. "Let's get down to business. How do you read these polls, Homer? Give me your gut reaction. You have a feel for these things," the Senator said.

Tunstall believed, not without reason, that Homer Wade, for all his rural, down-home behavior, was just about the wisest reader of political riddles he knew.

"Ah understand what you want, Leader," Wade said. "No question but what the numbers have bottomed and are going to start going up. President's had his balls in a vise for so long, guess maybe it is just a matter of time 'fore the hurting stops. Mah judgment is that when the new inflation numbers just out today start seeping in, and when his trip to Geneva gets the right play, the lines on the graph will rise. Anytime inflation and interest rates look like they're heading down, that's pocketbook news that's mighty good, and interest rates ought to follow. On the other hand, that Geer mess can't hep him. But, Leader, you know, and damn near everybody in this town knows, that it was all such a dumb fool thing, most folks are going to pass it off as a kind of rebirth of Nixon's dirty tricks. Know what ah mean?"

Tunstall nodded appreciatively. That was precisely how he judged it. The Majority Leader had pondered carefully what had happened. Terry Geer's arrest made no sense. Tunstall's conversations with the FBI and with his own contacts in the Washington police force had convinced him something was awry. He knew that Toni Georgihu was investigating a woman's death in Mexico City that seemingly had some connection to Geer. His source at the FBI, usually voluble with the Majority Leader, was hesitant and obviously passing along only the barest outlines. Tunstall also knew with an animal certainty that in politics there are no such phrases as "can't win" or "can't lose." Twenty-four hours was a millennium in any political campaign. Time was measured in minutes, and anytime anyone took a poll its findings were already out of date.

There stirred inside him coarse forebodings. He had a five-seat margin in the Senate. There were eighteen Democratic seats up in the next election, contrasted with fifteen Republicans. He figured three Republicans as live prospects for defeat, but four, maybe five, of his own party were, as Homer Wade might put it, hanging by their knuckle joints. Too thin, too thin.

But what gnawed at Tunstall's political entrails was the Hobson's choice which confronted him. A weak candidate, as Kells seemed at this moment to be, would put to hazard the future of some Democratic incumbents and squeeze the chances of some very good senatorial prospects, two of whom Tunstall had personally persuaded to run, to upset Republican incumbents. But, and here his stomach growled, the likelihood of Bill Rawlins and the President in a national primary brawl, bloodying up the countryside until the Convention in late July, had a dismaying odor about it.

Tunstall shook his head. Civil war must not be allowed to explode. His plan all along was for the President to withdraw, and so far the plan was not working. Tunstall had a positive revulsion to anything that malfunctioned. The more certain became a primary war, the larger his misgivings. It was never a question of whom he liked the most, or which man was the nearer to him in friendship. To the Leader, the game was a Senate Democratic majority, with a

President in the White House who was beholden to Raymond Tunstall. All else was of meager value.

The primaries were about to begin. The time had come for a new assessment. He remembered what General Tallant, the Chairman of the Joint Chiefs, had once remarked in a briefing. War, Tallant had said, quoting the German battle strategist Clausewitz, is full of friction. Friction was all the small things that go wrong, accumulating and building up, as they do, which in turn produced what the war planners had never conceived. Friction, Tunstall concluded, was what separated war from war games. Same thing in politics. Which was why this Kells versus Rawlins battle was brimming over with friction.

"Course," said Senator Wade, "Ah got to say that if the primaries were held today, Bill Rawlins would kick the grits out of the President. Ah'm not glad to say such a thing 'cause ah am one of those Democrats who grew up believing you stuck with the girl you brung to the dance and didn't get seduced by some new gal dressed up in one of those gowns with no straps. But today there is no such thing as loyalty anymore. Changing world, Leader, and sometimes ah'm not real sure if ah like it any more than ah know what to do about it."

"I understand, Homer, and I thank you," said Tunstall. "As usual, you are on the mark."

The Chairman of the Senate Foreign Relations Committee stood up, his paunch protruding over his suspender-held baggy trousers.

"Always glad to try to hep you, Leader."

The twelve tables of ten people each were elegantly dressed with exquisite china and colorful floral arrangements. The lights were bright enough in the State Dining Room of the White House so that each person in the room was recognizable to everyone else, but dimmed enough to flatter appearances. The hum of conversation ended as the President rose to deliver a toast to the guests of honor, the King and Queen of Spain, after which the guests erupted into applause, chairs raking back as each person in the room rose, glasses of champagne held high, and "To the King and Queen of Spain" resounded through the dining hall.

The President moved among the guests, now on their feet, the dinner at an end. An orchestra beckoned them to the East Room's dance floor.

Touching Clem Barkley on the arm, the President said, "Get John, Mike, and Willacy and meet me on the second floor. I'm going to dance with some of the ladies. I'll be about ten minutes."

Clem nodded.

In the East Room, the President took the hand of the Queen of Spain and guided her to the dance floor.

Upstairs, Willacy Hughes and John Wingate sat on the couch. Clem and Mike Carson drew up chairs so that they would all flank the President's wing-backed chair.

"Willacy," Clem asked, "what's the latest on Terry Geer?"

"The U.S. attorney can't find one witness who ever saw Terry take anything stronger than a martini. No evidence of Terry either dealing drugs or taking drugs, or selling secret documents. What they have is the so-called evidence they found in the house, but not a sliver of corroboration. If we could somehow connect that murdered woman in Mexico City, we could probably get the damn thing thrown out."

Clem nodded. "I talked to Toni Georgihu today. She said the Bureau questioned this Wayne Malloy, who's thick with the Soviets. They drained him pretty good, but he doesn't seem to know much. He was a sort of courier. He picked up this woman, Greta Hulved, at JFK on her arrival; got her the invitation to the Corcoran."

"Why would the Soviets want to do this?" Willacy wondered. "Would they go this distance to try to infect Donald Kells? Hoyle Henderson, yes, but where would Hoyle get a top-secret document like that? There's no evidence Bill Rawlins could have gotten his hands on it; it wasn't in his 'need to know' area."

Wingate nodded. "The only people who could have access would be two people on my staff, plus you, Clem, Terry Geer, and of course the Secretary of Defense, Sam Harcourt, and possibly three or four in the Secretary's inner circle."

"I doubt if we could track down the leaker," Carson said, "and to try, we'd have to go after our own people, and that doesn't play well in this town."

"Meanwhile," said Clem, "the Rawlins people are like locusts. They're everywhere."

"You know," Willacy said, "Rawlins had a good reception in Iowa." He smiled conspiratorially. "We have two people there who've infiltrated the Rawlins organization, including one who's made some hefty contributions so he's invited to everything. Hate to spend money on Rawlins, but it's a prudent investment."

Mike Carson lifted his head sharply. "Who've you got in the Rawlins camp, Willacy?"

"Don't worry about it, Mike," Willacy said.

"That's not good enough," Carson said sternly. "Trouble with us is, the right hand doesn't know what the left is doing, so we screw up. You can't say that about the Rawlins crowd."

Before an irritated Willacy could respond, the President walked briskly into the West Hall sitting room and took the wing-backed chair.

"About forty-five minutes before I greeted the King tonight," he said, "Sam Harcourt called. Tomorrow morning on my desk'll be his resignation as Defense Secretary. He will simultaneously announce he's heading a citizens' group for Bill Rawlins."

"Ouch," Clem said. Willacy Hughes groaned. John Wingate's jaw muscles tightened. Only Mike Carson seemed unperturbed.

"I can't believe that Sam Harcourt thinks Bill Rawlins will put him on the ticket," Willacy said.

"Sam does believe it. Count on it," Clem said.

"How does this play, Mike?" the President asked. "Is this crippling, or just a two- or three-day story?"

"This could linger," Carson said.

Clem broke in before Carson could expand. "I don't agree. Harcourt has no political organization. He lives in New Jersey, comes from Indiana, and in neither place is there anything resembling a Harcourt legion. He's rich, successful, and has an ego the size of an eight-wheeler, but that's it."

"My guess is, Mike's more right than wrong," the President said. "The press will play this as rats leaving a sinking ship. My guess is, Sam's betting it all on Rawlins because he's greedy for fame and power. My guess is, this *will* hurt."

"Then we should move fast," Clem said.

"I agree," the President said. "John, call a meeting for nine tomorrow morning. I want Winthrop MacIver and the Chairman of the Joint Chiefs. I'm appointing Fernando Carrera new Defense Secretary. He's done a superlative job as Deputy Secretary, and with a Harvard MBA, Vietnam-era Medal of Honor, and a leg lost in combat, he's not going to catch too much flak from our Loyal Opposition in the Senate."

"It won't hurt that he'll be the first Hispanic head of the Defense Department," Clem said, unable to disguise his glee. "With Roncalli as Vice President and Carrera as Defense chief, I like our chances better."

The President had a touch of grit in his voice. "Don't confuse talent with playing the ethnic game. I don't work that way."

Clem become somber. "Sorry, Mr. President. I didn't mean . . ."

The President smiled. "Well, maybe just a little. As a former President once said, 'A little demagoguery never hurt anyone.' "

Bungalow Five sits elegantly on the Crescent Street entrance to the newly rebuilt Beverly Hills Hotel. Inside, some forty reporters and cameramen were crammed into the spacious living room. The air was already going stale.

The former Vice President had flown directly to Los Angeles from Iowa. He sat in a straight-backed chair next to the fireplace. Leaning against the closed door of a bedroom was Hoyle Henderson, tapping the eraser end of a pencil against his teeth.

"Richard Multon, Los Angeles *Times*. Mr. Vice President, can you tell us the objective of your visit?"

Rawlins smiled easily. "One eighth of all the nation's electoral votes are in this lively state. So I've come to plead my case. A calendar at home tells me California will have a vote in the primaries. And that, my friends, is why I am here." Rawlins was enjoying himself.

"Mr. Vice President"—a pretty blonde with white teeth and bangs raised her hand—"Madge Winfree, San Francisco *Examiner*. I note that Mr. Henderson is here with you. There've been rumors that Mr. Henderson may have had something to do with the recent unhappy events surrounding Terence Geer, Assistant to the President. Would you comment?''

Rawlins' jaw tightened. He turned. "Care to comment on that, Hoyle?"

"Ms. Winfree," Hoyle drawled, "since when do I have to deny every idiot rumor that someone in the President's camp peddles all over town? And what's wrong with the notion that a certain Presidential Assistant might be trading dope and stealing secrets? Wouldn't be the first time somebody in the White House misbehaved."

A stocky, bearded black man held up his hand and, at Rawlins' nod, said, "Damon Hite, Channel 11. How do you react to the opposition mounting in Germany to the Chancellor's bid for reelection?"

"I have no desire to get involved in Germany's elections; I have enough to do in my own campaign. But I continue to say we ought to get on with nourishing relationships, not torturing them."

Hite persisted. "With counterrevolutions in eastern Europe, and the Middle East in turmoil since the fall of Saddam Hussein, isn't a more formidable Soviet Union a legitimate concern of any President?"

Rawlins stood. "Of course—but shouldn't we concentrate on getting inflation down, and interest rates down, and put our guns away until we do something to help the average family in this country?"

Hite was not through. "One more question, Mr. Vice President. Defense Secretary Sam Harcourt has resigned. Is this a signal he's going to be your candidate for Vice President if you win the nomination?"

"Secretary Harcourt's resignation is a signal, all right—a signal to the nation that this Administration is fading fast. The Secretary's recommendations for sane and sensible redesigning of our foreign policy have been ignored."

Half an hour later, the reporters departed, leaving behind a litter of coffee cups and soiled paper cups on the large coffee table and carpet.

"Not bad, Bill, not bad at all," Hoyle said. "That Winfree dame sure needs a large dick in her, though. I'd volunteer except I got to keep zippered up these days, else we get goosed by nosy reporters at every stop."

Rawlins said coldly, "I don't need any morality lectures from you, Hoyle. You're sounding like that dork preacher friend of yours."

Hoyle was unfazed. "Just doing my job, Bill. I'm your conscience *and* your button man. Dual responsibilities that I take mighty serious. Why don't you get a little rest? We head out in two hours. We got three hundred heavy wallets waiting in a lean-to in Bel Air for that five-thirty reception, and then two hours later at the Beverly Hilton, two thousand more."

Rawlins said nothing.

Hoyle waved at him and said, "I'll let myself out."

Bill Rawlins heard the front door slam. He sat quietly for a few moments. He walked slowly through the entrance foyer, took out a key and unlocked the door to the bedroom hallway.

She stood by the bed in a light-blue nightgown made transparent by soft light filtering through the window. He held her hand, drew her close, and kissed her, slipping the straps of her gown down. It slithered to the floor.

As he embraced her, Bill Rawlins lifted the phone by the bed. "Refer all my calls to Mr. Henderson in Suite 379. Thank you."

He drew the nude Laura Hurley down on the bed, turning so she was on top of him. Her hair fell about his face, as she kissed him desperately.

Hoyle Henderson snuffed out his cigarette. He read the twelve telephone messages left at the front desk. Ariel Graves, who traveled with Hoyle as a member of the campaign headquarters staff, sat in the living room of Suite 379, managing the two phone lines from the hotel switchboard, as well as the direct line Hoyle had installed earlier. There was a walkie-talkie beside her. She handed him another stack of messages.

"These callers are going berserk, Hoyle," she said, as the phone jangled again.

Ariel Graves picked it up.

"Oh, it's you again. Hold on a sec." She turned to Hoyle, hand over the phone. "This guy's called about six times. Won't give his name. Says it's urgent."

Hoyle nodded, on the move. "I'll take it in the bedroom."

"Yeah," Hoyle said into the phone. "Where you calling from?"

"Never mind," said the voice. "The Los Angeles *Times* has fingered the woman, or they think they have. It's a certain visit a certain lady made in New York City after a certain TV interview. If she's anywhere around, you better catapult her to hell and gone. They'll be swarming all over you."

The phone clicked in Hoyle's ear.

Hoyle bit down hard on his cigarette. He looked at the copies of the phone sheets in his hand: Rick Gleason had called three times.

He sat on the side of the bed. The Kells people must have alerted Gleason.

Laura Hurley was a beautiful woman. Unbelievable figure. Very rich. To Hoyle these were all mighty fine assets, though not necessarily in that order. Jesus, running for President was a hellaciously indelicate moment to play grabass between the sheets.

He picked up the phone. "This is Hoyle Henderson. Put me through to Mr. William Rawlins in Bungalow Five. Emergency."

Rawlins' voice was low. "Yes, Hoyle?"

"A report from our Washington outpost. Rick Gleason has his pit bulls on the trail of Laura Hurley. They know about New York, claim she's with you here in Los Angeles, and, as far as I know, have a stakeout on your bungalow. Gleason won't go with any story like that unless he has it nailed. I'm sending Ariel Graves downstairs. She'll wait at the back door of the bungalow. Let her in. She'll have some clothes ready to get the lady out of there. If we move quickly, I can handle Gleason. I'll get our driver to meet you at the front door of the bungalow and take you on to Bel Air. I'll join you there."

Rawlins merely said, "Fine," and hung up abruptly.

Hoyle picked up his walkie-talkie. "This is Mesquite calling Pilot."

Within seconds, Charlie Embaugh's thick voice was coming through the receiver. Embaugh had taken leave of absence from the Secret Service to personally manage the privately financed security apparatus for Rawlins.

"We got a crisis, Pilot. The boss will be leaving in a few minutes. Have another car parked at the far end of Crescent and be ready to move when Ariel appears with a friend. Get a couple of your biggest guys to the back of the Bungalow, and clear that area of any hangers-on. If they don't want to leave, a poke to the gonads'll explain why they ought to."

Within eleven minutes, Ariel Graves, short, plump, arm in arm with a rather tall, unsteady gentleman wearing a brown fedora, gray slacks, and an oversize jacket, glided out of the back door of Bungalow Five and walked casually along the tree- and brush-lined pathway back of the hotel. They turned off to the right and walked, now faster, along the rear pathway of the outermost bungalows way up Crescent Street, a short distance from the intersection of Lexington. There, Ariel and her companion got in a black Lincoln Town Car and sped away.

Hoyle dialed Rick Gleason's number on the private line.

"How you doing, Rick?" he said, and listened as Rick Gleason spoke rapidly.

"You're on heavy stuff, Rick," said Hoyle, "if you believe that shit from the Kells crowd. You go with a story without solid proof, and you and your bosses will spend the next five years in depositions and courtrooms, which your stockholders will just love, since it will cost you a frigging million in lawyer fees."

Within half an hour, Hoyle was in Bel Air, pulling into the gate-guarded spacious driveway of the Chief Executive Officer of one of the largest bank holding companies in the world. Rawlins was sitting in his car, Charlie Embaugh and two scowling companions standing idly around the shiny black four-door Lincoln Town Car.

Hoyle waved at Embaugh, and slid in the back seat next to Rawlins. "I bought us a little time. Gleason almost has the story—almost, but not quite . . ."

"Cut the preface," Rawlins said abruptly. "Bottom line?"

"The bottom line is that he lacks corroboration, which means the *Times* ain't going with any story. Willacy Hughes or Clem Barkley fed him. But they got no smoking gun. What Gleason has is that her limo dropped her off at the Kells building in New York. He knows that she was at the Lambert dinner party, and somebody, probably Clem, says you and the lady were cozy, and walked together to the Lambert cottage. I told Gleason we'd sue the ass off his paper if he prints anything without proof. I told him not only would we haul him and his whole goddamn Board of Directors into court, but we would publicly claim that the White House put him up to it. And then we would tear out some eyeballs as extra fun. Gleason says he has more, but I doubt it. Doubtless there'll be a tail on the lady from here on in. Need I say more?"

Rawlins absorbed Hoyle's comments silently. Then he tapped on the window. His door opened. Over his shoulder he said with a wide grin, "Let's go in and charm the populace, Hoyle."

Thirty-three

SILENCE HUNG like a shroud in the Kremlin offices of the new Politburo in Moscow. Danil Kirsanov, aide to the Executive President, watched his chief read the note Kirsanov had delivered.

The Executive President moved slowly to a giant desk. "How was this confirmed?"

"Werner Haffenstorn's lover could not hide the truth once matters were . . . properly explained."

"Haffenstorn, that neo-Nazi swine! Who was this lover of his? Was she German or Soviet?"

"*He* was German, Comrade Executive President."

The Executive President looked pained. "Oh," he said. The Soviet chieftain had a puritan distaste for such sexual matters. "Is that your proof, the lover's confession?"

"The penitent lover soon offered other names and facts, which we've corroborated."

"And the lover, where is he?"

"I regret to report he is dead. The exhaustion of confession was taxing. Heart failure, our physician reported. But then, it was an affair of the heart that caused his difficulty in the first place."

A wry smile creased the Executive President's face. "You have a lethal wit, Danil Vasilievich."

Kirsanov bowed ever so slightly.

"Is Haffenstorn's exposure known by Viktor Zinyakin and his associates?"

"No—I am confident it is not. If Zinyakin knew, we would know he knew. Everyone in the Special Security Elite Guard, which conducted this inquiry, is loyal and circumspect." The Special Security Elite unit, organized by the Executive President, was contemptuous of the KGB, and collectively found them and their Chairman odious.

"And they're standing by now?"

"Ten of the Elite Guard officers are in the privileged area, just outside the Conference Room."

"And Viktor Zinyakin?"

"He will arrive in a few minutes to attend a small Politburo meeting. The subject is China and he will be prepared—except he will be operating off the wrong agenda."

"Will he come alone?"

"He will doubtless bring with him his pet ape, Ryzinsin. He is supposed to be the Chairman's China expert." That Lev would be an expert in anything except wielding a clawhammer on a captive in the KGB detention center was absurd to Kirsanov.

The Executive President was somber. "I find it odd that Viktor Anatolevich could be so careless. Until now, the reports from Germany disclosing Werner Haffenstorn's political activities haven't proven any involvement with our KGB. But this new information gives us no choice." The Executive President turned abruptly to Kirsanov. "How do you gauge Federof?"

"I do not count him as part of this cabal, Comrade Executive President. Filipp Vladimirovich is a patriot. I cannot believe he has been corrupted by the KGB Chairman."

The Executive President's expression was troubled. "Federof is our man in Washington. Do we know precisely what orders Viktor has issued him?"

"No, we do not."

The Executive President looked pensive. He looked down at his hands, palms up. "We have to do what we are doing with the United States, even as we have to do what we do tonight. My grandfather used to say that one must seem to be contrite, else we make others suspicious. And then, when our aims appear pacific, we strike, swiftly, surely."

Kirsanov said nothing.

The buzzer on the huge desk came alive. Kirsanov picked up the phone.

"Yes? Thank you. Escort him to the Conference Room."

He put the phone down. "The Chairman of the KGB is here, and with him is Lev Ryzinsin."

The Executive President strode to the door to his right and entered a corridor, leading to another door, which opened onto the large, dimly lit Conference Room. Kirsanov followed.

At the far end of the Conference Room were the KGB Chairman and bulky Lev Ryzinsin. They both smiled broadly as the Executive President approached.

"It is good to see you, my Leader," Zinyakin said expansively as he embraced the Executive President.

"Thank you, Viktor Anatolevich," the Soviet leader stiffly replied.

Ryzinsin shook the Executive President's hand. "It is my pleasure to be with you, Comrade Executive President."

"And I with you, Lev Panfilovich." He gestured to the KGB head to sit down, then motioned to Kirsanov, who took a seat beside Zinyakin.

"The agenda tonight is China?" Zinyakin asked.

"The agenda tonight, Viktor Anatolevich, is more than China. It concerns the Soviet Union's future. That, you will concede, is a larger agenda than China." No glacier could have been colder than the Executive President's voice.

Zinyakin's neck went rigid. He looked quickly at Lev, who was now on alert. "The future of the Soviet Union is always at the top of our agenda. Can you be specific?"

The Executive President nodded at Kirsanov, who rose, swiftly strode to the smaller door at the rear of the room, opened it, and four immaculately uniformed officers, in the garb of the Special Security Elite unit, poured in.

Zinyakin flinched. Ryzinsin half-rose to his feet.

The tallest officer stood at attention before the seated Zinyakin.

"You are under arrest, Comrade Chairman, for betrayal of your oath to the Motherland."

The officer drew a burnished 9mm weapon from its holster, leveling it against the forehead of the Chairman. The other three officers withdrew their weapons as well, two of them pointing glistening 9mm automatics at Lev Ryzinsin, who began to sputter, "This is a lie, this is wrong!"

One of the officers swatted him with a gun barrel.

The other officer patted Ryzinsin down; another searched the KGB Chairman. No weapons were found.

Then the tall officer bowed slightly to the Executive President.

"Spare us any rebuttal, Viktor Anatolevich," the Executive President told his KGB Chairman.

Zinyakin, trembling, said nothing. He wiped his forehead with the back of his left hand. "May I request that the Executive President not act hastily. There are many questions he may want answered, and many services I can perform for our country."

"Services, Viktor Anatolevich? You have been skillful at performing services, though not for your country: for your own blind ambition. What instructions have you given Federof?"

Zinyakin said nothing. He drew himself to his full height and stared at the Executive President.

"I can tell you what you want to know!" yelled Ryzinsin, an officer's gun barrel pressed against his nose.

"Keep your mouth shut, you spineless coward," snapped Zinyakin.

Kirsanov moved quickly to Zinyakin's side. He held out his hand. The tall officer placed the 9mm automatic in his open palm. Kirsanov put the gun's snout against Zinyakin's right temple.

"Answer the Executive President."

The KGB Chairman stared at the wall in front of him, the nose of the gun pressing against his head. "You cannot shoot me," he said. "You must put me on trial."

Kirsanov smiled. "I cannot shoot you? Because you deserve a trial? How nicely you now remember legal obligations."

He pressed the trigger.

The sound shook the room. Bone, blood, and brain flew from Zinyakin's head and he fell like a pole-axed animal.

Ryzinsin almost fainted.

The Executive President shook his head sadly and left the room.

Kirsanov moved to the now totally distraught Ryzinsin, who held on to the back of a chair to keep himself upright. The gun was still in Kirsanov's hand as he came to Lev's side.

"You and I will now depart these premises, my dear Lev Panfilovich, and we will talk of many things. You will tell me all that you know. You will be happy to do so because you know that when I tell you I will do something to you, you know I will do it."

He motioned Lev out of the room, following him with weapon at the ready. Over his shoulder he said to the tall officer, "Get this room cleaned up, now."

The next day's edition of *Pravda* announced the hospitalization of the KGB Chairman and his aide, Lev Ryzinsin. The cause of their illness was not specified, but it was implied that a contagious virus had struck them down. The story did not reveal the name of the hospital to which they were taken. Though their families had been notified of the swiftness of the illness, because of the contagion family members could not visit either man. The Executive President praised them highly and hoped they would be free of their malady soon to return to their duties, where they were so sorely needed.

On the leased Gulfstream IV flying east, Bill Rawlins, Hoyle Henderson, Peter Weymouth, and three campaign staff members paid scant attention to the story on page six of the New York *Times* which revealed that the KGB Chairman was in the hospital with an undisclosed illness.

What they did read with mounting interest was the report of a speech given by Senator Gifford Gray at the National Press Club in Washington, carried live by C-Span, and excerpted by all three national network evening news shows. "NBC Evening News" allotted almost two minutes to Gray's remarks, a lavish time expenditure inside a twenty-six-minute newscast. Even the *Times* reporter found that convincing evidence that Senator Gray's critical assessment of Rawlins' run for the Presidency was beginning to take public root.

Weymouth said, "With the exception of Senator Gray's entry into the debate, we are moving pretty good, Bill. But frankly, we have a nagging running sore that comes from what Senator Gray has been peddling around the country, that there is something diabolically wrong about a Vice President turning on his President. Like marking the cards or lying to your family. Because Senator Gray has this latter-day God reputation, it is beginning to hurt among the commentators, who in turn are infecting the public. I thought your old man used to be a buddy of his. Can't we turn him off somehow?"

Rawlins turned to Hoyle. "Hard to turn Gifford Gray off of anything, eh, Hoyle?"

"Well," said Hoyle, "I don't have any plaster-saint worship fetish like most of the Senate has about Gray. Hell, Bill, even you get a little ticky in Gray's presence. As far as I am concerned, he's a worn-out old man who is past his prime and ought to get the hell out of public life and go back to that farm in Tennessee that he keeps on saying how much he loves. If he loves it so much, how come he spends so damn little time on it?"

"What you don't understand is that taking on Gifford Gray is like getting into a fight with your father," said Rawlins. "Not very appetizing. So my killer instincts cool when it comes to Gifford."

Hoyle said, "All right, Bill, but this friend of yours and your late father's is kicking the living shit out of you, and I tell you it hurts."

Weymouth changed the subject.

"By the way," he said, "our band of roving reporter brothers is on our backs about who accompanies Bill on campaign trips. They want to know the names of each staff member who is with you. What is this all about?"

Hoyle threw a quick glance at Rawlins, who was now deeply engrossed in the *Times*.

"What else, Peter, except the same old crap," said Hoyle. "Those nosy reporters are sharking in and out of the woods, trying to nail down something, figuring if they bury their snoots deep enough in dirt, they'll smell something funny. But all they are going to really get is their breath backing up on them, and that'll be as rancid a smell as they will ever sniff."

Weymouth wasn't mollified, but he had two packets of material he needed to go over with Rawlins, so he gave a short nod to Hoyle and said, "Bill, I have some speech drafts we need to take a look at, as well as a detailed story-line for the next five weeks. We are suggesting that we tackle one issue at a time for a week, hit the President hard on each one, making several speeches on each issue so that even the hard-asses will finally come to understand what we are saying, Senator Gray or no Senator Gray."

He passed a folder to Rawlins, and an extra copy to Hoyle. Bill looked up, grinning. "Okay, to work."

He tossed the *Times* over to Ariel Graves, who was sitting on the sofa back of Rawlins. She caught the paper in mid-flight. She flipped the pages, glancing only erratically at the story on page six about the illness of the KGB Chairman. She flung the paper down beside her and looked out the window at the wispy, glaringly white landscape. It is so peaceful up here, she thought.

Andrew Collingdown, Director of Central Intelligence, sat stiff-backed in the Oval Office. Winthrop MacIver, the Secretary of State, Clem Barkley, Mike Carson, and John Wingate were seated in a half circle around the President's desk.

"What do you have for me, Andy?"

"Mr. President, there's been a massive upheaval in the Soviet leadership. We don't know at this time precisely why, but Viktor Zinyakin, the KGB chief, is definitely out. *Pravda* says he's hospitalized with a contagious disease; our experts think he's already been liquidated. It may have something to do with Germany as well. The Chancellor, we are reliably informed, received a message from the Kremlin reporting some treasonable activities by leaders of the newly organized Democratic Alliance Party, the neo-Nazi seedbed threatening the reelection of the Chancellor. Werner Haffenstorn, the neo-Nazi ringleader, has also disappeared. Underground or dead."

"This may have a bearing on what Clem and Toni Georgihu are working on," the President said. "Go on, Andy."

"This is not a casual turn of events, Mr. President. When you meet with the Executive President next month, the Zinyakin ouster will, in my judgment, affect your agenda. Zinyakin was a first-class hard-cover, brutal and remorseless."

Clem said, "Apparently Zinyakin had aims to become the all-powerful Soviet leader, in a throwback to the old regime, and wasn't averse to making alliances that would have been unthinkable some years ago. His fall, if he's really fallen, has got to have foreign policy linkage."

The CIA Director nodded.

The President turned to MacIver. "What's your judgment, Winthrop?"

MacIver cleared his throat. "Well, sir, we have been examining the material the Agency has uncovered. I do believe that Zinyakin was an evil force within the Soviet leadership, and that the Executive President might have in the future been threatened by his ambition. But what is still puzzling is what triggered this precipitous move. As we plan for the meeting next month, we will surely insert this new development into our briefing papers."

Clem was amused. Briefing papers were the gristle and grain of State Department life. What an archaeological treasure is the State Department archives! He often mused that 95 percent of what he read in CIA briefings and State Department secret books would be better learned with more clarity within the pages of the Washington *Post* and the New York *Times*. He knew that the President had small cause to celebrate the phrase "top secret." Any time more than two people gathered in any meeting or read any document, short of sequestering them and cutting out their tongues, whatever was said or read always leaked.

"You agree, John?" the President asked.

Wingate fumbled with his tie. "My estimate tracks Andy's. That is, we may assume that with the hard-liners absent from the table, the Executive President has more leeway in his future policy. But, Mr. President, one is never certain about the Byzantine corridors of Soviet decision-making."

"Therefore?" said the President.

"Therefore, sir, let us wait. When you meet with the new Soviet leader, you can address this presumed development face to face. For myself, I don't place much stock in the Haffenstorn part of this tale. The Chancellor is running scared, but then, as you have often instructed, all candidates should do that very thing."

"You're taking instruction well, John," the President said affably.

"Mr. President," Clem said, "this man Federof at the Soviet Embassy is a former high-ranking KGB general under Zinyakin. There's also an agent named Vaslansky whom we've picked up on taps and intercepts. I've suspected for some time that Federof, or Vaslansky under Federof's instructions, killed those two Bulgarians. And I also believe that all this relates somehow to the Rawlins campaign. I just can't make the connection."

Clem noticed the puzzled look on the faces of MacIver and Wingate. Ouch, he thought, I have said more here than the Boss would have chosen. He glanced quickly at the President, but there was no hint of anything on his face.

"Maybe," said Mike Carson acidly, "because there's no connection to make." He turned to the President. "I'm worried, Mr. President, that the hardball we're playing of late will surface in the press and bite us in the ass."

The President nodded. "Point well taken, Mike. I don't want our side of this campaign getting personal or mean."

He stood.

"John, keep me fully briefed. I'm asking Mike Carson to keep a lid on all this. Winthrop, you and John play this discreetly with press inquiries. Use your instincts, but under no circumstances do we allow any expression of anxiety or puzzlement to seem part of our response. And it's really premature to treat this Soviet upheaval as good news."

"The good news," Clem said, "is that the latest ABC poll shows a slight upturn in our report card."

The President smiled. "Now, let's not insert any crass political canvassing into this meeting . . ."

Federof and Vlady Miektor strolled in the courtyard of the Soviet Embassy. Federof had the antibugging device in his outer lapel pocket switched on.

"We are at a turning point, Vlady Aleksandrovich. And we must turn quickly, else we will regret everything."

Miektor stopped.

"Keep walking," Federof said. "I have heard directly from the

Executive President. He has informed me that Viktor is ill and cannot return to his duties."

"What . . . ?"

He drew closer to Miektor. "Listen closely, my old and dearest friend. You and I will act decisively, now. Listen carefully."

As they walked, Federof spoke slowly, watching Vlady closely to assay his understanding of the orders.

Then Federof steered Miektor back to the Embassy proper. "Be about your tasks, Vlady Aleksandrovich. I count on you."

Miektor gave him a bear hug.

"Remember," Federof said, "Vaslansky is your first stop. Make sure he understands, and if he doesn't, let me know and I will deal with him."

As Federof approached his apartment door, Berisov hailed him.

"Filipp," the Ambassador said anxiously, "do you have a moment?"

Federof smiled almost deferentially. "Of course, my friend. Shall we go to the Secure Room?"

Inside, an agitated Berisov sputtered, "What is the matter with Viktor Zinyakin? Has there been a coup attempt? I am in the dark. I have received only a dispatch which parrots what was in *Pravda*."

"My friend, I know nothing more than you. We will continue with our duties as we have in the past. Have you received any orders instructing you to do otherwise?"

Berisov paced. "I have been dispatching reports to the Foreign Office, but they only reply: 'Your report received.' Nothing more! Am I a robot?"

Federof put a hand gently on his shoulder. "You are a diligent and competent Ambassador. Your services are appreciated, else you would have been recalled. Have you not considered that?"

Berisov nodded slowly.

"Why seek anxiety when there is no need for it?"

The Ambassador smiled weakly. "Filipp, perhaps you are right."

Federof then went to his apartment. His hand on the doorknob trembled slightly.

. . . .

Toni Georgihu sat in Clem Barkley's office. "You sounded odd on the phone, Clem."

She looked so appealing he found it difficult to concentrate on what she was saying.

"Clem, are you listening to me? What did you want to tell me?"

"Well, it's kind of a funny, strange story. About two hours ago, my secretary told me I had a call from a man who would not reveal his name, but asked me to leave my office, go to a pay phone in the lobby of the Willard Hotel, and call a specific number. He also told my secretary that no one should wire the Willard pay phone in advance because there would be someone watching it until I arrived. Isn't that funny?"

"So far it is hilarious enough for Jay Leno's monologue," Toni said. "You didn't go, did you?"

"I did, because the caller said this was a follow-up to the gentleman who worked for Crown Broadcasting."

"Roy Hickey?"

"Precisely. I walked across the street to the Willard and made the phone call as requested. He asked me to go to Room 712 in the Willard, at that moment. I was to knock on the door twice and I would be admitted, where I would become privy to information that would be most valuable to me and the President. I called the Secret Service, told them where I was going, and if I didn't call back in fifteen minutes, to come fetch me."

"Did you go to the room?"

"I did, and there I met a certain Mr. Vaslansky whose dossier, as well we know, is longer than *War and Peace*. By the way, I have reported all this to the President."

"Well?"

"You and I have a rendezvous."

"Ah, sounds romantic."

"Except this is a menage à trois."

Toni frowned.

Clem was clearly enjoying the scene.

"To answer your unspoken question, you and I have an appointment with the much-discussed Filipp Federof!"

.   .   .   .

Laura Hurley wept. Racking sobs shook her body; her head was in her hands, thick hair falling in disarray about her face.

She'd spent two days making phone calls to a ghost. Of the three numbers she had, one had been disconnected, the second never answered, and the third eventually got her a hollow, unfamiliar voice that took her name and abruptly ended the call.

When the phone finally rang, an hour ago, she picked it up so eagerly her trembling fingers fumbled it to the floor. She hastily retrieved it. "Hello, hello!"

Another unfamiliar voice said, "Mrs. Hurley, your friend is unable to speak with you. He believes it's wise for there to be no contact between the two of you for the time being."

"For the time being? What does that mean? When can I talk with Bill?"

Silence.

Then the voice said, "For the time being. That's all I can tell you."

"That's not good enough! I want to speak to Bill. You tell him he's got to talk to me!"

"I'm sorry, Mrs. Hurley. Please don't bother calling again. This number is being disconnected at the end of the day."

Then she heard a click.

She screamed.

Thirty-four

WHEN NO ONE answered her knock, Laura Hurley's frightened maid called Laura's wealthy father, Malcolm Kent, who rushed to his daughter's apartment on Fifth Avenue in New York City.

The pills Laura had taken would have done their fatal job had paramedics not acted with dizzying speed. Kent flew Laura in his private jet to the Mayo Clinic in Rochester, Minnesota, registering her under an assumed name. Saving his daughter's physical being was only the start. Ahead were years of psychiatric care. His little girl had been severely wounded.

Rage burned in Malcolm Kent like carbolic acid. He wanted to hurt Bill Rawlins, but he wanted the pain to linger and last . . .

In his hotel suite in Rochester, Kent dialed the number of Senator Raymond Tunstall. He had to start somewhere, and the Senate Majority Leader was the first stop.

B. J. Brackenfield lingered over his coffee at Duke Zeibert's restaurant at Connecticut Avenue and L Street, sitting at a table with Mitchell Joyner and Willa Hammond. He had launched into a new story, when Duke Zeibert ambled over. "You got an emergency call, B.J. Why don't you get with the twentieth century and put a phone in your office so I don't have to be your switchboard?" Duke Zeibert laughed gleefully.

B.J. rumbled to his feet, saying, "Considering the food you serve, Duke, free phone calls are necessary."

He picked up the phone. "B. J. Brackenfield here."

"How you doing, B.J.? You giving the Lord a bad time?"

"Jimmy Winger, you wizened little fart. How come you always call me when I am taking lunch? Don't ask for money, Jimmy, my bank is giving me shingles every day about your loan."

"No asking for money today, B.J. Remember that story our grandpappy used to tell about John Nance Garner, how old Cactus Jack would always stick with his troops until the fire got too hot, then Cactus would call his cronies together and say, 'Boys, I aimed to stay with you, but this shit is stinking too bad, so I want you to know I'm about to cut and run.' Remember that story, B.J.?"

"Course I remember. You practicing a sermon on me, or what, Jimmy?"

"Not a-tall, B.J. I am just saying to you, in the words of Cactus Jack Garner, I am about to cut and run."

"Jimmy, I don't know whether it's the fault of AT&T, or maybe Duke Zeibert ain't paying his phone bills, but I got trouble hearing you just right. You cutting and running from what?"

"I got reporters all over my backside, asking pesky questions, and mostly about you, B.J., about my finances and about our fine friend who aspires to be the leader of the free western world. Since my vocation in life is saving souls, I don't want to lose mine. Fact is, I'm suddenly getting lockjaw and am not sure I can continue to talk up our former Vice President and friend to mankind. As I said, B.J., I'm hauling ass, cutting and running, adiós amigos, have a good day, and all the rest of that good gospel."

B.J. pondered what he had just heard. He knew just about every newspaper on the North American continent was trolling the waters. He had been called by a most persistent reporter, even had her hanging out in his reception room, but he figured that unless someone gave him a court order, his tongue didn't function for reporters. B.J. didn't talk to the press. When he got the last call from the unrelenting scribe, he merely said, "Young lady, I am not in the interview business. I'm in the law business. Now you want legal counsel, I'll recite for you my fees and we can do some talking, but otherwise the alum in my mouth is beginning to stick to my gums. Good-bye, Miss or Miz or Madame, as the case may be."

"Jimmy, you and I need to talk. You better not go off doing damn foolish things, which you and I know you're capable of doing about every twenty minutes. You hear me, Jimmy, you stand hitched until you and I talk face to face, though right now I'd like to bash yours in."

"You do explain things so sweetly, cousin B.J. I'll be around Washington next week. You want to manhandle some spirits with me so that we can, as you say, with your usual disregard for God's commandments, talk turkey? Meanwhile, I suggest that you find some way to get these reporters off my sore back."

B.J. decided it would not be prudent to burden Willa and Mitch with Jimmy Winger's blatherings.

Clem Barkley and Toni Georgihu stood in the small parlor of a suite in the Willard Hotel. Filipp Federof lounged no more than six feet from them, inspecting Toni with an unmasked admiring gaze.

Toni Georgihu was a thoroughly indoctrinated agent of the Bureau. She knew her craft. She had fought tradition, callous treatment by men who had no intention of becoming acclimated to a woman agent however qualified or intelligent, and she had triumphed. But at this moment she was engaged by a truant, bizarre thought. She was fascinated by this man, who leaped out of the pages of the Bureau's sterile prose. She was curious about him— that part which the files did not disclose.

Federof surveyed Clem carefully. This man was close to the President, very close. He knew the secrets guarded by the White House. He was definitely the man Federof intended to penetrate. His appraisal of Toni was less professional and more personal. She was very tall, pridefully erect, not too bad-looking, and doubtlessly quite handsome without her severe clothing. But Federof dismissed these exploratory fleshly probings. Too much was at stake.

Clem said calmly, "Perhaps we should all sit down first, and then we would like to hear what you have to say, Mr. Federof."

"Yes, that would be suitable to me," said Federof, in the cultured tones that one expects from someone who might have gotten a First in Classics at one of the British public universities.

Federof bowed slightly to Toni, nodded to Clem. They took seats at a small table in this suite, which had been swept earlier by the FBI for bugs and cameras.

"Let us, as you Americans say, get down to brass tacks, though," Federof said with a smile that Toni found, to her dismay, alluring, "I have often wondered why it is that brass tacks are supposed to be serious business. Your language is so pliable."

"Let's cut the preliminaries, Mr. Federof, and save the English lessons for another time. Why are you here?" said Clem.

"I come to you with a gift," Federof said. "There is no reciprocity involved. It is a gift from my leader to your leader. We need to begin anew, to begin a period of trust, perhaps small at first, but later it will grow as your President and mine try to create something useful, valuable, and lasting for all of us."

He spoke quietly, without passion and seemingly without guile.

Clem spoke. "Before we go any further with gifts you bring us, let me speak candidly."

"Candor is a blood relative of trust, Mr. Barkley," said Federof.

Clem ignored the riposte.

"I have a question. How do you fit in with two very dead Bulgarians?"

Federof stared at him, then smiled slightly. "Yes, that was a bungled, stupid adventure. It was something that had to be done."

"Like Greta Hulved?" Acid burned in Clem's quiet words.

Federof shrugged aimlessly.

"But why was Roy Hickey killed, what was the purpose?" Toni asked.

"It was all part of a charade, to make you think that this man Hickey was the source of the leak of the secret trip to China."

"A charade? Hickey wasn't the leak?" Clem said. "I don't understand."

"Mr. Hickey was receiving funds from the KGB for minor services rendered. We wanted you to think certain things that were not so."

Clem folded his hands. "All right, now tell us about your gift."

Federof stood up, strode to the window, looked out, turned and faced them, leaning against the sill.

"There is a mole in your Government," he said, "in the most sensitive of all arenas. He is a servant of the U.S.C.R. and has for the last few years been supplying the former Chairman of the KGB with the most intimate information which you guard with much zeal. I will offer you this traitor, but only under the following scenario."

Clem Barkley and Toni said nothing. They exchanged blank expressions that concealed shock.

Clem said, "Mole? You mean a spy?"

"If you like that word better. Perhaps John le Carré is on your reading list." He nodded playfully to Toni. Federof was proud of his knowledge of western literature.

"The code name for our agent is Nightingale, the bird who sings in a clear, unambiguous voice. Indeed, you asked earlier about Mr. Hickey and his place in this scheme. It was Nightingale who designed the Hickey charade. We had to have someone to nail as the leak of the China trip. Someone you would accept as the leak without your really knowing who took the secret public. Nightingale is a most ingenious species, don't you agree?"

"Nightingale?" asked Clem. Though he was in the inner circle of the President, had sat in on interminable meetings with the CIA and assorted other intelligence agencies in the bosom of the Government, his knowledge of moles was pitifully small.

Clem pressed on. "What is this scenario you mentioned?" he said.

"First, that the source of your knowledge of the spy remain in this room. The President can take full credit for the unveiling of this man who betrayed the United States, except for one minor addition, and that is, the President should publicly declare that the Executive President knew nothing of the presence of the spy, that the spy reported to the former KGB Chairman and no one else.

"Second, the President should send a note to the Executive President confirming that the spy has confessed—and I assure you he will—that his mission in this country was to serve the KGB Chairman, thereby absolving the Executive President of complicity."

Federof paused. "Impossible as it may seem to you, the Executive President was never privy to the existence of Nightingale. This was, from beginning to end, Zinyakin's project, left over from his predecessor, who also neglected to tell his leader."

Clem said, "That's hard to believe, Mr. Federof. Truly hard to believe."

"Can you certify to me," said Federof, "that your President is totally knowledgeable about American agents within the Soviet Union? Does he know who they are and where they can be located?"

Clem said nothing. The impact of Federof's revelation was too stunning to readily absorb.

"All right, Mr. Federof, we've talked enough. Who is the mole?"

"Do you speak for the President? Do you, on his behalf, accept my scenario?"

Toni broke in, saying quickly, "You will truly deliver this spy to us, if he truly exists?" She hesitated. "It is a man we are talking about?"

Federof laughed. "Yes, Agent Georgihu, the spy is a man. We are not so 'with it,' as you might say. Next time, we will be an equal opportunity employer." Federof's smile was self-approving.

"I didn't realize the KGB specialized in wit," Clem said. "The question is, will you deliver this spy to us?"

"Yes."

Clem didn't hesitate. "You've got a deal."

Federof nodded, hands extended in a gesture of accord.

"Now," said Clem, "who is the mole?"

The Majority Leader sat with Vincent Canfield in the columnist's antique-laden library. Tunstall sipped the wine Canfield had provided.

"Vincent," Tunstall said, "I had a most disturbing phone call from Malcolm Kent. He was virulent in his denunciation of Bill Rawlins."

"Why?"

"He gave no reason. If I didn't know how shrewd and cool Malcolm is, I'd have sworn he was on the verge of a breakdown."

"Some business deal they were in together has taken a bad turn, no doubt," Canfield said dismissively.

"Perhaps. But he said he was prepared to spend millions to defeat Bill in the primaries and he wanted my help."

Canfield's alarm wasn't well disguised. "Your help, indeed! And on what b-b-b-basis does he apply for that aid?"

"He's been a generous contributor to my PAC, which supports Democratic Senate incumbents as well as Senatorial candidates. How else do you suppose I'm able to entice aspirants to run, and when they win, bind them to me?"

"I presume you refused him."

"Vincent, sometimes you presume too much."

"Raymond, I didn't m-m-m-mean it that way—just, why on earth would Malcolm Kent call you and make such an unreasonable request?"

Tunstall examined the wine in the glass as he held it up to the light. "I don't know. But the Malcolm Kents of the world don't drip venom over the phone unless there's ample reason . . ."

Less than twenty minutes after their meeting at the Willard Hotel, Clem and Toni faced the President in the Oval Office.

The President was more than just surprised by their report, he was shaken, blood draining from his face. His eyes pierced Clem. "I pray to God this information is false."

Toni spoke up. "Mr. President, I'm convinced Federof isn't lying. The Director shares my view. I respectfully suggest we move immediately to nail our mole."

Clem said, "Toni's right, sir. Federof has given us very explicit information on how to lay our trap. It's the proof you need. And we can get it."

The President shook his head, as if he were gesturing no, but he said, "Clem, you and Toni discuss this with the Director. Whatever the three of you decide, I'll go along. I have no problems with Federof's 'scenario.' But, as positive as this may wind up, I have to say right now I personally find it shattering."

Clem understood.

The buzzer sounded and the President picked up his phone. He listened intently, looking up at Clem and then at Toni. His face became gray.

"God, what more misery can be visited on this place?" his anguished query directed to himself more than the two in front of him.

He put down the phone and said, "Gifford Gray just dropped dead in the Senate Dining Room."

The panel truck bearing the name Mildred's Catering Service drove out of the Soviet Embassy gates and turned right on Tunlaw. In the truck, sitting behind the driver but well out of sight, was Filipp Federof.

The truck clattered over the cobblestone streets of Georgetown, turned down an alley, and stopped. The driver said, "We're here, sir."

Federof peeked over the edge of the seat and then briskly disembarked. "A bit silly to slouch about like this, but I suppose it's necessary," he murmured. He was at the back entrance. The door was open. He pushed it back.

A voice said, "You're punctual."

Federof said, "Thank you for receiving me. I've long wished to meet you."

"Come into the library," Bill Rawlins said.

Soon Federof was gazing at the Bingham landscape above the fireplace.

"Drink?" Rawlins asked.

"Thank you. Cognac?"

Rawlins nodded, poured Courvoisier into a tumbler. "I'll have a light scotch myself."

They lifted their glasses.

"I found your message intriguing," Rawlins said. "A bit surprising you'd want to talk with me. Is that wise? A Presidential candidate meeting secretly with a top KGB general. I doubt any explanation I could give would wash with the press."

Federof sipped his cognac. "I would not intrude if there were alternatives. I have come with information that will not be cordial to you. I report this to you because there is no other alternative."

Rawlins' eyes narrowed. He took a brief swallow of the scotch. "Somehow, I didn't figure you came here to tell me how charming I was."

"You must withdraw from the race."

The six words were spoken almost tonelessly. This statement, uttered with such finality by this Russian, was a hammer blow. Rawlins felt it. Hard.

"Withdraw? Come now, General Federof—"

"I do not mean to sound as if I come bearing truth from God, or whoever understands these things, Mr. Vice President. But I do have to tell you the facts. In the recent past, Boris Vaslansky, on behalf of the KGB Chairman, met very secretly with your instrument, a man named Henderson. The FBI knows Vaslansky consorted briefly with a Senator and a TV commentator. But they do not know about the meetings with Henderson. They were very carefully guarded."

Rawlins said nothing.

"The KGB Chairman in question," Federof said, "will never be in power again. Your man and his sealed a compact that is no longer functional. My leader has now determined that it is better for him to revise his relations with President Kells than appear to be intruding into an American election."

Rawlins remained silent.

"Mind you," continued Federof, "under different circumstances, and perhaps with different people in charge, I would be admiring of the design of your compact. Indeed, as I am admiring of you. But I now have no choice. I am telling you that you must withdraw because the consequences of your not doing so would be immense and tragic. Not to me and my leader, but to your own personal fortunes. Forgive me this brutal reporting of facts, but each of us must do what we have to do."

Rawlins stood. He was icily calm. "Care to have your drink freshened? I think I will." He poured two shots of scotch into his glass. He downed it in one gulp. "I noticed you looking at the Bingham. Handsome, isn't it?"

Federof nodded. "I like it very much."

"I own that work of art, although this is my brother's home—but

I assume you know that. Your file on me must be pretty thick." Rawlins sat down languidly. "And if I don't withdraw?"

Federof leaned toward Rawlins. "Then, Mr. Vice President, we will throw Vaslansky to the wolves. He will sing like a Siberian canary. They are the hardiest of birds and their song is long and sweet and memorable." Federof smiled sadly. "Both Henderson and Vaslansky made certain neither was doing any recording, but Vaslansky made meticulous notes, after the fact. It does pain me to reveal that there were photographs taken of your man and mine."

"That's hardly proof."

Federof shrugged. "Even if you denied our allegations, we would cast such doubt on your campaign that the questions would never stop. You would spend all your time explaining you are not in bed with the Soviets. We all remember Mr. Nixon having to say constantly, 'I am not a crook.' You cannot function as a legitimate candidate under such a cloud. It would destroy you."

"And if I go along with this fabrication, what can I expect?"

"The President—and the public—will never know why you have withdrawn. You may make whatever amends with the President you find fitting. No one in your campaign organization will know. How you deal with Mr. Henderson is your choice. We will not inform him or meet with him."

Rawlins nodded. He gazed into the glass in his hand. He slowly twirled it, the small amount of scotch splashing easily. "I am a bit puzzled as to why you guys are so passionate about reelecting Kells. I had the distinct impression he kicks your nuts in about every forty-eight hours. Am I missing something here?"

"Such questions are beyond my power to answer. I can only say that my leader now has different views."

"All right, General—let me think this over. Do I have a deadline?"

Federof spoke in a low voice. "Yes, you do, Mr. Vice President. I must know within a week from this day."

"When I was studying at Harvard," said Rawlins, "I took a course in Russian history. I learned that Peter the Great had a great zest for western ways and western living. His exertions killed him at an early age. I can now see that modern Russia is infected by the same virus."

"And what is that virus, Mr. Vice President?"

"An absolute blindness to logic and the main chance."

Federof nodded appreciatively. "I am not so learned as you are, Mr. Vice President. But I am careful in how I carry out my instructions. That is why I am a survivor."

Thirty-five

THE WASHINGTON CATHEDRAL is to the nation's Capital what Chartres is to the world.

This day in the Cathedral there were assembled the great and the near great to pay their tribute to Senator Gifford Gray. In the front row sat the President and every member of the Cabinet except two who were out of the country. A majority of the Senate and many from the House were also present. Bill Rawlins sat two pews behind the President, alone, not even his private security aides at his side.

The Cathedral hummed with the soft strains of a sixteenth-century English tone poem.

After the President had spoken and returned to his seat, there rose to the pulpit the towering figure of Senator Will Matthews.

He spoke of the life of Gifford Gray, his belief in public service as life's noblest and most rewarding adventure.

"The historians of science tell us of a divine continuum. Michelangelo died on the day that Galileo was born. And Galileo died on the day that Newton was born. No coincidence, say those who believe that God works his wonders in ways not known to mere mortals. So it is, I believe, that two days ago when Gifford Gray died, there was born somewhere in this land a child who will one day extend the nobility with which Gifford Gray so honorably provisioned the public life of our land of liberty."

The Senator bowed his head, then lifted his eyes to the assembly. The deep musical voice boomed and echoed throughout the Cathedral.

"I weep this day, as all this land should weep. We are drained of wisdom, of an indomitable will that refused to crack, of a mind that would not cringe, of a love for the bonds that hold this nation together, bonds that strain and move but never shatter. Oh Gifford, oh my friend, oh my brother, your genius it was to have done the best things in the worst of times, and to have hoped the best things in the most calamitous of times.

"And now we put you to rest, my brother. But we know, oh yes, we know, that in the days and years to follow, we will try to do what you would have done, and if we try, each of us will know we have been true to the people we have by solemn oath sworn to serve. That, my old and loving friend, is your legacy to this land . . ."

It was over. The din in the Cathedral grew louder as the guests, many wiping their eyes, rose to depart.

The President, flanked by Secret Service agents, moved toward the exit. He nodded to a Secret Service agent, who opened the door, and a cadre of agents enveloped the President as the horde of reporters and photographers raised their voices. Sensing something special was afoot, the President turned slightly.

Behind him, approaching rapidly, was Bill Rawlins.

The President stopped, half outside. The reporters and cameramen went berserk as Rawlins came to the President's side.

"Bill—I'm glad you came."

The two men shook hands.

"I know," the President said softly, "how much you and your family cared about Gifford."

"Mr. President, it's important that I trouble you for a private visit." Rawlins spoke quietly, his eyes fixed on the President.

"Of course. Early next week . . ."

"Today, if possible."

The President hesitated.

"I think you'll find what I have to say of importance, Mr. President. I wouldn't intrude otherwise."

The press and cameramen jostled, mobbed each other, mike booms stretched out to catch this conversation. The Secret Service became a wall, forcing the cameramen back, pushing aside the booms.

The President nodded. "In my office in one hour?"

"Thank you, Mr. President."

Precisely one hour after the President's departure from the Washington Cathedral, his buzzer sounded. Clem said, "He's here. I brought him through the West Basement. He's now sitting in the Cabinet Room."

"Escort him in. I want to see him alone," said the President. "Under no circumstances am I to be disturbed. No one is to be allowed in, no one."

Bill Rawlins came into the Oval Office, faultlessly clad in a dark gray suit, with blue stripes. The President waved him to a seat on the sofa. The President sat in his rocking chair.

"Mr. President, you were generous to allow me to come here. I am aware that the last few weeks have not been comforting to you and, for that matter, to me as well."

The President rocked slowly, elbow on the armrest, his chin cradled in his hand. He said nothing.

"I have come here to tell you that I plan tomorrow or the day after to announce I am withdrawing from the race."

The President stiffened. He forced himself to sit quietly.

"I have come to the conclusion that I have made a tragic error," said Rawlins. "My father's death, and now Gifford Gray. Even though Gifford had been taking me to task, and effectively, I might add, I admired and respected him more than I can say."

The President sat mutely, examining Rawlins carefully.

"What I have concluded, Mr. President, is that the country is damaged by my recent actions and I want to stanch the flow of blood as quickly as I can. Most of all, I want to apologize to you. However odd this may sound to you, I never intended to betray you. I honestly felt what I said. But to a good many folks, including Gifford, what I did was an act of betrayal. Therefore I am withdrawing. And I will tell the country of my decision as soon as possible. It's your call to make."

The President looked deeply into Bill Rawlins' soul. This is too sudden, too precipitous, the President knew that. But why?

He said in a very low voice, "I accept your apology, Bill. I must tell you I was deeply wounded by what you did. You caught me by surprise, as you do right now. You say this is my call? Then I suggest you announce this right away, no later than tomorrow."

Rawlins nodded. "I'll do it, Mr. President. I'll need several hours to make some calls around the country, and to construct a sensible statement. But I will try to do it tomorrow, no later than tomorrow evening."

The President stood up. He thrust out his hand. "Let us put this behind us, Bill. I bear no malice. This country and its problems are too large for malice."

He watched Rawlins leave the Oval Office, then he turned to the phone console. "Clem, get Mike Carson and Willacy Hughes in my office on the double. Find Willacy wherever he is. I need to talk to all of you, right now."

The President called the FBI Director. He instructed him carefully that the trap to be laid for Nightingale must be delayed for at least forty-eight hours. There was no need to lay two earthquaking pieces of news on top of each other.

The President sat wearily behind his desk. In the space of three days, he had played the role of a spectator, a fascinated observer. Strange and astounding events were exploding and unwinding round him, events over which he seemingly had little control and no sense of their approach. Strange how in politics so much resembles starting a heavy body down a hill. Once it moves, it takes on a life of its own and no matter who did the pushing, it can't be called back.

Political genius, he remembered from reading a biography of Bismarck, consists of hearing the distant hoofbeat of the horse of history and then leaping to catch the passing horseman by the coattails. That is precisely what he was doing now. Fifty years from now, when historians chronicled the last three days, they would probably write that Donald Kells, with his usual foresight and political dynamism, had deciphered the future with such skill that professionals still marvel at the dexterity of his countermoves. They'd get it wrong of course, as historians often do.

What he felt now was not so much pleasure as a huge feeling of relief, the kind that comes to the marathon runner who stayed the course to win only because his most favored opponents faltered and fell by the side of the road. Now he had to consider the next run, the one against the Republican candidate. Bobby Stonehaven, the little Governor, the overwhelming favorite of the other party. Stonehaven would not be so accommodating as Bill Rawlins, nor as forthcoming as the dashing KGB general, nor would he gasp and topple over in total fatigue. The bloody fight of winner take all lay ahead.

But at this moment the President came close to laughing. The hard part could come later. Now he would savor his momentary redemption.

Every newspaper in America erupted with headlines proclaiming the withdrawal of the former Vice President from the race for the Democratic nomination.

The anchormen of ABC, CBS, NBC, and Fox were a blur, so fast did each of them intersect with quick cuts to correspondents in the field. CNN unleashed a half hour of Pat Buchanan and Robert Novak snarling at the President for some undisclosed application of muscle, forcing a reluctant Rawlins off the scene, implying obliquely that some rascally and naughty things were in motion, even as they excoriated Rawlins for his liberalism. "Expert political observers" flooded the networks, with appearances by representatives of seven think tanks, four political consultants and media advisers, and five former White House assistants. William Booth Rawlins, on all three of the three morning shows, exuded charm and atonement with such telling effect that Kathie Couric of NBC, Joan Lunden of ABC, and Paula Zahn of CBS came perilously close to endorsing him for another run.

Why did he withdraw? To NBC's Kathie Couric he said with solemnity, "I realized that however much I thought I had a right to run, I came to feel it threatened to polarize the country, to break ties within the Party. Senator Gifford Gray's persuasions, plus my own—what shall I call it?—introspection, made me realize that I had acted too hastily. It's hard for any elected official to admit a mistake, but I admit mine. I care about this country, and I care about the Democratic Party, and I determined that my continued involvement in the race would, in the long run, be injurious to both. I intend to support President Kells with all the passion I can summon. I will work as hard as I can for his reelection."

To ABC's Joan Lunden, he said much the same, adding, "I made a terrible blunder. I want to own up to the American people what I did. And what I did, I have prayerfully concluded, was not in the long-term interest of this great country or my great party. So I have withdrawn, and I apologize to all those who worked so hard on my behalf, and I ask the forgiveness of the President and the people we both serve. I am human. Perhaps the citizens of America will be forgiving. I would be grateful for that."

It was an exhibition of contrition and humility not often seen on national television, by a famous and powerful political baron. If Ms. Lunden, Couric, and Zahn were absorbed by the former candidate's exemplary tone and rueful gaze, so were millions of Americans equally enraptured by an act of contrition which barely escaped a national absolution.

Thirty-six

THE PRESIDENT watched the performance, with an occasional approving look at Willacy Hughes and Clem Barkley, both seated in the President's office watching television as they sipped coffee and nibbled at toasted bagels.

Willacy wiped his mouth with his napkin. "It's hard to believe, even harder to figure out. What our noble friend neglected to tell the American people was we were closing a noose around his neck. My guess is, he figured to strike his tent before we tore it down for him."

The President waved away his comments. "No matter, Willacy. Bill's going to come on board. He's not without allies. We need him, and I want him. I'm not going to give him a urine test or ask him to take a polygraph. We have a long ride ahead of us, and it's going to get rockier once the conventions are over. You agree, Clem?"

"It'll be a mean campaign, sir. I say we ought not to close the door to anyone who wants to join us, and that goes for Bill Rawlins."

Willacy threw his hands in the air. "All right, sir, you're the boss. I follow orders. I'll endorse Clem's comments. Which means I will embrace our Texas friend and welcome him to the campaign bus. I will say this for him, he never bears a grudge against those he deserts."

"Willacy, let's hear no more of this," said the President. "I want to make sure that everyone in the White House has the party line. No divergences from anyone. The same goes for you and Clem and everyone else who is working in this campaign. Understood?" They both nodded.

"Meanwhile," said the President, "we have a bit of a problem on our hands. How can we best handle this exposure of Nightingale, which must be managed quickly?"

Within two hours of the announcement, the Senate Majority Leader was on the phone to Clem.

"My dear Clem, I don't want to bother the President, but I want to tell him how overjoyed I am at these most happy moments. We are on our way to victory, I am sure of that."

"Senator, please hold on one minute, will you?"

Clem buzzed the President. "I've got the Majority Leader on my line. Wants to tell you how happy he is."

The President said, "Come on in after you transfer him."

"Mr. President, Raymond Tunstall here. I cannot adequately convey to you my delight at Bill Rawlins' announcement. It is a glorious day for you, sir, and for the Democratic Party."

"Perhaps," said the President dryly, "for the country as well. I do appreciate your call, Raymond. You please me greatly." Clem, listening on the President's coffee table phone, could almost hear the wayward, unspoken thought of the President that the Senate Leader was the most punctual of men. He never allowed an opportunity to escape without taking at least some small advantage of it. Immediately.

"You may be sure, Mr. President, that I will work to the limit to make sure you are reelected. This nation needs you, and needs you desperately."

The President simply said, "Again, Raymond, my gratitude to you. You and I will miss Gifford very much, as will the country. I will lean on you even more in the future."

Clem was pleased. It was the delicately right touch. The Senate Leader beamed into the phone. "How gracious of you, Mr. President."

As the President put down the phone, he motioned to Clem. "Mark it down, Clem: 'Victory has a thousand fathers, defeat is an orphan.' Raymond Tunstall has no zest for orphans."

Willa Hammond dialed the phone number of B. J. Brackenfield.

"Yeah, Willa," remonstrated B.J. in a tone neither valorous nor festive, "I'm sitting here with Mitch and Maggie. I'm putting you on the speaker phone. Hoyle called me before Bill Rawlins went public. I told the little flyface I was so grateful that he let me know six seconds before every jackleg reporter in town knew about it. I tried to get you, but the only one I could find was Mitch, and he thought I had been firing up some bad coke. Jeessus Haitch Christ, I didn't have a chance to cover my ass with all my clients."

"I've got no time for limp, candy-assed excuses, B.J., and least of all now."

To say Willa's voice had an edge was to B.J. a little superfluous.

"My neck is out several furlongs," said Willa, fury uncontained. "Not to mention the barrel full of cash my clients' PACs poured out to Rawlins. And that's not counting the soft money. Right now, my panties are around my knees and I am doing my damnedest to scramble back to Kells and that charm-laden duo, Clem Barkley and Willacy Hughes, both of whom have the memory of an elephant on junk. Migod, some of my clients are looking at me as if I had become a ballet dancer. I am suggesting to them that Stonehaven is a better bet than the odds make him. What does our little weasel friend Hoyle say to all this?"

B.J. was solemn. "He's jumping around like a monkey in heat. Can you imagine Hoyle trying to peddle the line that Rawlins wants to save the country from a political bloodbath? I told Hoyle that he's got a better chance to win the DC lottery than find a taker for that crap. I can't figure it out. Either Rawlins is joining the Hare Krishna crowd, or he's got a bad case of Alzheimer's, and I'm willing to believe either of them than swallow the patriot line. Jesus, I'm doing the Jack Daw strut with every client I got, sounding like a guy putting the scam on old widows. What can I tell you?"

Mitch Joyner joined in. "We've all got deep doo-doo on our face,

Willa. Maggie here has been drowning in phone calls. As have I. I hate to admit how much Hoyle fetched from our PACs."

"Next time you get a candidate, B.J., would you please include me out?" Willa clicked off the phone.

B.J. turned to his companions. "Willa does have such a nice way of crapping in your face, doesn't she?"

Two days later, Federof put down the phone in his apartment in the Soviet Embassy. All he had heard at the other end was the woman's voice he now knew so well say, "Let's go. Start it moving."

He strode down the Embassy second-floor corridor. He flung open the door to a bedroom. Vaslansky was in the bathroom. He came out hurriedly as he heard the door slam.

"Boris Andreevich, the time is now. Do it." Federof was unsmiling and so was his voice. Boris Andreevich Vaslansky did not need to be reminded that his once-powerful mentor, Viktor Zinyakin, had become a nonperson. And Vaslansky understood that nonpersons have no value. Boris Vaslansky was a quick study when his own neck was in peril. When one was about to be pushed over the side, it did tend to concentrate the mind wonderfully.

At 6:30 p.m. the Safeway store on MacArthur Boulevard at 28th Street was doing its usual early evening business. At the Express Number 6 checkout counter, a woman stood behind the cashier and smiled heartily at the line waiting with less than nine items.

She looked for all the world like a Safeway supervisor checking up on how the beloved customers were being treated. None of those prepared to pay for their food noticed the slight bulge beneath the cloth jacket the woman wore. They would have been astonished to find their own cashier carrying a 9mm automatic.

The young couple, both wearing tennis sneakers, with their cart in front of them, sauntered along the packaged luncheon meat open freezer in aisle 6-7. They chatted merrily with each other, the man giving a slight pat to the weapon that was holstered in the small of his back under his denim jacket. His slightly plump brunette "wife" held a carryall in her right hand.

The gray-haired man in a brown business suit examining the display of colored balloons close by the floral section in aisle 6-7 buttoned his coat slowly. The store manager was a very tall woman who smiled graciously at customers. She stood a few feet from the gray-haired man and just in front of her office, which faced aisle 6-7, with her back to the entrance and the aisle. Both were armed.

At that very moment, an unobtrusive gentleman strolled in. He picked up a red plastic shopping basket and idly strode past the first four aisles. He wandered down aisle 5, where bathroom items were displayed. He picked up a tube of Crest and a new Sensor razor and continued to walk down the aisle and around to his right.

He walked past the open freezer containing luncheon meat on aisle 6-7, looked casually at a package of bologna, moved around the man and his wife holding her carryall, walked slowly toward the bread section. He stopped and examined loaves of bread, then moved ever so slightly in front of an array of Pepperidge Farm cookies.

Out of the corner of his eye, he spotted the store manager, her back to him as she bowed slightly to a fat lady pushing her heavily laden cart. A gray-haired man appeared to be asking a question of the store manager. Neither was seemingly aware of him. He slowly stole a gaze behind him, but the man and his wife were examining something in their cart. As he turned back, he quickly, almost casually lifted one hand to pick up a box of cookies, reading the label more closely as his hand flicked up behind the upper part of the shelf, found the tiny slip of paper, and palmed it. Still holding the cookie box, he turned to the floral section just behind him.

Instantly he felt an object in his back. He almost turned his head, but he heard a soft, stern voice say, "Freeze, mister, don't panic, don't move. Very slowly give me the piece of paper in your hand."

He was astounded. The red plastic basket dropped from his left hand, the Crest toothpaste and Sensor razor skidding across the floor. He dared to turn his head ever so slightly. It was the man in the tennis sneakers. There appeared in front of him the fellow's wife, only this time she was ominously brandishing a menacing automatic weapon.

The store manager bounded toward him, as did the gray-haired man, a cruel-looking automatic in his right hand. The store manager said in a clear, authoritative voice, "This is the FBI. You are under arrest." Whereupon she pulled out a card and read Miranda rights. The startled man looked keenly at the store manager. He suddenly recognized her.

The cashier at the express counter hit a buzzer on her belt. Three other shoppers raced to the last aisle, guns at the ready, where the man had been handcuffed. His face drained of color, an expression of dismay and anguish distorted his features. He tried to speak but could not utter a whispery gasp.

The store manager said to him, "My name is Antonia Georgihu, Deputy Associate Director of the FBI. You are under arrest for espionage. Give me the piece of paper in your hand. Now."

She reached behind him. He opened his palm and she took the scrap of paper to which was ingeniously taped a tiny piece of film.

"Please state your name," she said.

The man breathed deeply, once, twice. He did not answer.

"I am going to reach into your jacket pocket to see if you have identification." She thrust her hand into his inside jacket pocket and extracted a small wallet.

The man spoke for the first time. "That's not necessary. My name is John Wingate. I am the National Security Adviser to the President."

"I know," said Toni.

The President faced the reporters at his news conference in the press briefing room.

"I intend to read a statement. I will have nothing further to add. Mike Carson will stay on to answer those questions he can.

"At 6:42 p.m. last Tuesday, at the Safeway store on MacArthur Boulevard here in Washington, the FBI on my orders arrested a man who allegedly has been, for the last several years, a personal spy for the former Chairman of the KGB. He is John Wingate—National Security Adviser."

The momentary collective gasp rocked the room.

"We have not been able to ascertain precisely what information has been fed back to the KGB, but over the next weeks we will attempt to catalogue the loss.

"This alleged spy was revealed to me by sources I cannot disclose. Immediately I conferred with the Director of the FBI and his able assistant, Deputy Associate Director Antonia Georgihu. They planned the arrest with my full approval.

"We have learned that Viktor Zinyakin, the former KGB Chairman, has died from an undisclosed illness. The Executive President of the U.S.C.R. has sent me a message assuring me that he had not approved, and knew nothing of, this espionage. He is taking measures now to cleanse the KGB of those who were involved with the former KGB Chairman in what he terms a 'deplorable enterprise.' I have responded to the Executive President with my gratitude for his message, and I commend him for his actions.

"Moreover, the FBI has this morning informed me they have confirmed that my assistant, Terence Geer, was a victim of a plot to falsely implicate him. The drugs found in Mr. Geer's home, as well as the top-secret documents, were allegedly planted by Mr. Wingate, acting on orders from the former KGB Chairman. We have in custody a KGB agent named Boris Vaslansky, operating in Washington under the direct authority of the former KGB Chairman, who has confessed that he and Mr. Wingate were the sole perpetrators of this duplicity. With the charges against him dropped, I welcome Mr. Geer back to his duties in the White House.

"The Executive President has requested that we deport the KGB agent to the U.S.C.R., where he will be dealt with by the authorities there. I have agreed to the deportation, once the agent has been thoroughly debriefed by the FBI.

"I lament this terrible series of events. I am embarrassed and revulsed by this betrayal. But I am gratified by the work of the FBI, and the response of the leadership of the U.S.C.R. It may be that this treachery may bear within it seeds of a new rapport with the U.S.C.R. It may provide, as some tragedies do, a new beginning for both our countries. I pray that is so.

"Thank you for your attention. Mike Carson will now answer whatever questions he can."

The President turned from the lectern and strode quickly from the press briefing room, ignoring the frantic, shouted questions.

The spy in the White House blew the withdrawal of William Booth Rawlins out of the headlines. Those to whom politics was one huge yarn were suddenly riveted, searching out every newspaper article, every TV show for more information, relishing every Hitchcockian turn, veils lifted, shadows illuminated, darkened corridors now garishly lit.

Stories were written about the late James Jesus Angleton, obsessed chief of counterintelligence at the CIA who burrowed into every nook and cranny of the American Government in an unsuccessful quest for the mole he was certain existed. One TV commentator remarked, "In that great soundproof spy room in the sky, Jim Angleton is cackling, 'I told you so.' "

Perhaps most fascinating to the press and public was the President's own dilemma: betrayed by a man who was his colleague and, he had thought, friend.

The President's response to reporters on this subject was sobering. "If John Wingate is found guilty of espionage," said the President, "I favor his paying the price our country demands for treason."

In response, Vincent Canfield wrote a column condemning the death penalty.

Federof, with Vlady at his side, turned to Vaslansky.

"Tell the Americans everything that I have told you to say. The truth, Boris Andreevich, the truth, or perhaps I should say, almost all the truth. There are a few items we must leave unsaid. Vlady will go over everything with you before you meet with the Americans."

At Federof's request, the FBI allowed Vaslansky to return to the Embassy before he would be thoroughly and exhaustively debriefed by the Bureau.

Vaslansky frowned. "And what happens to me when the Americans have finished debriefing me?"

Federof patted him affectionately on the shoulder. "You will return home and you will be taken care of. Perhaps you will have to live outside Moscow, perhaps far from Moscow. But nothing is forever. In time, when all this inconvenience has faded, who can tell? But, Boris Andreevich, your alternatives at this moment are quite bleak. Consider that before you start sulking. Now, let's buzz Irina and have some tea. You do like tea, don't you?"

Federof smiled at Vaslansky, a cold, hard smile.

Thirty-seven

CLEM FELT the comforting warmth of the Acapulco sun on his bare chest on this February day. It was snowing in Washington, and Clem took unaccustomed glee in knowing the snow was there and he was here. With Toni.

The day after his divorce was declared final, they were married.

They lay beside a small swimming pool in their private villa at Las Brisas, on the side of a hill overlooking beautiful Acapulco Bay. She was clad in a skimpy bikini which was, to Clem, revelatory. Actually, erotic would more carefully define his feelings.

"What are you thinking?" he said, as she stretched languidly, with one arm fluttering just above the water.

"Clem, my darling, that is a cliché question. It's been asked by young men of women for a thousand years."

"Guilty as charged, but what are you thinking?"

She let a hand loll delicately in the warm pool water. She turned to Clem. "I am thinking that politics is a strange business. It brought us together, that's the best part. But in all my years in the Bureau, I have never encountered anything so unpredictable and so wound up in riddles and contradictions as the business you are in."

Clem leaned over, ran his hand lightly over her sun-browned skin, caressed her, kissed her. "What you will further learn, dear,

dear Toni, is that politics is both what is true and what is not true. You just have to leap into politics without really knowing what you'll find. It's all on faith."

Toni touched him tenderly on his arm. "Like marriage?"

Mike Carson smiled triumphantly. When the news of his resignation from the White House was made public, the stories in the press and on television hailed his labors as superior and lamented his absence from President Kells' next four years. "A major loss for the Administration" was the conventional press view.

He sat in first class on United Airlines' nonstop flight to Los Angeles, toying with a glass of red wine, reading the article about himself in the New York *Times*, which glowingly beatified him as the White House "golden child."

Tomorrow he would become Chairman and Chief Executive Officer of Olympian Entertainment, newly and fully funded by Roger Rawlins and a group of investors he had assembled. The press release heralding the formation of the new enterprise specifically noted that more than $200 million had been invested by the Rawlins group, and an additional $200 million inserted by one of Japan's largest conglomerates and $100 million from a German consortium. Together with bank loans, the new company would have equity capital of more than three quarters of a billion dollars. Roger Rawlins' group had the majority voting shares, and Carson's contract proffered him generous stock options.

Olympian Entertainment would be a rising, visible force in the American film and television production and distribution industry —so vowed the news release—and, with its new Chief Executive Officer as a prized asset, would grow larger and more influential in the years ahead.

The young Michael Carson, energetic, vibrant, and confident, would with his talent and integrity be the ideal new leader of this most important American creative industry—or so the news release implied.

The news release omitted what other ideas lay so restlessly inside Mike Carson. He mused to himself about the possibilities that lay ahead, including, as soon as possible, the supplanting of the Rawlins group as the control apparatus by his own band of brothers, wherein he would be the majority owner. He had some very definite ideas on how to shape that move. Mike believed that one always planned ahead, keeping in mind one should never turn away from friends until it was no longer convenient to stand with them.

While the sun shone so brilliantly in Acapulco, it was nowhere to be seen in Moscow, where it was bitterly cold. Snow had fallen in heavy rows, armoring the earth with a thick white quilt, now discolored as freezing rain and pollution debris streaked it and stained it.

The new KGB Chairman awaited the visit of the new American Secretary of State on this dismally inhospitable February day.

Moscow and the Soviet Government apparatus had watched with large interest the U.S. Presidential campaign. Soviet television carried news of that event, live from the U.S. on CNN and on Russian newscasts. Indeed, all of Europe, the European Community and those nation-states contiguous to the Community, found the American Presidential election irresistible theater.

All three U.S. networks had forecast the Kells victory by 11:35 p.m. election night. Governor Robert Stonehaven, the Republican candidate, conceded at 7:45 on the morning after. Stonehaven had waited until it was clear that California was in the Kells camp. That tilted an otherwise tightly contested election, as brutally close as Kennedy/Nixon and Humphrey/Nixon.

Yesterday morning, at a foreign policy meeting in the Kremlin, the Executive President had seemed pleased, or so it appeared to the new KGB Chairman. The meeting with President Donald Kells in the election year had mollified whatever cautionary feelings the Executive President might have had. He was rather impressed in this meeting—unlike his previous visit—with the openness of President Kells.

"Mr. Executive President," Kells had said directly to him, "I am hoping so very much that you and I find it possible to talk not as enemies but as leaders who have common interests. We will both concede that neither of us will do anything that does not serve our individual countries. I am as one with an old British Prime Minister, Palmerston by name, who said that England had no permanent friends and no permanent enemies, but England did have permanent interests. May the same be said of you and me. So, what I pledge you is, I will work very hard to make sure that whatever decisions I may make do not disserve your permanent interests, and I will pray that you would find it suitable to do the same for me. If that is so, you and I will become reliable and friendly adversaries, as well as honest activists."

"Yes," the Executive President had told the new KGB Chairman, "Kells is a man of candor. I can do business with him—until I am ready to do otherwise."

The new KGB Chairman lounged easily in the large chair behind his desk. He had expunged from the spacious office all memory of its previous occupant. Every stick of furniture, every vestige which bore the stamp or smell of Viktor Zinyakin had been cleared from the entire secretariat of the KGB.

The door opened and an alluringly formed woman with short dark hair approached him. She was clad in an appealing dress which had mysteriously appeared at her apartment, a gift from a not so mysterious dear friend who appreciated such finery.

"Comrade Chairman, the American visitor is at this moment being escorted to your office."

"Ah, thank you, Anya, my dear." He rose, touched her lightly on the shoulder—to which she responded with an affectionate gaze—and walked briskly to the anteroom.

As the huge doors opened, the new KGB Chairman held out his hands, exuberant smile widening.

"It is so good to see you again, and to be able to say, 'Welcome, Mr. Secretary.'"

Bill Rawlins, face flushed from the cold wind that assailed him as he alighted from his car, moved like a dancer across the room. "No one can be more pleased than I to see you again, Filipp Vladimirovich. Being here only proves that tomorrow always belongs to those who really want it, and I want it."

"Ah, Bill, at heart you really are a Russian poet," said Federof.

"No, Filipp, I am no poet, but if I resemble any other man in this country, you are that man. For the fact is, my friend, I am like you. I'm a survivor."